ANGEL,
ARCHANGEL

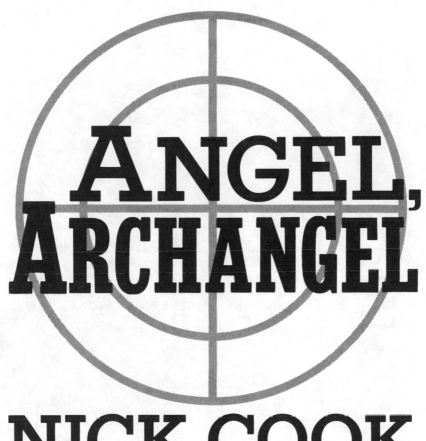

ANGEL, ARCHANGEL

NICK COOK

ST. MARTIN'S PRESS   NEW YORK

Design by Levavi & Levavi

Library of Congress Cataloging-in-Publication Data

Cook, Nick.
    Angel, Archangel / Nick Cook.
      p.   cm.
    ISBN 0-312-04322-8
    1. World War—1939–1945—Fiction.   I. Title.
  PR6053.05214A83   1990   89-77817
  823'.914—dc20   CIP

First Edition

10 9 8 7 6 5 4 3 2 1

To Julian Cook, my father

ACKNOWLEDGMENTS

It is impossible to list all the people who helped me in the making of this book. I hope you know who you are and will accept my debt of gratitude for much tireless encouragement and practical help over the past five years. Some names do stand out for special mention: Colonel Maurice Buckmaster, OBE, for advising me, some years ago now, that the concept of Archangel was within the realms of possibility; Harry Hawker for his excellent technical advice; and Sheila Mills for some incisive criticism. To Ali, family and friends for putting up with a would-be author over the past five years, heartfelt thanks and apologies to you all. The person who walks away with the credit, however, is Mark Lucas, without whom this book would never have got off the ground, or struggled to stay airborne. To him, the debt is incalculable.

PROLOGUE

The aide-de-camp to the chief of the general staff of the Red Army worked agitatedly to decipher the signal that had just come in from General Nerchenko on the First Ukrainian front, but long before he reached the end he reckoned that Plan Archangel was dead.

For a moment, the colonel considered flight, then thought better of it. How could he hide from the eyes and ears of the NKVD in Moscow?

Nerchenko said he could retrieve the situation, but it was still desperate news. Yuri Petrovich Paliev, whom they had entrusted with the secret of Archangel, was gone.

Colonel Nikolai Ivanovich Krilov did not feel any fear. After a year of burying himself in Archangel, Nerchenko's message merely served to trigger the exhaustion he had suppressed for so long.

If Paliev managed to reach the NKVD—the Soviet security force—the comrade marshal had friends in the Kremlin who could give them enough warning to let them take a walk with their revolvers into the woods off Komsomolsky Prospekt.

He wanted to see his wife one last time if it came to that. He would hold her a little more closely than he had done since the early days of their marriage, but it was essential that he did not arouse her suspicions. When they came to her with the news of his death, her shock would have to be genuine and absolute. He had not loved Valla for many years, that was true, but he cared for her too much to let her become another victim of the NKVD's interrogation techniques.

Krilov put the codebook down on his desk and folded the piece of paper, carefully placing it in the top pocket of his tunic. He doused the lights in his office and headed for the end of the great Kremlin corridor where he would find his commander and mentor of the last two years.

Marshal Boris Shaposhnikov, Hero of the Soviet Union, did not look up from his paperwork when Krilov knocked and entered the room. Krilov realized that months of listening to his footsteps on the marble floor of the great corridor told the marshal immediately that it was he who had entered.

Krilov had gotten to know his master well. When Shaposhnikov and he had first taught doctrine to junior officers at the Voroshilov Military Academy shortly after the relief of Stalingrad, Shaposhnikov had expounded the value of keeping a clear head through the small reversals that a commander inevitably faced on the field of battle. *This* reversal, however, was not small, nor, so far as Krilov could see, had it been inevitable. Still, Krilov would retain his composure; he would select his words to convey both gravity and steadiness.

"Comrade Marshal, Archangel has been badly compromised."

Shaposhnikov maintained his legendary ice-cold facade.

"What has happened, Kolya?" Still he called him by that diminutive of his given name. Usually he found it comforting, almost fatherly. Now it meant nothing.

The marshal had stopped writing and was looking up at Krilov's face. The blue eyes had not lost their luster, Krilov thought as he tried to keep his voice even.

"Nerchenko just reported in from Branodz. Paliev took the plans from his safe last night, commandeered a jeep, an escort vehicle, and a platoon, and was last seen heading east toward Ostrava."

"East? Are you sure?"

"Yes, Comrade Marshal. He is not taking them to Eisenhower. Not that. But he is, apparently, bringing them back here to Moscow. Yuri Petrovich has betrayed us."

"What made him turn?" Shaposhnikov had risen and was facing the window, seemingly more interested in the snow that fell on the Palace of Congresses than in the crisis that was unfolding in his office.

"Nerchenko's safe not only contained everything on Archangel, it also detailed the arrangements for deploying the Berezniki consignment at Branodz."

"He has been most careless," Shaposhnikov said.

"He can only conjecture about why Paliev is doing this. When he was first approached about Archangel, he embraced it wholeheartedly—but he was not at that time informed about the Berezniki element. He has since learned about it, and Nerchenko thinks it may have shocked him. The general does not know; he admits he is guessing. In any case he now believes Paliev wants to lay *all* the plans on the desk of the NKVD, use them as a bargaining chip to save his own life for having been part of Archangel in the first. Possibly Major Paliev intends to go directly to Stalin; who knows?"

Krilov studied the lined features of the sixty-two-year-old man in the reflection on the window. It displayed little emotion.

"And what is General Nerchenko doing to save the situation, Kolya?"

"He has dispatched one of his Siberian units after the traitor. He has also sent word to depot-level HQ at Ostrava that Paliev is a dangerous deserter who is likely to be making for one of the airfields or the railhead there. He has issued orders for Paliev to be shot on sight."

"Yuri Petrovich will find the road to Ostrava is longer than he thought," Shaposhnikov said.

Krilov saw the reflection smile.

Paliev had to negotiate some two hundred kilometers of hostile Czechoslovakian terrain before he reached Ostrava, the main marshaling point between the industrial heartland of Russia and their southern front. Aircraft and trains shuttled back and forth ceaselessly with their cargos of men, matériel, and munitions. In Krilov's mind, there was little doubt that Ostrava was Paliev's initial stop on the way back to Moscow.

Nerchenko would have ordered checkpoints on the larger roads, forcing the traitor onto mountain and forest tracks. It was the type of country where the Siberians performed best. They had to. Paliev was now a flea on a very large bear.

"It won't be easy to find him, Comrade Marshal."

Shaposhnikov turned to the younger man. His face, Krilov was still surprised to notice, wore an expression of complete serenity. But his voice, when he spoke, had the edge that had helped to maintain the marshal as Stalin's right-hand man throughout the Patriotic War.

"It is too late for doubt, Kolya. Our contact at Berezniki tells me the consignment is on its way to the front. We shall not stop the train now. So go back to your wife. Sleep well tonight. If Paliev reaches Moscow, I will see to it that he never delivers his cargo. And what if he does? No one will believe him. Go home, Kolya. Everything will be all right."

Shaposhnikov waited until Krilov closed the door behind him before slumping onto the rough wooden chair by his desk. He had been waiting for Paliev to make his move, but now that it had come, he was puzzled. Paliev had gone east, to Ostrava, and that was not what he had expected at all.

He thought of Krilov, newly reassured that everything was under control. He only wished he believed the words himself.

BOOK ONE

1

Fleming pulled the parachute harness tight over his shoulders and cursed lightly as his finger snagged on the rough metal catch.

The first stabs of light rising above the black hangar sheds at the far end of the airfield caught the condensation from his breath as it swirled momentarily in the cold dawn air. He watched the crimson tear quiver at the end of his finger, hang there for a second, then splash onto the crisp carpet of snow that lay on the tarmac outside the ops room.

He felt no pain. His hands had been numb ever since he had crawled from the warmth of his bed into the musty, chill air of the Nissen hut. He had welcomed the numbness that spread over him like an anesthetic, helping him forget the task that lay out there, somewhere between the frozen English countryside and the cloudless heavens.

Three patches of blood spread on the snow by his feet, like tiny cultures under a microscope.

The image cut him deeper than the subzero temperatures of the wintery morning. He tried to shut off the picture that began to form in his mind, but not before he caught a glimpse of the spreading stickiness on his sheets as the hemorrhaging began once more.

Fleming cursed himself for allowing his concentration to

drift. The hospital bed was behind him now. He was flying again.

He pulled the fireproof gloves over his hands and set off toward the slim, darkened shadow of his aircraft on the other side of the field. The single fitter, slouched against the side of the fuselage, straightened as Fleming approached him. Fleming caught the glow as one last drag was pulled from the precious cigarette, then a deft flick of the wrist, an athletic movement, and the aircraftman was on the wing of the Spitfire, reaching out to him.

"Morning, sir." Fleming caught the smell of sleep and tea on the man's breath as he bent down to pull him onto the wing.

He brushed aside the helping hand, anxious that the fitter should not feel him tremble.

He lowered himself into the armored bucket seat, his feet sliding effortlessly into the rests on the rudder bars, his hands clasping the spade-grip of the joystick. Nothing much had changed in the cockpit between the Mk XVI and his old Mk IX. As Fleming went through the checks, his eyes and fingers darted over the instruments even as the fitter struggled to strap him into the machine.

Concentrate on the aircraft, the job in hand, forget the past.

A voice, somewhere far away, tried to reach out to him, but his mind dismissed it, focusing on the task that now lay before him. The fitter's hand shook him gently by the shoulder.

"Tight enough for you, sir?"

Fleming nodded, embarrassed by his dulled reactions. The fitter pulled the clear bubble canopy forward until it rammed home against the forward frame of the cockpit. Fleming's hand moved up to the catch and brought it down with a click that indicated he was now sealed into the body of the Spitfire.

He pushed the starter button, heard the wheeze of the engine as the propellers moved through, one . . . two arcs, then the cough as the engine caught. A whiff of oil-smoke from the exhaust permeated through to his cramped cell. The Merlin engine thrummed against the firewall by his feet, the rhythm slowly stabilizing until he knew it was time to go.

As soon as the shuffling mechanic retired with the wheel chocks, Fleming flexed his fingers on the throttle lever and pushed it tentatively forward. The Merlin responded, sending a burst of power through the transmission system to the blades, which blew a blast of icy air past the cockpit and sent the fitter scuttling back to the warmth of the ground-crew office in the hangar.

Fleming watched the outside world drift by as if it were no more than a dream, an imprecision compounded by the shapes of trees, buildings, and other aircraft, strangely distorted in the slight curvature of his Plexiglas canopy. At the same time, the discipline forged by years of flying kept part of his mind on the mission. Elevators . . . free; rudders . . . fine; flaps . . . on half setting; engine oil pressure . . . normal.

He swung the aircraft onto the threshold and pushed the throttle through the gate to its take-off setting, his left foot instinctively tapping down on the rudder bar to counteract the vicious torque from the Merlin.

As soon as the aircraft came unstuck, Fleming felt a surge of relief that left him feeling drained and weak. The burst of elation disappeared the moment the cackle in his headset reminded him of the task ahead.

"Goshawk, this is Sunflower. Steer one-one-oh degrees and make Angels one-three." The static could not muffle the impeccable BBC tones of the Women's Auxiliary Air Force (WAAF) controller.

"Roger, Sunflower. Am climbing to Angels one-three. Vector one-one-oh." A slight tremble. "Is there any sign of the intruder, over?" The voice controlled, a little steadier this time.

"Not yet, Goshawk. We've lost him in the murk. Patience, my boy, we'll tell you the moment he breaks cover." A man's voice. Staverton. What the devil was the old fox doing there? He should have been tucked away in his basement in Whitehall. Fleming felt the claustrophobic flying overalls wrap themselves more tightly around him. He was being watched by everyone from the lowliest WAAF controller to the head of the bloody Enemy Aircraft Evaluation Unit (EAEU). And they were all waiting for him to make a mistake.

On his new course setting, Fleming could see the clouds building up from the west. He cursed again. The weather conditions would help his opponent, not him.

A crackle on the ether.

"Goshawk, we have your bandit on radar now. He's forty miles east of you, heading southeast. Vector two-seven-oh and climb to Angels three-oh, over."

He fought the constriction in his throat.

"Roger, Sunflower. Am making Angels three-oh now. Course two-seven-oh."

"Goshawk . . ." The WAAF again. There was trepidation in her voice; the WAAF controllers always sensed the frightened ones. ". . . He's somewhere between Salisbury and Warminster. Making a dash for the coast. Good luck."

Fleming increased the back pressure on the stick and saw the tops of the looming clouds disappear beneath the long nose of the Spitfire. The glare was brighter than he had ever known, but at least the sun was behind him. Something was going his way.

The supercharger cut in as he leveled off at thirty thousand feet, giving the Spitfire an extra burst of power in the rarefied atmosphere. He glanced into the mirror above his head.

Contrail.

Shit. He'd stand out a mile with a streak of moisturized air pouring out behind him. Might as well scrawl your signature across the bloody sky. He pushed the stick forward, seeking the invisible boundary layer of moisture-free sky where the contrail from his hot engine exhaust would melt away.

Five hundred feet lower he found it and allowed himself a quavering smile. Perhaps luck was with him after all.

Below, the unmistakable landmark of Winchester, its distinctive cathedral rising above the icy watermeadows by the river Itchen, slid beneath a gap in the thick, rolling cumulus. He did a few calculations. About twenty miles to intercept. At 400 MPH, he should spot the enemy in just over five minutes.

If his luck held.

Fleming pictured the control room, dark except for the green glow of the cathode-ray tubes that hummed beneath the glass of the radar screen. And there would be Staverton's face, ghoullike in the pulsing aura, peering intently into the electronic picture as the two dots converged. Staverton could see their every move, but Fleming knew he'd never shout a warning because the intruder might hear it, and the element of surprise, now on Fleming's side, would be lost. But deep down, Fleming also knew that even if the other aircraft had no radio to eavesdrop on him, Staverton would do nothing. It was part of the test they had set for him.

He felt like an exhibit at a circus sideshow. His freakishness lay not in some hideous facial deformity, but within, forged by two minutes of hell as his Spitfire tumbled burning through the sky, while he wrestled to open the hood with a lump of German 20-millimeter cannon in his belly.

It seemed everyone at Farnborough knew what had happened to Robert Fleming over Italy in 1944.

A flash of sunlight on metal. At ten o'clock. Higher than him. He screwed his eyes up against the glare, scanning the sector for another fix. Nothing. The trouble with the Luftwaffe's high-altitude recce aircraft was that for the last few months the Germans had taken to painting them blue all over. Bloody hard to spot unless you happened to know one was out there. At least he had that advantage.

Then he saw the contrail. It was no more than a few hundred yards, a short line made from millions of tiny water droplets as the hot gas from the German engine hit the layer of moisture that he had encountered minutes before. His adversary must have spotted his mistake in a second, correcting his flight path down into the lower stratum of the atmosphere where no trail would form. But it was too late. The contrail pointed with all the conviction of an arrow to the scudding silhouette of the duck egg–colored Junkers as it passed from right to left across his propeller arc. Two miles from him; that was all. Control was good.

Fleming pushed the throttle to the stops and slid in behind the tail of the Ju 288, the Luftwaffe's very latest armed and armored eye-in-the-sky. Despite the German plane's twin boosted Jumo engines, the Mk XVI Spitfire was faster. Fleming watched in wide-mouthed fascination as it grew larger in his sights. Another fifty yards and he'd have it in range.

And then it was gone. Fleming had a fleeting impression of ten tons of metal standing on its wingtip for a split second before spiraling down like a sycamore seed on an autumn wind to the sanctity of the cumulus below. He swore, fighting the needles of panic, then punched the rudder bar and whipped the stick over to the left in a vicious, synchronized action, struggling against the gs as the horizon disappeared. His head pressed against thc canopy, held there by the force of three times gravity as the Spitfire whirled earthward.

Spiraling.

As he had done over Monte Lupo with an FW 190 on his tail.

He fought to remain conscious, to beat the g-induced darkness, his eyes desperately trying to relocate the German aircraft. Must . . . find it. Must leave the past behind. Through the mist of his grayout the snow-covered earth and the clouds merged into a dizzying fusion of whiteness, punctuated every revolution of his turn by a flash of blue. Sky . . . ?

The Junkers. There it was, revolving past his cockpit once every half second. Still making for the clouds. Almost there. So was he.

Fleming responded automatically, kicking on the opposite rudder and pushing forward on the stick. Two more revs and he was out of the spin. His head swam from the effects of the gravity and his body was damp from the hot flush of sweat that oozed from every pore during his brief plummet earthward. The sweat of fear, not just physical exertion. Except this time he was going to beat it. He had to or it would consume him, Penny, everything. The remedy was here, in the clouds.

Fleming locked onto the tail of the Junkers, about three hundred yards behind, just as it entered the wall of stratocumulus. He followed, penetrating the cloud as close as he could to his opponent's entry point.

There was a moment of thick, cloaking mist swirling around the cockpit, then came a bright, searing flash as he shot out of it into the blue eye of the huge cloud formation. A great glint of silver shone as the Junkers split-essed away from him, downward, the sun catching on the thin film of water vapor on its glistening underside, like light reflecting off the belly of a game fish.

Fleming delved down again through the great tunnel of steam, keeping the Junkers within the frame of his windshield, tantalizingly close to his sights. And all the time the thought was tumbling through his mind: It shouldn't be able to do this. A Junkers shouldn't bloody well fly like this. How can a man throw a heavy fighter-bomber around the sky without tearing its wings off?

Fleming turned with the Junkers down a narrow chasm of clear sky, two great white walls on either side of him. The enemy aircraft banked into the cloud and disappeared. He felt sick with the exertion; he wanted to turn away, tell Staverton he had lost it.

No. Fight it.

The cloud was patchy, thinning out. The Junkers was split-essing away from him again, down . . . down, closer to the ground. He followed, leveling out as the Junkers pulled up over the New Forest. He was close now, closing faster. He had the speed.

His opponent knew it too, dodging his way over the contoured treetops, then going lower as the forest gave way to heathland. A group of ponies scattered as the heavy, icy air was split by the noise of the twin Jumos and the Merlin, the two sounds merging as the Spitfire closed in.

With a monumental effort Fleming inched his thumb along the spade-grip of the stick, seeking the gun button that would end the madness. The Junkers reared. Too late. He had him.

Then the Junkers dropped everything. Flaps and undercarriage lowered. Fleming froze. Monte Lupo; it was happening again.

It took place in an instant, yet to Fleming it was in excruciating slow motion, a replay of an earlier drama, an earlier battle, one that he had fought in his nightmares ever since. And the ending was always the same. He lost and there was nothing to do about it.

With flaps and wheels down, the Junkers shuddered, bucked, and slowed to the point of the stall, but it held there, and Fleming could only watch, rigid with fear as the blue belly slid by only feet above his cockpit.

He was dead. The German aircraft was positioned squarely in his mirror. The 20-millimeter cannon would rip into him any second.

"You're dead, Wing Commander. I've got you on gun camera. You'll have to do better than that." A voice in his head, echoing over and over again, tormenting him.

"I said you're dead, Robert. Break off." A sense of waking, coming out of the dream. Yet he was still in a hurtling piece of machinery, real machinery, with real ground whipping past him at 300 MPH a few hundred feet below. Real voices . . .

"Break off, Robert, goddammit. It's me, Kruze." The name burst through his headset.

Kruze . . . the exercise. Not Italian skies, but English.

He looked over his port wingtip to see the Junkers pull alongside, so close that Kruze was clearly visible in the cockpit. Kruze. It really was him. No nightmare this time, no FW 190, no cannon . . . As if to reassure him, the RAF roundels stood out proudly where once had been the stark crosses and swastikas on the 288.

Thick bile rose in Fleming's throat as the exercise was replayed in his mind. He felt as if he was going to retch into his mask, but nothing came up.

"Robert." Kruze's anxious face, thirty feet away, matched the tone of his voice. "Robert, for Christ's sake answer me. Are you all right?"

Fleming nodded once.

"Let's go home, then. That's enough for one day."

The Junkers peeled off toward Farnborough and Fleming banked after it.

□

Kruze jumped from the wing of the Ju 288 onto the slushy tarmac of the dispersal point. The snow of the previous night had turned to a light drizzle, altering Farnborough, crisp and clean at dawn, to a dirty, wet, miserable place.

Fleming's Spitfire had rolled to a stop several hundred yards away, parked untidily beside an otherwise immaculate row of test aircraft. Kruze started toward it, but was still a hundred yards away when Fleming emerged from the cockpit, threw his helmet to the ground, and moved back toward his Nissen hut.

There was no point in pursuing him.

Instead, Kruze set off for the hangar, looking for Sergeant Broyles. Inside the cavernous shed, technicians worked frantically on a dozen different types of aircraft. Most of them were new marks of bombers, fighters, and reconnaissance aircraft for the air force, but in the far corner were two that would never enter service with the RAF.

The Messerschmitt 110 night fighter stood alongside the spindly, awkward shape of the Fieseler Storch liaison aircraft under the intense gaze of the arc lights. Two fitters were busy in the cockpit of the fighter, making last adjustments to the backseat operator's console where the plots from the Lichtenstein radar were displayed when the Me 110 went about its work—stalking Bomber Command in the pitch-black skies over the Third Reich. It was a bloody good system. It was hardly surprising, therefore, that their boss, Air Vice Marshal Staverton, had got so excited when the news had come through a month ago that Monty's advancing army had come across an intact unit of the type. Staverton's message to his team was simple. Find out what makes the system tick, discover what its vices are, and within two weeks come up with a way to nullify the thing. Eleven days into the flight-test program—and 200-odd downed bombers later—the EAEU had the answer. That same evening a report was on the Air Vice Marshal's desk, and two nights later a jamming system was flown on a thousand-bomber raid to Berlin. Losses were 80 percent down. Not bad, they'd all thought. Not good enough, Staverton had said bitterly, pointing to Bomber Command's intervening losses.

Staverton was not an easy man to please, but each of them

would have followed him to the gates of Berlin and back if necessary.

Kruze found Broyles berating a young fitter for neglecting some minute detail in maintenance procedure on the Me 110. The sergeant, old enough to be Kruze's father, if not his grandfather, saw the Rhodesian out of the corner of his eye and dismissed the trembling aircraftman with a hard, but paternal, clip to the head.

Broyles wiped the grease from his hands onto his overalls. The lined, leathery face creased into a smile.

"I suppose you've been bending another of my bloody airplanes, Mr. Kruze."

Kruze pulled a packet of cigarettes from his flying jacket and tossed it to Broyles, who plucked it eagerly from the air. The big man appreciatively sniffed the bittersweet smell of the Lucky Strikes.

"Pipe down, Chief. A bit of tweaking here and there and she'll be as good as new." He took a cigarette from the pack returned by Broyles.

The chief snorted.

"Mr. Kruze, sir, Jerry don't build airplanes like we do." The chief's voice was laced with good-natured sarcasm. "Besides, when you go popping rivets and bending undercarriages, I can't very well get on the telephone to bloody Herr Göring and ask him to send over a few bleedin' spare parts, can I now?"

Kruze laughed. "Course you can, Chief. You'd scare the crap out of him and have the parts by morning." He clapped his arm over Broyles' shoulder and walked him over to the hangar door. The air outside was still as they strolled toward the Junkers, away from the sounds of activity within the maintenance shed. Standing before the aircraft Broyles whistled above the gentle pinging noise of the two, still Jumo engines as they cooled in the damp air.

"Sweet Jesus, there's furrows on the skin where the wings have bent," the chief said, burying his face in his hands. Kruze knew that this performance, though reflecting the concern of any maintenance sergeant at the impending repair work, was also tongue-in-cheek. It had developed into something of a ritual.

Kruze patted the nose of the Ju 288.

"I've got about six seconds of gun-camera film in here needs developing. Get one of your boys to take it over to photographic, would you, Chief?"

"Yes, Mr. Kruze. Got him, did you?" Broyles nodded to the distant form of the Spitfire.

"Yeah, I got him all right."

Broyles grunted satisfaction. "There's a bit of justice for you."

"What's that, Chief?"

If there was one thing Kruze had learned about Broyles, it was that he didn't pull any punches.

"I had Mr. Fleming in here half the night sticking his nose in my business. That Spitfire was serviced perfectly, the manifest said so. Only Mr. Fleming wouldn't have any of it. Kept getting us to check it over and over again. You should hear what my men have to say about him, the bloody stuffed shirt."

"Steady, Chief. He's had a rough time of it."

Broyles shrugged. "I dare say, Mr. Kruze. But why doesn't he just stay put in that place of his up in London? Put him near an aircraft and he's trouble."

"That's enough, Chief; I get the picture." Kruze realized it was a halfhearted admonition. His own view of Fleming wasn't that different from the seasoned old engineer's.

The chief scratched his head as he watched the tall Rhodesian amble over to the debrief center on the other side of the field. Funny bugger, Kruze. Wasn't like the rest of the officers, thank God.

□

Air Vice Marshal Algernon Staverton, head of the RAF's Enemy Aircraft Evaluation Unit, the EAEU, was standing with his back to the door, staring out between the peeling window frames toward the black maintenance sheds, when Kruze entered his office.

There was damp in the air, but Kruze had become used to that during the long English winter. Staverton turned slowly when the door was closed behind the Rhodesian. The brightness outside made the lines of the Old Man's silhouette appear even more gaunt than usual, Kruze thought. Staverton was hardly a man you could like, but his reputation as an RFC flier and the tough, efficient way in which he ran the EAEU made him someone to respect.

Staverton's career had been somewhat oddball. The Old Man had established the top-secret EAEU with little help from his RAF superiors, who in early 1941 had believed there was not much value in setting up a costly unit to test captured enemy aircraft. Staverton, then only a group captain, persuaded them otherwise. Since then, the reputation of the EAEU—and Staverton—had grown in classified circles.

Four years later, and Staverton's knowledge of enemy aircraft and Luftwaffe operations had made him one of the nation's leading experts in aerial intelligence. Recognition of his expertise came in early 1944 when he was recruited for Churchill's small team of special Cabinet advisers.

In the months preceding the Normandy landings, interpretation of enemy activity assumed vital importance, and Churchill wanted the very best advice from men who answered directly to him. Staverton was a natural for the job. Promoted to air vice marshal to give him equal status with the two other specialists, a major general from British Army Intelligence and a rear admiral from its naval counterpart, Staverton was reputed to be every bit as uncompromising with his superiors in Whitehall as he was with his pilots.

AVM Staverton had been allowed to retain command of the EAEU, even though, by rights, it should have passed to a younger man upon his promotion to Whitehall. He now divided his time between a dark basement office in the Air Ministry and the EAEU's headquarters at Farnborough.

The AVM scarcely concealed his ambition. There were few pilots in the EAEU who doubted he would advance to air chief marshal before the war was out. Provided he did not put too many backs up in Whitehall, that was.

"Well, what happened up there?" Staverton gestured Kruze to the chair in front of his desk and sat down himself.

"The Ju 288's good, there's no question about it. For a big airplane it's maneuverable—tight in the turn, good roll response, rugged . . . It'll all be in my report."

Staverton nodded.

"And Wing Commander Fleming, how did he do? Will we be seeing your Junkers on his gun camera?"

"I haven't had a chance to talk to him yet, sir." Not exactly a lie. "He followed me all the way down from thirty thousand feet to the deck, where he must have had me in his sights for a few seconds . . ."

"And then he had a problem." Staverton probed with the skill of a surgeon. "We heard something over the intercom. Sounded like trouble."

"It looked as if he had a block in his air-supply system. A touch of hypoxia, I reckon. It seemed to clear as soon as he got down on the deck."

Staverton waited until the rumble of a bomber taking off had subsided.

"You don't think it was a touch of something else? After all, Robert has been through more than most of us." Staverton's blue eyes were cold. "He's an extremely brave young man, but anyone who's suffered as he has can only expect to recover slowly. Piet, if you think he's been pushed too far, you have to tell me."

Kruze bristled, but said nothing.

"We had codes of silence in the last show too, you know, but it never did any good to some poor bastard who was too proud to admit that he had had enough. We operate a tight unit here, you know that. Robert has served it well, but if he's gone over the edge, he can be replaced."

"And we lose the best intelligence officer in the RAF."

"There are others. Perhaps they will take time to train for our purposes, but it can be done."

"Sir . . ." Kruze paused. "You know as well as I do that that's impossible. Fleming's work is indispensable to what we do down here. His presence may not always be welcome on the station, but it would take months to find the right man for his job, let alone train him."

Staverton sensed he hadn't finished.

"If there's more, man, get it off your chest now. You know rank counts for little here."

When it suits you, Kruze thought. "All right. Why the hell did you make him do that air test if you suspected he was unfit to fly?"

"Because he requested it himself."

"And you let him do it, just because you felt it might be good for him? Well, the answer to your first question is, yes, I do think he's had enough, but then perhaps we all have."

Staverton seemed unconcerned by the outburst. "You know his wife—"

"I've met her."

"How's she coping?"

Kruze's mind drifted back to the dinner at the cottage. It had been an awkward attempt by Fleming to get to know one of the Farnborough team a bit better. Just Fleming, his wife Penny, a recently widowed friend of hers, and himself. Fleming had been much as usual: withdrawn, shy almost, seeming as ill at ease with Penny as he had been at the base.

She had saved the evening. Attractive and vivacious despite

14

Fleming's clumsiness with her and his guests, Penny never seemed to show any resentment. Once during the evening, however, he had caught a look on her face, gently bathed in the candlelight, as she watched her husband try to make polite conversation. At the time, Kruze thought it was pity; only on the way home did he realize that it was a look of immeasurable sadness.

"She's fine, as far as I know. And so's he." As long as you leave him alone, he thought.

"All right, Piet, that'll be all."

Staverton rubbed his eyes. "Just get that report to me in London by mid-morning tomorrow. I'll not be staying here much longer today. Then take a few days of that leave that's owing to you while you're about it. It may be the last chance you get for quite a while."

2

The officer was lying on his back in the tall grass, arms folded across his chest. The dawn sunlight was streaming down on him, but the peaked cap cast a thin shadow across his closed eyes.

He looks dead, Oberscharführer Dietz thought, as he stood above him. The sergeant was seized by a desire to slip a shell into the chamber of his Mauser sniper's rifle, put the barrel up against his officer's head and blow his brains over the little grassy hillock on which they'd been holed up for the last two days. What'd be the point? They'd all be dead before long anyway. Every man of the platoon, or what was left of it. Killing the pig of an officer would probably be doing him a favor.

The officer was awake and fully aware of Dietz's presence. What did the fool want now? He had been thinking of home. It was almost seven years since he had been there, and it still haunted him. War hadn't eased the contempt he felt for his father, and his so-called friends would be first in line to slit his throat if he ever did get back. But he could never forget the place. If only things had been different.

It was the same for the platoon, God help them. They were tired, dirty, and sick, and they wanted to go home, but all of them knew that even if they survived this mess, home was out of the question. For all except Dietz, that was. The Bavarian still had a place to go back to, but he was the only one who

16

didn't care. That was the irony. Dietz had probably been quite a pleasant young man before this campaign, but by the time they had left Stalingrad he too was living on borrowed time.

They had been behind enemy lines now for five months, off and on. It had started when the big Soviet push came in November. His section had been cut off by the assault, but they'd managed to fight their way back to other German units a few weeks later. By that time the Germans had been pushed back into eastern Czechoslovakia, but his commanding officer had been so impressed with the havoc that he had wrought behind the Russian lines that he was promoted and told to go back and do it all over again. "Don't worry," the general had told him, "you're not the only ones who'll be there. There will be enough SS units behind Ivan's lines to cause real chaos. Supply lines will be cut and perhaps even their advance can be stemmed long enough to give our troops a chance to regroup and smash the Bolshevik army once and for all. Then the Third Reich will turn on the Americans and the British, and then Germany will be great again." That had been in November 1944 . . . five months ago, was it? It seemed like a lifetime to the officer. For every filthy Ivan he'd put down, another ten seemed to take his place.

". . . then Germany will be great again." My bloody ass, it will.

The officer watched through half-closed eyes as Dietz slipped his rifle strap over his shoulder, leaned forward and prodded him.

The officer's eyes flicked wide open, but he wasn't startled. He knew they thought he was too cool by half. Whereas the rest of them stank and were covered in dirt, the officer always managed to look clean and shaven every morning, wherever he happened to be. His face had become gaunt in recent weeks, though: the skin stretched tight over his hooked nose, and his cheeks gray, from the bout of dysentery that had gone around the platoon after their withdrawal from Boskovice.

The officer stared back at Dietz for several seconds. Sergeant Dietz served as a terrible reminder of the horror of the battle for Boscovice. The retreat from that provincial town had been a nightmare. The seven survivors of the once-proud platoon had withdrawn across country by night, taken to these foothills, and had remained here for two days without seeing any enemy activity.

Parts of Czechoslovakia were like that. The isolated valley in which they had taken refuge was off the main Soviet armored-convoy routes and they hadn't seen a soul. Except Dietz, of course, who had been surprised the previous night by some old peasant when he went down to that hamlet near Tryskov on a clandestine forage for food. The old man had spotted him coming out of a barn with two dead chickens under each arm and had rushed up to welcome his Russian liberator. Even though Dietz was wearing full forage gear—the camouflaged smock and over-trousers that they all used, with no insignia of any kind—the Slav couldn't help but notice the shape of his helmet even in the half-light of dusk. The old man's cry of alarm died in his throat the moment Dietz's combat knife hit him full in the chest.

When Dietz told the story later he had bragged that the man died before the chickens even hit the ground. Everyone had laughed, but he was still damned good with that knife. It had got them out of a few tight spots before.

The officer realized that his sergeant was standing there waiting for orders. He snapped out of his reverie.

"What is it?" He stared up at the broad, unshaven face and was about to speak again, when he heard the faint sound in the far distance and knew that it was beginning all over again.

"One jeep and an armored personnel carrier, sir. They're heading this way, but haven't yet come out of the trees. I saw them enter the other side of the wood two minutes ago."

The officer rolled onto his front and parted the grass so that he could get an unrestricted view of the flat expanse of land and the line of trees beyond. Dietz lay down beside him and studied the face once more, this time waiting for orders.

The officer had chosen his ground well. You could get a clear view of the plain that stretched away from their hillock as far as the pine forest in the middle distance. From where Dietz had been sitting on lookout you could even see the road that led into the far side of the wood. It was on this patch of the track that the sergeant had first spotted the vehicles.

It would only be a matter of seconds now before the small convoy would be in sight again. Thank God we're well hidden, the officer thought. At least Ivan won't have a clue we're here.

Dietz spoke again.

"As I said, sir. Two vehicles. One of them an APC. One of ours. Thought we must still have some armor left in this area, until I saw the red star on the side. It's a Hanomag, sir, and it must have had more than a full complement of men on board, because I saw two Ivans sitting on the front. The rear compartment must be full, sir."

The officer waved a hand impatiently.

"I'll make the damned judgments around here, Dietz. What about the other vehicle?"

The sound of engines was quite discernible now and growing louder.

"It was a jeep, sir. Two men in the back, plus driver."

The officer thought fast. The jeep, that was no problem, except for its speed, of course. The Hanomag, though, that was different. They were big brutes with drive wheels at the front and tank tracks on the rear six axles. There could be ten fully armed troops in the back, if Dietz's guess as to why the soldiers were sitting on the front proved to be correct. So that means there could be at least sixteen Ivans and only seven of them. Good odds. Christ, it was better than Boskovice. There must have been thousands of them there.

"Get back to your position and take out the driver of the jeep with the sniping rifle. Wait until he gets to the bend in the track and you can see the Order of Lenin swinging on his bloody tunic and then let him have it. Body shot. With any luck, he'll roll the car and that'll take care of the two men in the back."

The officer got to his feet and picked up his MP40 machine pistol, which had been propped against a nearby tree. He turned back to Dietz, who had already concealed himself behind an old tree trunk on the brow of the hill. He had unslung the Mauser and was drawing a bead on the point where the sandy track led out of the forest.

"I'll take the rest of the men and the panzerfaust and deal with the Hanomag. We'll hold our fire until you shoot the driver." Dietz gave the thumbs-up signal without looking at the officer. He may be a complete swine, the officer thought, but he was a damned good soldier and was the best shot in the Das Reich Division. For that matter his remaining six men were the best soldiers in the Waffen SS. They didn't like him much, and Dietz hated him—he knew that—but they had all survived, and that bonded them together.

The officer moved fast down the slope toward the boulders that would shield him and his men from the road. As long as the Soviets didn't leave the track, they'd get a clear shot at the Hanomag as it reached the slight bend fifty meters away from their position. Just don't get any big ideas about the roads being mined, Ivan, he thought.

As he approached the rocks the other five were already there with the panzerfaust. It was just as well they had trained for this over the last two days.

He hit the ground in the middle of the group as the Hanomag came into view. Two seconds later, the jeep followed it out of the wood. The officer watched with satisfaction as the two vehicles continued along the track. Just to his right he heard a faint click as the panzerfaust was armed, and out of the corner of his eye he could see the soldier raise the device to his shoulder. The bend in the road was right at the extreme of the rocket launcher's range, but there was nothing else for it. They would have been spotted a mile off if they left the cover of the rocks and got any closer. Let's just hope that hothead Dietz doesn't get an itchy trigger finger, thought the officer.

It was then that the Hanomag stopped.

"Scheisse." The word hissed under his breath. He didn't dare use the powerful Zeiss binoculars for fear the bright March sun might reflect off the lenses and alert the Russians. He squinted into the distance and could see an Ivan standing up in the rear of the Hanomag, flagging down the jeep. The man jumped over the side of the personnel carrier and wandered over to the smaller vehicle. Thirty seconds later he was back at the Hanomag; he walked ten meters past it and dropped to his knees.

He's looking for mines. For God's sake don't leave the track, he thought. The officer held his breath and felt his stomach knot and twist, until the pain was agony. Nerves and dysentery could incapacitate a man. Then the Russian stood up and beckoned the Hanomag on. He walked, scanning the ground, while the Hanomag inched along the track several meters behind him. Christ, if he carries on at this rate, the bloody war will be over, thought the officer. Worse than the tearing pain in his stomach was the awful realization that the Russian scout might be able to see Dietz, or even the whole group, as he got to the bend in the road. Then it would all be over. The Hanomag's heavy-caliber machine gun would pin them down among the boulders and they would fire back until their ammunition ran out. Without surprise on their side they would never be able to get a clear shot with the panzerfaust. One thing was for sure, he wouldn't be taken alive by those savages.

The officer's anxiety faded when he saw the scout jump back in the Hanomag, and then both personnel carrier and jeep proceeded swiftly along the track toward them. The scout must have satisfied himself that the patch was free of mines. They reached the bend. The panzerfaust wobbled briefly in the hand of the man on his right. Steady, steady, the officer thought. Come on, Dietz. Nothing. Come on, you Bavarian oaf.

Ten meters away, Dietz shifted the center of the cross on his telescopic sights from the driver's head to his left shoulder. He was briefly fascinated by the animated discussion that the two officers in the back seemed to be having. Then he fired.

The wheels on the jeep locked hard around to the right and the vehicle slewed over onto its side, catapulting one of the passengers to the ground ten meters away from the edge of the road. The officer saw one of the Russians on the front of the Hanomag crane his neck around to where the jeep had been behind them. His eyes were wide with terror.

There was a flash and a deafening crack to the officer's right. The rocket shell left the panzerfaust and hit the Hanomag just behind the driver's cabin. It was no coincidence that it had found the thinnest point of the vehicle's armor. Anyone who had traveled in the German personnel carrier never sat just behind the driver's seat. The metal there was so thin you could use it as cigarette paper; that had been the old Wehrmacht joke when the Hanomag made its first appearance during the Blitz-krieg in Europe. The corporal with the panzerfaust knew exactly where to aim.

The Hanomag evaporated. Ivan never learned. Those stupid potato-heads must have stored some ammo in the back of the vehicle.

Now they'd have to move fast before every Russian in central Czechoslovakia came down on them like a ton of bricks.

When the dust settled seconds later, there was no sign of movement around either the jeep or what was left of the Han-omag. The SS officer cocked his machine pistol and walked down the hill to the nearer of the two vehicles. His feet slipped once on the rough scree slope, but he kept his balance by grasping a clump of grass that was growing up through the rocks.

The rear wheels of the upturned jeep were still spinning furiously. The officer looked at the two bodies lying spread-eagled on the ground beside it and then beckoned to the rest of his men who had remained by the boulders. He put a boot under the belly of the driver and rolled him onto his back. Dietz had done a good job. The old rogue must have used a dumdum, because the bullet had blown off most of the Russian's left shoulder. There was no sign of his arm. The officer who had been behind him was also quite dead.

21

There was not so much as a forage cap to be found beside the burning chassis of the Hanomag as the officer and his men patrolled around it looking for signs of life.

Dietz had wandered down to the jeep and wasted no time in pulling off the Russian officer's watch. He then disappeared behind the vehicle and started rifling through the inside pockets of the vehicle's door. He emerged thirty seconds later with a khaki-colored, canvas dispatch case tucked under his arm.

The officer walked over to Dietz, who was admiring his handiwork with the Mauser.

"A good shot, sir?" Dietz looked up and was grinning from ear to ear, exposing an uneven row of brown teeth. "I keep a few of these beauties for special occasions." He was holding one of his specially doctored bullets between thumb and forefinger.

Then the officer noticed the dispatch case under his sergeant's arm.

"It was in the jeep, sir. In a compartment on the inside of the door. It's sealed."

"Give it to me." Dietz hesitated before handing the case to his superior officer. Several other camouflage-clad figures drew around the officer and Dietz, sensing in the air a showdown between them. If they disliked the officer, they absolutely detested Dietz. He was not only their sergeant and superior, but an outsider. Some even thought that he was a Nazi plant who'd been assigned to their platoon to spy on them.

If the officer's men had been less intent on the confrontation, they might have noticed a slight movement in the tall grass ten paces away from the jeep. As it was, the twitching arm of the second Russian officer who had been thrown furthest from the vehicle went completely unnoticed.

Major Yuri Paliev had been brought around by the sound of voices nearby. His rib cage felt as if a tank had driven across it, and he could taste blood in his mouth. He knew he was dying. Waves of pain were washing over him, but he was fighting them, motionless except for the twitching movement in his arm, over which he had no control. What bothered Paliev was that his mind was quite lucid—at least he thought it was—yet these men who seemed to be arguing a little way over to his left were not German. At first he thought that they had been ambushed by Slav partisans, who were not uncommon in that part of Czechoslovakia, but he knew some Slavic and he knew some German, and these men were neither.

22

He couldn't raise his head, but through the tall grass he could see a group of men. They were soldiers, all right, but it was hard to tell whose, for they wore camouflaged battle gear and even their helmets were covered in grass, twigs, and leaves. He couldn't get a look at the two men who seemed to be arguing, but one of them must be an officer, he thought, from the way he was barking out orders. With all his remaining strength, Paliev craned his neck for a better look. At the precise moment he spotted the peaked cap of the Waffen SS officer, one of his smashed ribs dug into his diaphragm and he screamed.

Seven heads spun around in the direction of the cry and three machine pistol bolts clicked in metallic unison as the guns were cocked.

One of the men ran over to the dying Russian and peered at his face. Blood was trickling from Paliev's mouth, but the soldier hardly noticed it. He was captivated by the quizzical expression, which furrowed the Russian's brow. It was as if the Ivan wanted to ask him something.

"Over here, sir! One of them's still alive!"

But it wasn't the officer who rushed over to the Russian's side first; it was Dietz.

"Who are you?" Paliev choked out in German. Dietz drew the bolt of his sniper's rifle back and slipped in a bullet. He cocked it and pointed the gun nonchalantly at the Russian's head.

"We're just about all that's left of the Second SS Panzergrenadier Regiment, Das Reich Division, Ivan, which is too bad for you." Dietz's finger tightened on the trigger.

The Russian's eyes looked imploringly at Dietz.

"What's bothering you, Ivan? Is it the others?" He laughed. "I am German. But these reprobates I've mothered for the last fifteen hundred kilometers, they're not. I'll show you."

Paliev could hardly understand a word the Bavarian was saying. He saw Dietz grab the soldier next to him and rip open his camouflaged jacket. The gray uniform underneath was the same as a thousand other SS uniforms he'd seen on dead Germans along the front. The young soldier did not resist as Dietz took off his battle smock. The others had all crowded around and some were laughing. It was as if they were playing a game that had been rehearsed many times before. Dietz grabbed the young soldier's arm and pointed to a little badge just below the elbow on the field-gray uniform.

"See Ivan? It's red, white, and blue." Dietz was reveling in the Russian's confusion. He could not have sounded more mocking. "We're a Freikorps unit. Very rare they are, too. You're a lucky boy." He laughed loudly again before reverting to the language that was the native tongue of his officer and those five other young idiots.

"Yes, we're a British Free Corps unit in the SS," he said slowly, mocking the aristocratic English accent of the superior officer.

He leveled his rifle once more at the Russian's forehead.

Paliev closed his eyes before Dietz's second dumdum bullet entered his cranium. He died without having a clue what the German had said.

3

Although it was raining lightly, Kruze chose to walk from Waterloo Station to the Air Ministry. The journey from Farnborough to the London terminus had taken well over an hour because of an unscheduled stop in a tunnel near Addlestone. Air raid, someone had said, and Kruze had not moved to disagree, even though he knew it was just another false alarm.

The rain fell more heavily while he walked down the Strand. He contemplated calling a cab as he dodged the pedestrians who weaved down the street of theaters and music halls, but dismissed the idea when the familiar sight of Nelson's column came into view. From Trafalgar Square the ministry was only a few minutes' walk.

Londoners seemed to have forgotten the war. The last German air raid on the capital was a distant memory. Although the buzz-bomb threat had been serious enough for the government to consider an evacuation of the city, everyone always referred to it as if it were nothing more than a mild nuisance. In the four years that he had lived among the English, he still had not quite got used to their vagaries.

Kruze paused by a crowd that had gathered outside the Rialto Cinema. The proprietor was shouting excitedly at a policeman and pointing at two lower-ranking officers, who joked and winked at the girls in the crowd when the policeman's back was turned.

"But I saw them do it!" The proprietor looked ridiculous in bow tie and ill-fitting impresario's jacket. There was loud laughter as one of the soldiers turned drunkenly and shrugged at his growing audience.

Kruze saw the object of the owner's displeasure. A poster, boasting the proud, manly figure of Errol Flynn in combat attire, had been defaced in a large scrawling hand with the word "pansy." The film was *Objective Burma* and it had caused quite a stir when it was first released in London, Kruze recalled. It implied that Errol Flynn had captured Burma from the Japanese single-handedly. An old woman caught Kruze grinning and frowned her displeasure. Kruze transferred his smile to her, touched his cap lightly, and moved on.

He skirted the edge of Trafalgar Square and looked up at the figure of Admiral Nelson. That the Germans had not flattened the center of London had been a miracle. The great buildings of Whitehall, the nerve center of the British war effort, bore few scars, unlike Waterloo. There, Kruze had seen workmen pulling down the shell of a huge warehouse, hit by a V2 attack some weeks before.

Approaching the ministry, Kruze patted the document in the inside pocket of his greatcoat. Once he'd delivered it he'd have more than enough time to take in a show or a film in one of the myriad theater halls that crowded the West End. Perhaps he would see the Errol Flynn film if the cinema had not been burned down by the mob he had just left.

The lobby of the Air Ministry was cold and gloomy, and a large puddle lay under the coat stand beside the main reception desk. Kruze took off his cap, exposing blond hair that was slightly longer than the regulation length. The middle-aged woman behind the desk smiled warmly at the Rhodesian.

"What can I do for you, sir?" The voice was from the East End of London.

"I'm carrying a dispatch for Air Vice Marshal Staverton. Special delivery." Kruze saw the heavily made up face crease for a second as she tried to place his accent.

"Right, sir, I'll have a pass made up for you right away."

"No, that won't be necessary," Kruze said quickly. The woman left the entry-forms drawer half-open and looked up at him in surprise.

Kruze lowered his voice. "Look, I'm on leave at the moment

and I've got a nasty feeling that if I see the old boy, I'll never get away. You know how it is." He leaned forward a little until he could smell the powder on her face. She blushed under the gaze of his bright blue eyes.

"Of course, sir. I'll see that this gets to the Air Vice Marshal all right. You'll have to sign for it, though."

Kruze printed his name on the form.

"Thank you, Squadron Leader," the woman said. "Enjoy your leave."

Kruze couldn't wait to get out. The thought of working at a desk in the ministry broke him out in a cold sweat.

He rushed headlong into the cold air outside and never even saw the person who collided hard with his shoulder. Before he knew it, the Women's Auxiliary Air Force sergeant was sitting in a puddle on the ministry steps, with rainwater splashed across her uniform.

"Aren't you even going to help me up, you ill-mannered oaf? No, on second thought, don't bother." There was something about that voice. The shapely legs swiveled around until her feet were positioned on a lower step. As she reached for her cap, fair hair cascaded down over her shoulders.

Kruze knew it was Penny Fleming even before she had turned around. She gasped when she recognized him, the mask of anger turning immediately to surprise.

"Oh, Piet, I'm so sorry. I'd no idea—"

He helped her up. "Don't apologize; it was my fault."

"No, really, I wasn't looking where I was going," she stammered. "Are you all right? I didn't mean to be so rude."

He smiled. "I hate to think what would have happened if you had."

She flushed and turned away from him. He bent down to pick up her cap, taking his time. When he handed it to her she seemed to have regained her composure.

"Look," he started, "if you need me to get you through security, I could go with you as far as the Bunker." The Bunker was the unofficial name for the basement nerve center of Staverton's intelligence effort. "You'll never reach Robert otherwise—you know what Staverton's like about guarding that miserable place."

"No, thank you." Her voice was firm, but her eyes seemed to shift nervously away from him. "I'm only leaving a message . . . a letter. They can take it down to him from the lobby."

He sensed she wanted to leave.

"I hope to see you both soon," he said. "I owe you a dinner . . ."

"That would be nice," she said, making her way up the steps toward the great door of the ministry.

Kruze walked back to Trafalgar Square and down the Strand again, searching out the cinema where *Objective Burma* was showing. He wanted as much to get out of the rain as to see the picture. He spotted the Rialto a hundred yards down the street. The crowd had disappeared, leaving only a few ticket seekers gathered by the foyer.

It exploded without warning. No one saw it and no one heard it coming. Kruze was lifted off his feet as the cinema and several buildings on either side disintegrated in a ball of flame. The rush of hot, choking air that swept over him a second later was accompanied by an eerie, high-velocity whistle.

Kruze tried to suck in the air that had been compressed from his lungs, then picked himself up and ran through the fog until he could see orange flames flickering through the clouds of dust and acrid smoke. As he stood before the epicenter of the blast, a cold breeze blew up from the banks of the Thames, driving the smoke away toward Piccadilly and fanning the flames to an intensity that forced back the few who had rushed to the building in the hope of finding survivors.

When the choking mist lifted, Kruze knew that few people would have survived in those buildings. A large store had taken the worst of the explosion, but the cinema was not much better off. Pieces of plush red seating poked through the shattered masonry. Broken pipes sprayed water over the entire scene, creating tiny, flame-free oases around them. A woman's body lay horribly mutilated a few feet from him, her limbs twisted and limp, as if every bone within them had crumbled into powder. Elsewhere, people attended passersby who had been caught by the blast in the street.

The crackle of the flames from the building mixed with the crescendo of pain from the survivors, until it was the human sound that dominated. A distant clatter of bells signaled the approach of the fire engines, and seconds later three arrived, weaving their way through groups of people in whose midst lay the wounded or dying.

When the fire engines fell silent, Kruze heard a cry from the far reaches of the cinema. At first he thought he'd imagined it, but then he heard it again. There was no one around him. The firemen were some distance away, bringing hoses to bear on the flames. Just then, two young soldiers appeared through the smoke and began pulling at the rubble twenty yards from him. Kruze called over to them, but they took no notice. Each had his own casualty to help. Realizing he was on his own, he darted toward the alley that used to separate the store from the cinema.

A moment later, the sound was distinctly recognizable as a plea for help, but Kruze could not see through the smoke. Then he saw the bright red sweater through the gray pall. For a second, Kruze was transfixed as the arms seemed to beckon to him. Then he realized that they were thrashing and clawing to be free of the wreckage. Kruze leapt over the smoldering velvet stage curtain between him and the obscured figure, and seconds later he was tearing at the bricks that had half-buried the young boy.

He could not have been much more than ten. When he stopped struggling, Kruze thought that he was too late, that the shock had killed him. He wiped the grime away from the small, bruised face and saw the tears squeezing out between tightly clenched eyelids.

"What's your name, feller?" Kruze tried hard not to transmit the slightest trace of panic in his voice.

The eyelids flickered open, but the reply was feeble. "Billy, sir."

"I'll have you out of here in no time, Billy. Can you move your legs at all?" The lad shook his head and began to cry, his chest heaving as the sobs convulsed his body. "I want my Dad," he whispered.

Kruze tore at the bricks once more and uncovered the beam that had fallen across Billy's legs, breaking both of them and pinning him to the floor. The Rhodesian bellowed at the top of his voice for assistance. On the other side of the ruins he could hear more bells: ambulances removing the dying and the wounded. There was little chance that any of the rescuers would hear him.

He tugged at the beam. At first it would not move, then it gave a little, but Kruze could only raise it a few inches off the ground. It was all he could do to prevent it from crashing down on the boy's pale and broken legs.

Kruze wiped the furrowed forehead and swept the matted brown hair from Billy's eyes.

"Listen to me," he said gently, "I'm going for some help. When I get back we'll have you out of here—that's a promise."

Kruze made a move, but the boy grasped him by the fingers and tugged with all his strength. "Please, don't leave me."

Kruze was about to soothe his fears when a gust of wind blew through the ruins, fanning the embers of the stage curtain, which had been slowly smoldering nearby. It burst into flames.

Kruze tore his hand free from Billy's grip and wrenched off his greatcoat. He tried to get close to the source of the flames but the wind whipped them into an inferno, which drove him back. He threw the coat over the boy and tried with all his strength to lift the beam high enough to throw it clear of Billy's feet. This time Kruze raised the thick wooden support almost a foot off the ground, but the weight of the masonry at one end made it impossible to do any more. Kruze screamed for more strength, but he felt the energy being sapped from his body. The beam started to slide from his fingers.

Kruze was startled when a pair of hands pulled Billy away from the smoke and the flames. The Rhodesian dropped the beam and ran, jumping over his fallen coat, which was now afire. He followed the figure that ran awkwardly with the boy through the smog-filled ruins in front of him, before losing them in a crowd of people who rushed forward to take the injured child to the nearest ambulance. As the white truck tore away, its bell clanging, the crowd parted to expose the anonymous rescuer.

Penny Fleming turned to face Kruze.

"I was just behind you when the explosion happened," she said. "I saw you dart into the building and knew you'd seen something."

"You could have been killed."

"So could you." She smiled. "I'm sorry I took my time, but it's hard to climb over rubble in high heels." She held up a battered shoe.

Away to the west the bell of an ambulance sounded above the din of the rescue workers.

"That poor little boy," she said, looking down the street. "Will he be all right?"

"His legs were badly broken, but he seemed like a brave kid. I think he'll pull through. Where are they taking him?"

"I heard one of the drivers say Charing Cross Hospital." She turned to the burning ruins of the cinema. "Do you think he had family in there?"

"He asked for his father once, but I don't know."

"Shouldn't we go with him? He'll be terrified, the miserable little thing."

"Penny, there's nothing we can do. He'll be unconscious by now, and in next to no time they'll be operating on his legs. He won't even wake up till tomorrow."

"Then I must go and see him. Tomorrow. " She paused. "What about you?"

He looked up at the scudding gray clouds, so different from the sky over the New Forest where yesterday he had almost flown her husband into the ground.

"Why not? I didn't really want to see Errol Flynn anyway." She looked puzzled.

"He was playing here at the Rialto."

"Oh, I see." She laughed. She studied him for a moment, unsure what he intended. He held her gaze. "What happened?" she asked, suddenly feeling conspicuous amid the rescuers picking their way through the rubble. "I heard someone say it was gas."

Kruze beat the dust from his cap. "It wasn't gas. The V2 is faster than sound, so there's no hint it's coming. Just an explosion, followed by that rushing sound. Once you've heard it, you'll never forget it." He looked back into the smoke. "Gas explosions are convenient explanations, not so bad for morale. Ordinary people don't like hearing about weapons that kill hundreds at a time with no warning."

She shivered. "I've never been so . . . close before."

The rain had soaked her hair, causing several strands to fall down over her face. The defiance that had been etched there when she had turned on him outside the ministry had disappeared, revealing soft, fair features instead. There was a look about her, he thought, that bordered on elation.

"It doesn't do to think about it," he said.

She shook her head and smiled. "Not death—my God, I hadn't really thought about that. I meant the war. It's happened, here, and I finally did something about it. I actually saved a life, instead of shuffling pieces of paper around for the RAF."

The Rhodesian remembered his dinner at their cottage, so English with its little gravel path, the wild roses over the porch, and, inside, glimpses and snatches of an alien life. Photographs of Robert at his pukka public school, studio portraits of her parents, staring from their frames in that way only the British

31

aristocracy could. Talk of racing, parties, picnics, large country estates, and the antics of eccentric friends. She was, and was not, a part of all that.

They stood watching each other, while a short distance away the firemen battled to keep the blaze under control. Kruze was suddenly struck by the absurdity of their surroundings.

"Look, we're going to freeze if we don't get moving."

"What do you suggest?"

"We could get a drink. I reckon I owe you one."

She looked at her watch. It was past closing time. "A drink? At this time of day? My dear Piet, this is London, not some Rhodesian country club."

He smiled. "Come on, I know just the place."

□

At that moment Robert Fleming was a hundred miles away, heading for the burns ward in the military hospital attached to the United States Eighth Army Air Force base at Horsham St. Faith in Norfolk, on some wild bloody goose chase.

A B-17 gunner, pumped to the eyeballs with morphine, had ranted about being attacked by a rocket fighter. Not that there was anything unusual in that. The stubby little Me 163B Komets had been knocking B-17s and Liberators out of the sky every day of the week for the last four months. They were highly effective, quick-reaction fighters, but their flaw was that they were short on range. Their modus operandi was simple: wait for the bomber waves to come over, light the rocket, pop up to thirty thousand feet, knock down a Fortress, or two, or three, and glide back to base.

The remedy had been fairly simple, too. Plot the Me 163B bases and stay well clear of them.

Now this gunner had gone and said that a 163 had pounced on his straggling B-17 over the North Sea—almost two hundred miles from the German coast. So the Americans, in their wisdom, thought the EAEU should hear about it. Hallucinations from a dying man. But someone had to check it out.

Fleming flipped the report shut. Poor sod. Probably just as well he'd lost his marbles. All the way to Regensburg and back, only to have his Fortress blow up over the field. Must have pulled his rip cord somehow. But the nine other crewmembers were all gone.

Horsham, one of the largest bases of the occupying U.S. forces, who had been present in Britain since 1942, took some of the worst casualties among the Fortress and Liberator crews during the course of the "Mighty Eighth's" daylight raids over Germany.

Fleming had been apprehensive on the train journey from London to Norwich, and the feeling did not disappear during the early part of the ride in the staff car that took him the few miles from the railway station. He had made a supreme effort to quell the pain that was welling up inside him at the thought of the visit ahead. From what he had seen of Marello's medical dossier, it read even worse than his own.

Fleming had become more relaxed the closer he got to the base. He had been raised in East Anglia and had spent a happy childhood in Wymondham, a market town close by. Many people hated the flatness of the countryside, but for Fleming it was an exhilarating place. Apart from a few remote cottages by the roadside, the scenery was devoid of habitation and the wild pine trees, separated by the rough, grassy heathland, had a strange, primeval quality, which he had always liked.

It was all infinitely preferable to the Bunker, which he shared with Staverton when the Old Man wasn't down at Farnborough. His office was situated twenty feet below ground and he hardly ever got to see the light of day. Trips like this were rare. Most of the data analysis that came with the job was carried out in the Bunker, as it was irreverently referred to by those who worked at the ministry.

Fleming had no idea what Kruze had said to Staverton during his debrief after the Junkers fiasco at Farnborough, but the AVM had been strangely conciliatory when he had eventually reported in, suggesting he should go to Horsham St. Faith to get out of London, enjoy the journey, get some fresh air. But Staverton couldn't seriously have placed any credence in the gunner's story. At the back of his mind he had the nagging feeling that this was another of Staverton's tests of his mental and physical condition.

His thoughts were interrupted as he caught a glimpse of a B-17 lumbering over the airfield perimeter about a hundred yards away, its flaps fully extended and four 1200-horsepower Wright Cyclone engines straining as it came in to land.

Once Fleming went through the double doors, the smell of aviation fuel would be replaced by the antiseptic odor of the burns ward. He hesitated for a moment at the threshold. To go back into a hospital was the one thing he'd never wanted to do in his life. He felt his stomach contract and thought for a moment he'd have to turn back. He fought the compulsion to retch. He breathed in hard and willed the panic to subside.

Fleming reported to a duty nurse and asked where he could find Sergeant Antonio Marello. As he followed her to the wounded airman's bed, he forced himself to turn from his own past.

One glimpse of Marello was enough to confirm the seriousness of his injuries. Dear God, Fleming thought, thank you for not letting me burn.

The man before Fleming had no hair. The flames that had seared his head had also taken lumps of his scalp. The combined effect of the wounds and the zinc anti-burn ointment made Fleming feel sick.

"That's the last goddamned time I ever wear a baseball hat on ops, sir."

Fleming was quite unprepared for the man's reaction to his stare. The nurse had told him not to be deceived by the patient's apparent well-being—morphine had that effect. The gunner, she said, was dying. Although she was angry at Fleming's intrusion, the base commander had been insistent that she should allow Marello to answer his questions.

"I'm sorry?" He looked fixedly into Marello's eyes.

"I'm never going to wear a baseball hat on ops again." Marello's accent, very slow from the drugging, betrayed his New York City upbringing, but not the slightest trace of pain.

Then he understood. The American had been wearing a cotton baseball cap, a common practice among U.S. crews, when the B-17 exploded. His goggles and oxygen mask had protected him from the worst of the flames, but his flimsy hat had disintegrated and his hair with it.

"I don't like having to do this," Fleming began, realizing how phony he sounded, "but if it helps you at all while we talk, I've been through some of what you've just come through." Christ, he didn't mean to sound that patronizing.

"You in bombers too?" The American was searching for a further bond between them. Fleming wished he could have said yes. He already felt a kinship with this man, but he didn't know how to express it.

"No. I was with a fighter squadron, until an FW 190 pushed me into early retirement."

"Fighters?" Marello queried with a sneer. "If the P-51s had been doing their job, *Gypsy Mae* would still be around today." He referred to his B-17 as if it had been alive.

The gunner had strayed onto the subject of Fleming's quest. He decided to capitalize on it.

"It's really your brush with the enemy aircraft that brought you down that I've come here to talk about. Tell me about it." Fleming feared he was being too brusque. His surroundings, the state of the crewman, had made him edgy. "I heard what happened to your crew. I'm very sorry." It sounded like the afterthought that it was.

Marello's brow furrowed and his eyes glazed over for a second. He shook his head. His voice sounded shakier than it had before.

"Well, sir, I didn't realize what I had seen at first, but I caught a sight of it at about twelve o'clock and high above us. How high, I couldn't say, but shit, was it moving."

"You say 'it.' What was it?"

"It was a long way away and I ignored it at first. I thought it must have been one of them inbound buzz bombs. I didn't even bother to tell the others. The skipper had his hands full as it was. We'd been shot up pretty bad over the target." He flinched uncontrollably. The reflex almost tore out the needle that fed the plasma drip into his arm.

"The first I knew the thing was coming for us was when the radio bust loose with shouts from the other guys. I caught something about a plane screaming at us like a bat out of hell . . ."

Fleming sat on the edge of his chair and heard how Marello swung his turret around to sweep the sky above the solitary B-17 to be confronted by a small, stubby aircraft, its wings swept back like a swallow in a dive.

"Jeez, it moved so damn fast. I couldn't even get a fix on him. And it kept on diving like it was going to ram us, but then it must've passed between the fuselage and the edge of the wing. The next thing I knew, the number three engine was on fire. Chuck Deller, the skipper, he did damn well to shut it down and get the extinguishers on, but I never saw the Kraut again." His voice trailed off; his head lolled on the pillow.

Fleming's skin prickled.

"But you'd seen these machines before, hadn't you?"

The American shook himself slowly.

"Sure, we'd seen 'em many times. But not when we were only a half hour from base."

"About fifty miles from our coast—you're positive about that."

Marello fixed his gaze on Fleming. For a moment the eyes ceased to swim in their sockets.

"Like I told the other guy, when you're that close to home you start counting the miles off."

"What happened next?"

The gunner winced as a spasm gripped his body. The returning pain helped to focus his mind.

"About thirty seconds later, an explosion hit the ship. Deller was yelling to the two waist gunners to tell him what had happened, but there was no reply, so he told me to go and check out aft. That Komet must have come back for us 'cause he left a hole the size of a house in the underside of the Fort that took Lieb with it."

Fleming had seen the crew roster back in the Bunker. Liebowitz was the ventral gunner, just about the worst job you could have on a Flying Fortress. Cramped in a fishbowl slung under the middle of the giant bomber, with his face nuzzling the breeches of the twin Browning machine guns, he was dangerously exposed.

Fleming looked down at his feet, trying to picture the awful scene. The rocket fighter's 30-millimeter cannon must have sliced up through the bomber and evaporated Liebowitz's turret. Marello was faced with a gaping gash where once there had been a manned defensive position.

"The two waist gunners, they were dead too . . . but it was the thought of Lieb stuck there in his turret . . . he just never stood a chance."

When Fleming glanced up from the floor Marello had started to sob softly. The morphine was wearing off. Fleming looked around for the duty nurse, but she was nowhere in sight. Marello had begun to moan. The low wailing sound grew as the man relived, over and over again, the last moments of his ship. Fleming moved from his chair to the bed and took Marello in his arms, holding him tightly while the spasms brought on by the memory twisted and contorted his body.

Fleming held the gunner as Penny had held him, night after night. Later, when the pain left him and the nightmares began, she still cradled him, until morning broke and he wasn't in the burning cockpit of his Spitfire, but between the sweat-soaked sheets of their bed in the cottage.

Penny watched him stripped of his dignity, layer by layer. In the end, there was nothing left of the boy with the public-school bravado, with whom she had first fallen in love. He had become a pathetic creature, at times unable to perform even the most basic bodily functions. That was when the rage began. God knows how he had summoned the strength for such emotion. He hated her for witnessing what he had become.

Fleming held Marello tighter and felt the gunner give.

He had never watched a man die. He had been surrounded by death on the squadron, but it had never touched him physically, like this. When he had been stationed in Italy, an aircraft or two failed to return some days. That night, the survivors would get drunk and the next day ops continued. There hadn't been much time for mourning.

Marello would die a long way from home with no one by his side. Fleming shuddered. He had been a whole lot luckier.

His urge to hold Marello had been instinctive, just as hers had been with him. Yet he had thrown it all back in her face. He had wanted to retreat, to run away from his image of what he had become. He knew now that if he had been in the American's place, frightened and alone, he would never have found the will to live.

Fleming bit his lip as the panic rose again. All along he thought it had been his own efforts that had pulled him through. That somehow he had reached into himself and tapped a deep reservoir of strength, which had enabled him to claw his way back.

His marriage had been the price of that selfishness.

When he found her, crying in their bedroom one day, his anger had exploded. She had no right to feel sorry for herself. No bloody right at all. He remembered the quarreling. Voices raised. He remembered hitting her, hard. Watched as she recoiled, put her hand to her face, then stared wide-eyed at the blood on her fingers. He tried to shut out the picture, but it was no good.

A few days later he started work at the Bunker. Three months ago. It seemed longer.

With him in London and Penny commuting between her job at the fighter control station and the cottage, they had seen each other a handful of times since.

Marello convulsed again and Fleming squeezed him gently. Long minutes crawled by before the nurse returned with a syringe, to administer another shot of oblivion. But as Marello was approaching darkness, his comforter Fleming was approaching the light.

4

When Kruze opened the door for her, the boozy, smoke-filled atmosphere of the Trocadero Hotel's Almond Bar hit Penny a few moments after the cacophony of animated voices.

Kruze led her toward the bar through a maze of uniforms she had never seen before. There were men sporting the shoulder flashes of the Polish Air Force and the Norwegian Army. She picked out snatches of French from the conversation around her and saw American uniforms brushing against the deep blue tunics of the Royal Air Force. There were girls too, wild and exotic-looking.

To Penny, it seemed as if everyone knew each other, although she knew that could not be so. The party throbbed with a gaiety she had never experienced before. She watched one of the girls detach herself from a group and walk across the room, an empty glass held conspicuously in front of her, as she searched for company and a fresh drink. A free French officer was the first by her side, much to the annoyance of two British soldiers. The Frenchman caught Penny looking at him over the girl's shoulder and winked at her mischievously. She smiled and waved back.

Kruze, at last at the bar, turned and saw a different woman from the one he had knocked to the ground on the ministry steps barely an hour before.

"You like this place?"

A song had started up in the corner so she moved closer to him.

"You like this place?" He was almost shouting in her ear.

She nodded vigorously. "I love it. How on earth did you find it? I thought I knew Shaftesbury Avenue, but I've never heard of the Almond Bar, let alone the Trocadero Hotel."

"Word-of-mouth stuff. Unfortunately the jungle telegraph works a little too well. Last time there were just a few forty-eight–hour passers and some Windmill girls. Now look at it."

"Windmill girls?"

Kruze nodded to the woman in the clinging, expensive-looking evening dress, who now had one arm around the Frenchman and a new drink in her other hand.

"They're chorus girls from the Windmill Theater around the corner," he said. "Help to liven the place up a bit. What are you going to drink? They've got just about everything."

"I'll have a whiskey—a small one; lots of water."

They made their way over to a corner where it was quieter. Kruze was about to raise his glass in a toast, but somehow the gesture seemed wrong. Instead he gazed past her through the window, watching passersby scuttle out of the wind and the rain in the approaching darkness.

"Suddenly worried that somebody on the squadron might see us here?"

He was surprised at the ease with which she had guessed his thoughts.

"Not for the reason you think."

"And what might that be?"

"I couldn't give a light if one of the boys were to round the corner and see me with you. It's not as if talking is against the law. I was thinking of Robert. And this place. Somehow the two don't go together. Perhaps it was wrong to bring you here."

"It's all right." She smiled. "Just because Robert might prefer his club, there's no need for you to feel guilty."

"How is he?" The words came before he could stop them. He didn't want to talk about her husband, but the picture of him running from his Spitfire at Farnborough suddenly filled his mind.

"I don't know. To be honest, Piet, Robert and I see very little of each other these days."

He sensed her awkwardness.

"Staverton's a tough old bird," Kruze said, trying to fill the void. "He works Robert to the bone. I expect it must be difficult for him to get away."

"That wasn't what I meant," she said softly.

He looked her in the eyes. "I didn't think it was. I was merely trying to . . ."

"I know; thank you." She looked back into her glass. "I don't think he cares too much about us anymore." She shook herself slightly. "Anyway, enough of that."

"For what it's worth, I don't much like your husband, but he's damn good at his job, even if he is sometimes a pig to deal with. But please don't think I'm trying to stick my nose into things that don't concern me. Domestic rows aren't any of my business."

"Piet, I'm not talking about a tiff. I'm divorcing him."

Kruze faltered. "Then what were you doing in the ministry?"

"I wanted to tell him it was over. No more nights on my own. No more rows. I wanted to tell him we both had to let go."

"And did you?"

She shook her head. "I resorted to Plan B and left a letter at the main desk. The time for talking to Robert is over." She stared into the middle of the room for a moment. "That's not exactly true. I meant to, but I'm afraid I didn't have the courage to tell him to his face. So much for the heroine of the Strand."

"Does he know it's gone this far?"

"If he doesn't, things are even worse than I think they are."

"I'm sorry," he said. "I should have known better than to ask after that night I came over for dinner."

"Was it that bad?"

"No, I enjoyed it." He smiled. "I'm not so sure about your friend, Anne Fairhall, though. We didn't exactly see eye to eye. Different cultural backgrounds, you might say."

"Anne?" She looked at him for a moment, her head cocked slightly to one side. "I have to admit now that it was a bit naughty. When Robert described you as the silent type, I thought I'd ask her over to liven things up a bit. The only trouble is, she does go on a bit."

"Silent? Is that what he said?"

She thought for a moment. "Not exactly; I think that was my interpretation. If I remember right, 'dangerous' was the actual word he used. Only he didn't mean it in a derogatory way, I don't think. He said you're an exceptional pilot, aloof from the rest of the chaps, but loved by the noncommissioned men. Anyway, I was wrong. And I'm sorry I subjected you to a whole evening with Anne. It won't happen again, I promise."

She thought about that for a moment. "I think dinner parties are going to be off the agenda for a while."

"Have you got somewhere to stay?"

"Yes, thank God. My sister has let me use her apartment for a day or two. It will allow me some breathing space while I get myself together. Then I'll go back to the cottage and keep busy until I go back to work in a few days' time. The CO's been very understanding. I really don't want to talk to Robert. It won't do either of us any good." She let out a deep breath. "I'm sorry to burden you, Piet. I've fought it for months now, but I just can't live with him anymore."

Kruze tried not to show his discomfort. "Time for another drink," he said.

When he returned with two Scotches, Penny looked composed.

"What now, then?" he asked.

☐

It was shortly after seven o'clock when Fleming emerged from the underground station and set off on foot for the ministry. The cold weather that had prevailed since the beginning of the year had eased a little, although the light rain still made the capital look drab and miserable. He felt an urgent need to get to the cottage, to Penny, and he reckoned with any luck he would be able to catch a train out of the city the following day, Staverton permitting.

He was both tired and revived after his visit to Norfolk. Marello had deeply disturbed him, but that moment of holding him, and in turn having the vision of himself being held by Penny—this had had the impact of an epiphany, a turning point. He wanted to go home to explain, to tell Penny it had not been all in vain. To tell her what a selfish bloody fool he had been all these months, that it had been she who had pulled him through.

A corporal standing guard on the north door of the ministry scrutinized Fleming's pass before clearing identification with his department in the Bunker. While he shuffled from foot to foot waiting for authorization to proceed into the building, he was surprised to see that tape had been crisscrossed over the windows since his departure that morning.

"Rocket, sir," the corporal said as he stamped the papers. "It landed just over there in the Strand."

There hadn't been a V1 or V2 strike on England for several weeks. He hoped that this latest attack was not a signal for another missile blitz on London. With the Russians pressing at the gates of Berlin, he, like many other Londoners, had become complacent about the Germans.

Then there were the implications of what Marello had said. They already knew the Germans had a fighter that could outfly anything in the RAF or USAAF inventory, but its limited range had confined it to a local nuisance. If the American's report was accurate, they could bring the air war back to Britain's doorstep, something they hadn't been able to do in force for almost five years.

Staverton was often hard to track down among the maze of corridors that riddled the huge building. As one of the select team of technical advisers to the Cabinet, there was no end of senior brass, civil servants, and ministers who wanted his time. In view of the afternoon's V2 attack, Fleming was surprised to find the AVM at his desk, hunched over some papers. Staverton did not divert his attention from the small pool of light shed by the lamp as the door closed, so Fleming coughed lightly.

"Ah, Robert. Didn't hear you come in, I'm afraid. I was a bit wrapped up in the business of this afternoon's raid. Doubtless you've heard about it—probably even seen the mess in the Strand."

"I came by underground, sir. I didn't know anything about the attack until I got into the building . . . How many came over?"

"Just two, thank God. There were about forty casualties at the home store and that picture house next door. The other one fell on a warehouse on the Isle of Dogs. That one didn't kill anyone, luckily. Funny thing, though. The police discovered that the warehouse had been crammed full of cigarettes, cans of food, stockings, you name it. All burned to a crisp now. Some black marketeer is going to be cursing the Germans tonight."

"Where did they come from?" Fleming asked. "I thought we'd destroyed their missile plants weeks ago."

"We did; and that was exactly the same question Number Ten put to me earlier this afternoon. Intelligence reports suggest that this was a one-shot. I heard just before you came in that our people on the Continent have traced the firing position to a small town in southern Denmark. Apparently some garrison commander decided to loose off his old stock before his position was overrun by our troops. I told Churchill not to worry about it. I hope I'm right."

He was rarely wrong, Fleming thought.

"Now, Robert, Norfolk. How did you get on?" Staverton gave Fleming a look that suggested he was not interested in the intelligence-gathering part of the exercise. It confirmed Fleming's suspicion about why he had been sent.

"The Germans have developed a long-range rocket fighter," Fleming said, not giving an inch.

"You don't mean you were actually taken in by this gunner's delusions? My dear Robert, I only sent you up there to placate a rather hysterical USAAF intelligence officer."

"I don't think they were delusions."

"Let's hear it then."

"The gunner had been pretty badly knocked about, that's true. And he had been given morphine—he was in a lot of pain."

"Come on, Robert. Was it or wasn't it a 163? And, more to the point, where was it?"

Fleming sensed that Staverton could see he had survived his brush with the medical profession remarkably well.

"The Flying Fortress was attacked about fifty miles off Blakeney Point on the north Norfolk coast," Fleming said, determined not to let Staverton get the better of him. "And I'll tell you why I believe that. Marello was a very experienced gunner. He was halfway through his second tour and he'd come up against 163s before, several times, over Germany. Having been through hell over the target and having nursed the aircraft back over the North Sea, they thought they were safe. And that's when they were attacked. He described the aircraft perfectly. It was a 163, all right." He tossed a buff manila folder on Staverton's desk. "It's all in the report."

Staverton sucked his teeth. "That's all we need," he said. He would have a lot more to tell Churchill and the Cabinet tonight.

"Very well, Robert, we'll talk about this again in the morning. If you're right, the next few days are going to get damn busy."

Fleming saluted and turned for the door. There went the prospect of some leave.

"Oh, Robert . . ."

Fleming paused with his hand on the door knob. Staverton looked levelly at him.

"Nice work," he said.

□

Since he had been working in the Bunker, home for Fleming had been a small, rented, studio apartment in Courtfield Gardens.

Once inside, the strain of the trip to Norfolk caught up with him. He felt a sudden, searing pain where the worst ridges of scar tissue crisscrossed his chest and stomach. He breathed deeply and massaged the point where it seemed worst.

He walked into the kitchen, found a drop of whiskey in a bottle at the back of a bare food cupboard and poured himself a last, stiff measure. He intended to call Penny at the cottage the moment the alcohol had settled in and loosened his tongue enough so that he could bring himself to say that he wanted to see her as soon as possible, and to explain why.

He walked back into the sitting room and collapsed in a chair, cursing as he crumpled the smartly pressed tunic that he had thrown over the seat back. When he pulled it out from behind him, the small brown envelope fell from a pocket to the floor. He had not opened it when he had found it in his pigeonhole on the way out of the ministry. He always savored her notes and letters. He realized again that that was something else he had never told her.

He smiled to himself. It was just like her to use their best vellum and seal it in a shabby, official-use-only envelope.

The smile left his face before he had even started to read. The needles of panic, the same ones that had jabbed his flesh through the sweat that covered his body in the Spitfire's cockpit the day before, were there again. But this time he managed to fight them.

The writing was bold, rounded, in keeping with the finality of the message. She exhorted him to read the letter through, not crumple it into a ball and throw it away. In that moment he felt the change in himself more acutely than ever. It was what he would have done, pretended it was not happening.

He read, carried along by the conviction in her words and wondered, in some faraway part of his mind, why it was that he already felt jealous. He had never felt that way about her before. She had always been there; he never imagined she wouldn't be. He had seen men looking at her—longing for her, even—but it had never concerned him. He cursed his arrogance, and understood a little better why she was doing what she was.

He turned the pages, looking for evidence of self-doubt, or a weakness in her hand to tell him that she didn't mean it, but there was none. A terrible thing had happened to him; she didn't shrug it off. Another man would have died, but the price of his survival had been their marriage. It was the frustration of not being able to help, for in everything she had done before she had never known failure. She too had started to become bitter, try as she had to fight it. She saw it starting to twist her in the same way that it had him. She didn't want it to take them both. She hoped he would try, in the months ahead, to understand. There was no mention of the day he had hit her, no outpouring of emotion, no recrimination at his failure to let her in during the last few difficult months. It was a practical decision.

"You left it just a little too late, didn't you, old boy?" he told himself.

His hand fumbled for his glass and he brought the whiskey to his lips. When the alcohol permeated his stomach wall, he began to feel calm enough to think it through.

It had been almost a fortnight since he had last been at the cottage and, following a pattern that had been set since his convalescence, things hadn't exactly been cordial between them. He couldn't blame her. He had been nothing short of cruel. And with that realization came the knowledge that he had not only the strength to live without her, but the determination not to give her up without a fight.

When he felt steady, he walked into the hall and asked to be connected to Padbury 278.

It rang for two minutes before the operator apologized and told him that she would have to disconnect him. Wartime rules prevented her from allowing him the line any longer. Perhaps he could try again the following morning? The caring female voice persuaded him that that was the best course of action.

He replaced the handset slowly and walked down the narrow corridor to the bedroom, taking his cigarettes and the dregs of the whiskey with him.

□

Kruze knelt beside the fire. He blew on the glowing logs until the warmth began to spread to the corners of the sitting room.

No light was on in the small, low-ceilinged room, but when

he turned around he could see the slight mist of perspiration on Penny's brow as she stood watching the flames. She was wearing her blue WAAF skirt and shirt; the jacket had been thrown over the small sofa by the hearth rug.

Her tie was off, the collar open. The glow from the fire played over her face, its soft light making her look even more beautiful. She had let her hair down and the long, gently waving curls fell over her shoulders and down her back.

They had spent the last three hours at the dinner table talking the lighthearted banter of two adolescents discovering each other for the first time. Kruze was startled to realize that three hours was time enough to start what was, probably, falling in love.

She looked at him and smiled.

He moved to her and ran his hand up her back, felt the heat of her skin beneath her shirt. She held him tightly and looked into his eyes.

"I need you," she whispered. "I hope you don't think that's—"

He kissed her before she could finish the sentence.

He explored her mouth. She responded, slowly winding her tongue around his. Then her hands were combing his jacket, undoing the buttons, tugging at his uniform. She managed to get it half off before he helped her. It fell on the ground between them. She ran her hands through his hair, then traced a long nail down his scalp, his neck, across his back. She felt the perspiration that soaked the top of his shirt, smelled the fresh, outdoor smell of him as she twisted and turned in his embrace.

He stopped and held her at arm's length. She opened her eyes and watched him as he stared, questioning, into her face. She smiled and opened her mouth a little. The flames flickered in the grate and reflected momentarily on her glistening lower lip. He ran his hands down her back and pulled at her shirt. Then his fingers moved over her bra strap, seeking the catch. He tugged and it seemed to give. She had undone her buttons so that when he slipped his hand over the cups of her bra, both it and the shirt fell to the floor.

She stood standing before him in the semidarkness with only her skirt on. He bent down and put his mouth around her nipple and sucked.

She moaned softly.

"Take me to bed." Her words were choked. He could hardly hear them.

They took the rest of their clothes off slowly, watching each other all the time, neither wanting to rush in case they broke the spell. Kruze felt as if he were drugged, or dreaming. Suddenly he prayed this was real, that he wasn't about to wake up and find himself in a strange place, without her.

5

The Focke Wulf 189 was a curious-looking aircraft. Between its twin engines the cockpit area was covered almost completely with Plexiglas for maximum visibility, designed as it was, exclusively for observation and tactical-photo reconnaissance.

In the nose of the German plane, Oberleutnant Rudi Menzel felt cold and vulnerable.

Cold, because his electrically heated flight suit was not functioning properly and because the damned FW 189 was more full of holes than the Wehrmacht's boots. He had remonstrated with the ground crew before the last flight for not patching up the aircraft following its brush with a Soviet La-9 several days before. Now the icy slipstream cut into his face as it was forced through the bullet holes and into the cabin at 280 kilometers per hour.

Vulnerable, because the FW 189 was slow and underarmed and he quite expected to see more Lavotchkins, Yaks, and any other Red Air Force fighter he hated to think about, between their present position and Chrudim, their destination, east of Prague.

His headset crackled. At least that seemed to be working; Menzel almost allowed himself to smile as he listened.

"Keep a lookout for enemy fighters. Especially you, Freddi, you dozy sod. No slipups like last time or I'll put in a personal

48

recommendation to the kommandant that you join our ground forces in the defense of the Reich. If we get bounced by Ivan we can't expect any help from our own fighters. Just remember that." The pilot, Hauptmann Pieter Klepper, sounded edgier than usual, Menzel thought, but he was right about Frederik Lutz. The idiot had let the La-9 get really close to them two days before because he'd thought it was one of their own FW 190s. The La-9 didn't look anything like the radial-engined German fighter, and there was Lutz, almost blowing kisses at the pilot until Ivan started shooting at them. Lutz deserved to be posted to a slit trench at the front. Then he wouldn't mistake Russians for Germans in a hurry.

Menzel got back to reading his map, every so often peering through the clouds for a landmark that would point them accurately to the Chrudim sector.

The Army had received reports of an unusually large Soviet presence in the area and had contacted the Luftwaffe to go and take a look-see. The twenty-year-old Klepper, being one of the most senior and experienced pilots on the squadron, had been tasked with his crew of two to take off from their airfield at Altenburg, forty kilometers south of Leipzig, and fly to Chrudim to establish the validity of the reports and, if they were substantiated, to bring back pictures.

Fucking marvelous, Menzel thought. Here he was, suspended four thousand meters above the earth and heading for one of the hottest sectors on the eastern front. All on the say-so of some madcap intelligence officer who had received spurious reports about a Soviet armored and logistics buildup in some shithole near Prague. So what. The Russians had been building up their forces in the region for months, and he hadn't noticed any sign yet of a German counteroffensive.

Menzel had no faith in the Wehrmacht's intelligence corps. For a start, Chrudim had been behind enemy lines in Czechoslovakia now for weeks. So what did the army know? The nearest an intelligence officer or a scout party had ever got to Chrudim in the last month was by staring at it on a map.

Since the big Russian breakthrough in eastern Czechoslovakia several months before, all had been chaos in the squadron. Things had become so desperate in the last few weeks that some joker at Luftwaffe staff headquarters had given orders for their FWs to be equipped with bombs. The mechanics jury-rigged racks under the wings and, the same afternoon, the lumbering aircraft had set out to bomb Soviet armor. Mercifully, their supply of bombs had run out ten days ago, so the squadron's remaining six aircraft went back to their observation duties. It was up to the Wehrmacht and the SS to defend the homeland against the Russian T-34 tanks now.

Below their port wing Menzel caught a gleam of sunlight on metal. Shit! Yaks scrambling to meet them. He was about to alert the others when a gap in the clouds showed him that it was water and not airframe on which the early morning rays of sun had reflected. Menzel glanced at his charts.

"Crossing the Elbe now, Herr Hauptmann. We should reach Chrudim in twenty minutes."

"Good," Klepper said. "Both of you. Keep alert. The Soviets must be worse than we think they are if they haven't spotted us by now. If we get bounced by fighters I'll head for the nearest clouds and try and shake them off. Once we get to Chrudim, the important thing is to take a look, take pictures, and get the hell out." Klepper's intercom clicked off.

Menzel scanned the sky, looking for a Soviet air presence, but saw none. Every so often he shot a quick glance at the cloud cover above them. The cumulus had never taken on such significance before. When the Yaks came for them Klepper would have a hell of a time finding cover.

As the March sun climbed higher into the sky, the clouds around them evaporated one by one.

□

So far, the major of tanks concluded, the *maskirovka*—the deception—had been a complete success.

As the engineers erected the last of the dummy T-34s in the town square of Chrudim, Major Kirill Malenkoy sat back in the rear seat of the jeep and ordered his driver to return to HQ.

The road that led from the little provincial Czech town was lined with T-34s and even the new Josef Stalins, their barrels stowed to the rear in readiness for rapid mobilization, their drivers' cupolas pointing northeast. The dirt track met the main Prague highway about ten kilometers from their present position. But this was one armored division that would never make it to the Prague-Berlin road, and Malenkoy smiled with satisfaction. General Nerchenko would be pleased with the progress. Who knows, maybe even Marshal Konev himself would hear of his handling of the *maskirovka* if the final maneuver proved a success. The major gazed down at his smartly pressed uniform and tried to imagine how the Order of Lenin would look among the other glittering medals that were pinned to his chest.

There was plenty more work to be done before the prized Order was his, though. The engineers had been instructed to erect another hundred tanks from the rough scraps of wood that had been sent forward from Ostrava by special convoy, and the major could also have done with another fifty engineers to ensure that he would finish the job on time. But judging by the speed with which his existing men had put together the first four hundred dummy vehicles, he estimated that he would be finished in a few days, easily within the deadline that had been set by Nerchenko.

As the GAZ jeep wound along the muddy track that led toward Branodz, Malenkoy cast a quick glance skyward to see if there was any sign of aircraft in the vicinity. He was pleased that the thick pines that lined the road almost totally hid the track from the air. Only a crazy Nazi would take his plane low enough to see any enemy activity on that road.

Nerchenko said that he had picked him for the *maskirovka* because Cadet Officer Kirill Malenkoy had passed out top in his year at the Red Army Academy at Smolensk, and *maskirovka*, the general noted, was the part of the training course for which Malenkoy had shown a particular aptitude. Malenkoy had shrugged it off modestly at the time. As a peasant's son, one who had spent his life in the forests and fields of Georgia, he had found the art of concealment, camouflage, and simulation very easy. When *maskirovka* became adopted as a formalized tactic of the Red Army, Malenkoy saw an opportunity for himself to shine in this uniquely Soviet technique of deception and disinformation. He was now something of a specialist in the field, having masterminded several similar operations in the early part of the "final offensive."

There were over fifteen hundred real T-34s hidden in the forests forty kilometers west of Chrudim at Branodz—the simple town also dubbed as Konev's HQ—which could wipe the Wehrmacht in this sector off the face of the globe if they were to roll toward Berlin now. Even the SS offered little resistance, except for the maniac Waffen SS terrorists who operated behind their lines.

Trying to flush them out was a job that the *stavka* left to the Siberian divisions. Fight fire with fire, Nerchenko had told him.

Maybe, but Siberians . . . he was damned thankful that he didn't have to work with them.

Among the junior officers at HQ the topical horror story was the tale of the Siberians who had murdered their young platoon commander, who had arrived from the academy only two weeks before. All fifteen of them had deserted and headed for the hills above the central Czechoslovak plain. The officer had pursued them across country and caught up with them after several hours. Picking up their tracks couldn't have been difficult. The trail of rape victims, both male and female, had considerably narrowed the search. The commander's attempts to bring them in had resulted in his death, too, but only after he had been tied, tortured, and screwed by each easterner in turn. The officer had had no choice but to find them, Malenkoy knew that. He had either to bring them back for trial, or to face the prospect of a bullet in the base of the skull for gross failure in the field.

Malenkoy's driver slammed his foot on the brakes and the jeep slewed across the road.

The first bullet splintered the windshield, the second tore a hole the size of a man's fist in the gasoline can that was strapped to the inside of the jeep next to Malenkoy's legs. He threw himself flat on the other rear seat, but not before he caught a glimpse of something in the middle of the road about fifty meters from them.

Malenkoy's mind screamed. He fumbled for his pistol. The driver was crashing the gears trying to find reverse. The smell of gas burned his nostrils. Why couldn't he get the fucking pistol out? Just as he felt the reassuring rough texture of the pistol grip, the driver found reverse and Malenkoy was jolted forward. Another crack, but no telling where the bullet found its mark. Malenkoy took a deep breath and came up from the seat letting four shots off in quick succession at the figure further up the track. The jeep shot forward and Malenkoy's fifth shot went wild. The driver tore off down the road back to Chrudim and Malenkoy fired the rest of his clip at the single assailant who had ambushed them like some sort of maniac, standing unprotected by cover, in the middle of the track.

The hunter had the last word. Malenkoy saw the flash from the panzerfaust just within the tree line and then the searing blast of hot gas caught him on the side of the face as the explosion tore into a pine only meters to his left. The jeep lurched onto two wheels and Malenkoy thought they would go over. The wheels spun, then gripped the surface of the road. Two seconds later they rounded a bend in the track.

Malenkoy and his driver never exchanged a word. The speed of their departure almost took them off the road at several points. The Russian kept his eyes on the dark interior of the forest, scouting the shadows for signs of movement or a hint of sunlight reflected off metal. They could be anywhere. It was the first time in three years of fighting that he had felt shit-scared. If one bullet had found the gasoline-soaked interior of the jeep, he would have been roast meat by now.

Shit! The fucking SS were in his sector. It hadn't been a partisan who had attacked them. He had seen the camouflaged battle smock and the coal-scuttle helmet. He had better place a call through to HQ when they got back to Chrudim. This was another job for the Siberians.

☐

Half a kilometer back up the track, the soldier was still swearing loudly at his comrades about the failure of the ambush.

They ignored the tirade of profanities. So two more Ivans had got away. There were probably half a million others in the area to choose from, judging by the enemy activity they had seen.

The officer was chastising the burly sergeant for his bungling stupidity. What had he hoped to achieve by darting into the middle of the road and taking on the Russians alone? Another act of disobedience like that and he would be shot.

As the small party of insurgents set off in single file through the forest, the sergeant smiled to himself. They would not dare to shoot him. Without his battle experience, they would never be able to make their way back through enemy territory to their own lines.

He slid back the bolt of his rifle and pulled out the unspent bullet with the soft snub head. He'd better go easy on those. He had only about ten left.

☐

The officer tried to control his anger as he joined the rest of the platoon. Dietz's decision to ambush the GAZ could not have come at a worse moment. As if they did not have enough problems getting back to their own lines, every Russian in the sector would now be on the lookout for them; and there would be search parties.

The dispatch case they had taken off the Russian major offered them a chance, but the officer needed time to study it and to think. He had been examining its contents when he heard the first shots from Dietz's Mauser.

What he saw had made him catch his breath. The maps inside the case seemed to show the exact positions and strength of all the Soviet units ranged along the eastern front. More than that, they highlighted areas of Allied strength and the location of his own forces. If they were genuine. It was most unusual for a mere major to be carrying such highly classified material.

He needed time to think.

□

"Fire off the port beam, Herr Hauptmann!"

"I see it. Let's take a look."

Klepper banked the Focke Wulf gently around to the north until the thin wisp of smoke emanating from the carpet of forest below was straight in front of them.

Menzel, in the nose of the Uhu, peered down through four thousand meters of icy-clear air at the source of the smoke trail. No sign of any activity down there, but according to his maps they were only twenty kilometers or so from Chrudim itself, so it was worth checking out. Could be some crazy Ivan patrol cooking a meal on an open fire in the middle of the great forest, reckoning themselves to be safe from any Germans. Klepper should take the plane down to treetop height and let him and Lutz spray the area with machine-gun fire. That would do something for their appetites. Menzel knew that Klepper would never give way to such a futile gesture. Their orders were simple. Take photographs of Chrudim and get out. No Ivan patrol was going to jeopardize the mission for Klepper, of that Menzel could be sure.

He checked his maps again. There should be a road down there. It was hard to see, but he could just make out a trail through the forest. Only then did he realize that the fire below was burning right beside the road that snaked its way off to Chrudim in the middle distance.

"Herr Hauptmann, that smoke is coming from a fire beside the main road into Chrudim. I think there must be a burning vehicle. Could be part of the reason we came here. Mind if we take a look?"

Klepper nodded. "We'll check it out. I'll continue on up the trail until we reach Chrudim. Make sure your weapons are armed, both of you. And Menzel, get ready with the cameras. You'll only have a few seconds over target."

The FW 189 went into a shallow dive. Menzel suddenly didn't notice the cold anymore. His heated flight suit still wasn't working, but he could feel the sticky perspiration soaking his back as he lay prone in the clear Plexiglas dome at the front of the aircraft.

He grasped the St. Christopher medallion that was swinging from his neck and squeezed it, his lips mouthing a silent prayer. His sweetheart had given him the charm when he had last been home on leave. Was it this year or last? He couldn't remember.

They were now skimming over the tops of the trees at 210 KPH. He felt an urge to cover his face with his arms as a bough danced crazily in front of his eyes before flashing past him in a green and brown blur.

The trail of smoke was straight ahead. Closer . . . closer.

They were already several hundred meters beyond the fire by the time Menzel radioed through to Klepper that there was nothing there, only a clump of trees burning beside the road.

Ten seconds later, the voice of Lutz, in the rear of the aircraft, cut in.

"Herr Hauptmann, we just passed an enemy jeep going like shit towards Chrudim. Disappeared before I could get a shot at him."

You moron, Menzel thought.

When he looked up, he could just make out the tower of the church of Chrudim on the skyline ahead of them and slightly to port. At that moment, Klepper turned to the left so that he was lined up directly with the landmark. It was then that Menzel noticed a needle-thin line of tracer bending around toward them from the top of the tower. He tried to get in a deflection shot with his MG 81, but was way off. The firing stopped, so the Russian must have gone for cover.

Klepper raised the nose of the Uhu and climbed to one hundred meters as they swept over the town. Menzel pressed down on the button at the end of the cable. Beneath the fuselage the twin Hasselblads clicked in concert, each snapping away at the scene below them at five frames a second. Menzel was dimly aware of a large square in the middle of the town that was filled with armor. He looked back as they passed over the target area. Jesus, the streets of the town were a mass of olive-green vehicles . . . trucks, armored cars, tanks.

The aircraft rocked in the turbulence as the FW was straddled by bursts of antiaircraft fire.

Klepper cut in over the din of the muffled explosions outside.

"I hope you got everything on camera, because that's it. No sense in risking our necks if we're going to get another reception like that."

The icy slipstream bit even harder into Menzel's face. The High Command would have to bring together all its reserve strength to have any hope of fending off an armored assault of that magnitude.

As Klepper set a course back for Altenburg, Menzel spared a thought for the troops that were preparing to defend the Fatherland from the Russians' spearhead assault from the south.

6

It didn't take them long to find the hospital, its red brick gothic towers and crenellations looming high in the mist above the small, terraced houses of west London.

"Poor little mite," Kruze whispered.

He paused by the railings, momentarily appalled that anyone could put an orphan of a few hours in a place like that, but she tugged him gently by the arm, urging him on.

They entered the hospital through the big, vaulted arch that was the main entrance. The duty nurse's face lit up the moment Penny asked for Billy Simmons.

"Oh, I am so glad," she said, "he's been asking for you." She strode down the corridor in the direction of the ward.

The boy seemed to be asleep as they moved awkwardly to his bed. The nurse touched the Rhodesian on the shoulder and whispered.

"He's been very badly shaken. Not surprising when you think what he's been through. Lost both his parents, poor little rat."

"I know," Penny said quietly. Kruze seemed not to be listening. He was studying the face that protruded from the sheets. Billy's eyes were screwed tightly shut and furrows were etched across his brow like gashes. The nurse continued in a hushed voice.

"His legs will heal. It's the deeper wounds that worry us."

Kruze pulled up the chair by the bed.

"I'll leave you three alone for a little while," the sister said. "Call me if you need anything." She walked out of the room. Kruze took in the high ceiling and the pistachio-colored walls. The two other patients in the ward seemed to be taking little notice of him or Penny. There was a coldness in the room which made him shudder. He had never spent a day in a hospital and hoped he never would.

For a second, he wondered what he was doing there. What would he say to the child when he awoke? There had been few children within the small farming community around Ellingworth where he had grown up, and they had had a maturity beyond their years. You got old fast in the bush, especially in the hostile country of the Mateke in Southern Rhodesia.

He turned to Penny, but she nodded toward Billy. When he looked back at the boy, the young eyes were open and staring boldly back at him. His lips moved.

"I knew you'd come." The words were barely audible, but he tried to smile. "Who are you?"

"I'm Kruze." He tried to smile back. He took Penny's hand and urged her gently toward the edge of the bed. "And this here is Penny." She bent down and moved a strand of hair out of his eyes.

The boy's blue eyes never left Kruze's face. "How are you feeling, feller?" Kruze asked, disturbed by the intensity of Billy's gaze.

"My legs don't hurt—I just feel thirsty; always thirsty. They tell me I can't drink, though. Why is that? Why don't they tell me things, Kruze? I kow my mother and father are dead, but they don't tell me." The lower lip began to pucker, but he managed not to cry.

"I suppose they just want you to try to get better . . ."

"I knew you would come, though."

"How was that, Billy?" Penny asked.

The boy's face tightened in concentration.

"Nurse told me I was very lucky. She said that if I hadn't had a pair of guardian angels watching over me I might be . . ."

"Anyone would have done it," Penny said, squeezing his hand.

The boy's concentration seemed to lapse for a moment as his eyes roved slowly around the room. There was nothing there to remind him of home. He looked back to Kruze.

"Are you a pilot?"

"Yes, I fly fighters mostly." The boy's eyes seemed to sparkle for an instant and he pulled himself a little way up the bed.

"I bet you've shot down a lot of Germans."

"What makes you think that?"

"Well, you've got a lot of ribbons on your chest, so you must have shot down a lot to have got them."

"Actually, I got most of these for testing new fighters and you don't have to be too brave to do that. If anybody deserves a medal, it's you."

Billy fell silent.

"I'd never get a medal. You don't get medals for hating people, do you?"

"What do you mean?" Penny asked.

"I know that when I leave here I'll have to live with my gran. I'd rather die than live with her. She just makes rules all the time. I won't stay. I'll run away the moment I get the chance." He was on the verge of tears.

"I'm sure she's not that bad."

The boy winced. "She beat me once. Mum never beat me."

"What had you done?"

"Nothing. Nothing at all."

Billy turned his head away from Kruze and looked through the window and out over the rooftops. Almost a minute passed before he spoke again.

"I was with some friends outside her house. We were playing in the street. One of them kicked a ball and it went through her window. Everyone ran 'cept me. She beat me for it with a stick."

"Hey, you listen to me," Kruze began. "I knew a kid like you once, who lived on a farm back in Rhodesia, where I come from. He even looked a bit like you. His parents had a small airplane they used for flying around the farm. It was a pretty big farm." He gestured expansively with his hands.

"One day they flew into a cloud and never came out—they just disappeared. The plane must have crashed somewhere in the hills, but no one ever found the wreckage. The boy, who wasn't much older than you, was brought up by his grandfather and, from the start, the two of them just never saw eye to eye. Much later, when he grew up, he met this girl and told his grandfather that he was going to marry her. The old man went through the roof and told him that he was young and foolish and that he should know better. The boy decided to run away with the girl. But it didn't work out."

"Did he go back to his grandfather?" The boy was captivated, his eyes wide.

"No, he couldn't. You see, he couldn't bear to face that old man who was right all along."

"What happened to him, then?"

"Well, he drifted around the country for a while, working on farms here and there. Then the war broke out in Europe. A lot of people from Southern Rhodesia joined up to fight the Germans and he saw it as a chance to get away from the past. He enlisted with the RAF and came to England."

"Was he very upset about the girl?" Penny asked.

Kruze turned around and looked at her. There was the trace of a smile on her face.

"It all happened a long time ago."

Billy frowned, lost in thought.

"Did you ever hear from your grandfather again?" he asked.

Kruze laughed and shrugged his shoulders. Billy's enthusiasm showed that Kruze was more than his savior now. He was an ally, someone who understood.

"I tried to write to him from England a few times to explain, but the words always seemed to come out wrong and no letter ever got sent. He never will get any explanation now, because he went and died a few years back; a lonely old man in the African bush. I was all he had, and in the end, he had nothing."

The old nurse walked back in and put a thermometer in Billy's mouth.

"I'm afraid it's time for rest now," she said.

As Kruze rose to leave, Billy held his hand out and Kruze shook it.

"Will you come and see me again, Kruze?" The thermometer became dislodged from under his tongue. The nurse clucked irritably and put it back in place.

"I'll be back, feller. Don't worry."

When the nurse pulled the thermometer from Billy's mouth, she was surprised to see that he was smiling.

□

Staverton picked up the folder. The words "Arado Ar 234 Blitz" were printed across the top left-hand corner. He opened the file and read the first paragraph. It was a resume of the detailed report that would follow in the ensuing pages.

THIS TWIN-ENGINED GERMAN JET BOMBER, CONCEIVED BY THE
ARADO FLUGZEUGWERKE COMPANY OF BRANDENBURG DURING THE
CLOSING MONTHS OF 1940, IS NOT ONLY 100 MPH FASTER THAN ANY-
THING THE RAF CAN MUSTER AT PRESENT (FEBRUARY 1945), IT CAN
ALSO MANEUVER IN RINGS AROUND OUR OWN FIGHTER AIRCRAFT.
WHEN FITTED WITH THE DETACHABLE MG 151 20-MM BELLY-
MOUNTED CANNON PACK, IT BECOMES A LETHAL ADVERSARY AND WE
ESTIMATE HERE AT FARNBOROUGH THAT, PROVIDED IT IS GIVEN A
REASONABLY SKILLFUL PILOT, IT WILL SCORE A KILL EIGHT TIMES
OUT OF TEN WHEN PROVOKED.

Staverton closed the folder on his desk and tried to rub some
of the weariness from his eyes. The Arado was a production
bomber, for God's sake, and yet it was better than their own
Spitfires and Tempests. And the Arado dossier was only one
such report that Staverton could remember having seen in recent weeks. There were plenty of others. The Me 262 and He
162 jet fighters were now both operational and offered the Luftwaffe a phenomenal new capability. The only jet that the RAF
had to throw into the fray was the Gloster Meteor, but it was
slower and less maneuverable than its German counterparts.

Then there was the Komet rocket fighter, the most radical
combat aircraft of them all. The prospect of a new, long-range
variant had allowed him little sleep.

Staverton poured himself another cup of coffee. Churchill's
reaction to Fleming's report had been succinct and to the point.
The prime minister's grasp of technical and operational mat-
ters never ceased to amaze him. His support for Staverton's
plan of action had been unequivocal.

He looked at his watch. Nearly nine o'clock. When Fleming
arrived, things would really start popping.

□

Fleming had never seen his boss look so bad this early in the
morning. His tunic was rumpled, he was unshaven, and his tie
and collar were loosened.

"Come in, Robert, and get some coffee. Some for me too,
while you're about it." Fleming called in the WAAF orderly
from the adjoining office and asked for two—both black.

"Had a bit of a late night, as you no doubt guessed." Staverton gestured at the state of his clothes. "I didn't finish with
the prime minister until the early hours. He's very concerned
about your 163 report and has communicated the need for

direct action. It turned out that he was seeing Tooey Spaatz last night. Spaatz is heading back to America tomorrow and was getting the treatment over at Number Ten. It's his boys who are going to catch it in the neck if you're right about this rocket fighter."

Fleming did not often rub shoulders with the top brass, but he knew of almost all of them. General Carl "Tooey" Spaatz, Commander of the U.S. Eighth Air Force, was one of the most influential men in Allied High Command. He had openly come into conflict with the British air staff over the strategy for the bombing of Germany. Spaatz favored precision bombing by day. The British argued that it was saturation bombing by night that would bring Germany's population and its industry to submission. Spaatz had got his way for his own forces, but at immense cost to the B-17 Flying Fortress wings in East Anglia. Until the long-range escort fighter had come into service the previous year, many U.S. day missions had ended in decimation for the Fortresses. The new 163 was set to start that process all over again.

"Anyway, about an hour ago, this arrived." The AVM held up a piece of paper bearing the seal of Churchill's office. "This makes it official. The general and the PM feel the long-range 163 could severely damage the morale of the American Fortress crews."

"I think that's putting it mildly, sir. If that aircraft out there is what we think it is, it could destroy the Eighth Air Force. It gives the Luftwaffe the ability to hit the Americans almost all the way to the target and back."

"Yes, I'm inclined to agree with you," Staverton said. "But Churchill's main concern, based on the latest intelligence reports from Germany, is that the Nazis have a plan to pull their armies back from Italy and northern Europe and get them dug into Austria and southern Bavaria. Basically, it would terminate the possibility of a swift conclusion to the war. Personally, I've never bought the idea of Hitler's alpine fortress. Now I'm not so sure."

Fleming's mind raced. "The performance of this new 163— let's call it the 'C' variant, because that's what it must be— suggests that it could operate from small strips in the Bavarian and Austrian mountain valleys and deal out a hell of a lot of punishment to any bombers trying to locate and bomb their airfields from high altitude."

Staverton nodded. "We cannot take any chances. Reconnaissance photos show they've been steadily pulling their forces back into the region. There's evidence of intense tunneling activity in the mountains, too."

"But even if they do manage to establish fighter squadrons in the mountains, surely it would be impossible to get any large-scale manufacture of the 163 going?"

"One of our chief faults in recent weeks has been underestimating the capability of the Nazi as he retreats into his corner. Our armies have constantly been coming across empty factories throughout their advances into Germany. The Nazis have just moved the entire operation lock, stock, and barrel further on down the road, if necessary. There is no reason why they shouldn't move it just that little bit further away into the Bavarian and Austrian Alps."

"But could they build even short runways in time?"

"With their infuriating ability to hide things away underground, they could build hangars for these airplanes deep into the mountains and launch them off straight country roads. It would be a nightmare even trying to find their bases, let alone destroy them."

"And it would be suicide for the army to try to storm those mountains and valleys," Fleming said.

"Exactly, Robert, suicide. The alternative is to put the Alps under siege and starve them out, but that could take years."

The drone of the air-conditioning system suddenly seemed to fill Fleming's ears. "What can we do?" he asked.

Staverton sucked the end of his pencil.

"I agree with the conclusions in your report. We have no way of knowing whether this new aircraft is a prototype, or fully operational, but we need to find out fast. Churchill has made it clear that it's up to us at the EAEU to produce an answer to whatever it is that's out there. I think there is only one."

Staverton paused. Fleming was used to such dramatic gestures. There was still something of the showman in the Old Man.

"We will have to recover one from the Reich. We must find out if we're right about the 163C, and what makes it tick."

Fleming went still.

"You can't mean it, sir."

"It's the only way, Robert."

"I know that one of the EAEU's responsibilities is to ensure that as many German aircraft, aircraft-engine, and armaments factories get captured by the Allies before the Russians get hold of them, but isn't this taking our duties a bit far?"

"Not at all. We came within a hair's breadth of pulling off a similar operation several years ago. It was late 1942 and a new version of the FW 190 was making mincemeat of our latest Spitfire. We had to capture one and take it apart at Farnborough. We had a test pilot ready to parachute into France close to an FW 190 base, but at the very last minute the whole thing was called off."

"Why?"

Staverton smiled.

"It was a remarkable stroke of luck, really. An FW 190 pilot got completely lost over the channel, took a reciprocal bearing, and landed his brand-spanking-new Focke Wulf in the mist at RAF St. Athan in Wales. He was so stunned when they came to arrest him that he didn't even attempt to set fire to the aircraft."

"But that was an operation to bring a conventional aircraft out of France," Fleming said.

Staverton was unperturbed. "This operation is certainly going to be different. It's required a great deal of planning and we haven't got much time. So this is what we're going to do."

Fleming put the coffee down.

The Old Man got to his feet and walked over to the map of western Europe that adorned most of the wall behind his desk. He pointed to a small area south of the Danish peninsula.

"As you know, the Nazis have carried out most of their rocket research on the Baltic coast at these two test centers—Peenemunde, here . . ." Staverton stabbed his finger at a spot on the north German shoreline. ". . . and Rostock, here.

"We've had a crew on a Danish trawler keeping Peenemunde under surveillance for several weeks and it's been dead. Not a squeak since they did their last A4 rocket tests there over two months ago. So it's not Peenemunde—I double-checked with the trawler last night.

"That leaves Rostock." He stabbed his finger once more on the map.

"This morning, at three o'clock, an RAF Mosquito took off from a captured airfield in Germany on a routine recce mission of Rostock harbor, only the docks were not its real objective. The pilot was briefed to cause a hell of a stir above the harbor, attract a bit of flak, and then to all intents and purposes head home, hugging the trees until he was beyond the range of Rostock's gun batteries. By sheer chance, his course takes him slap over the test center just outside Rostock and that's where he really gets busy. Those cameras work like hell over the airfield, but the enemy, of course, doesn't know that. He's convinced that it's the harbor that we're interested in."

Staverton halted for a moment, pleased with himself. It was a favorite trick of the reconnaissance boys.

"One of our own chaps from the EAEU at the Mosquito's base sent back a coded message just before you got in. The photographs are positive. At least, our man Bowman has good reason to think so. The only trouble is, he has no data with which to compare them."

That was logical enough. Fleming was one of only a handful of people, even within the EAEU, who was allowed access to archive material on new enemy equipment. He'd given up counting the number of bloody evenings he'd spent peering through stereoscopic pairs at a maze of black and white dots that some expert claimed formed the image of a new enemy weapon.

He was half expecting what came nest.

"I want you, Robert, to get over to Germany right away and positively identify those photographs, one way or another. Find out if that thing is the long-range rocket fighter."

"Yes, sir." He thought of Penny.

But Staverton hadn't finished. "And if it is, I want you to coordinate the extraction operation. I've already set the wheels in motion. I need to ensure that it's carried through to the letter, and you're the best qualified man to do it."

The drab walls of the Bunker seemed to cave in for Fleming, but the AVM was in full stride.

"There's a Dakota waiting for you at Northolt. Your travel documents are at the airfield. With your papers are a further set of instructions, which set out all the objectives of the trip. Read them carefully. I don't have to tell you how important this whole thing is."

Fleming wanted to move, but his legs felt like lead.

"I've got great faith in you, my boy. I know you can do it."

The Old Man, now with his back to the wall chart, arms crossed, stared fixedly at Fleming, who had not moved from the hard, straight-backed chair.

"That'll be all, Robert. There's a car waiting outside that will take you to Northolt. Good luck."

Fleming got to his feet and left. For once, he forgot to salute.

☐

As the Riley staff car swung off the Oxford road into Northolt airfield, Fleming felt a tinge of sadness. The wide highway slid out of view and was all but obscured by the guardroom where they drew to a halt.

He turned around for a last look at the road. Endless convoys were sweeping into the center of London, only a few miles away, but there was little traffic heading in the direction of Oxford. It was ironic that Staverton had chosen Northolt as his point of departure. In better days, Penny and he passed it regularly on the way home to the cottage.

The corporal tapped on the window.

"Wing Commander Fleming?"

Fleming pulled back the glass and let the raw wind catch him full in the face. He nodded.

"Papers please, sir."

On the far side of the airfield Fleming could see his DC-3 transport taxiing over to the dispersal point. A ray of sunshine broke through the clouds and raced across the runway, passing directly over the Dakota as it drew up alongside the control tower.

"Thank you, sir," the corporal said, as he handed back Fleming's papers. "Please make your way over to the tower and report to the duty orderly. You can pick up your travel documents there."

Fleming entered the tower building and found few signs of life. A middle-aged WAAF corporal was typing with her back to him, behind the reception desk. The room was shabby. Fleming straightened a picture of the king, which had been blown crooked by the wind as he had opened the door. The WAAF turned around to see who it was.

"I'm Wing Commander Fleming. I believe you should have some travel documents for me."

The WAAF delved her hand into a pigeonhole and produced a thick bundle of papers, which she handed over. Fleming went through them. A travel pass that would give him rights of passage through northern Germany, and a thin carnet with his photograph on the inside front cover, which was the standard-issue passport. Also, a thick manila envelope with NOT TO BE

OPENED UNTIL AIRBORNE typed on the top left-hand corner. That would be from Staverton. He tucked the papers into his inside jacket pocket.

"Corporal, I wonder if you could do me a favor?"

"I'll try, sir."

"Could you mail a letter for me?"

The corporal shifted nervously.

"I can't, sir; it's against base rules."

"I understand that," Fleming said, "but it's only a few words to my wife. If it makes any difference, you can censor it yourself." He smiled warmly.

The WAAF hesitated, then nodded.

Fleming scribbled a note, sealed it in one of the WAAF's envelopes and handed it over to her. He dug deep in his pocket and came up with two pennies for the stamp.

"Thank you,"he said. "I'm deeply grateful." He sprinted for the door.

Outside, he could see the pilot of the Dakota waving him over to the transport. The aircraft was already taxiing to the runway threshold when Fleming was pulled aboard by one of the aircrew kneeling by the open cargo door.

As the DC-3 lumbered into the sky two minutes later, Fleming looked to the west one last time. On a clear day you could probably see Padbury from two thousand feet.

□

Inside the control-tower building, the WAAF shivered as the wind blew through the door by which Fleming had left. She walked over and closed it, and sat back at the typewriter. Her husband had been killed almost a year ago on the Normandy beaches, but she hadn't been too upset. She had been having an affair with a GI sergeant for several months by then. She was looking forward to seeing the American later on that evening. He had promised to take her to a show in town.

She had failed to notice the wind lifting Fleming's envelope and casting it down behind her desk.

7

The DC-3 rolled to a halt beside a wrecked hangar at the northernmost end of the airfield. Coming in to land, the plane had first been buffeted by the strong crosswind that whipped across the North Sea as it began the descent over the Frisian Islands; then the rain came down.

When the pilot finally shut down the engines, Fleming's battered eardrums took a few seconds to register the new sound. The rain that was being driven against the aircraft's metal skin sounded like sticks rapping on a kettledrum.

As a crewman wrestled to open the Dakota's door, Fleming pulled his greatcoat tight around his body. The icy blast that hit his face was a chilling welcome to Kettenfeld, an ex-Luftwaffe airfield on the outskirts of Emden. As he jumped down onto the grass, Fleming felt a surge of adrenaline.

A jeep screeched up beside the Dakota. The driver pulled back a canvas flap and shouted against the wind.

"Wing Commander Fleming? I'm Bowman. Jump in."

The vehicle sped off onto the concrete perimeter road, which led to a cluster of buildings on the far side of the field. Bowman, a stocky, balding squadron leader, squinted hard through the windshield. The wipers were fighting a losing battle against the rain.

From what Fleming could see, Kettenfeld was chaos. Aircraft of all types littered every inch of available space. Fitters, their collars pulled up for protection against the wind and rain, scuttled around their charges, filling empty tanks with fuel, replenishing reserves of oil and hydraulic fluid, checking that rudders and elevators had not iced up. They passed a recovery team trying to raise the nose of a Havoc whose starboard leg had collapsed as it was being bombed up for a mission. All around, British and American aircraft were landing and taking off, their wings waggling precariously as the pilots fought to keep control in the strong winds.

A week before, Kettenfeld had been in the hands of the Luftwaffe's NJG 1, a night-fighter unit with the hopeless task of intercepting the hundreds of Allied bombers that poured into the German heartland almost every night. At one point, Fleming thought he saw some Junkers 88s parked in a distant corner of the airfield, but they could have been Mosquitoes.

They reached a row of Nissen huts and the brakes squealed as the jeep skidded to a stop.

Bowman pointed to the door of the corrugated iron building and then made a run for it. Fleming was right behind him, but something made him pause by the door. A hundred yards away ground crew were busy attaching tow lines from troop-carrying gliders to four-engined Halifax tugs. Staverton hadn't wasted any time. Looking at the gliders, Fleming tried not to think about how many men would die. For a moment he hoped that Bowman's photographs were not of a 163C, but a trick of the light or an act of deception by the Germans. Then he could rid himself of the whole affair, catch a plane back to England. He shook his head and moved after Bowman.

It was warmer inside, but just barely. Bowman led the way down the central corridor and into the office at the far end. The walls were still covered with the regalia of the previous occupants. A recognition chart with the silhouettes of a dozen British and American planes was pinned to one wall and a Luftwaffe squadron photograph tilted at a crazy angle on another. Someone had pushed pieces of newspaper into several bullet holes that dotted the large iron-framed window, but the draft still forced its way into the room, rustling the papers on Bowman's desk. Fleming hung his coat up on the back of the door while his companion poured two cups of coffee from the pot that had been gently simmering on the coal-fired stove.

"I'm sorry the weather couldn't have been a little nicer for you, sir, but then Kettenfeld's a bloody awful place, I'm afraid. I can't say I blame Jerry for leaving here in a hurry."

Fleming put the mug to his lips and sipped the dark, bitter liquid. The coffee burned his stomach. He hadn't eaten since the previous evening.

"Would the Germans' hasty departure explain what looked like some Ju 88s out there?" Fleming gestured with his thumb out the window.

Bowman nodded as he gulped down a mouthful of coffee.

"We found six of them, all pretty much intact. One of them has even got the latest variant of their Lichtenstein radar on board. We've been wanting to get our hands on one for months to see how they've improved the system."

"It seems odd the Luftwaffe didn't destroy them before they left."

"In this instance, we were lucky," Bowman said. "The Canadians who overran Kettenfeld advanced so quickly that it was all the Germans could do to get their personnel off the base. We found the Ju 88s with their tanks almost dry, so there was no possibility of flying them out and there couldn't have been any time to place demolition charges on them. London radioed this morning to say that a team from Farnborough is on its way over here to fly them back to England. Best of luck to them in these conditions.

"I seem to spend the entire bloody time briefing army officers about the value of German equipment. The trouble is, their men just look on it as target practice, or a piece of junk that they can vandalize. The EAEU doesn't mean a thing to them. And as for Montgomery, all he wants to do is get to Berlin as quickly as possible and if that means destroying anything that gets in the way, it's too bad."

Bowman was bitter. It was the Russians who had captured all the really good stuff so far. Rocket scientists, aircraft designers, electronics specialists: the Soviets had them all. The British and the Americans had little to show for their efforts. Apart from anything else, it distressed Bowman that few people outside the EAEU appreciated Germany's military technology, the role it could play in a postwar world. The Russians knew, all right.

"I think," Fleming said quietly, "that we're going to have a bit more cooperation from the army over the next few days."

Bowman looked puzzled.

"Don't ask me how he did it, but Staverton has somehow managed to convince the top brass that we need to get our hands on the 163C, if that's what that thing is, sitting on the tarmac in your photographs."

"So it really is the 163C, eh," Bowman said. "They finally got that beast into production. We've been hearing rumors out here, but no one actually believed the Germans could do it."

"Maybe that's moving a little fast," Fleming interjected. "We're not totally sure, but Staverton's told me to find out."

Fleming tapped the papers as he placed them on the desk. "These are Staverton's instructions in the event there is a rocket fighter at Rostock. We haven't got much time, so let's have those photographs from the recce Mosquito."

Bowman produced a cardboard folder from a drawer and handed it and a set of stereoscopic glasses to Fleming, who had settled into the chair at the desk. Before he pulled out the photographs, Fleming stared out over the cold German airfield.

"If this is a 163C, two hundred-fifty glider troops will take off at dawn tomorrow for Rostock. Their objective is to capture the airfield and hold it until I can get the rocket fighter out of there."

□

HQ came back to Malenkoy with the reaction that he had been dreading. It was his *maskirovka*, and if the security of that exercise was in jeopardy, it was his responsibility to find the insurgents.

It had not taken long for the garrison commander at Chrudim to muster three hundred Siberians from the Third Guards Army and send them down the Branodz road to the point where he had been ambushed by the SS terrorist. And if there was one, there had to be others.

It was over two hours after the attack took place that the convoy of trucks rounded the bend in the track and Malenkoy saw the smoldering tree that had taken the full force of the panzerfaust's detonation.

Two hours! What was wrong with the Red Army these days?

It was obvious the solitary German aircraft was on a reconnaissance mission, and this obviousness, though its lucky crew never knew it, was the only reason they were left so unharassed. They were *meant* to see Malenkoy's tanks, and to live to tell the tale. After all, that was what the *maskirovka* was all about. But a Waffen SS unit studying the tanks from the ground would not be so easily fooled.

Malenkoy had been given a fleeting and blurred glimpse into the grand strategy of which his *maskirovka* was a part. The Germans were to believe that the Red Army, supported by hundreds of tanks, was massing near the main Prague-Berlin highway. Hitler would divert hoarded divisions from the Berlin perimeter, sending them south toward Chrudim. Zhukov, poised with the First Belorussian east of Berlin, would then drive southwest, behind Hitler's Chrudim thrust, and thus prevent them from getting back to Berlin where they would discover that Malenkoy's armored divisions were wooden decoys. Meantime, the real Russian force, at Branodz under Konev, would charge: first southwest and then northeast, hooking around the baffled Nazis and slamming into Berlin from a totally unexpected angle. Brilliant plan!—provided luck stayed with them. If it didn't, both Zhukov and Konev, in making their moves, would be exposed to the very kind of flanking move they intended for the enemy.

Malenkoy, in the truck at the head of the convoy, told the driver to halt. He jumped down from the cabin and walked alone along the last fifty yards of the track to the place of the ambush. The panic that he had felt only hours before welled up in him once more. He flashed a glance to the place where the madman had stood in the middle of the road, firing at will, while his driver struggled to heave the jeep around in a two-point turn. He now saw his attacker with a clarity that had been missing in the mind-numbing moments of the ambush. He was tall, huge in fact. He had a rifle held firmly to his shoulder and he had fired single rounds at them. Single rounds, while Malenkoy cowered on the rear seat! Even when he had come up from the back of the GAZ and scattered half his pistol clip at the man, the attacker had not moved. Malenkoy's hand moved instinctively to his holster. The cold metal of the Tokarev jolted his senses back to reality and the spell was broken.

He stepped over the boundary line that separated the road from the forest. Even though he was now only ten meters into the wood, its size and darkness chilled him. Two fucking hours! If there were a rogue SS unit at large, it could be anywhere by now.

He ran back to the rear of the lead truck and spoke to a lieutenant. The young officer in turn briefed his troops in the local Irkutsk dialect that was their first language. Not all of them could speak High Russian. It was all lost on Malenkoy, who could not understand a word of Siberian.

All the platoon commanders were given a similar message. Fan the troops out and try to find tracks. Anyone who picked up the scent was to radio through to Malenkoy immediately so the search could be concentrated. As long as they found the trail before sunset, Malenkoy was confident that they would have the SS by the following afternoon at the latest.

It was now four o'clock. That gave them two hours to find out the direction in which the SS were heading.

□

It took little more than a minute for Fleming to identify the blurred object in the middle of the photograph as the C-model 163.

The differences between the C and its predecessor, the fully operational 163B, were subtle, but the evidence was clear after Fleming had scrutinized the recce photograph under the stereoscopic glasses.

No wonder Bowman had been unable to establish a positive identification. The photograph was grainy and the actual image of the aircraft was smaller than his little fingernail, so you had to know exactly what to look for to differentiate between the two types.

But there it was. The streamlined fuselage between the two stubby wings set against the mottled surface of the airfield made the rocket fighter look like a hawkmoth clinging to the bark of a tree. The 163C did not have quite the same bulbous body as the standard 163B, but to the untrained eye, referring to grainy photos of minute scale, the aircraft would have appeared identical.

Fleming had one last look through the glass, before he was satisfied. One Me 163C at Rostock. It seemed a tiny thing for which to launch such a massive military operation.

Later, when he asked himself why he had not noticed it straightaway, he put it down to fatigue. He knew, as he tilted his chair back and examined the pitted ceiling of the old Luftwaffe ops room, that the 163C was hiding something from him. There had been an unnatural kink in the leading edge. A dark shape, a shadow, somehow familiar, but unexpected on an aircraft of this capability.

His pulse quickened.

Fleming put his face back over the framework of the stereoscopic pairs and slipped a higher power lens into the base of the device. His fingertip, looking blimplike under the magnification of the lenses, traced its way clumsily across the airfield until it hovered by the rocket fighter.

Not a change in the shape of the wing profile, but something beneath the wing. He could see its shadow on the concrete. Its tip was just visible; not part of the leading edge, as he had first presumed, or a trick of the light.

A fucking bomb.

A fighter-bomber for the defense of the Alpine Redoubt, one that could hit back from the sanctuary of the mountains.

He reached for the phone on Bowman's desk, but thought better of it.

"What is it?" Bowman asked.

Fleming looked into the face of the other man, aware that Bowman would know of his reputation and had seen his excitement.

"Take another look at the aircraft. Notice anything strange under the wing?"

Bowman peered into the optical device for a long time. Fleming knew he was desperate to find something. Eventually, Bowman sat up, his face devoid of expression.

"I can't make anything of it. The leading edge has got a funny line to it, that's all. Could be a smudge on the negative."

Fleming bent over the glasses again. Could it be that the enemy was developing a dual-role rocket fighter, one that could hit the Fortresses at twenty-five thousand feet, then swoop down over Allied lines and deliver ordnance at phenomenal speeds against tanks, command bunkers, and bridges? Silently, without warning?

If he were an EAEU field officer like Bowman, perhaps he would have put it down to an abnormality on the print. But after several months of analyzing reconnaissance shots in the Bunker, he'd learned fast. He was sure it was a bomb, but that wasn't enough.

He breathed in slowly and tried to think it through. Staverton's briefing notes had been specific. Immediately upon identification, Fleming was to send the coded message. The Old Man did not want any halfhearted crap. He had tagged the aircraft as the latest Messerschmitt rocket fighter; that would do for now. If it was a fighter-bomber, he would find out when he arrived at Rostock.

The mission left no room for uncertainty. Rostock was caught between the advancing Canadian First and British Second Armies and the Soviets' Second Belorussian front, pressing eastward at an incredible pace. It was touch and go who would get to Rostock first. Current estimates put the Western Allies two days' march away from the German test establishment. The Russians were probably three to four days away, but they had been known to storm through fifty kilometers of enemy territory in twelve hours under Marshal Rokossovsky's leadership.

If the Russians discovered that British paratroops had leapfrogged beyond their front-line troops to take Rostock, there would be one almighty diplomatic row. Churchill promised Staverton that he would try to hold Stalin off, but he could only stall for so long. It would therefore be up to Colonel Jewell's paratroops to take Rostock, hold it for long enough to airlift the 163 out, and then retire with the help of the Royal Navy from Rostock's Baltic shore.

Once the airfield was secured, Fleming's handpicked unit was to fly in, supervise the dismantling of the 163, and fly it out.

Fleming had the solution as he lifted his face off the stereoscopic pairs.

Bowman had been standing in the corner of the room watching intently for his reaction.

"I want this message sent to London straightaway," Fleming said, scribbling on a pad. "Transmit it in Morse, twice. No encryption. That'll tell Staverton we're in business."

Bowman hesitated. "You all right?"

Fleming did not answer at once. He hardly heard the question. He just wanted to sleep.

"Yes," he replied at length. "Listen up, Bowman. I think that your 'smudge' is a bomb strapped to the wing of that thing. If I'm right, Staverton should know about it as soon as I've made a positive identification at Rostock. If the 163C does turn out to be dual-capable, I'll see to it that you get word from the airfield. Then I want you to put a call through to the Bunker and tell Staverton. It's important that you do it straightaway."

Bowman took the scrap of paper and ran through the rain to the communications hut, some fifty yards away. "The star shines in the east." The message was quite innocent, but there was one man in an office deep below the streets of Whitehall for whom it would have a special significance.

□

Long after the message had been sent to the Bunker, Fleming lay back in the deep armchair in Bowman's office and tried to snatch some sleep. Everything was in place, but it was hard not to think about the things that could go wrong.

Staverton's signal had come from London, acknowledging his identification, confirming that the mission was to go ahead. A second reconnaissance Mosquito had flown over Rostock an hour previously and checked that the 163 was still there. It had not moved from its position on the tarmac, although Fleming was quite ready for the Germans to wheel it into one of the hangars, out of the bitter temperatures that still hit the Baltic coastline in early spring.

Bowman had been busy during the last hour getting together a small team of engineers who could accompany Fleming to Rostock. Outside, Fleming could hear work continuing on the Halifax tugs and gliders, and the constant drone of engines as aircraft taxied to their dispersal points in readiness for the signal that would trigger the mission in just over eight hours' time. But it was not the sound that kept Fleming awake.

He was afraid of death, not because of the pain and suffering—he had already beaten those two enemies on the hospital bed—or for fear of what lay beyond. He did not want to die because he did not want to leave Penny behind with only a couple of lines on a letter to tell her that perhaps they did have a life together after all.

All he could see was her running away from him, into the night.

8

The Siberians had been searching the forest floor for a clue for the last two hours, but had turned up nothing that could point them in the direction of the Waffen SS terrorists.

Malenkoy had been sitting in the back of one of the trucks—at the spot where he had been ambushed earlier that day—waiting for news of progress over the radio. The last bulletin had been made by a young officer who sounded clearly jumpy at having to scour the dark, wet forest for a tiny group of bandits who could be anywhere by now.

Malenkoy pulled back the canvas flap at the rear of the truck and peered at the darkening sky. Normally they would have had a little more light at the end of the day, but the ever-gathering rain clouds had hastened the onset of dusk and he knew he had no choice but to summon back the Siberians and resume the search the next day. If the Germans decided to press on during the night, the chances of picking them up tomorrow were even more remote, but what could he do? His men marching through the pitch-black wood with torches to light their path would present easy targets if the SS decided to turn and fight. They would have to be recalled. He only hoped that the Siberians weren't baying for blood, for rumor had it that they could turn on their own officers when they were pulled off the scent.

Malenkoy flicked the power switch and gave the call sign that signaled a general return to base.

□

It was raining heavily, but the rivulets that ran down the officer's neck, soaking his coarse, gray shirt, did not bother him. The attention of SS-Obersturmführer Christian Herries of the Britische Freikorps was seized by the two maps spread out on the ground in front of him, but he couldn't work out what the hell they meant.

Both charts showed the same topography to identical scales. Chrudim, in the southeast of the map, stood out as the largest town, although it was closely followed by Branodz, some forty kilometers away to the west. The rest of the twenty-five hundred kilometer area was covered by a forest, which clung to the slopes of the broad range of hills that separated the two towns. Herries could see that they would reach their own lines quicker if they followed the network of valleys that crisscrossed the area, but he also knew that the valleys would contain the largest troop concentrations and thus they had to be avoided where possible. Their only real chance lay in sticking to the hills and moving under cover of the trees. It would be an unpopular route with his severely weakened men, but it would make them hard to find for Ivan.

It was the positions given for the Red Army that bothered him. They were different on each map, even though both charts showed the same date in their top right-hand corners, clearly indicating that they were both still current. But were they valid? What was confusing was the fact that one showed the huge concentrations of tanks and troops ringing Chrudim that he had just witnessed with his own eyes one hour before, while the other did not, depicting instead an almost identical armored buildup around Branodz. Herries would have dismissed it altogether had not the route back to his own lines depended on whether Branodz was heavily fortified or not. If the Red Army was there in the same strength as it was at Chrudim then he would have to give it a wide berth, and that would add at least another day's march to the trip. One thing was quite obvious whichever of the two maps told the truth: Ivan had nearly half a million troops in the area and Herries wanted to be as far away as possible when the tanks rolled toward Germany.

There was one other small difference between the maps. The

one that showed Branodz as the center of the buildup had been given the title "Archangel." The simple word, scrawled in a shaky hand along the northern edge of the map, provided the best clue so far to unraveling the mystery. Herries delved into the Red Army–issue dispatch case looking for some text that he had noticed earlier with the maps.

He found some soggy and crumpled pages in the bottom of the bag. They were typed and barely legible, but he leafed through them, searching for the information he required.

The words on the pages seemed strangely unfamiliar. Herries had spoken plenty of Russian over the last few years, mainly interrogating prisoners or beating information out of local civilians, but this was almost the first time since Oxford that he had picked up a page of Cyrillic. There was just not enough time to go over the whole of the twenty-page document so he scoured down the lines for "Archangel," his index finger weaving a precarious course through words and sentences which gradually built up a picture of a pending Russian assault. At the back of his mind Herries kept on wondering what a lowly major in the Red Army was doing with such sensitive items of strategy. Ivan must be getting complacent.

Archangel jumped out at him from the middle of the fifth page. He picked up the text from the top of the sheet, praying that there had been some mistake and that Branodz was an insignificant and poorly garrisoned town that did not require them to make a massive detour. That way, they could be back behind their own lines by the day after tomorrow. Picking a path through both sides' frontlines would be a nightmare he would worry about when the German positions were in sight.

It should have taken Herries five minutes to absorb the details about Archangel, but instead he reread the account twice, at first thinking that his grasp of the Russian language had left him, then that the lack of food and sleep over the last few days had caused him to lose a grip on reality. When he had finished, he rolled onto his back and let the rain fall on his face. Herries was past feeling the freezing-cold droplets and the dampness of his clothes. His mind raced at the information that he now knew he had interpreted correctly.

Herries sprang to his feet. He started to break into a run, but slowed as he passed the two men on watch. When he had left McCowan and Dyer out of sight further up the hill, Herries charged through the trees, ignoring the pine branches that whipped and stung his face, until he reached the spot on the edge of the forest where they had first spotted Chrudim. Just before he approached the clearing he slowed to draw breath, cursing himself for the way he had breached one of the most elementary rules for survival behind enemy lines. So often the insurgent who momentarily took his eyes off his surroundings wound up dead, taken by surprise by a Soviet patrol for failing to look and listen.

Herries crouched behind a tree trunk and watched the dark interior of the wood for signs of life. It was still, apart from the sounds of the raindrops that had managed to penetrate the foliage, splattering the leaves on the forest floor around him. Satisfied he was on his own, he unslung his Zeisses and turned his attention to Chrudim, nestled in the middle of the valley floor almost a kilometer away. Nothing much had changed in the last hour. There were no tanks on the move, only a few jeeps scuttling in and out of the square in the center of the town. Eventually Herries found what he wanted, a line of T-34s several hundred meters from his position, which unlike all the other tanks in the area, had not yet been covered with camouflage netting.

He raised the binoculars.

He had seen hundreds of T-34s on the eastern front, and they had never failed to chill his soul. But there was something strange and unmenacing about this one. It was too clean, even for a vehicle that had left the factory that morning. It had none of the trappings that made up a fully functional and operational tank. Usually they brimmed with oil cans, spades, pickaxes, spare pieces of track, but this one was bare. There wasn't even the customary slogan painted on the side of the driver's cupola. "For Moscow," "Long Live Stalin," "To the Front from the Kolkhoz Workers of Novosibirsk District," or some other such crap was usually daubed on tanks by workers before they left the factories for the front.

Then there was the gun. It was far too big for a T-34, unless the Russians had suddenly equipped the type with a long-barrel ninety millimeter instead of the standard seventy-six millimeter. After Herries had focused on the length of the barrel he knew that what he had read about Chrudim was valid. The T-34's gun had not been forged in a factory, but sculpted from wood. Ivan had done a good job with the telegraph pole; it was hard to tell that it had been lashed to the front of the turret with rope. Herries went down the rest of the line before he was satisfied. They were fakes, all of them. Impossible to identify as such from the air, but unmistakable at close range. He picked out other armored vehicles at random, but it was the same story. None of the tanks in or around Chrudim was going anywhere—just as the documents had said.

So he could trust them. And that meant he could use them.

Two maps. One showing a mythical assault against the German positions, the other all too real.

He sat back against the nearest tree and scarcely moved for the next half hour. When he got up and started to move back toward the camp, every nerve ending in Obersturmführer Christian Herries' body was tingling.

Archangel was not a plan to feint the Germans toward Chrudim and then outflank them from Branodz. Archangel wasn't aimed at the Germans at all.

Ivan was poised to launch a preemptive strike on the west—against their own allies, the British and the Americans, for God's sake! The Red Army was going to bulldoze its way through the crumbling Reich to Paris and, if the momentum was still there, push to the Channel ports, driving the British and the Americans into the sea.

Herries felt a smile crease his face.

Archangel was his ticket home.

☐

Just before he reentered the clearing where most of his men were asleep, his jacket caught a branch, snapping it with the noise of a gunshot. Before he could even curse, Herries heard two machine-pistol bolts being drawn back as McCowan and Dyer prepared themselves for ambush from a Russian patrol.

He threw himself flat.

"It's Herries," he said through clenched teeth.

When he heard two more clicks and knew that the MP40s had been made safe, Herries picked himself up and walked into the clearing that housed their makeshift camp.

The two men on watch were standing with guns at the ready on each side of the open patch of forest. The other four, who had been huddled around a small fire, were also prepared for a fight. Dietz, Herries observed wryly, still held a bead on him with his rifle.

"All of you get some sleep, and that includes you two." Herries looked at McCowan and Dyer. "We're all edgy, but we must be rested when we break out of Chrudim later tonight. Any nervous behavior like that could bring a whole Siberian division down on us. In the meantime, I'll take over the watch."

Herries felt the tension ease. He was satisfied that his voice had not faltered. If the plan was to work, he had to maintain their respect. Even Dietz, at any time a moment away from insurrection, had lowered his rifle and was settling down to rest again.

"Do the maps show a way out of here, sir?" It was Gunnersby, the Freikorps' youngest and last recruit.

Herries grunted. "I've seen a way."

Gunnersby's mouth twitched at the edges, then broke into a thin, faltering smile. Herries watched him as he lay down between Berry and Wood, the three of them drawing close to each other for warmth. They were joined by the two sentries who unfurled their groundsheets close to their fellow Englishmen, shunning the open space next to the leprous Dietz.

Herries chose a spot on the edge of the clearing and sat back against a pine, cradling his MP40 in his lap. Darkness was falling rapidly and it was now possible to see the faint glow of the fire, its intensity checked by the rain that still fell lightly over the central Czechoslovak foothills.

He had to be sure before he made his move.

The main thing was that work was continuing on Archangel at Chrudim, that he'd seen with his own eyes. Yet it was over forty-eight hours ago that they'd carried out the ambush and Ivan must have found the jeep and its Hanomag escort by now. It had to mean that they were satisfied the documents had been destroyed. The slightest hint of trouble and the dummy armor at Chrudim would have been dismantled by now.

Herries glanced back at the six forms hunched around the dying fire. It would be difficult negotiating his way back without them, especially without the skills of the master predator Dietz, but there was no other way. Archangel's value was that it was his, and his alone. There was no room for anyone else.

Herries checked off everything he would need for the march ahead. He had three grenades, four clips for the MP40, his compass was in his pocket and he had the maps—accurate German maps, as well as the Soviet charts they had found in the jeep. Food would be a problem, but the SS training school at Bad Tolz and three Russian winters had taught him how to live off the land.

Another long look at his men told him that they were asleep. It was time to go.

□

Dietz's eyelids flickered open when he heard the slight rustle.
The cold, gray eyes followed Herries as he slipped from his post
into the impenetrable gloom of the surrounding forest. The
sergeant's upper lip curled in a sneer at the thought of Herries'
discomfort as he squatted in the dark forest. If the officer's
dysentery kept up like this, it would kill him. Then he, Dietz,
could lead the others back to their own lines and get the promotion that was long overdue to him.

The last embers from the fire threw out just enough light for
him to catch a glimpse of the stick that tumbled and spun as
it arced through the night air toward him. Dietz knew what it
was even before it landed in the middle of the group of bodies
on the other side of the fire. It was too far for him to reach it
and hurl to safety, so he rolled away, trying to scramble to his
feet so that he could launch his body that few extra meters
from the center of the blast. But his feet caught in the blanket
and he was trying to pull it free when the stick grenade exploded.

The flash momentarily turned the night into day, but Dietz
did not feel the shrapnel that tore through his shoulder. His
mouth gaped as he tried to refill his lungs with air that had
been squeezed from his body by the viselike pressure wave that
accompanied the explosion. Something heavy fell across his
body, pinning his back to the ground; and then all was still.

When Dietz came to, Dyer's headless body was still twitching
on top of him as the blood pumped from the neck and coursed
over his face. Then with one last spasm it writhed and rolled
onto the ground beside him. The warm stickiness that covered
his face made him want to get up and run forever from that
place, but his survival instincts told him to stay down.

Despite the ringing in his ears, he heard the figure draw near,
he felt the breath on his cheek and he wanted to scream as the
boot lashed into his rib cage. But still he made no sound or
movement.

Soon all he could hear was the ringing again. Then he knew
that Herries had gone.

□

Herries moved swiftly down the hillside, trying to put as much
distance as he could between him and the camp before the
Russians arrived on the scene.

Not that it really mattered. To Ivan it would just be a case of another faulty grenade going off and six less SS terrorists to worry about.

And they were all dead, there was no doubt about that. It wasn't even necessary to put a bullet into Dietz just to make sure. The bastard must have lost half his body weight in blood, judging by the mess that covered his face and body.

□

Almost seven kilometers away, Malenkoy heard the distant rumble of the pressure wave as it rolled through the valleys toward his position.

His first concern was that one of the Siberian platoons had been ambushed in the same way that he had been earlier that afternoon.

He flicked the radio on for clarification from his men in the field, but the airwaves were jammed with the excited cries of his officers as they reported the explosion and, more important, the direction from which it came.

Malenkoy hit the transmit button and bellowed for silence.

"Malenkoy to patrol leaders. Turn back and head for the source of that explosion. I don't know what's going on out there, but it has to be them. There are no other patrols reported in the area."

The three officers acknowledged that they were proceeding in the direction of the sound of the detonation.

Then he was out through the back of the truck and making for the nearest of the patrols. The trouble was, if he could pick out his own troops by the light of their torches, so could the SS.

9

They stopped by the Serpentine on their way to the underground station at St. James' Park. A group of boys were sailing their homemade boats by the water's edge and Penny paused to watch, absorbed by the sight of the toy yachts with their delicate paper sails bobbing precariously among the geese and ducks.

"They're coming home," she said.

"The birds? It's still winter. Feels like it, anyway." Kruze turned to face her.

She laughed. "The children. They're returning to London. Perhaps it really will all be over soon."

The youngest boy, a scruffy child, with dirty hands and a face that had not seen soap in days, splashed his friends with muddy pond water and ran off laughing as they chased him across the park.

"You mean you've missed all that noise?" the Rhodesian asked. "I thought you English frowned on kids who misbehaved in public."

"Don't be so stuffy," she smiled. "This hardly sounds like the man who was sitting anxiously at Billy's bedside this morning."

"We were just talking."

"No, you weren't." She smiled.

Kruze shuffled, as if to get some circulation back into his frozen feet. "He was just a frightened kid responding to a friendly face. As you said, it could have been anybody. We just happened to be there."

She touched his arm. "A good try, Piet. It's not against the law in this country to show emotion, you know."

"I thought you'd probably seen quite enough of that already."

"That was something quite different." She took his hand and moved toward the path that led to the station on the other side of the park.

The late-afternoon sun was slipping behind the trees. Despite the cold, they walked slowly, her hand resting lightly on the crook of his arm.

"What was she like?" Penny asked, suddenly.

"Who?"

"The girl you told Billy about."

He laughed. "I never said she was my girl."

"I'm afraid you didn't cover your tracks very well, my darling."

Kruze lit a cigarette. "We were very different. I was young and so was she. End of story."

Penny shook his arm lightly. "She hurt you. I'm sorry."

He shrugged. "A little. I hurt him more."

"Your grandfather? He meant a lot to you, didn't he?"

"Yes, I suppose he did, the stupid old so-and-so. After my parents died, he raised me as his son—and that's not easy for an old man. My father had no brothers or sisters and his own wife had been long gone, way before I was born. It was just him and me, from my early teens to the day I left the farm in Mateke. Looking back, they were good years."

They reached the edge of the park and paused to get their bearings, before plunging down a darkened side street that led to the station.

She said, "Don't you think they were for him, too? If he was the man I think he was, he would have understood."

"Penny, how can you know? He was a Rhodesian, born on the family homestead and buried there seventy-six years later. A tough, sinewy, old man who'd seen three-quarters of a century filled with nothing but heat, a business that just about broke even, and a social life that consisted of having the neighbors over for a drink at Christmas, so long as they could be bothered to make the 250-mile round trip. You don't find people like that in the towns and villages of Kent or Gloucestershire."

Her eyes flashed. "I know what he was like. He was honest, professional, sometimes moody, proud, arrogant even. He'd be awkward, a fish out of water with people of his own kind, but he would enjoy a drink with the boys after a day's work. He'd be hard with anyone who didn't pull his weight, but he'd walk through hell to save a man who was good and true."

He had not seen her this angry, even on the ministry steps the day before. The memory of it made him smile.

"Damn you, Piet. I'm right, aren't I?"

When he spoke the smile was gone. "I take it all back. How did you know?"

"Somehow I knew he would have been just like you."

He paused in the street for a moment and looked into her eyes. "You're a remarkable woman, Mrs. Fleming."

"I believe guilt is a wasteful, destructive emotion. And if I'm right about your grandfather it's a luxury he would never have allowed himself."

"You seem to know him better than I do."

"I want to get to know *you*," she said, urgency and frustration in her voice.

They rounded a corner and he saw the dim glow of the sign for the underground station almost at the end of the street. The journey was almost ended and she didn't even know when or whether she would see him again.

"You'll be going back when this is all over, I suppose," she said, turning the question away from the immediate future.

She thought it ironic that in under two days she had probably got behind his eyes as no one had in a long time, yet a moment before they parted, she didn't know the answer to the one question that mattered most to her.

"This place, the air force, they've been home for five years. What's there to go back for?"

She stopped him by the entrance to the station. "I'm surprised at you, Piet. The one way to assuage any remorse you may still have would be to go back and run that farm."

He walked over to the window and bought two tickets, one for Waterloo, the other for Marylebone.

"I belong here now," he said, turning to face her.

"Is that what you really believe?"

They passed through the barrier and paused at the point where their paths divided.

"Don't run away, Piet," she whispered, and kissed him lightly on the cheek.

She disappeared down the steps, the sound of her fading footsteps drowned by the sudden approach of her train.

Dawn was breaking over Chrudim when Malenkoy's platoon found the Freikorps' last camp. One of the other patrols had stumbled across the clearing several hours before and had guided Malenkoy and his Siberian search party to the spot over the radio.

The young officer who had first come upon the scene had described the situation to Malenkoy, but he had not prepared the major of tanks for the carnage that surrounded the long-extinguished camp fire.

Malenkoy fought to control his heaving stomach as he surveyed the mutilated bodies of the SS terrorists. Two of the five corpses had lost limbs; a third had no head. The sight of it chilled his body beneath the thick, sheepskin *polaschubuk* he wore over his uniform.

He strolled to the middle of the clearing and raised his head to the clear, ever-lightening sky, trying to suck in cool mountain air that was not polluted by the stench of death that already pervaded that lonely place.

SS shits. Whatever had happened, they deserved it.

His bitterness came not from his own brush with them the day before, but from the memory of what the SS had done to the people of his country, especially in the two years that it had taken to retreat from Stalingrad to the edges of Berlin. Malenkoy looked quickly down at the cadaver of the youngest. He looked like any one of his fellow graduates from the academy all those years ago.

Malenkoy glanced up at the sky once more and muttered an oath that went unremarked by a group of Siberians who were standing nearby, joking together in some unintelligible tongue. To what depths had the human race sunk over the last four years? It was obvious, even ten years ago at the academy, that war would come to Europe, but the totality of the conflict had not been imagined by anybody at the time. He had thought about it before, but now the feeling boiled in him so strongly that he wanted to shout it out. How could men do this to each other?

A lieutenant appeared and handed him a muddy, blood-stained piece of cloth, ripped from the tunic of one of the SS. Malenkoy wiped away the grime to see the faded, but unmistakable colors and pattern of the British flag. He let the badge fall, grinding it into the mud with his heel.

He had heard tales from comrades who had fought along the front about the exploits of the Britische Freikorps, but he had dismissed the reports as the exaggerations of men who had been too long fighting a tough and ruthless enemy. Now he could scarcely believe that the soldiers who had attacked him on the forest track were men whose brothers were fighting the common Nazi enemy less than seventy kilometers from where he now stood, according to the latest reports back at HQ. Total war. At times it had got to the point where he was uncertain who the enemy really was.

Malenkoy left his thoughts behind and returned to the present. A nagging feeling told him that it was not over, that there was something very wrong about the scene before his eyes. He turned to the officer who had escorted him to the clearing.

"Search these bodies for papers. Anything that gives further clues to their identity, I want to see it."

The younger man screamed, waving his PPSh submachine gun excitedly at his troops, who immediately set about searching the pockets of the dead.

Was it possible that these were not the men who had attacked him yesterday? It had to be unlikely that there were other SS units operating in the vicinity, but where was the one who had stood unflinching in the road while he had fired off a whole magazine in blind terror? It had to be the headless one. Malenkoy walked over to the monstrous form and looked it over from the boots to the shoulders, trying not to let the Siberians see his revulsion. He thought hard for several minutes, before calling over the junior officer who had just barked the orders.

"How tall would you say this man was, Comrade Lieutenant, taking into account, of course, that he was once in possession of a head?" The junior officer flashed a glance at Malenkoy that showed he did not know how to handle his superior's sarcasm.

The lieutenant looked at the body hesitantly, sensing a trick in Malenkoy's question. He answered nervously and in a low voice, worried that Malenkoy would show him up in front of his troops.

"About one meter seventy-five, sir."

"That's what I was worried about. It means, then, that we have at least one man still on the loose." Malenkoy once more saw the figure standing astride in the middle of the road. He had been tall and broad across the shoulders. This . . . thing by his feet had been a much smaller man. He winced at the thought of having to report the news to Nerchenko at HQ. A platoon was hard enough to locate in a densely forested area twenty times the size of Moscow, but one or two men would be next to impossible.

Malenkoy heard the rough cough beside him and saw the sergeant with the Order of the Red Star pinned on his quilted *telogreika*, who had been standing there for the last few minutes, not daring to interrupt the thoughts of his senior officer. Malenkoy turned to face the lieutenant, who was holding some documents up to him.

"Yes, Comrade Starshina, what is it?" He had tried to hide the weariness in his voice.

"One of my men found these, Comrade Major. They were in a pocket on that man over there, sir." He pointed to the broken body of Wood. "They're the papers of a Red Army major."

Malenkoy took the bundle of documents and began to leaf through them. The face in the photograph, slightly obscured by a large bloodstain, was someone he knew. It belonged to Paliev. So that was how Yuri Petrovich had met his end, poor son of a bitch—ambushed by this outfit. There had been much speculation among his comrades back at HQ as to what had happened to Paliev since his disappearance a few days ago.

At least this was one piece of useful news that he could bring back to Nerchenko. Rumor had it that the general had been very upsest by the loss of his personal aide.

☐

Even though it was still about ten miles away, Fleming could see the column of smoke billowing up from the airfield and he braced himself for the reception they would receive when they came into Rostock.

Sitting on a jump seat behind the copilot on the flight deck, he craned his neck for a glimpse of their escort, eight heavily armed Hawker Typhoon fighter-bombers. Four of them hung slightly back on the York's starboard beam, each aircraft lumbering under the weight of the sixteen air-to-ground rockets racked beneath the wings. Just behind the fighters, Fleming could see the second Avro York. It was an ungainly-looking thing, but was the only aircraft the Allies possessed that could accommodate the principal parts of the 163C without a major dismantling operation on the rocket fighter. If they ever made it into Rostock, and provided the 163C was still there, both transport aircraft would be needed to ferry the German rocket fighter's partly dismantled components back to Kettenfeld and on to Farnborough.

Fleming's headset crackled.

"Jewell to Metal Bird, Jewell to Metal Bird. Believe we have you in visual contact. Do you receive? Over." The voice was clear, the signal strong. Fleming prayed that the landing and the storming of the airfield had gone according to plan.

He held his mask up to his mouth and shouted back over the roar of the two propellers, whose tips cleared the cockpit wall by mere inches on either side of him.

"This is Metal Bird. Can confirm we are ten miles downrange of Rostock. Do we have clearance to come in? Over." This was the moment that would determine whether they went into the furnace, whose smoke and flames now filled their field of vision through the York's windshield.

"Jewell to Metal Bird. Land on first thousand yards of runway. I repeat. Only use the first thousand yards of the runway. Enemy still has far side within range of mortar and small-arms fire. Once you are down we will put up a smoke screen to shield you on taxiway to hangar." The pilot gave a thumbs-up to show that he had understood the instruction. There was now only one more thing Fleming needed to know before he could authorize their descent. He hit the transmit button, but Jewell came back before he could send the message.

"Metal Bird. Thought you might like to know we have found the 163C and it is intact. I repeat, 163 okay. But situation critical here. Get down as quickly as you can. Jewell out."

Fleming had no time to praise the fact that the 163 was still there and in one piece. He tapped the pilot on the shoulder and stabbed his forefinger down in the direction of Rostock. The pilot nodded and pushed the control column forward and the plane's nose dropped, momentarily exerting the effects of negative gravity upon his stomach.

It was time to start the diversion for their landing.

Fleming twisted in his seat. The Typhoons were level with the right-hand window of the cockpit.

"Metal Bird to A and B flights. You heard Jewell. The enemy is concentrated in the eastern end of the airfield. They're all yours."

The Typhoons peeled away in a shallow dive, heading for the far end of the runway at over 400 MPH. Fleming watched the leader down to fifty feet, saw the flashes under the wings as the rocket motors ignited and the projectiles sped away from the rails toward an invisible enemy. Eight weblike threads of smoke stitched their way through the sky, each pulling a Typhoon after it, until the aircraft disappeared into a pall of black cloud that belched from something burning brightly on the ground below.

The runway grew before their eyes until it filled the entire windshield. Several hundred yards to port, through the smoke, Fleming could just make out the white tops of the Baltic waves as they lapped at the wide, dune-filled beach bordering the airfield. Between the beach and the runway were two immense hangars and a group of outbuildings. Fleming refrained from pointing out their quarry to the pilot, who was keeping one eye on the runway and one on the far perimeter fence where the enemy's forces were concentrated. The copilot turned to Fleming and signaled that he knew where to head once they touched down and had slowed to a speed where they could turn the aircraft off the runway.

They were now down to fifty feet. The pilot wrestled to keep the aircraft steady in the strong crosswind before dropping the wheels down hard on the tarmac. The two crew stood on the brakes, which immediately transmitted a shuddering protest through the whole airframe.

Fleming caught a needle of light out of the corner of his eye and watched in a trance as a line of tracer curled out from a group of trees to their right, but the gunner had not accounted for the deflection and the shots went wild. As he watched the source of the machine-gun fire, holding his breath for the second burst, the copse disintegrated in an enormous explosion. The shock waves rocked the York and his earphones filled with the cries of the Typhoon pilots who had scored one more kill in their quest to keep the York's approach to Rostock free from ground fire.

The York slewed left and right off the runway centerline as the crew fought to slow the aircraft enough for a violent turn down a slip-road that led to the two hangars. Fleming's heart missed a beat as he saw smoke pouring from the hangar area, the thick clouds swirling and expanding as they were pushed across the airfield by the breeze coming off the Baltic. But the hangar complex, which housed the 163, had not taken a hit. Fleming could make out Jewell's paratroops as they activated smoke canisters during the most vulnerable part of the York's journey; the aircraft was beyond the protection afforded by the buildings and clawed its painfully slow way along the exposed taxiway.

Fifty yards ahead, a soldier leapt in front of the York and signaled for the pilot to head toward the second and largest of the buildings. Then the immense doors slid open and Fleming could make out the figure of Colonel Jewell within, his stocky frame dwarfed by the interior of the empty hangar. He was gesticulating wildly, beckoning for the York to taxi toward him. The copilot looked at his captain who shrugged before inching the throttles forward and coasting the transport aircraft inside. Switches were thrown and the propellers spluttered to a stop.

Fleming had already thrown off his straps and was scrambling out through the flight-deck door, past two ashen-faced engineers who would shortly assist him in dismantling the 163 and crating it up for the return journey. As long as the paratroops could stave off whatever the Germans threw at them over the next few hours. Fleming jumped to the concrete floor of the hangar, and the crackle of machine-gun fire, punctuated intermittently by the dull crump of a mortar explosion, echoed around the immense building. It was the first time he had heard the enemy, but far from experiencing the nausea of fear that should have gripped him, he felt exhilarated and drawn to the action.

Jewell was striding over to him, his right hand extended as if he were a long-lost chum spotted at a cocktail party. But as the colonel drew close, Fleming noticed that the eyes that had sparkled the day before looked tired, the face drawn. Jewell's handshake told him that things were not under control. The initial bravado could not hide his anxiety.

"Morning, Fleming. Glad you made it. I'm sorry we couldn't get the whole airfield cleared for you as planned, but we judged it safe enough for you to make an approach and landing. It turns out that there's a bigger garrison in Rostock town than we anticipated, but I think we can hold our position long enough for you to get your contraption out of here. Provided the Russians behave themselves, that is."

"Russians? What do you mean, Russians?" Fleming had to shout to make himself heard over the second York, which had safely arrived at the hangar and was being positioned just behind the first aircraft. He thought he might have misheard what Jewell had said.

"According to prisoners, the Russians broke through the German front lines last night and are now only about seven kilometers from here. The reason the Germans haven't thrown the book at us is because they're more preoccupied with stemming the Red Army's advance westward. It's a bloody irony that we're pinning the Germans down at the far end of the airfield, while I'm actually praying that their troops don't throw in the towel and let the Red Army catch us on what the Russians see as their territory."

"Christ, how long do you think that gives us?"

"Impossible to say. It could be a day, it could be two hours before they're here. You'd better get your men to take that aircraft apart and loaded up on the Yorks as quickly as possible."

Jewell led the way to a corner of the hangar that had been cordoned off by a large screen.

The sight of the 163C took Fleming's breath away. Up close, it did not seem to retain any of the qualities—the short, moth-like body and the stubby wings—that he had recognized in the reconnaissance photographs. It was beautiful in the way a racing car was, and quite the opposite of its operational sibling, the squat and ugly 163B, even though the relationship between the two was obvious. Fleming found it hard to believe that this graceful machine was the same as the one that had almost destroyed the mind and body of the B-17 gunner in the hospital bed at Horsham St. Faith.

Walking around the aircraft, he remembered the bomb and his fear, and how he had almost called Staverton on the spot, so acute was his concern at the thought of a rocket-powered fighter-bomber going into production in Germany. The 163C was clean.

It was then he spotted the slight protuberance beneath each wing. He threw himself under the aircraft, like a mechanic at a garage, and saw the hardpoints, the mechanisms that held the ordnance in place until the pilot triggered the release of the weapon. A bomb had been there; it had simply been removed during the night.

He scribbled out a note on a piece of paper and handed it to Jewell.

"Colonel, I need this message transmitted to a man at Kettenfeld called Bowman. It's very important. Could one of your men handle it?"

Jewell nodded. "Consider it done," he said. "Just concentrate on getting that thing packed up and out of here."

At least it was smaller than Fleming thought it would be. As long as they could get the wings off cleanly and the fuselage into two halves, front and back, the 163C would fit into the Yorks with room to spare. But dismantling the aircraft quickly, and without damaging it, would prove to be a bitch; of that Fleming was sure.

And there were only seven kilometers between them and the Red Army.

Fleming never thought he would find himself praying for the Wehrmacht to hold its ground.

□

Dismantling the 163 was taking far too long, so Jewell's find was the answer to a prayer.

Fleming looked up from his work on the aircraft's wing root as the colonel came toward him, a motley selection of individuals in tow. Several paratroopers walked behind holding guns to their backs, but the prisoners did not look like soldiers to Fleming. There were five altogether. Two of them were no more than twenty-five years old, while two more were in middle age, the last in his late sixties. They looked confused and frightened.

"They're scientists," Jewell said to Fleming. "My men caught them skulking in one of the outbuildings behind the hangar."

Fleming wiped some hydraulic fluid off his hands onto his trousers. The Komet was a mechanical nightmare. The fuselage was made of metal, the wings of wood. Without carefully removing the skin covering the airfoil sections first of all, it was impossible to find the main pins that held the wings in place on the fuselage. And tearing the wing panels off too suddenly could cause untold damage. It was slow, back-breaking work.

"They're the engineers and scientists who were working on the Komet when we landed here this morning. I thought you might need a little advice on how this thing should be taken apart."

Fleming laughed.

"Colonel, what makes you think these men are going to assist us in taking away their latest secret weapon? Just how politely do we have to ask them?"

"We don't have to ask them anything. They'll do it. They know that the Russians are about five kilometers from here and I gave them a choice. Either they help us dismantle this thing so that we can all get away before Joe shows up, or we leave

95

on our own and tie them up for the Russians to find. I think you'll find they're actually quite eager to help." A thin smile spread under Jewell's well-clipped, graying moustache.

The eldest scientist stepped forward from the rest of the group, casting an anxious glance back at the corporal in charge of the prisoner detail who was still training his Sten on them. The other four Germans seemed to be willing him forward, urging him to act as their spokesman. His English was halting, though more through nervousness, Fleming thought, than because his grasp of the language was poor.

"We will work for you, but only because we do not want to go with the Russians. If we take apart the Komet, you must promise to take us with you. We know what the Russians will do with us."

Fleming looked at Jewell and nodded. The corporal, seeing the sign, preempted his colonel's command and ushered the Germans over to the rocket fighter and watched, his eyes darting from one to another. Unlike Fleming, the corporal did not appreciate the threat of Soviet techniques in persuasion.

With the assistance of the technicians, it took just under a half hour to remove the Komet's wings. Fleming was pleased with their progress.

"What next, Doctor Hausser?" He turned to the frail but dignified man, the senior scientist.

"We need to get the Komet off the ground . . . on jacks." The old man stammered as he searched for the right words. "The skid must be raised into the belly and the wheels removed if the Komet's fuselage is to fit in the transport aircraft, I think."

"Where are the jacks?"

"Under those sheets, there." Hausser gestured toward a jumble of machinery, half-hidden by a tarpaulin, over by the hangar wall.

"Get them," Fleming said.

Minutes later, the Komet was raised, its wheels a few inches off the ground. Another German scientist, a young, nervous-looking man, worked with a wrench to free the jettisonable undercarriage dolly from the skid.

Hausser flipped a catch and pushed the canopy hood open. Fleming turned to find the old man trying to pull himself up onto the wing, the only stepping stone to the cockpit in the absence of a ladder.

Hausser winced. "I must now raise the landing gear," he said.

"I can do that," Fleming said. "Just show me what to do."

He sprang up onto the wing and was settled in the pilot's seat a moment later. Hausser, on tiptoes, leaned over the cockpit wall and nodded to a lever by Fleming's right hand.

"Push it hard forward and the skid will come up."

Fleming reached out, gripped the lever and pushed. He felt the heavy clunk as the skid retracted.

Then he saw a movement out of the corner of his eye. He turned to see the scientist with the wrench running for the door.

"Oh God," Fleming heard himself say, "it's booby-trapped."

His hand went down again to the lever, found the thin strand and traced its way along the length of the wire to the underneath of the seat. He felt the grenade, grabbed it by its wooden stock and heard the rasp as the tape ripped away from the metal pin.

He threw it with all his might at the large windows halfway up the hangar wall, then ducked back into the cockpit. There was a crash of glass, followed by a deafening explosion.

The Komet rocked on its jacks, then steadied.

Fleming came up to see half the assembled company lying prostrate on the floor. He tried to stand, but his legs gave and he fell back, drained, into the seat.

There was a scuffle away to his left. The man with the wrench had been knocked to the floor by a paratrooper standing guard by the door.

Jewell sprinted over to the Komet.

"What the bloody hell happened?"

"Our friends decided to make things a little more difficult for us," Fleming replied, trying to force a smile. "A grenade was rigged to explode as soon as the skid was retracted."

"The little shits!" Jewell barked. "We'd better round them all up."

"I don't think that will be necessary," Fleming said. Slowly his breath was coming back. "If Hausser had known it was booby-trapped, he wouldn't havc bccn talking to me from the edge of the cockpit."

"Then what do I do with him?" Jewell jabbed his finger at the scientist by the door, who was struggling against the paratrooper's headlock.

"Ask him if he's got any other surprises. Then tie him up and dump him. The Russians can have him."

"Done!" Jewell said.

"I hope one of your men wasn't having a quiet smoke outside when the grenade went off, Colonel."

Jewell smiled. "More likely to be one of yours, Fleming. The paras haven't got time to stand around, unlike the RAF." He clapped Fleming on the shoulder. "You're a cool customer, Fleming. We'll make a paratrooper of you yet." Then he was gone.

Hausser, his face a death mask, pulled himself off the floor and looked into the cockpit.

"I never realized," he whispered.

Fleming touched him gently on the arm. "I know," he said. "But from now on, we take no chances. Have the rest of your men search the Komet for any more of those things. Then get the fuselage apart. We've got to be out of here in twenty minutes."

Jewell watched, trying hard to be patient, as the twin Walter rocket engines were detached. The front and rear halves of the fuselage easily fitted into the two Yorks, once the cargo doors had been removed. The pilot set about getting the major components arranged around the aircraft's center of gravity, so that the extra weight exerted as little effect as possible on flight characteristics during the return leg.

Colonel Jewell's calm finally evaporated.

"Look, man, if you don't get these two aircraft out of here now, you're not going to have to worry about any fucking return journey, because the only trip that you'll be making is to Moscow."

Fleming made sure their prize was secure then told the two pilots it was time to move. Paratroopers swung the two aircraft around to face the hangar's great sliding doors. The magnetos whined as the propellers started to turn, then the motors caught. Fleming waited an eternity for the engines to stabilize. Jewell was already on the radio preparing to stage his tactical withdrawal to the beach where his men would be picked up by boats from the Royal Navy destroyer.

The York led its stablemate out of the hangar. Fleming, sitting by the open cargo door, saw the first of Jewell's troops making their way toward the beach. Many were being supported by comrades, others limped or bore field dressings. Staverton would tell him it had been worth it, whatever the cost to the paratroops, but right now Fleming wondered how many of them would not be leaving that remote and desolate Baltic shore.

The engines roared to the response of opened throttles, taking Fleming by surprise. The pilot must have decided to take off on the shorter secondary runway, without bothering to line up into wind. It was risky, but the alternative was overflying the German positions at the far end of the airfield.

The crates holding the 163 shifted with each bump under the York's wheels until the ropes went taut with the strain. Fleming tried not to look at his own men or the two German scientists under their charge, for the fear on their faces did nothing to soothe his own tattered nerves. At last the York clawed its way into the air and Fleming stared at the ground below, agonized at the slowness with which it receded. Away to the left he could see a procession of olive-green tanks rolling down one of the slip-roads that led to the airfield. The red flashes on their turrets were barely discernible, but they were obvious enough to show that the Soviets were only minutes away from catching Jewell's men in the act of highway robbery.

Fleming undid his safety harness and squeezed past the crates until he was at the flight deck. He grabbed the spare headset and microphone and tried to raise Jewell on the radio. No reply. He gave up after two further attempts. The colonel was cutting it fine if he wanted to rendezvous with the navy.

10

"**S**o there's one Nazi on the loose in our sector. So what?" Nerchenko had not even bothered to address Malenkoy to his face. He carried on writing his report, the thick, gold embroidery on his cuff scratching the paper noisily as his hand moved across the page. "You think one SS insurgent is going to cause a problem? A platoon, that's a problem, but one man . . . go back to building your dummy tanks, Malenkoy."

Malenkoy shifted nervously.

"There may be others, Comrade General—we just cannot be sure. Their camp was close to the *maskirovka* at Chrudim, too. Shouldn't we at least try and find this man and make sure?"

Malenkoy braced himself for the explosion, but it never came. Instead, the general put down his pen, wearily removed his wire-rimmed glasses and rubbed his eyes. He continued to talk while he kneaded his eyeballs.

"I thought that the whole point of assembling armored divisions out of wood was that the enemy would notice them and believe that we were mounting a massive attack in that sector. Or maybe I'm wrong. You're the camouflage and deception expert, Comrade Malenkoy; you tell me."

Malenkoy decided to back down. He had seen the general in this mood before. Anyway, his superior was right. What was the point in making a fuss? Nerchenko had used his own argument about the consequences of this renegade Nazi spotting the *maskirovka* and seemed quite relaxed about the whole affair. It was time to get back to Chrudim and put the finishing touches to the dummy tanks. He had had quite enough of chasing fascists around the dense forests of Czechoslovakia. If he could finish the job by tomorrow he would get back into Nerchenko's favor again.

"Oh, we did solve one mystery, Comrade General."

He had almost forgotten about it, but the thought of currying favor had jogged his memory about Yuri Petrovich. He reached into his pocket, pulled out Paliev's battered ID papers and placed them on the general's makeshift desk.

Nerchenko stopped massaging his eyes and studied the bloodied document. The room was as silent as a mausoleum, disturbed only by a row of Nerchenko's medals, two Orders of Lenin and three of the Red Banner, which sounded like distant bells as they danced on his chest. Malenkoy noticed his general's complexion turn a shade of grayish white.

Malenkoy was surprised to see that the general had a heart after all. Paliev had been his trusted aide for almost two years, that was true, but he never would have guessed that Nerchenko had been this attached to him.

Malenkoy waited several seconds for Nerchenko to regain his usual ice-cold composure, but instead he appeared to be sickening.

"I'm sorry, Comrade General, that it had to be me who broke the news. Yuri Petrovich was a good man. We were friends, you know."

"Where did you find these?" The voice was low and almost quavering.

"We didn't find these on him, Comrade General; they were in the pockets of one of the SS. He must have kept it to show to their intelligence people. Well, he won't be showing it to anyone, now."

"Did you find anything else of his? Papers, plans, I mean. Things that the enemy could use." Malenkoy could hardly hear the general now. His voice was little more than a whisper.

"No, Comrade General. The SS terrorists were clean. They did not even carry ID papers of their own. It is possible that the survivor tried to destroy all evidence of their identity before he left the camp. Perhaps he overlooked Paliev's papers."

Nerchenko's hands shook as he tried to light a cigarette. He was clearly too upset to speak any more, so Malenkoy dismissed himself, leaving him alone and deep in thought.

It was a measure of Nerchenko's desperation, Krilov thought, that he had sent two coded messages about Archangel to Moscow in one week.

Archangel had been given a reprieve as soon as the news came in that Paliev's charred body had eventually been found by his burned-out jeep, the victim of a random partisan attack—or so they had thought. The plans, it seemed, had gone up in smoke with him.

The marshal listened carefully, his chin resting on his clasped hands, while Krilov read out the decoded transcript of Nerchenko's latest bulletin. When he finished, Krilov held the paper over his lighter and dropped it, burning, into the wastebasket beside his master's desk.

"It sounds as if Comrade General Nerchenko is upset by this latest development," Shaposhnikov said calmly, watching the smoke rise from the wastebasket. Krilov had never seen his mentor quite so resplendent as he was today, in his bright-green uniform, with its red piping and heavy gold embroidery.

"And not without some justification this time," Krilov added.

"Let us go over what we know, and I stress 'know,' Kolya, before we do anything rash. We know that Paliev took the plans from Nerchenko's safe and we know that he was prevented from carrying out his treachery by, of all things, an SS unit operating behind our lines." Shaposhnikov smiled, perhaps because he knew what the SS did to their Russian prisoners, Krilov thought. "Now we also know," the marshal continued, "that Paliev's identification papers were found on the body of one of the Germans who foiled our traitor's plans, which were probably to inform Stalin exactly what is happening on the First Ukrainian front. However, that is where the firm evidence ends."

"What about the report by the major who found the SS commandos' bodies that there may be survivors from the unit still at large?"

"This is only the belief of a major of tanks, Kolya; it is not backed by proof. But let us suppose that it is true and, worse still, that this survivor, or these survivors, have the plans to Archangel. What can they do? They are some fifty kilometers behind our lines, and even if they do make it back to their own troops, which I very much doubt, as the sector is crawling with our own men, they will be powerless to stop the plan going ahead."

"Not entirely, Comrade Marshal. If the Archangel document does end up in Berlin it would be simple for the Nazis to deliver this plan to Stalin, perhaps in return for some sort of cease-fire. They still have agents who are active in Moscow, according to the NKVD."

"Kolya, you helped me to prepare the plans for our generals in the field and you know that to an outsider Archangel would appear to have the full backing of the chiefs of staff and Stalin himself. You forget that it is only we and a handful of loyalists at the front who know that Stalin does not have an inkling about Archangel. No, it will go ahead, but the plan will have one significant change." Shaposhnikov moved over to the window and paused to watch the first shift of workers arrive by truck at the construction site on the other side of the square.

"Change, Comrade Marshal?"

"Yes, Kolya." Shaposhnikov turned to face his subordinate. "I agree that there is some risk to Archangel between now and the great day. But there is a simple remedy. We will bring the attack forward. That will be our insurance in case these insurgents do make it back to their lines and drop Archangel into the lap of the German High Command, or what's left of it."

☐

Krilov was impressed. Once more he had come to Shaposhnikov, urging him to exercise caution in the face of another setback to their plans. Yet the marshal had brushed off his concern as he would a piece of fluff from his uniform. Instead of playing safe, he had gone on the attack.

"There is, of course, an alternative," Krilov said. "If Archangel is compromised, then we could always play our ace right at the start. If the enemy is mobilizing to meet us, then we hit them on day one with the special . . . means at our disposal. Even as I speak, the Berezniki consignment is approaching Ostrava."

The marshal smiled, his lips thinning out until, to Krilov, they seemed almost opaque.

"It should never need come to that, Kolya. The Berezniki consignment is a fail-safe, a weapon of last resort. That should be enough."

"Indeed, Comrade Marshal."

The older man clapped Krilov on the shoulder.

"Go, Kolya. Get word to our men on all three fronts. Archangel has been brought forward by a week, to the 17th. The tanks roll in five days' time. That and the Berezniki consignment should be all the insurance we need."

□

As soon as he entered the village he knew that evil lay in wait for him. The horse sensed it too, at first shaking its head violently from side to side, then rearing up on its hind legs, uttering a cry that sounded more human than animal. He looked around for the rest of his cossacks, but they were not there. He tried to turn back, but the horse broke into a gallop and carried him down the path he had known so well since the early days of his childhood.

And then he was on the ground. He looked up just in time to see the horse galloping away. He was quite alone in that place; there was not a soul in the entire village—except in his house. He was outside the house and he could hear her moaning. He had to go in to save her, but he knew that evil was there and he cowered on the ground, sobbing quietly, begging to be allowed to stay away. Her cries for him cut right through his head, but he did nothing, save to block his ears and try to escape the sound of her pleas for help.

He was inside now. He was trying not to look at the door to her room, for he knew that it would only take a glance for it to open. But he had to see, he had to know what they were doing to her. He had to save her. The door swung on its hinges and he saw the soldiers on her, writhing over her, tearing at her clothes. He tried to turn away, to avoid her twisted face as the men in brown uniform went down on her again.

Then they finished, laughing at him as they pulled up their trousers and walked from that room. When they had gone he rushed to her, but the bed was a sea of flames and he couldn't get near. She was still alive, calling to him, while all he could do was stand there and sob and cry out her name.

"Yulia!"

Boris Shaposhnikov, Hero of the Soviet Union, found himself wailing like a baby in the early hours of the dawn that was breaking over Moscow, calling out his wife's name again and again. He felt weak and sick, as he always did after the dream had gripped him and thrown him like a rag doll around the bed.

And then his mind returned to the calm and ordered discipline for which he was known and admired by all those who saw him by day. Marshal Boris Shaposhnikov, Chief of the General Staff, friend and adviser to Josef Stalin himself. Shaposhnikov, the inscrutable, who had never been known to make a mistake in his life.

Except one.

But they would pay this time. It had taken twenty-five years for him to execute his revenge, but it was worth the wait. Archangel was almost complete. It was now only a matter of days.

11

Kruze lay in the darkness, his eyes open, trying not to think of anything in particular, but his thoughts always returned to her. It bothered him that he could not shake her from his mind. His two days in London had been intoxicating—pulling the boy from the movie theater, the rush of feeling for Penny. But now he was back in Farnborough, the EAEU, and the two worlds could not go together.

That she was still technically married to Fleming bothered him less than the fact that because of her he was now just like all the other guys with domestic worries. Unfaithful wives, families that had been evacuated to the far reaches of the country-side to escape the flying bombs. All the uncertainties, the problems of domestic life. The confusion and the fear that always returned after a pilot had one too many beers in the mess.

His detachment from that world had so far kept all his faculties razor sharp. Until now he had lived on that edge, so fine between life and death, which kept him the best up there, invulnerable. And now Penny had entered his life and he loved her and cursed her for it at the same time.

He swung himself off the bed and groped his way to his trousers, slung casually over the back of the chair the night before. He walked over to the window, wiped the chilled condensation off the pane and stared out. The pre-dawn mist still hung thick over the airfield and it looked the sort that wasn't going to clear when daylight came. Part of him wished he had stayed away.

He shook his head, switched on the light, and pulled on the rest of his clothes. He moved to the basin, ran the tap, and splashed the freezing water onto his face. He felt old, much older than his twenty-nine years, but under the mop of fair hair, the features he saw in the mirror were still brown from the years of working under the hot African sun. The eyes were still a deep, shining blue. There were lines on his forehead that he hadn't previously noticed, but then perhaps he had not really cared before.

He pulled on his cap and strolled outside, glad to get away from the confines of his room. There was an air of expectancy about the station. He had been dimly aware of it when greeted by Mulvaney, the station commander, the previous evening. He was chirpier than usual, smug almost. It was infectious, the others had caught it. There was definitely something in the air.

The crackle of cutting equipment interrupted his thoughts. Even though there was some light, he still could not see the huge sheds for the mist. He knew that shifts of mechanics had been toiling through the night to try to unmask the secrets of aircraft that still patrolled the skies above the disintegrating Reich.

Kruze reached the great sliding doors of the hangar and found the small access hatch.

The brightness of the place almost blinded him. On his left, fitters scrambled over a four-engined Halifax bomber, making it ready for its next flight to test the new radar-jamming equipment contained in the black box in the belly of the aircraft.

Next to the great bomber lay the Me 110 he had seen there a few days before, its crosses and swastikas in the process of being removed for a set of Royal Air Force roundels. Stencils were taped to the wings, the fin, the fuselage. The smell of oil-based paint and thinners was heavy. Two great heaters at each end of the hangar blasted out warm air, which remained trapped beneath the roof despite the numerous cracks in the corrugated iron paneling.

Moving down the line, Kruze came to the Junkers he had flown against Fleming during his last dissimilar combat test. The memory brought a momentary crease to the furrows by his eyes. Then the feeling was gone, leaving only the professional interest in what was being done to the armed reconnaissance airplane.

The wing skin had been removed, the panels lying on the ground beside him, buckled in parts where the stress from his overzealous aerobatics had acted on the airframe. Two aircraftmen shone torches over the mainspar that ran the length of the wings, checking for signs of fatigue. Others stripped the Jumos down, laying the intricate pieces of the cylinders carefully into boxes, numbering them for easy reassembly. Unlike aircraft at other RAF stations, the airplanes with the EAEU at Farnborough did not come with manuals.

Kruze found Broyles at the far end of the hangar lying on his back under the jacked-up frame of the Fieseler 103 that Bowman's team had discovered on a small satellite airfield in Denmark a few weeks before. The chief swore as a nut slipped from his greasy thumb and forefinger. Kruze retrieved it from the floor and handed it back to him.

"Morning, Chief. You ever sleep?"

Broyles squinted against the glare of the arc lights. "Sleeping's for pilots and officers, Mr. Kruze. I've got to keep these bloody things in the air."

Kruze laughed. "Cigarette?"

Broyles slid out from under the tiny wing of the Fi 103.

"Thank you, sir," he said, wiping his hands on his boilersuit before pulling out a Lucky Strike from the proffered pack.

"Up a bit early yourself, aren't you, Mr. Kruze?" Broyles' oil-streaked watch told him it was a little before five o'clock.

"Couldn't sleep, Chief. You know how it is." Concerned that Broyles might ask him why, and suddenly bereft of any easy answer, Kruze looked down at the Fieseler.

Bowman's outfit had been attached to a Canadian infantry regiment in the forefront of the drive into German-occupied Denmark. Of special interest to the EAEU was a satellite airfield at Grove, where, according to resistance reports, a newly formed unit of KG 200, the Luftwaffe's special operations division, was being trained on a specially adapted, piloted version of the Fi 103, better known outside the Reich as the V1 doodlebug. What the EAEU found at Grove chilled them. The Germans were close to declaring the Fi 103 Reichenberg IV operational. Instead of fielding a flying bomb with an often unreliable guidance system against the Allies, the Nazis' refined system would permit the destruction of high-priority targets, thanks to the specially trained pilot staying with the missile right to the end. Staverton wanted to know how it worked, down to the last nut and bolt.

"I hope you never have to fly this," Broyles said. "I wouldn't wish that job on my worst bloody enemy. Gives me the willies just to work on it. And that's without the warhead installed."

Kruze sat down on a workbench next to the chief and sucked hard on the loosely packed end of the Lucky Strike. "What about the poor dumb German who's going to fly it for real?"

The chief snorted, utter contempt on his face. "If a bloody Nazi is mad enough to get into this thing in the first place, then he deserves to be damned, damned to hell."

Kruze cursed his stupidity.

"Sorry, Chief, I forgot." He pulled again on the cigarette. "Maybe this is one job you should be taken off."

Broyles ground the stub under his heel and wriggled his way back under the Fieseler. Kruze saw the pain and the anger ebb from the seasoned engineer's face. The old Broyles, the professional, twenty-five years in the service, looked back at him.

"Pass us that wrench, would you, Mr. Kruze?"

Kruze did as he was asked.

"To tell you the truth," the older man said, "it's just another job. And that's what I live for now, you see. The service. That's all the family I need now. Thanks." He passed the tool back to Kruze. "Now, I just hate Nazis and bloody officers." He grinned back at Kruze, exposing an intermittent row of nicotine-stained, unbrushed teeth. "English bloody officers, of course."

Kruze smiled back. "Of course," he said.

He watched Broyles remove the paneling, going about his work as if the Fieseler were a sedan brought in for a routine oil change at a garage. He tried to imagine Broyles the family man, with a wife and two children living in the outskirts of London. Sending his paycheck to them once a week, until a faulty guidance system determined that a V1 should overfly its target in the center of the capital and crash twenty miles off course, in a suburb where Mrs. Broyles and family went about their routine, ordinary lives.

"Better to have loved and lost, Mr. Kruze."

The panel, with the stark serial number on the inside face exposed, was discarded noisily on the concrete floor.

"I'll be seeing you, Chief." The words disappeared as the first cough of a twelve-cylinder Daimler-Benz from the Me 110 ripped through the hangar.

Kruze headed for the sliding doors. His mind was full of thoughts about the chief, first family man, then widower, now remarried to the service. For the rest of his life. He thought of

109

himself—and he hadn't done that for a long time—Piet Kruze . . . orphan. Not much to stay for. Nothing to return to, winding up a bitter old man after a lifetime's dedication to the job, to flying. And nothing else to show for his life. What a bloody waste.

He emerged into the damp, cold air. The mist was still heavy; no chance of it lifting that day. He yearned for the warmth of the hangar again, then thought of the heat on his back from the open fire in the room of the small apartment in London where he had held her for the first time.

Penny Fleming. He loved her, didn't he? She had made him feel good inside, good about himself—and he hadn't felt that way since he turned his back on the small homestead, on an old man who loved him, hundreds of miles from nowhere in the African bush.

Penny. The future.

He quickened his step, moving now with purpose to rouse Marlowe, get him to cover for him for the day. Shouldn't be too difficult, he persuaded himself. There wasn't going to be any flying done. And Marlowe had the car that would transport him to the cottage in Buckinghamshire where he could once again glimpse the future and, this time, catch it in his hands.

□

Dietz was so close that he could smell Herries, even though he could not see him. The SS sergeant lay down by the dense trees beside the main highway and waited.

His shoulder hurt like hell, but at least the shrapnel wound had been clean. The metal had torn through the flesh leaving no chunks of the antipersonnel grenade inside to turn the wound gangrenous. In some respects, the injury had proved advantageous, as its painful throbbing had kept him from succumbing to the exhaustion that had racked his body during the march of the last two days.

He was going to find Herries and kill him, whatever it took. His hatred of the man over the last two years was now justified and it felt good. When he found his officer, he would put him to his death slowly and, furthermore, he'd get a medal for doing it once headquarters was informed that Herries had turned. He always knew that the man was a fucking traitor. He had always been the Englishman through and through. Some of his preciousness had been ironed out by the long Russian campaign, but unlike the other English, who had joined the SS until death,

Herries had been looking for the right moment to jump ship. And Dietz had merely been waiting for him to do it. Now that he had, he was going to pay.

It had been so easy picking up Herries' scent. The man had left a trail through the forest as wide as Ludwig Strasse, the main street of his home city, Munich. The only reason he had not caught up with Herries sooner was because he had had to wait until light on the morning after the explosion to see enough to pick up his tracks. That had been dangerous, because Ivan had arrived at the camp just before dawn and Dietz had had to lie low until they went on their way, all the time hoping that they would not find and follow Herries' trail themselves. The sergeant had seen the Siberians with the Russian officers and knew that they were more than capable of tracking down Herries in that forest. He did not want them to remove his pleasure of hunting the turncoat himself.

When the Russians left, it took Dietz a few minutes to find the path that Herries had cut through the trees. Thereafter, his only problem was maintaining the stamina to catch up, but he knew that Herries was partially incapacitated by his chronic diarrhea, and that had spurred him on in his quest.

And now he was very close. The tracks were fresh, not more than a few hours old at the most. Now that he had reached the end of the forest, found the Strakonice-Pilzen highway, he would wait, listen, and watch. Herries would show himself, sooner or later.

Dietz was grateful for the opportunity to rest up. He must have marched thirty kilometers in the last two days. From what Herries had said at the camp they must be approaching their own lines by now. It was another fifteen kilometers to the front, maybe less. Judging the points of the compass from the position of the sun, he calculated that Herries would be heading north and west, which would mean following the road that lay before him off to the right. He reckoned that it would pay to stick to the forest, on account of the occasional Russian convoy that used the road, but if Herries had any sense, he would keep the road in sight as a permanent navigational reference point.

Where was Herries?

Dietz resolved to wait for one more hour, before searching for Herries' tracks on the other side of the road. But he was still convinced that Herries was on this side; it was only a gut feeling, but his instinct had served him well when he had called on it before.

The sound of a vehicle approaching from the front caught his ear. He picked it up several hundred meters away on the long, straight highway. It was a jeep moving at high speed, its bright-red star clearly visible on the hood. Dietz hugged the ground a little closer and merged with the grass and the bushes.

The open-topped vehicle passed so close that Dietz was able to distinguish the lone occupant as a lieutenant from the silver flashes that twinkled on his epaulettes. His bored expression reflected the tedium of driving along the straight, flat roads that crossed the great Czechoslovak plain that lay beneath the mountains. The German twitched at the opportunity he was missing; an officer riding alone in a jeep without escort was a rare sight that close to the front. But to expose his position now would be to alert Herries, and the Englishman was a higher priority than any Russian.

He watched as the vehicle shrank in the distance. It was well over five hundred meters from him when he saw its brake lights sparkle and then glow red. Two pinpoints of light at the extremity of his vision.

Then he heard the shot.

Dietz was on his feet and running for the jeep while the single report was still echoing off the mountain.

□

Malenkoy was satisfied that the construction phase of the *maskirovka* was all but complete. There was just time to finish it before the operation entered the new phase tomorrow. Nerchenko had seemed especially eager for him to start adding the final master-touches during their meeting earlier that morning and Malenkoy had been in no position to argue. If he had had the power of veto, he would have advised holding back on the bogus radio transmissions for a few more days, but Nerchenko had seemed anxious for activities to be stepped up now. And no one argued with General Nerchenko.

By tomorrow evening, if German aerial reconnaissance pictures hadn't already shown it, the intensive radio traffic under Malenkoy's supervision would make the Nazis really believe that Chrudim was brimming with Soviet armor just waiting to roll toward Berlin.

Deception and disinformation—that was Malenkoy's trade. Instead of putting his skills to good use in this area, he had been made to hunt SS diehards for a day and a night in a cold, wet, and threatening forest. The experience still made him feel jumpy.

He needed a drink and knew just where to find one.

Sergeant Sheverev was exactly where Malenkoy expected him to be. As he entered the vehicle-maintenance park, he could hear the burly starshina bellowing at an unfortunate private who had mislaid one of Sheverev's precious wrenches. The private explained that he had put the tool down for a second beside the truck he had been working on and the next time he looked, it was gone. It was now probably changing hands on the black market for local wine or brandy, Malenkoy thought.

Sheverev looked over the private's shoulder and caught Malenkoy's eye. He sent the private back to work on his mechanical charge. The private passed Malenkoy, relief that he had escaped so lightly etched on his face. Sheverev was not known for his leniency in the maintenance park.

"Comrade Major, to what do I owe the pleasure? No, don't tell me. I can guess." Sheverev let out a long, throaty laugh, his bearlike frame heaving with every intake of breath.

"Quiet, Oleg Andreyovich, and give me a drink. Vodka is what I feel like, so please, none of that local wine which does such terrible things to my stomach." Malenkoy gave him a pained expression.

"To please our new hero, the major, would be an honor." Sheverev bowed to Malenkoy in mock reverence and disappeared behind one of his trucks.

Sheverev was Malenkoy's best ally in Chrudim. Malenkoy had tacitly agreed to turn a blind eye to Sheverev's racketeering on the understanding that he could use the sergeant's tools and resources when he needed them. Sheverev also kept his major happy with a liberal supply of vodka whenever Malenkoy felt like a drink. There was one other advantage of keeping in with the sergeant; he knew all the gossip there was to be had in the sector.

He reemerged carrying a bottle and two dirty, metal cups. Sheverev poured a good measure into each container and handed one to Malenkoy.

"To you, Comrade Major," he said, raising his cup. "A damn good engineer and scourge of SS terrorists to boot. *Nastrovya*." He knocked back half the contents.

"Spare me the compliments, Oleg Andreyovich," Malenkoy said, yawning. "I only coordinated the hunt, because the fuckers were in my sector and ruining our little game here. It was really the Siberians who found them."

"The Siberians . . . yes, I knew that actually," Sheverev said, shaking his head slowly. "Those sons of bitches have had a busy week."

Malenkoy took another swig of the throat-burning vodka. Already he felt his body relaxing. Soon the *maskirovka* would be finished and then perhaps he could apply for some leave. He was hardly listening to the old gossip.

"Busy?" Malenkoy felt he had to humor the other man. He didn't want the vodka supply to dry up. "Busy doing what?"

Sheverev leaned forward. Malenkoy could smell the alcohol on his breath.

"Well, a sergeant friend of mine who looks after a bunch of Siberians over in Branodz told me that our good friend, Comrade General Nerchenko, commissioned his platoon to track down a major from headquarters who took a jeep and an armored car for escort and deserted, just like that." The starshina whistled through his teeth. "I mean what would make a man run away like that? It was a nice, comfortable job being aide-de-camp to the general."

Malenkoy stiffened.

"You don't mean Major Paliev?"

"Yes, Paliev; that was him." Sheverev nodded.

"Oleg Andreyovich, Paliev didn't desert; he was ambushed on official business for the general. He was killed by the SS insurgents we found on the mountain. We found his papers on one of the bodies."

"Well that may be, Comrade Major," Sheverev said, slurring his words, "but Nerchenko told my friend and his Siberians to kill your Major Paliev when they caught up with him. Nerchenko must have really hated this Paliev. He ordered them to burn the body, the jeep, everything. Only deserters get that sort of treatment."

Malenkoy stopped drinking. He thought of Yuri. He saw the headless body at the Freikorps' camp. He saw Nerchenko's face drain of its color when he told him that it was the SS who had killed Paliev. Yet he'd wanted Paliev dead all along. It just didn't add up.

Sheverev continued to drone on.

Malenkoy looked intently at him and put his finger to his lips.

Sheverev looked affronted.

"What's wrong?"

"Nothing. I've got to go."

"So suddenly?"

"Yes."

Malenkoy walked off, but stopped after a few paces. He turned to Sheverev.

"You should watch your mouth, Oleg Andreyovich. One day you might get it shot off."

Sheverev shrugged.

"Me? No chance. I'm a survivor. Like you, Comrade Major. We use our heads. We'll be all right; you'll see."

□

Herries had forgotten to put his MP40 on automatic, but it did not matter. The single shot killed the Russian instantly.

The plan had worked perfectly, but he had had to wait a good two hours before the right opportunity presented itself. He had first spotted the jeep and the lone occupant through his Zeisses at a range of several hundred meters. When it reached a dip in the road, Herries jumped from behind his cover and lay down beside the crumbling edge of the concrete highway.

For an agonizing few seconds, he had thought the Ivan was not going to stop, then he heard the whine of the engine as the gears slowed the jeep's speed and he held his breath, his thumping heart almost blocking out the sound of the approaching vehicle. Before the occupant had time to get out of the car and remove his pistol from its holster, Herries had the gun trained on his chest. One shot, and it was all over. The young officer's surprise was etched on his now-lifeless face, showing the traces of those last emotions—anger at being duped, agony that it should all end this way.

Herries scrambled up to the jeep and inspected his work. Playing dead had been a desperate ploy, but he couldn't go any further on foot. His stomach felt as if it were being pulled inside out by the dysentery. Had he not reached the road at that precise instant, he would have collapsed in the forest and elected to stay and die there.

Herries was relieved to see an officer's greatcoat over one of the jeep's rear seats. It would cover up the bloodstain that was now spreading over the man's tunic with the rapidity of ink on blotting paper. He had to get the uniform off him, but it was too dangerous to do it in that exposed place. Better to drive further along the road and swing off into the trees, where he would have time to change into the Russian's clothes and dispose of the body.

He pushed the corpse onto the passenger seat and cast a quick glance around to familiarize himself with the controls. The ignition caught the engine straightaway and first gear engaged with no difficulty, but he lifted the clutch pedal up too quickly, and the jeep hopped forward with such a jolt as it stalled that Herries was thrown back in his seat.

At that precise moment, Dietz, one hundred meters behind, fired.

The bullet hit the frame around the windshield and whined off into the trees. Herries saw the point of impact out of the corner of his eye.

Then he saw the movement reflected in the windshield.

He already knew who it was before he spun around and saw the massive frame of Dietz pounding down the road toward him. It took two seconds for Herries to make a choice between turning to face his sergeant with a machine pistol on single shot or trying to restart the jeep. His dithering took Dietz fifteen meters closer. Herries made his choice, but his reactions were dulled by the sickening panic that caused the blood to pound in his head. His eyes raced over the dashboard. Where was the fucking ignition key? His fingers groped around the base of the steering column until he felt the angular edges of the key. He turned it and the engine coughed and died. In the mirror he could see Dietz, very close now, raising his rifle to his shoulder for a second shot on the run. He turned the key again.

The vehicle hopped a foot and stalled. The limp body of the Russian slumped forward onto his lap. Shit! He had left the bloody gear in first. Herries' mind was numb now to anything that was going on outside the jeep. The blood rushing in his head made his eardrums feel as if they would explode, while everything on the periphery of his sight grayed out until he was left with a narrow tunnel of vision whose only point of focus was the ignition key. He did not even hear the report from Dietz's next shot, nor the bullet that screamed past his head by inches.

Dietz knew that he had Herries. He pounded his legs with all his strength along the potholed surface of the road, over the final twenty yards to the jeep.

Herries turned the key with such force that his clammy thumb and forefinger slipped off the shiny metal surface, but the engine caught, the clutch engaged and he shot back in his seat as the jeep surged forward. Dietz hurled his rifle into the rear of the vehicle and lunged for the tailgate, grasping it with one hand, then two. Herries was into second gear, the engine screaming as he brought the speed up to 40 KPH, but Dietz held on, slowly hauling in his dragging feet, preparing himself for the final effort, which would propel him into the rear of the vehicle.

Herries could see it all in the mirror. The two white hands on the tailgate and between them the grotesquely twisted face, blood and dirt still caked to the stubble on the cheeks and chin, wincing with every jerking movement of his body which brought him one second nearer to jumping onto the back seat.

Herries threw the corpse off his legs and groped for the MP40, which was lying between the two front seats. He grabbed it by the barrel, took one last look at the needle on the speedometer as it nudged past 55 KPH, and then swung around, crashing the stock of his machine pistol down onto Dietz's knuckles. The mouth curled back silently with the pain, and the red eyes bored into Herries' for a second; then he was gone. Herries watched in the mirror as the body rolled, bounced, and fell along the road, before coming to rest. Then he rounded a corner and it was gone.

Herries drove fast for another two kilometers before he felt he had put enough distance between himself and the man whom he was sure he had killed two days before. This time he would take no chances, even if Dietz had hit the road hard enough to break every bone in his body.

Herries swung down a muddy track lined with high pines and, when he was satisfied that the vehicle could no longer be seen from the road, he slowed to a halt. His body trembled with deep convulsions as the events of the last few minutes caught up with him. He leaned over the side of the jeep and retched until his stomach was emptied of the berries and leaves that had been his only nourishment for the last few days.

Ten minutes later Herries was back in the driving seat dressed in the uniform of the Soviet lieutenant. He wrapped the greatcoat around his body to hide the large dark stain on the chest and was about to set off back for the road when he noticed the wretched appearance of his face in the mirror. He jumped out of the jeep and went over to his bundle of clothes, which partially hid the body of the Russian behind the nearest pine. He found his razor and set about shaving his dry face, his cheeks and chin still too numb to protest as the rusty blade scraped away the two-day-old stubble.

Satisfied that his cleaner image would not draw undue attention from passing factions of the Red Army, Herries drove off in the open-topped jeep, paused at the main road to make sure the coast was clear, and then took a left in the direction of Pilzen.

□

Shaposhnikov and Krilov settled back into the canvas seats in the rear of the Ilyushin as the pilot opened up the throttles and the bomber trundled down the long runway before lifting off from Kubinka, the military airfield fifty kilometers from Moscow.

It was a four-hour flight to Ostrava, the main Soviet railhead and logistics station for the Red Army buildup in Czechoslovakia. There they would pick up transport for the two hundred-kilometer journey to the front, but not before Shaposhnikov ensured that the consignment from Factory 497 at Berezniki, a facility at the base of the Urals, had arrived safely at the marshaling yards. Shaposhnikov wanted to oversee some of the unloading operation personally.

As Krilov stared out the window at the receding city of Moscow, he felt an immense wave of relief. Every minute that passed put another five kilometers between them and Beria's internal security police, the NKVD. The events of the last few days had made him anxious. Paliev's attempted defection, Nerchenko's jitters, the coded exchanges between Moscow and Branodz—they had all risked exposure unnecessarily. Finally there was the news that Paliev had been ambushed by the fascists. But somehow the leadership of Shaposhnikov had kept them as one, kept them strong. He relished the moment when they would all be together; Shaposhnikov, himself, and the three generals, Badunov, Vorontin, and Nerchenko, from each respective front. Five men who would change the face of the world. His whole body tingled with excitement.

The village of Krazna Hora had long been ordained as the meeting place for the final briefing on Archangel. Krilov had had to send out urgent dispatches within the last few hours to the three generals in the field to tell them that the plan had been brought forward. It would be up to Shaposhnikov tomorrow to tell them by how much the scheme had been affected.

Archangel would work because good men, pure Bolsheviks, committed to the ideals on which their revolution had been founded, were behind it. It would work because their mentor was not only true to those beliefs, he was also the best strategist in the Allied command—Western or Eastern. It had been planned down to the last detail.

By the time Generalissimo Stalin, once a great man, now paranoid and divorced from reality, realized they were gone, the steamroller would be heading for Paris.

It would work because they had the ultimate weapon known to man, the last resort if all else failed. And they had the balls to use it.

Krilov reclined a little more, no longer caring about the sharp discomfort of the seat. It felt good to be going into action again.

12

Herries' few hours in the barn could have been his most comfortable since his arrival on the eastern front, but he chose not to sleep.

He wasn't afraid of being discovered by the peasant who owned the barn, for he could easily have bluffed his way through any encounter with a rural Czechoslovakian simpleton.

Herries' restlessness centered on the tenacity of the Siberians whom the Russians used to hunt insurgents behind their lines. If they were on to him, they could have picked up his trail from the point where Dietz's body lay broken in the road. He was pretty sure that such clues as he had left were minimal, but now that he was only a matter of miles from his goal, it paid to stay on his guard. If he had been discovered, there would have been no question of bluffing his way past the Russians who controlled their Siberian hunters. They would have cast one look at the jeep hidden inside the barn and taken him away to be shot, as a spy, a deserter, or a black marketeer—jeeps commanded a high price with the partisans.

As soon as he had caught his breath, Herries arose from his bed of straw, heaped in one of the corners of the dry, stone building. He knew the most dangerous part of the journey was yet to come.

He had survived the two-day trek through the dripping forest, avoiding its dangers with the skill of a seasoned poacher. He had skirted Branodz by about three kilometers along the way and crept up to a bluff, which overlooked the center of the town, to see for himself Ivan's preparations for the invasion of the west. Squinting through his Zeisses he had seen the armor, the preparations, the hive of activity around the headquarters. There had been patrols, but none had come close to him. He was still good, even without Dietz.

But this morning he was heading into the beast's lair. Today would signal the end of the journey, one way or the other.

Herries stood in the middle of the barn and dusted the straw off his uniform. He walked over to the jeep and inspected his face in the rearview mirror. Stubble was returning to his sallow cheeks, but he scratched it off with his razor; the light that streamed through the cracks in the wooden roof was just sufficient to show him what he was doing.

He had needed cover, a place to go to ground for a few hours. He had not been long on the road when he spotted the barn down the muddy track. It was the perfect place to hide the secret of Archangel.

Herries placed his officer's cap on his head and inspected the face that stared back at him in the jeep's mirror. He reckoned that with the greatcoat to conceal the reddish-brown mark that stained his chest, he could pass unchallenged into Pilzen.

He walked back to the corner where he had rested and pulled back some of the straw until the base of the stone wall was exposed. He removed the loose rock that he had found the night before and stuffed the small package into the dark recess that lay behind. He wedged the stone back into its position, satisfied that it looked undisturbed and then heaped the straw back into the corner.

The job finished, he pulled back the twin doors of the barn and paused to scrutinize the surrounding woods to make sure that he had not been observed.

The jeep started up the first time. He coasted down to the end of the track and resumed his journey along the last few kilometers that led into Pilzen.

Before the radio was destroyed during their retreat from Boskovice, Herries had reckoned the German-occupied town in western Czechoslovakia to be the next to crack between the viselike squeeze of the converging Soviet and American armies.

When he crossed the town's limits in his jeep, he wasn't so sure. His eyes darted in and out of the columns of Red Army troops that lined the streets, looking for signs of a Western presence. He was in the center of the town and on the point of turning around when he spotted the Stars and Stripes fluttering reassuringly in the wind on a building at the far side of the main square. His pulse quickened as he steered the vehicle straight for it.

He drew up outside the building and hailed the burly U.S. military policeman who was standing guard outside. Trying hard to keep his nerve, he mustered a halting Russian accent.

"I have signal for the British liaison officer. Please to tell me where is the British delegation." Herries prayed that the American would not run a spot-check on his papers.

The MP ambled down to the jeep.

"You want the British mission? Jesus Christ, another one?" The American gritted his teeth. "You're almost there, bud. See that gray building on the other side of the square? You'll find the British in there. Why the hell they can't put a flag outside their building same as we do, I don't know. That way I wouldn't have to give fifty goddamned guys like you the directions every day."

Herries put the jeep in gear and tore around to the other side of the square, scattering a group of U.S. and Soviet personnel who were bartering in the road outside the British building. Herries leapt out of the vehicle, bounded up the steps, and was through the door.

"And where the bloody 'ell do you think you're going, Joe?" The hand that had grabbed him prevented him from reaching the officer who was sitting at a desk on the far side of the room. He turned around to confront the sentry. The clipped, English public-school tones of his voice echoed throughout the sparsely furnished lobby.

"I am an officer of the German armed forces and I have come to surrender myself to your commanding officer. I have vital, urgent, information to convey."

Amazement registered on the soldier's face before he drew the bolt back on his Sten and held the muzzle firmly up against Herries' chest. The corporal didn't need to summon the captain over. In a moment he was beside the sentry, his startled eyes searching Herries' haggard face.

"What the devil's going on here? Who are you?" The voice was pure Sandhurst.

"My name is Herries. I am an obersturmführer of the Waffen SS. I have come to turn myself in to the British authorities, because I have some vital information which I must report to your commanding officer." Herries cast a sidelong look through the open door, beyond which Russian and American soldiers were trying to get a glimpse of him. The corporal also noticed the prying eyes and slammed the door shut.

"Hold on a bloody moment; let me get this right," the infantry captain said. "You're a German officer, wearing Russian uniform, talking to me in King's English, and you want to surrender to my commanding officer with urgent information?"

"That's right," Herries said levelly. "And if you value those pips on your shoulder, Captain, you should take me to him now."

The officer looked at Herries for a long time. Then his mouth cracked into a smile. "Well, how do you do," he said. "And I'm Winston fucking Churchill. Corporal, lock this man up in the storeroom and keep him under armed guard while I fetch the colonel. He's not going to believe this."

□

Colonel Jackson listened at first impassively and then with increasing distaste to Herries' story.

The picture that Herries painted made him sick—an actual regiment of British volunteers fighting on the Russian front. Alone in the storeoom with Herries, Jackson would have gladly put a bullet through the traitor's head but for the startling information he was holding.

Herries, made to stand in the corner of the dim room with only his trousers on, was shivering convulsively. He was clearly ill, but Jackson felt no compassion.

"I don't have the authority to grant what you ask, but even if I had, why should I believe you?" Jackson asked with a sneer. "The fact that your Reich is on its last knees obviously would not have escaped your attention, so you came up with this incredible tale to save your stinking neck."

Herries clutched his bare chest with his arms, trying to warm himself against the cold and damp of the room. His words came between intermittent sobs and shivers.

"Colonel, why the hell should I give myself up to you, right out of the blue, when I could have taken off to Turkey, or Switzerland, or any other fucking place you care to think of where there aren't British, American, or Russian troops to hunt me down? I have come to you because I have information which

123

you cannot afford to ignore, but I have put a price on that information. It's full immunity from prosecution or no deal."

Jackson, who had listened to Herries whine for the best part of an hour, exploded with rage.

"How dare you talk to me of deals, you damned traitor? If we want any information we can beat it out of you right now."

Herries stepped forward into the light of the single lamp, which hung from the ceiling. He gave Jackson a wry smile.

"Do you really think I would have neatly memorized the plan just so that you could make me cough it up, Colonel? You must be joking. The original documents—giving names of participants, dates, times, and so forth—are hidden in a very safe place just outside the town. And you'd never find it in a month of Sundays, Jackson, so you can put that idea right out of your head."

The colonel took a step forward to strike Herries across the face. Herries retreated back into the gloom of the corner.

"Colonel, you can't beat the location of that hiding place out of me either. You see, I'm going to die unless I get medical treatment for this dysentery very soon and any persuasive techniques used by your men are only going get me there a little quicker. I really have nothing to lose by keeping my mouth shut under interrogation."

Jackson reluctantly lowered his arm. He would have to take guidance from General Styles. He just hoped the general was in the mood to listen. He turned on his heels, but Herries' cracking voice made him pause by the door.

"Remember, Colonel, I want a signed affidavit of immunity before I tell you anything. But you'd better hurry. I can tell you that time's running out."

Jackson slammed the door behind him and called for the sentry.

Herries passed out, unable to fight the fatigue any longer.

□

For a split second the reality of the door crashing open mingled with Herries' tortured nightmare. Dietz wasn't dead; he had finally caught up with him. Lights and noise exploded inside his exhausted mind.

Herries pressed his bare back against the damp wall in a vain effort to get away, but rough hands pulled at his body and dragged him to his feet. He opened his eyes and squinted under the light of the lone lamp to see not Dietz, but Colonel Jackson before him. Two soldiers gripped him tightly by the arms.

Jackson swiped Herries hard across the cheek with the back of his hand.

"You'd better wake up, you little bastard, because you and I are going for a ride."

The slap drove some of the fatigue from his body, the stinging sensation giving way to a dull throb at the point where Jackson's signet ring had partially torn the soft flesh of his lower lip. But it was not so much the pain as Jackson's words that jolted Herries out of his exhaustion.

"I told you," Herries croaked, "no signed affidavit, no deal."

The soldiers' grips tightened on his arms. Jackson nodded at a third soldier whose fist crashed into Herries' stomach, driving upward into the base of his rib cage.

"I warned you, you traitor. Don't talk to me about deals."

As Herries slumped, the soldiers let the body sink to the floor. Herries looked up at Jackson to see him holding up a piece of paper.

"You deserve more than that," Jackson sneered, "but General Style's signature on this forbids me to treat you too roughly."

"Give me that." The pain shot through Herries' ribs as he grabbed desperately at the sheet of paper. Clenching it with shaking hands, he saw the official stamp and the scrawled hand of General Styles. It was what he needed. It was his passport home.

Jackson waited till he could see Herries tasting immunity. Then he pulled the paper from his grip.

"Oh no," he said, shaking his head at Herries. "We need proof that what you've been garbling about for the past few hours is fact. Then you can have your miserable reprieve. Show us your evidence, Herries, if you can."

Herries, still on his knees, brought the blood up from the back of his throat and spat at Jackson's feet. "Before I lead you there, we're going to pass by the nearest Red Cross outpost and drop off that letter. Only that way do I get to trust your promises of freedom."

13

Kruze wanted to reach out to the trousers that were lying tantalizingly close to the bed and pull the pack of cigarettes from his pocket, but he resisted the temptation because he knew that the motion would stir Penny from her sleep.

It was a lovely little room, exactly as he'd always imagined the bedroom of an English country cottage should look. The bunched curtains, with their floral pattern, allowed a thin stream of late-afternoon light to play across the bedspread and cast shimmering reflections off the brass bedstead onto the faintly undulating surface of the old ceiling.

He shifted slightly, as if trying to shake himself out of the sudden depression that gripped him.

"What are you thinking?" Her voice wasn't tinged with sleep and when he looked into her face, close to his, her eyes were bright and alert. He realized that she had been awake all the time.

"I was trying to imagine how it would be to wake up in a place like this every morning." It was part truth. "I'm not sure I could."

"I could take that the wrong way."

"You shouldn't," he smiled at her. "It's nothing to do with you . . . us. Nor the cottage. It's a perfect place."

She rolled onto him and brushed away a lock of hair that had fallen across his eye.

She kissed his forehead lightly. "England isn't for you, is it? It's not where the future lies."

"Isn't it? You tell me."

"You already know how I feel."

"Do I?"

She stretched across him, her breasts brushing across his stomach, and pulled the cigarettes and lighter from his trousers. She produced two cigarettes, putting one in his mouth and one in her own. The glow from the flame bathed her face in soft, orange light. It reminded him of the time he had first been struck by her beauty at the dinner party.

"I see you on a homestead, a farm—"

He rolled her onto her back. "We're not getting into that again."

She took a light draw on the end of the cigarette. "I never mentioned Rhodesia, did I? It could be in Australia, or South America, perhaps. Somewhere far from here."

"Do you figure in that picture?" He put his arms around her and smiled to defuse the gravity of the question.

"Darling, at the moment we're in the depths of the English countryside, huddled beside each other for warmth." She laughed. "Those places don't exist right now. We've got to win a war first."

He laughed with her. "I've come too far to get caught out now."

Her expression changed so suddenly it shocked him.

"Robert said that once," she whispered. The words hung heavily in the room. It was as if Fleming were there, watching them.

"Do you still love him?" He hadn't meant to say it, but the vacuum left by her words compelled the question.

She rolled away from him, resting her head on the pillow.

"The man I loved died in a hospital ward over a year ago."

He had pried too deeply and cursed himself for the intrusion.

"A divorcée," she said presently, putting on a brave smile. "I wonder how my parents will take it."

"As long as you're happy, surely they'll . . ."

She smiled again, the sadness of the previous minute gone from her face. "Tell that to my father."

"But will they back you, your parents, if it gets rough? It might, you know. Perhaps we should be more careful—I don't mean for me, it's gone beyond that. The worst the RAF can do is reduce me to the ranks."

"And stop you from flying. Could you live with that?"

"I've thought about it."

"In any case," she added quickly. "It's not going to come to that. Robert's not going to contest it. If he had wanted to, he would have called me, or written."

The drone of an aircraft, somewhere far above them, probably searching for a gap in the mist through which to land, was the only sound to be heard.

"As for my parents, they'll be disappointed, but they know what things have been like for the past year or so. I've tried to hide it, to put on a brave face, but they know."

He was about to speak, but she put her finger to his lips.

"No more of this talk. We live for now, you and I. I haven't had a chance to do that in a long time."

She jumped out of bed and pulled a dressing gown over her shoulders.

"How about a walk? It's so beautiful around here, you'll see." Her enthusiasm was infectious and he smiled. "I'd love to bring Billy when he's better, have him to stay for a while. You would come, wouldn't you?"

"Yes, I'd like that," he said. He thought of the boy from the east end of London and wondered whether he would feel out of place too. A stranger in a strange land.

"We'll pass by the baker's on the way back. If we're lucky they might even have some bread. The rationing's not nearly as bad as it is in London."

Kruze threw back the sheets and moved over to where she was standing, half-dressed, by the window.

"You're right," he said, and kissed her softly. "No more talk about tomorrow."

◻

Herries, washed and in clean clothes, was ushered from the back of the truck by an officer and four military policemen.

The DC-3 was already lined up on the runway, its propellers turning. The pilot watched nervously out of the window as the POW and his escort jumped into the back of the aircraft and the door was closed. He didn't waste any time in opening up the throttles. He'd seen too many pilots caught on the ground, and knew that it was madness to loiter at an exposed airfield so close to the front.

He'd tried to find out what all the fuss was about while they were waiting for the truck to arrive, but the officer had told him to mind his own business. Now he was simply glad to be flying a plane out of that sector, heading for England. With a bit of luck, they would be there in just four hours.

□

Staverton sat alone in his office, chewing over the events of the last hour in Churchill's Downing Street bunker.

When the PM's private secretary had phoned, ordering him to get over to Number Ten straightaway, his immediate thoughts were for the Rostock raid. He knew Fleming had pulled it off; he had received the signal along with the supplementary message from Bowman that the Komet was capable of air-to-ground ops as well. And, God knows, that had given him enough cause for concern.

This gave him a great deal more.

Churchill called the special Cabinet advisers together whenever there was a crisis. While the career soldiers on the general staff talked tactics, Staverton and his two counterparts came up with unconventional answers to unconventional situations.

Except crisis wasn't the word, Staverton thought.

A man was being brought to London from Pilzen, western Czechoslovakia. An Englishman, a traitor, with a story—and documentary evidence—that outlined a Soviet plan to launch an attack on all three fronts in eleven days' time. They would be in Paris in three weeks and at the Channel ports perhaps three weeks after that. And no one knew why.

Until Herries and the documents arrived they were only dealing with a few facts. The most important was that they had the name of the man who was coordinating the front-wide assault. Staverton had heard of Shaposhnikov, but he wasn't much more than a name. The AVM's army counterpart on the Cabinet advisory team had become terribly excited the moment it had been mentioned. So the Kremlin was bringing Shaposhnikov, the arch-strategist, more or less out of retirement for this one. There had to be very special reasons for that.

The marshal's right-hand men were less well-known in intelligence circles. A quick review of the text by General Styles' staff in Czechoslovakia had highlighted three additional key players. General Vorontin would lead the Second Belorussian front to the far north, General Badunov would head up the First Belorussian in the center, and General Nerchenko the Second Ukrainian to the far south. Shaposhnikov was going to take personal charge of the First Ukrainian. But what of the existing front commanders, Marshals Roskossovsky, Zhukov, and Konev?

The plans appeared to have been drafted by Shaposhnikov; they were certainly signed by him. They pinpointed where Shaposhnikov would establish his HQ. In addition to leading the First Ukrainian's thrust, he would personally direct the entire six-hundred-mile front from a place in western Czechoslovakia called Branodz. That also gave them something to play with, though not much.

There was one further possibility—that it was not the product of the Soviet High Command at all, but of a rebellious faction within the Red Army operating beyond its control. The theory dovetailed neatly with the fact that the three existing marshals at the front appeared not to be part of the plan. But where did that leave them? Should Stalin be informed, or was he the architect? Would a tip-off to the Soviet leader merely precipitate the advance of their tanks? And heaven knew, Staverton thought, there was little that the battle-weary Allied troops could do to stop them, even with eleven days' warning.

In the end, everything hinged on Shaposhnikov. Stalin's chief of general staff would trigger Archangel from the front. Churchill wanted to know everything about the man and, when they next convened, to have an idea of how to stop him.

To Staverton, sitting at his desk under the dimmed electric lighting of the Bunker, it was a bad dream. His sleep-starved mind wandered to the man who had first supplied the information. The report said that he was an Englishman serving in the Wehrmacht—no, the SS. How could they trust intelligence from such a source?

But those who had seen the Archangel documents believed it. And, more to the point, the prime minister believed it too. Churchill had long said it was almost inevitable that the Russians would turn their attentions to the west. That the Yalta agreement was just another piece of paper.

☐

As soon as they entered the sitting room they paused briefly, relishing the warmth of the fire over which they would soon toast the bread that the village baker had saved for her. Penny went through to the kitchen to prepare the plates for tea.

Kruze's gaze was drawn to a picture of Fleming on the table by the window. He was sitting in the cockpit of a Spitfire, posing easily for the camera, a smile creasing his eyes in the hot Italian sun.

Kruze heard Penny starting back and he put the picture down. Only then did it strike him that it was the only time he had seen Fleming really happy.

Penny came into the room holding a tea tray. Then the phone rang.

Penny jumped at the sound. She looked at Kruze for a moment and he could see the anxiety etched on her face.

She put the tray down, lifted the receiver slowly, and listened. Kruze saw her features soften.

"It's for you," she said. "Somebody called Marlowe."

Kruze went to the phone. Marlowe was barely recognizable, but the crackle could not hide the urgency in his voice.

"You'd better get your ass back down here fast; Mulvaney's holding a briefing for all aircrew at eight. You were right; something is up."

Kruze knew better than to ask for details over an open line.

"I'll be there in two hours," he said, and hung up.

Penny had stopped slicing the bread.

"When will I see you?" she asked.

"I don't know. There's a flap on at base. It could be days, more . . ."

"But . . ."

He reached for his cap and coat, still damp from their walk.

"When there's a flap on, it means that the Old Man wants answers quickly. That can take days or it can go on longer. Now listen, I'm not telling you what today has meant to me. You know all that."

He moved over to the door. "I'll call you."

"But I may not be here, darling. I'm expected back at work. Leave's almost over." She felt almost frantic. There had been so much she, too, had wanted to say.

"Then I'll leave a message for you. You'll be getting up to London to see Billy, won't you? Somehow I'll see to it that word's left there." He smiled and winked at her. "Sorry about the bread. Make sure they save some for next time."

And then he was gone.

BOOK
TWO

1

The eleven pilots on secondment to the EAEU at the Royal Aircraft Establishment at Farnborough were in the briefing room a few minutes before eight o'clock. All were present except Kruze, but only Marlowe noticed he was missing. The others attempted to second-guess Mulvaney's announcement. After days of bad weather, all the talk was now about getting back in the air.

Marlowe looked up from the second hand of his watch just as Kruze walked in. He was followed almost immediately by Mulvaney. As they rose for the station commander, Kruze took his place next to Marlowe.

"Christ," Marlowe whispered, "you cut that a bit fine."

"Got stuck behind a bloody armored convoy just outside Camberley." Kruze fought to control his breathing. "What's up?"

"No idea. Mulvaney's been looking like the cat that got the cream, most of the afternoon. He's been busting to tell us what this is all about."

Mulvaney gestured for them to sit down and cleared his throat.

"Gentlemen," he began, "in just under an hour, two Yorks will land here with a rather special cargo. As you know, up to now we have concentrated on testing aircraft which have more or less fallen into our hands. But the one now on its way to us was packed up into crates and flown here from the enemy's secret rocket-research establishment at Rostock."

He paused, waiting for the whispering to subside.

"I'm also pleased to tell you that it was the EAEU which masterminded and carried out the entire operation—with a bit of help from the army."

There was an outbreak of spontaneous cheering from the back of the room. Mulvaney beamed with pleasure.

"Now I expect you're all itching to know how and why this operation came about." Mulvaney scanned the faces before him once again. "Gentlemen, I haven't even been told all the details myself, such is the high level of classification on this one. Suffice to say this. We managed to snatch a new version of the Me 163, the 163C, while Rostock was still in enemy-occupied territory. A special military operation was mounted to allow an EAEU team in to dismantle the aircraft, pack it up, and fly it out."

Kruze let out a low whistle. Mulvaney held up his hands to silence the burst of voices in the room.

"I don't think I need to tell you gentlemen that Rostock has, with Peenemunde up the coast, been the home of the Messerschmitt 163 Komet for the past few years. We are now going to take over that research where the Germans left off."

There was more muttered approval from the pilots.

"That's all I can tell you, at the moment," Mulvaney said, winding up his speech. "The Bunker wants answers fast on this one, so testing is due to start early next week. The bad news, gentlemen, is that all leave has been suspended until we get the job done. That'll be all."

Chairs scraped across the floor as they all rose to leave. Mulvaney watched over them, something akin to pride in his eyes. As Kruze started to go, the station commander called him over.

"Piet, I want to give you first refusal for the 163's maiden flight. You have had more experience in high-speed flight than any other pilot in the unit and it could well be invaluable when it comes to flying the Komet."

Kruze walked to the window and looked out over the blacked-out airfield. With uncanny timing, the last vestiges of the mist had cleared, leaving only a light drizzle sweeping across the runway. He thought about Penny for a moment, about their day together, her face, the smell of her body, the color of her hair. He tried to hang on to the image, but it slipped away from him.

He turned to face Mulvaney.

136

"I'm ready to go."

"Good man," Mulvaney said, in his stiffest public-school voice. "I want you to work up a high-speed flight program before you take the Komet up. Use the Meteor. She's not as fast as the Komet, but at least she should have some of the same flight characteristics."

"Yes, sir."

"Excellent, excellent," Mulvaney said, rubbing his hands. It was a mannerism that always irritated Kruze. "More details tomorrow. In the meantime, I'd like you to get down to the flight line and take a look at the merchandise when it comes in on the Yorks." He looked at his watch. "Any moment now and they'll be here. We'd better get cracking."

Kruze followed Mulvaney out to his car. The EAEU's secure hangar, used for all its most sensitive work, was over on the far side of the airfield.

□

The Yorks' propellers were windmilling to a halt in front of Kruze and Mulvaney, their landing lights cutting a swathe through the darkness and the drizzle that still blew in light squalls across the secure area of the RAE. One of the aircraft was heavily battle-scarred, and judging by the number of shining metal plates that had been welded over the bigger holes on the brown and green camouflaged body, some poor crew chief and his team must have been up all night patching her up.

As Kruze got out of the car in which he and the station commander had been sheltering from the rain, Mulvaney was already striding over to greet the aircraft. Ground crew swarmed around the two transports. The freight doors were pulled open and a gantry was wheeled into place. Inside, Kruze could see the large wooden crates that held the 163's principal components. He was surprised to see four dazed-looking characters in scuffed civilian suits wandering around the tarmac beside the aircraft. They looked incongruous among the blue uniforms and frenetic activity of the ground crew.

"Who are they?" Kruze asked as he walked over to Mulvaney.

"They're some 163 project scientists who chose to come back on the Yorks rather than get captured by the Russians."

"Uncle Joe was that close?"

"The Russians were practically breathing down the necks of our paras toward the end of the operation," Mulvaney said. "I

137

think there's going to be a hell of an uproar in diplomatic circles about the way we moved in there." He coughed. "Keep that to yourself, by the way."

"How long do you think it will take to get the 163 reassembled?"

"I don't know. Why don't we go and get some answers from the man who pulled this whole thing off? He should be around here somewhere."

Kruze followed Mulvaney over to the nearest of the two Yorks and crawled into the forward access hatch after the station commander. Mulvaney peered through the darkness and the throng of people milling around the oily interior of the cargo hold. Outside, a tractor and trailer drove past, the engine noise deafening in the confines of the fuselage. Mulvaney spotted Fleming, but Kruze, that much farther behind, could only see the silhouette of a lean man with a gaunt yet good-looking face, who was sitting on a crate and watching the comings and goings of the ground crew. Mulvaney walked briskly over to him, his hand outstretched, his voice lost to Kruze in the din.

"Robert, my dear chap, congratulations. I could scarcely believe it when the air vice marshal told me about the operation. It's an outstanding success for you and, I might say, the EAEU as well."

At that moment the headlights of the tractor lit the interior of the fuselage and Kruze saw it was Fleming. Then the tractor drove on past and the cargo hold was plunged into darkness once more. Kruze had a few seconds to compose himself, but he could not stop the questions that tumbled through his mind. Fleming was finished, wasn't he? Staverton knew he was washed up; the AVM had as good as said it the day of the air test on the Junkers. It was then that Penny's words came back to him. If Fleming had really cared, she'd said, he would have called her from the Bunker. Jesus Christ, he'd been behind enemy lines for the last two days.

Fleming seemed to be embarrassed at the brashness of Mulvaney's approach. He rose and shook hands a little self-consciously.

"Thank you, Paddy. I had excellent backup from our men, and the army. The paratroopers were the real heroes."

"I look forward to hearing all about it, especially the way you handled that booby-trap," Mulvaney said, turning around to find Kruze. "Meanwhile, it's been decided that Kruze, here, will be first to fly this thing." He patted the top of the crate.

Fleming smiled, something Kruze couldn't remember him doing in all the months that he'd known him.

"That's one job I don't envy you," Fleming said. He held out his hand. "How are you, Piet?"

Kruze flinched, then took the hand and shook it.

"Fine, thanks. Congratulations." The handshake was firm, Kruze noticed, and the smile was warm and friendly. This was not the Robert Fleming that Penny had described, the one he had always known. The bitter, introspective person who couldn't come to terms with the world after his ordeal in the cockpit of a tumbling, burning Spitfire.

Fleming got to his feet and stretched.

"If you'll both excuse me, I'm going to get some shut-eye. I'll catch up with you tomorrow."

Kruze watched him stroll easily across the hangar floor and out through a door on the other side, his coat slung over his shoulder.

"There goes quite a chap," Mulvaney said. "Cool as a bloody cucumber." Mulvaney was rubbing his hands together again. "It's hard to believe that six months ago he was in a hospital bed. An FW 190 got him over Italy, you know."

"Yes, I heard about that," Kruze said, trying to control his voice.

□

Staverton must have written Shaposhnikov's name out a dozen times on his desk pad. Each entry had a question mark after it. He had circled the name in every case and drawn an arrow down to the bottom of the page. A dozen lines leading to a single word. Remove. Yes, the Soviet chief of general staff had to be removed along with key members of his command, if possible. But how? He was tired, horribly tired. He dropped the pencil and rubbed his eyes.

At best, assassinating Shaposhnikov would put an end to Archangel. At worst, it would buy them time.

He had the germ of a plan, but his main doubts centered not on the scheme itself, but the reaction of the Cabinet advisers to it. It was bold, certainly, but the rudiments were well established.

His mind drifted back to that other time of sleepless nights, thrashing out the details of the Berchtesgarten raid. Hitler's hideaway in Bavaria was one of the most heavily fortified locations in the Reich, but Churchill wanted to show his allies, especially Stalin, that no target in Germany was beyond the reach of the RAF. Staverton was told to get to work on a plan that would strike the führer where he felt least vulnerable, high in his protected lair in the Bavarian Alps. After examining a number of alternatives, Staverton concluded there was only one that might work without incurring huge losses to Bomber Command.

Operation Talon: to steal a Luftwaffe bomber from an airfield in the Reich, dodge through the multilayered defenses around Berchtesgarten and put two thousand-pound bombs through the drawing room windows of the Eagle's Nest, Hitler's Bavarian hideaway.

Within the EAEU, he had pilots experienced with Luftwaffe machines. He had, with the help of Special Operations Executive, the means to get a man into the Reich and then to an airfield in Bavaria that operated the Ju 188E-2, which in early 1944 was an almost unbeatable Luftwaffe medium bomber.

The plan foundered because the Cabinet advisers, especially that pompous oaf Welland, questioned the very basis of Staverton's central argument for Talon: that Luftwaffe technology was in most respects superior to their own and was, therefore, right for the job.

Before the D-Day invasion, the EAEU was a shadow of its present strength, operating a few worn-out fighters and bombers that had either fallen with little damage onto English soil, or had inadvertently been put down by disoriented pilots. The EAEU of March 1944 was not the sort of fleet that would have prompted the Cabinet advisers to change their minds. It was a different story now; or was it? Their prize, the Me 262 jet fighter, had exploded a few months before, following a catastrophic turbine failure in one of the engines. Kruze, through his tenacity and skill, had barely escaped with his life.

There were other impressive German aircraft still at Farnborough. Impressive to Staverton, that was, and to the rest of the EAEU. To people like Rear Admiral Welland, they were just angular lumps of metal, no different from the RAF's machines.

In the end, 360 Lancasters went to Berchtesgarten. Only three hundred came back.

Just then the phone rang. It was Mulvaney.

"Back at Farnborough? What is, man?" Staverton barked into the receiver, with no idea what Mulvaney was crowing about.

The station commander seemed taken aback. He didn't want

to mention the 163C by name, even though they were supposed to be speaking on a secure line.

Staverton banged his fist on the desk the moment he remembered Fleming, the 163C, and Rostock. He looked at his watch. Fleming and the cargo would have been back at Farnborough for over an hour by now. He hadn't thought of them in a long time. For some months, Churchill had been pressuring him to let go of the EAEU and devote all of his time to his special duties as Cabinet adviser. So far, he had resisted all attempts to tear him away from his creation at Farnborough. Perhaps it was time to reconsider.

At least he'd have Fleming back in the Bunker to help him try to sort out this mess. The 163C flight-test program could go on without him. Archangel had priority over everything.

"Is the package safe and sound?" Staverton asked, more out of courtesy than interest.

"Yes, sir. We're just unwrapping it now," Mulvaney replied. "If you're going to put Fleming up for a decoration, you know you can count on my endorsement."

"Of course," Staverton said, by now anxious for Mulvaney to get off the line.

"I'd like to add for the record, sir," Mulvaney continued, "that he has proved himself not only to be a very able intelligence officer, but also a decisive man of action. The way he acquitted himself over the booby-trap incident has placed him high in our admiration."

Staverton had also felt a surge of pride when he was told about Fleming's courage at Rostock. "Your opinion will be recorded, Paddy."

He thanked Mulvaney and put the telephone back in its cradle.

The long-range rocket fighter, wonder-weapon of Hitler's Alpine Redoubt. A few days ago it was all he could think of. The corner of his mouth twitched into a smile. Funny how it just wasn't important anymore.

And then he had an idea.

He picked up the phone and asked to be put back through to Mulvaney at the Royal Aircraft Establishment.

□

The GAZ that Krilov had commandeered at the airfield jolted its way over the potholes that pitted the streets on the outskirts of Ostrava. Its gears crunched uncomfortably, because the driver had never escorted anyone more senior than a colonel, much less a marshal, and he was having difficulty controlling his nerves. The private weaved his way precariously through the thousands of Red Army troops, many of whom sang the folk songs they had known since childhood, as they marched through the night toward the front.

The sight of these men swarming toward the final battle, the condensation of their breath illuminated in the glow of the headlights, was magical to Krilov. The last time he had seen action, the fascists had been pouring through the rubbled remains of the Moscow suburbs. Now that the tables were turned, the atmosphere of impending victory all around them was intoxicating.

At last they reached the sprawling marshaling yards where the machinery and munitions that had been forged and assembled in factories deep behind the Ural Mountains arrived by train on its way to the fighting. Krilov had never seen anything like it. Despite the blackout imposed on the town, clouds of steam produced by the trains that pulled in and out of Ostrava every minute glowed a deep orange, illuminated by the raging coal fires that powered the heavy locomotives.

At each of the checkpoints that took them deeper and deeper into the marshaling yards, Krilov did the talking. One glance from the guards into the interior of the GAZ, the instantaneous recognition of the marshal's stars on Shaposhnikov's shoulders, was enough to see that they were swiftly waved through to the correct siding. Krilov stared in awe at the still-hissing locomotive and its drab, olive-colored wagons, indistinguishable from the hundreds of other munition trucks lined up in the military railway yard, but for one thing. The moment the jeep drew near, the elite VKhV troops that surrounded the train bristled, guns pointed menacingly at the GAZ, the source of the intrusion.

Krilov spoke once to the driver, words that were lost to Shaposhnikov over the venting water vapor from the boiler of the train, but the look on the petrified private's face told him that Krilov had cautioned him to say nothing about what he had seen that night. Krilov told the driver to wait, then the two of them stepped from the back of the GAZ.

The major in charge of the VKhV company snapped to attention the moment he recognized the two men. He had only met them once before—the day they had come to him with top-secret orders for a mission of vital importance to the state.

"Identify yourself," Krilov barked.

"Major Donitriy Vasilevich Ryakhov, Military Chemical Forces."

Krilov cast a sidelong glance at Shaposhnikov. The marshal smiled coldly back at him.

"What is your strength, Ryakhov?" Krilov continued.

"One chemical defense company of fifty men, Comrade Colonel."

"Is the consignment intact and, as important, does anyone know it is here?"

Ryakhov looked affronted. "All containers are present and accounted for. No one has questioned us or examined the wagons. Even if they had, Comrade Colonel, my men knew what to say."

Krilov cocked an eyebrow at the VKhV major. Ryakhov felt compelled to continue. "Sanitation equipment for the front," Ryakhov blurted, beginning to feel hot and sticky beneath his uniform. "My men are taking cleansing facilities and delousing fluid to Branodz, regional *stavka* HQ, just like the papers say."

"Any trouble with your travel documents, your new aliases?"

"None, Comrade Colonel."

Krilov drew closer. "You have never questioned your orders, have you, Ryakhov?" The major shook his head violently. "If not you, then perhaps your men have seen fit to discuss what is going on here."

Ryakhov felt the sweat dribbling down his back.

"Comrade Colonel, neither myself nor my men have breathed a word about this to anyone, of that I can swear. They all appreciate, like I do, that if word of the impending fascist chemical attack reaches our troops on the front line, it would have a disastrous effect on morale."

Krilov patted Ryakhov on the shoulder. "Good. It is important for your men to realize that this shipment is nothing more than a sensible precaution, a deterrence to any aggression on the part of the enemy to resort to chemical attack."

The sweat began to freeze on the major's back.

Shaposhnikov stepped forward from the shadows. "Have you ever seen the effects of a chemical bombardment, Comrade Major?" He asked flatly.

"Of course," Ryakhov stammered. "We have practiced extensively against live subjects."

"Live subjects, really? Criminals, or racial subhumans, I suppose."

Ryakhov hid his disgust. "No, farm animals. Sheep, goats, and pigs, Comrade Marshal."

"Then you know nothing," Shaposhnikov said. "In 1916, I lived through a Prussian chemical artillery bombardment that lasted the best part of an hour. I never found out what type of gas it was, I just knew it killed you rather quickly. In my trench we only had five masks per platoon and I was one of the lucky ones. I watched the man next to me cough his guts out, until after two minutes he begged me to put a bullet through his head, so I obliged. Do you know what kind of gas could do that?"

"It was probably phosgene, or one of the other lung irritants," Ryakhov whispered, not sure where all this was leading.

Shaposhnikov grunted. "What have you got in there?" he asked, pointing to the long line of wagons stretching out behind the locomotive.

"Hydrogen cyanide, Comrade Marshal. It attacks the blood-stream."

"Tell me what it did to your goats and pigs," Shaposhnikov asked with a sneer.

"Severe vomiting within seconds, incapacitation within minutes, and, shortly afterward, death from internal bleeding."

The marshal of the Soviet Union seemed unmoved.

"What would happen if we were compelled to use it against the enemy?"

"Well, Comrade Marshal, assuming there were wind at our backs, it would carry on the wind killing everyone in its path. It has a persistency of about an hour; that is to say, it would be safe for us to advance any time after that. I don't think we would find many people alive. Ten percent, at the most."

"How far does it carry?"

"It depends on the wind-strength, Comrade Marshal. If the bombardment were very heavy, it could perhaps reach one hundred and fifty kilometers behind enemy lines."

Shaposhnikov looked down the line of wagons, then turned to Ryakhov. "Good. Very good, Ryakhov. I just wanted to know." He nodded to Krilov, then stepped back into the shadows.

"Get this stuff loaded up into the trucks and be on your way to Branodz, Ryakhov," Krilov said. "I want it stored in the most secure area of the *stavka;* I will show you where. There are some outbuildings there away from prying eyes. As you say, we don't want our valiant comrades on the front line to see it. Not good for morale at all."

Ryakhov snapped to attention. "Yes, Comrade Colonel."

"Let us hope we are not provoked into using it," Krilov added.

Ryakhov nodded, glad only that his ordeal with the two senior-ranking officers was over.

Krilov and Shaposhnikov walked back to the GAZ, which had been parked out of sight of the train containing Ryakhov's chemical forces and cargo.

"Do you think they will believe that story about the fascists threatening us with chemical weapons?" Krilov asked.

Shaposhnikov shrugged. "What does it matter, Kolya? Ryakhov is more worried about what will happen to him than being hit by German mustard or chlorine gas. He'll never talk. Besides, I don't think he has the imagination to seriously believe that it is we who are considering first use."

Shaposhnikov thought back to his days in the czar's ragged army. A long time ago, a different era. Now the Red Army was the best equipped in the world.

One man, one rifle, one gas mask.

They climbed into the GAZ and the driver gunned the engine into life. It was time to link up with Nerchenko, Badunov, and Vorontin. Time to put Archangel into action.

2

At close to midnight, the special advisers to the War Cabinet gathered in the underground chamber beneath Downing Street for the second time that night. There were five of them altogether: Staverton, plus the two other intelligence chiefs and their respective aides. Had Fleming been there, the AVM would have had his own assistant, but as it was, he was just going to have to do on his own.

Staverton took his seat at the back of the room, one row behind Rear Admiral Welland and his aide from Naval Intelligence. The blue-black navy uniforms, the low ceiling, the stuffy atmosphere, and the great, steel air vents, gave Staverton the impression he was in the bowels of a vast warship.

Major General George Deering, assisted by his number two, a major from Army Intelligence, Eastern Section, pulled the sheet off the board on the wall in front of them, exposing the tattered maps and charts that had arrived that evening on the special flight from Pilzen.

Though principally commissioned to analyze the activities of the Wehrmacht, Deering also doubled as Churchill's expert on Soviet tactics and strategy.

"Gentlemen, this is Archangel, the Red Army's battle plan for the defeat of Nazi Germany and the invasion of western Europe," Deering said, without any trace of emotion. "It is what the PM and the rest of us monitoring Soviet activity have feared most since the tide turned against the Nazis in the winter of 1941–42."

Staverton craned his neck for a better look at the plans. Deering's team had cleaned them up as best they could, although there was not a lot they could do about the rips and tears.

"You all know by now how Archangel fell into our hands," Deering continued. "The fact that we have had to promise amnesty to the man who brought them in, a traitor to this country, is regrettable, but necessary."

"You mean Herries is going to get off scot-free?" Welland asked.

Deering was poised to turn his attention back to the board. "Amnesty was guaranteed by Randolph Styles and underwritten by the Red Cross in return for his information."

"That's a pity," Welland said. The navy being the senior service, he was nominally the most superior officer in the room, despite his equal ranking with Staverton and Deering. "Where is he now?"

"He's being debriefed by military intelligence at a safe house on the other side of Green Park."

"Debriefed? You made it sound like he's one of our own."

"You're missing the point, Admiral," Staverton said. "George is right. Herries isn't the issue. We can deal with him later."

"All right, point taken," Welland sighed. "But how do we know that he didn't forge the plans to save his hide?"

"I have had the very best men in this building putting these maps under the microscope. It is their conclusion that they are neither an elaborate German forgery nor part of some sort of Soviet deception," Deering said, trying to hide his animosity toward Welland. "I can give you the details if you wish—"

"No, that's quite all right, Deering. Carry on." Welland's was the question on everyone's lips. They had willed the forgery theory to be true.

Deering tapped the largest of the sheets pinned to the board with his swagger stick. "I would like to draw your attention to the main assault plan. As you can see, Archangel hinges on four initial moves, which if they are to be executed successfully, could totally wrong-foot both the Western Allies and the Germans. I think it is important to remind ourselves, gentlemen, that Shaposhnikov is a brilliant military strategist.

"Eleven days from today—although I'm afraid we can't necessarily depend on that date—will see a concerted barrage from forty-one thousand howitzers ranged along the six hundred–mile eastern front. The Second Belorussian front in the north sector, here, under General Vorontin, will advance along the Stettin-Bremen axis, where it will meet little German resistance, and will soon encounter the U.S. Ninth Army, whose lines of supply are already woefully stretched." Deering turned to his major. "That's not being too pessimistic, is it, Bill?"

"No, that's a fair assessment," the major said. "The Ninth is straining to get to Berlin before Zhukov, but, like our own boys, they know the war is almost over. They're willing to do mopping up, but none of them has the stomach for more heavy fighting."

Welland sank back into his chair. Deering paused. The sound of the ventilation system seemed to grow to a crescendo. Deering forced himself to turn back to the map.

"The Second Belorussian would probably take about three to four days to reach Bremen, whereupon the First Guards Tank Corps, supported by men from the Nineteenth Army and the Second Shock Army, would peel off toward the Rhine. Shaposhnikov estimates in the text that they would make it to the river two days later."

Deering pointed to the great cluster of red dots that almost ringed Berlin.

"Now to the south and the First Belorussian front. I am under no illusion that its part in the plan is quite achievable. While the Sixty-first Army and the Polish First Army advance north and west to support the left flank of the Second Belorussian front, five army divisions will envelop Berlin. In the meantime, the Second Guards Tank Army and the First Guards Tank Army will head west of Berlin and take on northern elements of the U.S. Twelfth Army.

"Further to the south, the First Ukrainian front under Shaposhnikov himself would push along the Leipzig-Cologne axis, engage German Army Group Center, and then proceed to tackle Montgomery's Twenty-first Army, which has all but defeated Model's Army Group, and also take on parts of Bradley's Twelfth Army. I believe that we would be able to contain the First Ukrainian but for one thing. The southernmost front, the Second Ukrainian under Nerchenko, has orders to march on the Nuremberg-Stuttgart axis where it would surround German Army Group G, and then move up behind the U.S. Sixth Army Group, cutting off all escape for General Devers."

Deering turned to face his small audience. "In short, after

one week, Shaposhnikov would have control of all land east of the Rhine. He's got the resources and the men to do it."

"Then what?" Staverton asked.

"He regroups and takes Paris."

"Just like that?"

"Once he's driven a wedge through our forces, there's precious little we can do. He's got more than three million troops under his command, his tanks outnumber ours by almost three to one, he's got four thousand fighters and fighter-bombers—"

"Dammit, Deering, you've got to have some ideas! You're the Soviet specialist . . ." Welland paused. "We've got to bring in the Americans."

"It's a no-win situation," Deering's voice was flat. "The PM does not want the Americans brought in yet, maybe not at all. And the only way of stopping Shaposhnikov once he's on his way is to mobilize more troops into Europe from the United States."

"But that would take weeks, months perhaps. Look how long it took us to prepare for Overlord."

"Precisely my point, Admiral. It's hardly the best way to exploit the one advantage we have—surprise." Deering, devoid of answers, turned the floor over to Welland. "What do you suggest, Admiral?"

"Well, without the Americans blocking the attack, it's obvious that Shaposhnikov has to be removed. The text tells us that he'll be coordinating the First Ukrainian's advance from this place Branodz. All we need to know is when he arrives and that shouldn't be too difficult to find out. I suggest we send a team into Czechoslovakia and have him killed. If he has Stalin's backing and we manage to get rid of him, the architect of Archangel, then it will buy us time. If he's a maverick, operating on his own, then we stand a bloody good chance of nipping this thing in the bud."

"What sort of team have you in mind, Admiral?" Staverton asked.

"This is exactly the sort of mission that the Special Boat Squadron is trained for. We parachute them in and have them kill Shaposhnikov. They would be in and out in forty-eight hours."

"And if one of them is taken?" Staverton cocked an eyebrow at Welland. "Admiral, the merest whiff of British intervention is going to bring Stalin down on us like a ton of bricks."

"What's the alternative?"

Staverton sucked his teeth. "He has to be killed, you're right in that, but we've got to make it look as if the Germans did it."

"My dear Staverton," Welland said disparagingly, "you don't think I was suggesting that the SBS should go in wearing full mess dress? They would be disguised as German paratroops, SS, traffic police for all I care . . ."

Staverton stood up, walked to the map and stabbed his finger on the spot that marked Shaposhnikov's HQ. "Admiral, do you have any idea what your men would be up against? There are close to one million Red Army troops in this sector alone and, if that isn't enough, around fifty thousand partisans in these forests, all of them looking for Germans to butcher."

Welland stared back impassively. He disliked the AVM, because Staverton was everything he wasn't: brash, short on etiquette, risen from the ranks, still with a trace of that northern accent.

"So, even if your men could get in, they couldn't get out. And think what happens if one of them is captured. If you were faced with the prospect of having your eyes gouged out by some swarthy Slav peasant, Admiral, would you stay silent?" Staverton stressed the word "peasant" in a way that made Welland feel uncomfortable. It was as if the AVM knew what he had been thinking. He shifted his gaze to Deering.

"What about you, Deering?"

The army intelligence officer looked at the maze of Soviet forces ranged along the eastern front. "With the all-out military option closed to us, I think we should resort to diplomacy, tell Stalin what's going on in Czechoslovakia. We must get him to take control of the situation."

"You're making the assumption that Stalin doesn't know about Archangel," Welland said. "For all we know he might actually be behind it. Just because Archangel appears to be Shaposhnikov's baby, it doesn't mean it hasn't got the Generalissimo's blessing."

"Basically, George," Staverton said, "we're on our own, whichever way you look."

Deering seemed to sag.

"What's your solution to all this?" Welland asked, turning to the AVM.

"Well, it's a modest idea, but I think it could work. It's the sum of a number of proposals discussed in this room tonight.

Like you, Admiral, I believe Shaposhnikov should be eliminated. However, in my opinion, the only way to accomplish that is by an attack from the air—not an airborne assault, but one that masquerades as a German air raid."

"It sounds strangely familiar," the admiral said, sarcastically.

"It should," Staverton said. "Berchtesgarten, remember?"

Welland averted his eyes.

"What on earth has Berchtesgarten got to do with Archangel?" Deering asked.

"Before your days here, George," said Welland. "It's a long story. This isn't the time or the place." He switched back to Staverton. "Don't tell me it involves that flying circus of yours at Farnborough."

Staverton ignored the jibe. Temperatures were already high. "The EAEU is almost tailor-made for this job. My men are trained to fly German aircraft, to think like Luftwaffe pilots and, in some cases, to speak like them."

Deering suddenly saw a glimmer and could no longer contain his enthusiasm. "My God, that's it. But how many German bombers have you got down at Farnborough, Algy? Surely you can't muster enough to mount an air raid?"

"I don't have to," Staverton said. "I only need one."

The AVM saw the surprise on every face in the room except Welland's.

"We've been through all this," the admiral said. "The answer is still no."

"I want to hear him out," Deering said. "The PM needs a plan of action on his desk tonight and the rules are the same as they've always been. The three of us have to agree on a plan and a majority vote carries the day."

"Only to be overruled by the PM tomorrow," Welland said. "Why bother? I've heard it all before. It's not worth it."

Deering ignored him. "Speak, Algy. Let's hear it."

Staverton nodded his appreciation. "I could probably gather a dozen German medium or heavy bombers for this job, but they would be cut to pieces by Yaks in minutes. None of them would get within fifty miles of Shaposhnikov's HQ."

"Yaks?" Welland asked.

"Soviet fighters," Staverton said. "Swift little buggers. Pack a nasty punch, too. The Russians have got hundreds of them in Czechoslovakia."

"Then why would one aircraft stand a better chance of getting through?" Deering asked.

"It wouldn't be just any aircraft. The one I have in mind is rather special: capable of 550 MPH at sea level, armed with thirty-millimeter cannon, two thousand-pound bombs, and crewed by just one man." He reeled off the figures Mulvaney had given him over the telephone. "Cuts down the risk of unnecessary exposure if anything goes wrong, don't you think?"

"Five hundred-fifty miles an hour?" Welland choked, thinking about the 450 MPH maximum speed of a navy Seafire. "What the devil can do that?"

"The Messerschmitt 163C Komet long-range rocket fighter-bomber," Staverton said.

"The thing your man went to the Baltic for?"

"Yes, Admiral. It's currently undergoing final assembly at Farnborough."

"But that thing's a fighter, quite unsuitable for a penetration mission."

"That's what we thought at first," Staverton said. "We only discovered yesterday that, in addition to giving the thing longer legs—more range, Admiral—they've also added a precision bombing capability, as well."

"That's a stupendous leap forward," Deering said, unable to hide the admiration in his voice.

"Are you sure about this?" Welland asked.

Staverton smiled to himself; Welland was hooked. Now all he had to do was reel him in. "Whether you like it or not, Admiral, German technology has the edge over ours. If we approve a plan like Operation Talon with Shaposhnikov as its objective this time, it will work."

"I'm not convinced," Welland said.

"Then come down to Farnborough tomorrow morning and watch the rocket fighter in action. If you're not impressed, I'll drop my plan."

"Which is?" Deering asked.

"Ship the Komet to a forward operating strip, fly it under the Soviets' defenses to Branodz, and hit Shaposhnikov in his headquarters with two thousand pounds of torpex."

"But," Deering objected, "even if your man did get through in this wonder-airplane, how on earth could he surprise Shaposhnikov, let alone be sure of hitting the target?"

"Speed, George, it's all about speed. At 550 MPH, Shaposhnikov would never see him coming. Even if our man only came close—and remember, Ivan's going to believe it's the Jerries doing it, not us—Shaposhnikov's going to think twice about launching Archangel without supremacy of the skies."

"But there's no guarantee—"

Welland's aide, a bespectacled commander from naval intelligence, never got any further. After almost forty-eight hours without sleep, Staverton snapped. "Of course there's no fucking guarantee. There's no guarantee that this madman is going to carry through with Archangel; there's no guarantee that Shaposhnikov is on his own in all this; there's no guarantee that an antidote will work. But we've got to stop pissing in the wind and do something. If nothing else, this will buy us time." The aide withered under Staverton's hostile gaze. He looked to his boss for support, but found none.

"What I'm offering you tomorrow," Staverton said, his composure returned, "is a chance to see German technology in action—a demonstration flight of the 163C rocket fighter." All eyes were on him. "If you're impressed, we go ahead and I run the show. If it leaves you cold, then I concede we have to stop Archangel by some other means."

"How long before the rocket fighter's ready?" Deering asked.

"I've got my men working flat out on it right now. They're preparing it for testing tomorrow and I want you to be there to witness the flight. You must be convinced before we get the PM to sanction a mission into Czechoslovakia."

Deering said, "Do they have any idea what it's been readied for, your people?"

"None," Staverton said. "I would only need to bring two of my staff into the picture, if the plan is sanctioned."

Deering removed his glasses. "I, for one, like the sound of it. But before I'm convinced, I'm going to have to be persuaded by the performance and reliability of this rocket fighter of yours at Farnborough."

"You hold the deciding vote, George," Staverton said, simply.

"Well let's see what happens tomorrow, then," Deering said. "I'll be there."

Welland nodded, grudgingly. "Very well. So will I. I'll see to it the PM is notified as well. Any slipups, Staverton, and we kill the plan."

Staverton felt a surge of relief. "Agreed," he said. "The preflight briefing's at nine o'clock. I think both of you should attend it. The flight is scheduled for midday."

Chairs scraped across the floor, papers were shuffled into

piles and into briefcases and folders. Deering's aides were taking the pins out of the Archangel map and preparing to fold it away.

"There is one more thing we should do tonight," Deering said. An uneasy silence fell across the room. "I think we should put a routine call through to our embassy in Moscow and get someone to monitor Shaposhnikov's whereabouts. At least when he makes a move for the front, we know we have to start worrying."

"Good idea," Welland said. "I'll see it's done straightaway." He picked up his papers and walked from the room.

As the others followed the admiral, Staverton drew alongside Deering. The army man had never seen the AVM so drawn.

"Thank you, George," Staverton said, with uncharacteristic humility.

"Don't thank me, Algy; just make sure you get it right. I stuck my neck out for you tonight. The old sea dog has got it in for you, it seems."

Staverton headed down the long, dark corridor that led to the Bunker and his camp bed. For the first time in two days and nights, he felt he might be able to snatch some sleep.

3

Fleming awoke with a start. He expected to find himself in the freezing tin shed at Kettenfeld, covered by the dirty blankets that Bowman had managed to dig out.

Instead, he felt clean, warm sheets against his skin. There were curtains on the windows and sunlight showed through a crack between the blackout material and the windowsill. He lay still, listening to the sound of voices and aircraft engines in the distance.

He had slept soundly; no, better than that. He couldn't remember waking so well rested, with such a sense of well-being, in over a year. Sometimes he had woken with the same feeling of excitement when he was a boy, when he just knew in his bones that something wonderful was about to happen.

There was a sharp knock at the door. Fleming looked at his watch. A little before eight. They had let him sleep in.

The door opened and Staverton stuck his head into the room. He looked like he had aged ten years in the few days Fleming had been away.

"How are you feeling?" the AVM asked.

"I'm fine, sir." Fleming was still trying to hide his surprise at seeing the Old Man. "Never felt better. I could ask the same about you."

"It's been a busy few days," he said. Staverton had slept during the night, but not for long. Before the sun rose he had commissioned a car to drive him from Whitehall to the RAE. The 163C's maiden flight was all he could think of. He needed Fleming badly as backup.

"You've done a great job, Robert; I'm proud of you." He hesitated. Fleming had never seen him so tense.

"Thank you, sir. Any word from Colonel Jewell?"

"They all made it to the ships. They're on their way to Chatham, so we heard."

Staverton seemed to regain some of his composure. He went over to the window and drew the curtains. "A damn fine job," he said, looking out over the airfield. "But there's work to be done."

"What sort of work?" Fleming asked. He expected to be debriefed on the operation that day back in the Bunker, but he was not sure that that was what Staverton had in mind.

"We're flying the 163C today. Here, at Farnborough. Get some clothes on. There's a briefing I want you to attend in an hour."

Fleming sprung out of bed. "But that's madness. I know we have to move quickly on this one, but there are checks to do, manuals to read, pilots to prepare."

Staverton swung around to face him. "You're right, it is madness. But the Komet's the only answer." He ignored Fleming's look of incomprehension. "The aircraft's been assembled, we've got fuel, and we've got a pilot. And now I need you, so get dressed."

Fleming grabbed his clothes, which had been thrown carelessly over the end of the bed. "What the bloody hell's been going on here while I've been away?"

"This isn't the time," Staverton said. "As soon as we see the thing fly, we go back to the Bunker. I'll tell you all about it then, in the car. For the moment, as far as you are concerned, this is a big day. We fly the aircraft that you stole from the Nazis. People will be excited. So will you, and quite rightly, laddie. But I don't want a word of this conversation to filter out beyond these walls, do you understand?"

"But you haven't said anything yet, sir."

"I will, boy, I will." Staverton walked to the door.

Fleming stopped him just before he turned the handle. "I wanted to get word to my wife, sir. She must have been worried sick these past few days not hearing anything from me."

Staverton paused. "I'm afraid that's out of the question, Robert. The classification on this one is so high I'm not even going to allow you to talk to yourself until it's over."

Fleming gritted his teeth.

"And when will that be?"

"If we're lucky? Ten days at the most."

□

Kruze was leaning against the door at the mouth of the huge flight-test hangar at the far, most secure, end of the airfield, studying the stubby little aircraft in the center of the concrete floor. He had been there for the best part of an hour, just watching it and the team of riggers, fitters, and Rostock scientists who had labored through the night, under the fierce direction of chief Broyles, to get it assembled and ready for the flight.

Sleep had not come easily to Kruze. When Mulvaney had told him late the previous night that he was to take the Komet up so soon, he had stared at him in disbelief. The station commander almost sounded apologetic: the orders had come directly from the Bunker. There was to be a demonstration and Kruze was to fly it. And that was it. No work-up flights and little time for familiarization. Mulvaney had wrung his hands and told him that, if it was any consolation, Luftwaffe Komet pilots were accorded the same training procedure. Next to none.

He became aware of a presence beside him.

"Taking a last look at her, eh?" Mulvaney's words echoed throughout the hangar. "Did their scientists tell you everything you wanted to know?"

"Their scientists?" Kruze smiled. "They're ours now."

Mulvaney shuffled uneasily. "They promised full cooperation, you know. I'll tear the hide off them if they don't play ball."

Kruze had a sudden absurd impression of a younger Mulvaney leading the Rostock scientists out onto the school cricket field. He smiled again. Perhaps he was cracking up. First Penny, then Fleming's return, now the Komet.

"Don't worry," he said. "They gave me their full cooperation. They seemed quite decent chaps, actually." He thought it was the sort of thing Mulvaney wanted to hear. "Told me it was just like flying a glider." He waited for his own echo to come back to him, before adding, "With a bloody great firework shoved up the tail."

Kruze detached himself from Mulvaney's side and ambled around the Komet, occasionally tugging at a control surface or running his hand along its smooth skin. Sergeant Broyles watched him for a moment, before leaving by the rear exit, ushering his ground crew with him.

The Komet was tiny. Its fuselage, nose-to-tail, was no longer than the length of three men, while its swept wings were probably less than thirty feet in span. There was no horizontal tail surface, just a vertical stabilizer that extended to a height of about eight feet from the ground. Perhaps its most unusual feature was the undercarriage, which consisted of two unnaturally large wheels to be jettisoned, the Rostock team told him, as soon as the rocket fighter lifted off from the runway. Landing was carried out on a long skid, mounted centrally under the belly. Right at the back were the two tiny exhaust ports for the twin Walter rocket engines.

The crosses and swastikas stood out starkly against the mottled green and brown surface of the wings and fin.

Kruze made sure they were alone. "What's it about, Paddy? I mean, why all the fuss? Yesterday evening we were assured a decent test period—at least, by Staverton's standards—then, bang! It's all go. It doesn't add up."

They were on first-name terms at the EAEU, so small was the team, but it was the only time Mulvaney could remember Kruze actually using his. "I don't know, Piet, and that's the truth. But it can only mean one thing."

Yes, one thing, Kruze thought. "So what's the target?" He didn't expect an answer.

Mulvaney shook his head. "I really don't know. All I do know is what you'll hear me say at the briefing and I think you will find that startling enough." Mulvaney looked at his watch. "My word," he said, "the delegation from the ministry will be getting impatient. Piet, it's time," he said. "Shall we go?"

Kruze followed Mulvaney through the door at the rear of the hangar, which led to the propulsion laboratories. At the end of one of the immense testing chambers, Kruze saw a group of people assembled. The Rostock scientists had exchanged their scruffy suits for white laboratory coats and seemed not the least put out by their new surroundings. Among the rest Kruze saw the various bigwigs from the ministry, a stern-looking admiral, a bespectacled army general and, finally, Air Vice Marshal Staverton himself. He cast a quick glance around for Fleming, finding him before long at the back of the room with several other middle-ranking officers. Their eyes met, and before the Rhodesian could look away, Fleming gave him a casual, friendly wave.

Mulvaney asked them to take their seats and then led one of the German scientists to the small stage at the end of the room. On the podium was a table, behind which was a blackboard. It reminded Kruze of the backdrop to the single classroom in the little schoolhouse he had attended in the bush. As Mulvaney rubbed his hands and looked around him, the German donned an asbestos suit, thick white gloves, and a protective hood and visor of the sort used by RAF crash-truck crews. Mulvaney, aware that he was no longer the center of attention, coughed to signal he was about to speak.

"Gentlemen, I don't think I need tell you of the unqualified success of the mission which has resulted in your trip down to Farnborough today. Guided largely by the efforts of Air Vice Marshal Staverton, we have managed to obtain the Nazi's most advanced aeronautical development to date, the Messerschmitt 163C Komet long-range, rocket-powered fighter-bomber. For those of you who have not yet seen the aircraft, there will be an opportunity to inspect it after the little demonstration that we are about to lay on for you here."

Kruze looked from Staverton to the two other senior officers beside him. Just what the hell were they doing at Farnborough?

"The Messerschmitt 163B Komet has been an all-too-familiar sight to our bomber crews over Germany, particularly our friends the Americans," Mulvaney continued. "But what we have in the next-door hangar represents an even greater threat. We believe that this version is about to go into series production in deep underground factories in southern Germany and Austria and will be used to defend these territories if the Nazis make a tactical withdrawal there. With its air-to-ground capability and its longer range, it will be able to strike deep into our own territory. It is a very worrying development indeed.

"With the 163C fighter-bomber geared as the basis of an air defense system for the so-called Alpine Redoubt, it became of paramount importance for us to obtain one of these aircraft in order to find ways to counter the threat. I very much hope that our test pilot, Squadron Leader Kruze here, will be able to identify its key weaknesses while we put the Komet through its paces over the next few weeks. Such an evaluation will be crucial if we are to neutralize the weapon in the future.

"What makes the Komet unique is its rocket-propulsion system. As those of you who are familiar with Farnborough and the work of the EAEU will be aware, Britain has made significant advances in the field of jet propulsion. But when it comes to rocket research, gentlemen, I am afraid to say we know next to nothing. We have, however, been fortunate enough to secure the services of a number of German scientists who have, in the very short space of time since our recovery of the Komet, given us a remarkable insight into its performance. I would therefore like to hand you over to Doctor Hausser. I would like to stress that he and his colleagues have no sympathy for the Nazi regime . . ." He paused. "I'll leave him to explain exactly what gives the Komet its awesome performance."

Mulvaney stepped down from the podium and took a seat alongside the brass who watched in silence as the oldest of the scientists from Rostock took a step forward to the front of the stage. He removed his protective headgear and, as Fleming had discovered at Rostock, spoke hesitantly but with a good command of English.

"The Komet can reach a speed of over a thousand kilometers an hour—that is six hundred and twenty-five miles per hour. Remarkable you will agree, yes? I will now show you what sort of fuel produces the energy to make this possible."

While the German moved behind the table and replaced his headgear, two of his colleagues brought forward an enormous sheet of Plexiglas, which they held between the table and the audience. The chief technician then produced two glass vials, no bigger than the top of a fountain pen. When he showed them to the audience, pinching the glass gingerly between thumb and forefinger, Kruze could see the surface of a clear fluid dancing delicately inside each container.

His voice was muffled behind the mask.

"In my hands I hold two different fluids—in the left, C-Stoff and in the right, T-Stoff. The Komet's internal tanks contain eleven hundred and sixty liters of T-Stoff and four hundred and ninety-two liters of C-Stoff. That is around two tons of fuel altogether. Remember these quantities when I show you what happens when only a centiliter of each is mixed together."

He poured a drop of C-Stoff into a flat, glass dish and then gently eased off the metallic lid of the T-Stoff vial. He held it for a few seconds over the dish while his hand steadied and then, in a quick, precise movement, emptied the liquid onto its shimmering counterpart.

The second the two made contact, there was a blinding explosion, sending shards of glass flying up against the Plexiglas screen. When the smoke from the table started to dissipate, the scientist took off his headgear and looked with some satisfaction at the faces of his audience.

Admiral Welland was the first to speak. "What the devil is that stuff?"

"C-Stoff," the German said mechanically, "is mainly methyl alcohol and is innocent enough on its own. But when mixed with the T-Stoff, or hydrogen peroxide, it produces a massive cryogenic reaction. The chemicals are easy enough to produce. It's controlling them once they are mixed that is difficult, very difficult."

"You mean those two substances are mixed in the engine's combustion chamber and burn on their own to give the aircraft its rocket power?" the admiral asked.

"Precisely."

The room filled with the excited murmurings of the dozen or so spectators.

"It is hardly necessary for me to add," Hausser said nervously over the hubbub, "that this fuel is highly unstable. We had several instances at Rostock where the T-Stoff leaked into the cockpit and literally dissolved the pilot. T-Stoff will instantly decompose anything of an organic nature; clothes, skin, rubber—even iron and steel. For this reason we had to make the fuel tanks out of aluminum. Even then, we could not prevent all leaks."

The demonstration over, Kruze wandered alone back to the Komet. The technicians were still working frantically to prepare the aircraft for its first flight. It was the haste of the flight-test program that alarmed him. On previous occasions he had taken captured aircraft up on the day they had arrived at Farnborough, but this little bitch was different—a rocket fighter that could fly at over 600 MPH, laden with two tons of liquid explosive.

He climbed into the cockpit and eased himself into the tiny bucket seat, casting his eyes over the simple instrument panel. The intruding bay containing the cannon squashed his legs together to the extent that he had difficulty operating the rudder pedals. He called over Broyles, who was working on the wing behind him.

"Hey, Chief, couldn't we take out the weapon bay to make a bit more room for me in here? I can hardly move my damned legs."

The seasoned old engineer grinned ruefully. "That's no

weapon bay, sir. It's the fuel tank that houses the hydrogen peroxide for the rocket motor. I'm afraid there's nothing we can do about it."

□

The ground crew were strapping Kruze into the cockpit of the 163C when Staverton walked into the hangar. Welland's last words were still ringing in the AVM's ears. He had threatened to cancel the demonstration on the spot, so acute was his concern about the fuel.

Utter chaos appeared to surround the Komet. Technicians were pumping water through the steam generator to prevent any inadvertent mixing of the two cryogenic rocket fuels. Other engineers played hoses over the ground directly beneath the aircraft in case any spilled.

As Staverton drew up alongside the cockpit, he could see wraithlike wisps of noxious T-Stoff gas venting out of the safety valves on top of the aircraft's fuselage. All the crew who had spent the night and morning working on the Komet wore masks to stop them from ingesting the deadly hydrogen peroxide. Kruze was wrapped in his asbestos flying suit and had his oxygen mask clamped firmly across his face.

The hangar doors were winched back to admit the little tractor that would tow the Komet out to the end of the runway.

Even after his extensive briefings from the Komet's designers and engineers that morning, Kruze was still poring over the dials and switches that dotted the instrument panel.

He looked up and saw Staverton's outstretched hand; he shook it and went back to his instruments.

"I know this air test is only meant for checking out the speed and range of this thing," Staverton shouted to make himself heard, "but could you pull out all the stops over the airfield? For the brass from the War Ministry, you understand. It could be important."

If the AVM had asked him before he had climbed into the aircraft, Kruze would have told him to take a running jump. If he was to take risks, he wanted answers. But in the cockpit, Kruze was a different person. He felt no negative emotion now, just a desire to get on with the job, mingled with excitement and trepidation at the awesome power of the aircraft he was to ride and break like a wild steer at a rodeo. He gave Staverton the thumbs-up.

As the Komet slid out of the hangar, Kruze waggled the control column from side to side and looked down the wings to check that the ailerons were responding to his commands. If he noticed Staverton's wave, he never acknowledged it.

The head of the EAEU started the long walk to the far end of the runway where the invited VIPs were waiting, and watching.

□

The tractor positioned the Komet at the end of Farnborough's main runway so that all Kruze could see was concrete stretching into the distance over the aircraft's nose.

Everything was quiet in the cockpit, except for a slight hissing sound from the two idling Walter rocket engines, which were waiting for the command to explode into life.

Kruze sat bunched in the bucket seat, preparing himself for the signal from the tower. An image of Penny sprang into his mind, her eyes sad, and her lips mouthing silent words. Kruze shook his head to clear the picture. It felt like a bad omen.

His headset crackled.

"Tower to Kruze. You are clear to take off. Good luck."

Kruze nudged the throttle lever to its first position. There was a muffled sound from the rear of the aircraft and a dull vibration shook the airframe. The turbine tachometer read around 50 percent. All systems normal. Kruze pushed the lever to the second stage. The Walters roared, their thrust pushing the little aircraft hard against the two chocks in front of the wheels. One final glance at the instruments and Kruze banged the throttle to its last stage. The reaction was instantaneous. The Komet bounded over the chocks and a wall of gravity pushed Kruze back into his seat. Straining to keep his eyes level with the instruments, he watched the needle on the airspeed indicator surge forward while, outside, the concrete rushed past in a blur at the periphery of his vision. The control column went loose and then, with a slight application of back pressure from the wrist, the Komet was airborne.

Kruze's whole body tingled with excitement. The power was phenomenal.

Concentrate, man. He had forgotten to jettison the wheels. He pushed the selector forward and felt the Komet jump again as the heavy undercarriage dolly fell the fifty feet to the ground. One more check of the instruments told him that he had 100 percent boost while he was still over the airfield.

He thought of the stuffed shirts from the ministry who were

gathered below, and Staverton's last-minute, somewhat awkward, instructions that they should leave Farnborough impressed. Climbing rapidly, he swung the aircraft toward the west.

As the noise of the rocket motors receded, Staverton glanced at the other delegates to gauge their impression of the takeoff. Welland, the most influential of the party, seemed more interested in the final resting place of the take-off dolly, which had bounced its way into a thicket on the other side of the airfield. Deering pulled his fingers out of his ears, with a look of mild irritation on his face, as if a child had just exploded a firework nearby. Staverton turned back to the part of the horizon where he had last seen the Komet and swore softly. He had hoped that Kruze was going to scream low over the airfield.

Deering walked over to Staverton and tugged him by the arm. They strolled over to the edge of the runway, safely out of earshot of the others. Staverton looked back and saw Welland walking toward them with an expression on his face that told him his verdict was already prepared for delivery.

"Damn noisy machine," Deering said. "The Russians would hear something like that coming a mile off, wouldn't they?"

Staverton resisted the temptation to raise his voice. "George, as I tried to explain before, with Kruze going at high speed and low-level, they wouldn't have a clue until it was too late. As the Komet approaches the target the sound wave would be a mere two or three seconds in front of the aircraft itself. It would give them no time to react."

Deering looked at Staverton. "I'm not so sure I like the idea. Besides, this thing was designed as a fighter, wasn't it? How is Kruze going to have time to learn how it operates as a bomber?"

Staverton felt his control of the situation slipping away. "Kruze is already familiar with the aircraft's on-board bombing aids. The Komet uses much of the same equipment as the Messerschmitt 262, which he flew extensively here at Farnborough."

Deering nodded. "The 262 is their jet fighter-bomber, isn't it? It's supposed to be quite a machine."

"That's right." Staverton shifted uncomfortably. He had set the trap up for himself.

"Then why don't we use that for the operation?" Deering asked.

"We can't," Staverton said, watching the approach of Welland out of the corner of his eyes. "The 262 suffered a bad midair engine failure. We lost the aircraft."

"You lost it? One of the things I did pick up at the briefing this morning was that rocket power is inherently more dangerous than jet power. And now you're telling me that you lost the jet fighter because of engine failure."

"It's not quite as simple as that, George," Staverton started.

Deering cut him off; Welland was almost upon them. "Look, Algy, I wanted to support you in this; I wanted it to work. Much as I hate to admit it, perhaps the admiral's right. We drop an assassination team into Czechoslovakia instead."

Staverton crashed his fist into his open palm. "At least do me the courtesy of waiting until the test's over."

Welland confronted them. "Too noisy, too dangerous, too risky," he said briskly. He drew breath to deliver the death blow, but never even began the sentence. His eyes caught a slight movement behind Staverton, somewhere on the edge of the airfield. Suddenly the Komet was upon them, so low, that in Welland's split second of awareness, he thought it would destroy them all. He threw himself to the ground, his warning to the others drowned by the deafening sound of the Komet's engines as it flashed overhead.

On the other side of the airfield, flying at just over fifty feet, Kruze pulled the control column hard back. The Komet sat on its tail and blasted through a gap in the wispy clouds, leaving a vertical column of fire and smoke behind it.

Staverton bent down and offered Welland his hand. "Of course it's dangerous and risky," he said, a trace of a smile on his lips, "but a rocket fighter's only noisy once it's gone past you, Admiral."

The admiral took his hand and was pulled to his feet. He tried in vain to find the Komet in the clear blue sky between the clouds, but Kruze was already far away, heading toward the north Welsh coast and the Irish Sea beyond, where he would put the rocket fighter's range and endurance to the test.

"Rather than stand around and hear my apologies," Welland said, "I suggest we all go back to London straightaway. I'm going to support this low-level bombing scheme of yours to the PM, Staverton, so you'd better start getting down to the nitty-gritty at once." He adjusted his cap. "Congratulations," he added. "You were right. I just hope you can organize this thing in the few days we have left."

They headed for their separate staff cars. Staverton managed to catch Fleming's eye and stabbed a finger in the direction of the parking lot. At least by the end of the journey he would have enlisted some extra help in his crusade against Archangel.

☐

From the tiny window of his attic room in the safe house maintained by military intelligence, down a narrow alley in Shepherd Market, Herries could see a vignette of London life that a few days before he had never expected to see again. Directly below, a line had formed outside a shop that had just taken delivery of fresh vegetables. An old lady at the front of the line seemed to be having difficulty in finding her ration card, but no one seemed to mind as she fumbled myopically inside her bag for the elusive document. Ah, the patience of the English, Herries thought.

The iron bars, which hindered his view, did nothing to dampen his elation. If they had made him a prisoner since his arrival in London, at least he had the status of a highly prized captive. A doctor had treated the last traces of his dysentery and the questioning had been very civilized. They wanted him alive. They were cooperating and behaving like gentlemen, which was more than could be said for those ignorant squaddies who had tried to beat the shit out of him in Pilzen.

The key rattled in the door of the cell. When it was pushed open, Herries recognized the silhouette of the MI6 colonel who had interviewed him until the early hours of the morning. He could readily detect the distaste that the man felt, but it had never openly manifested itself in taunts or insults.

White-Smith pulled a chair up to the table in the middle of the room. He motioned for Herries to sit down.

"I hope you're not going to keep me here much longer, Colonel?"

"Oh?" White-Smith looked with disdain at the ill-fitting suit that intelligence had given Herries on his arrival in London.

"I made a deal," Herries said. "I gave you the biggest bloody military secret of the war and now I expect to see you start honoring your part of the bargain."

White-Smith lit a cigarette, but did not offer the pack. "Do not push us too far, Herries." He did not look up. "Agreements made in time of war have a nasty habit of turning sour."

"Then perhaps I should remind you," Herries snarled, "that you need me if you stand any chance of stopping Archangel."

"Why? We have the charts and the plan. What more can you do for us?"

"Don't play games with me, Colonel. If you were going to kill me, you would have done it by now. No, you need me, because you don't know what to do about a certain gentleman who is threatening to roll several thousand tanks and millions of men across Europe. Oh yes, you'll tell me that you're negotiating and that there is a diplomatic solution to this mess, but you know as well as I that the Russian is a conniving bastard. He'll promise you one thing and then do the bloody opposite. I know the Russian, Colonel. I've lived with him. Yes, literally. Gazing up at the stars from my beautifully proportioned, shit-filled trench outside Stalingrad, I could hear them talking to each other. Sometimes we'd throw cigarettes to them—yes, we were that close. Then all we'd have to do was wait for one of them to crawl into no-man's-land, then we'd fire a star shell and put a bullet up his asshole. Five minutes later and, hey-ho, another one would pop up, only to be dropped like the first by one of my snipers. All for one lousy cigarette." He chuckled. "From time to time we'd take them prisoner. Some wouldn't even blink as we put revolvers into the back of their heads and pulled the trigger. Others would try and do deals, side with us, denounce Stalin, offer their services."

"Have you quite finished?" White-Smith ground the stub of his cigarette under his heel.

Herries laughed. "Ah, the English stiff upper lip. It makes you feel good to be back."

"There are some things about the area we need to know," White-Smith said, trying to contain his anger. "The dummy buildup at Chrudim, for inst—"

"Didn't I make myself clear to you?" Herries banged his fist on the table. "No more information until you've got something for me. When do I get out of here?"

"You'll be leaving here shortly."

"Just like that, I suppose."

"We'll give you a new identity, of course. Effectively, you'll be able to start a new life, Herries. I hope you make a better job of it this time."

Herries snorted. "What do you know of my life?"

"Quite a bit, actually," White-Smith said.

"Get to the point, damn you. When do I get out of here?"

"There are certain conditions you must observe before we release you."

"Such as?"

"We want to know the names of all the members of the British Freecorps that you came across during your training and operational service."

"That shouldn't be too difficult," Herries said, smiling. "I find your conditions acceptable."

"Then you can start by telling us what you saw at Branodz. And leave nothing out. Every detail could be important."

Herries reached across the table and took a cigarette from White-Smith's pack. "My dear colonel, I thought you would never ask," the traitor said.

□

Kruze waited until his altimeter read ten thousand meters before shutting down the twin Walter motors and leveling off. The roar of the rocket engines gave way to an eerie whistling as the wind sped by his clear bubble canopy at over 550 MPH.

The north Welsh coast and the familiar outline of the island of Anglesey slipped past below him. He had traveled the width of the country in just over half an hour and he still had well over half his fuel left. He double-checked the T-Stoff and C-Stoff gauges and scribbled down the figures on the scratch pad strapped above his right knee. Test the range, he'd been told, push the aircraft to its limits. Well, he'd done that all right. The Komet was proceeding swiftly and silently toward the coast of the Irish Republic and now Kruze was getting nervous. Marlowe was nowhere in sight.

He put the stubby fighter into a wide turn to the left, searching the revolving scenery before him for a trace of his escort. Marlowe had been dispatched to the rendezvous point half an hour before he took off. The Spitfire pilot was to serve a dual purpose. He was to act as chase plane, monitoring the performance of the Komet from the outside. He was also fighter-escort and guardian. With only a handful of people on the ground aware of the demonstration, Kruze did not want to be bounced by an overzealous pilot from Fighter Command. He decided to break radio-silence.

"Sunflower, this is Kingfisher. Can you hear me? Over."

Farnborough came back to him on medium strength.

"Go ahead, Kingfisher."

"Any sign of Hummingbird? I'm getting lonely up here."

The controller's voice crackled in his headset. "He should be with you any moment now. Slight icing problem. Keep calm, Kingfisher."

Kruze glanced out over his wing but could not see very much. The asbestos suit and the protective headgear were severely hampering his freedom of movement. He craned for a look over his shoulder and caught a glimpse of something rising up through the clouds to meet him. It was either Marlowe or someone with rather more hostile intentions. Kruze drew comfort from the knowledge that his rocket motors could get him out of trouble in the blink of an eye. All he had to do was make sure he was not caught by surprise.

He deployed the air brakes momentarily and the speed dropped further still. He was now registering just under four hundred knots.

He hauled the Komet around in a tight circle to bring him into a position to meet the other aircraft. Suddenly a Spitfire broke through the intermittent cloud, its green-gray camouflage prominent against the patchy carpet of cumulus and the shining sea below.

Moments later, the sleek shape of the Spitfire slid alongside the 163, fifty feet off its starboard wingtip. Marlowe gave the Messerschmitt a visual inspection, paying particularly close attention to the area around the tail where the Walters' searing hot gas had blasted out of the two tiny rocket-exhaust ports. The Spitfire weaved around to the other side, where Marlowe carried on with the examination. At last he gave Kruze the thumbs-up.

Kruze went through one more instrument check before satisfying himself that all was safe for the next part of the evaluation, a high-speed power dive to find the Komet's critical Mach number. Marlowe was to try to follow him down for as long as possible. Only if he spotted any problems from the chase plane was he supposed to break the strict radio-silence and warn the Rhodesian.

Kruze flexed his fingers before grasping the throttle with his gloved hand. Despite the altitude, he felt hot and sticky under the numerous layers of clothing and the protective hood. He was tempted to tear the whole cumbersome apparatus off his head, but the suit would perhaps just give him time to take to his parachute if anything went wrong. Perhaps.

Concentrate. Use the fear. Feed off it. Work the adrenaline to your advantage.

He eased the throttles forward.

Marlowe saw smoke belch from the 163's exhaust ports. By the time he reacted, the rocket fighter was rapidly pulling away from him in a shallow dive.

Kruze relayed the progress into his microphone, even though no one could hear him. It was partly force of habit, partly a way of keeping his nerves in check.

"Four hundred eighty MPH. Smooth ride. Turbine pressure looking good. No buffet. I'm opening up the motors to 80 percent." Calm, steady tones. Like the voice of the bomb disposal expert, Kruze thought. At any moment a split second away from total annihilation.

Concentrate.

Marlowe was losing him. He held the 163 in his gunsight as best he could, flipped off the safety catch above the firing switch on top of the control column, and pressed the exposed red button. Within the wings, the gun cameras whirred into life, catching the motions of the rocket fighter as it receded from view.

"Five hundred-fifty MPH. Still looking good. All instruments appear normal." Kruze continued to talk into his microphone.

Turbulence shook Marlowe's aircraft. At first the motion was barely perceptible, then it grew in intensity as the speed built up and the air that rushed to meet the Spitfire could not get out of the way of its long, graceful wings. Marlowe's plane rocked with vibration as it reached its critical Mach number. He pulled the nose up and let his speed fall off, but continued to monitor the Komet by tracing its path of smoke down toward the sea.

"Five hundred-ninety MPH and accelerating." Kruze was still counting. "Just gone through six hundred MPH. Slight buffet at six hundred ten, but only momentary. Six hundred twenty now. Smooth ride."

Marlowe watched in horrified fascination as the 163 carved an inexorable path toward the turgid sea, pursued by its angry, fiery trail. He found himself shouting into his mask for Kruze to ease back as he saw the aircraft head for a gap between the clouds. He knew that the cloud base bottomed out at a few thousand feet. A few seconds later and he broke RT silence to issue the warning.

Kruze heard, but decided to press ahead. Something was driving him on, pushing him harder than he had ever gone before. It was a force deep inside that told him this aircraft had to be taken to the limits, no matter the cost. He looked at his altimeter. Five thousand feet. Just a little bit more. He flicked a glance at the airspeed indicator positioned above his height dial. He read out 640 MPH. Then the buffet hit him again. It came so suddenly that it took Kruze by surprise. The tiny aircraft shook like a leaf in a raging tempest. The instruments blurred till he could no longer read them. He tried to call out, but the vibrations were so strong that he couldn't form any words. He was unable to read off his height but he could see the sea rushing up to meet him. To pull back on the column now would exert enough gravitational force to rip the wings off. He had to get the speed down first.

He fumbled for the throttle lever, found it, and shut the Walters down. He inched back on the control column and felt the 163's nose rise a fraction before the g-forces compressed his body, forcing the blood into his feet, and building until his head felt heavier than a sack of coal and the sea rushed to meet him.

Marlowe, in pursuit, broke through the clouds expecting the smoke column from the 163 to lead straight into the gray waters below. Instead there was nothing. No trail. No wreckage. No oil. The Komet had disappeared.

His gaze focused on a seabird far away, skimming the waves, pulling up, hanging there, falling, twisting and turning back toward the water. In that moment of disorientation and anxiety, it was one of the most beautiful things Marlowe had ever seen. Mesmerized, he squinted against the sunlight that streamed through the clouds. Then he laughed until the tears rolled down his cheeks.

It wasn't a seabird. It was the 163.

□

At eight thousand feet Kruze pulled around in a wide turn that would bring him back on a heading for Farnborough's long runway. Because of the Komet's high sink rates on the glide path, he knew he would need plenty of height for the approach; the Rostock scientists had warned him it was an unforgiving aircraft to bring in to land. He glanced out over his wing. Marlowe was there, his hand raised in salute.

The test had been a complete success. Not only did the 163C have the considerable range of which Mulvaney and Staverton had spoken, it was also the most maneuverable aircraft he had ever flown at high speed—and its speed was awesome.

171

This was where he really felt alive, where every nerve ending was ready to respond within a split second to any situation that could develop in the cramped confines of a high-performance fighter aircraft. The world outside was fickle, ever changing; but here, he knew where he stood. The elements were unforgiving and a moment's lapse on his part could spell disaster. It was a constant challenge, but it was the way he liked it.

Farnborough's runway grew in his windshield. It was time to extend the landing skid.

At first he thought he was flying through thin cloud. Then he realized that the smoky wisps were inside the cockpit and seemed to be emanating from the floor. He looked past the cumbersome asbestos suit and felt the hair rise on the back of his neck; he saw the source of the trouble.

He called up the tower.

"Sunflower, I've got a big problem. The T-Stoff tank appears to have ruptured inside the cockpit."

"Say again, Kingfisher."

Kruze cursed. "I've got a split fuel tank, dammit, but I'm coming in to land. Alert the crash trucks."

Before the youthful officer in the tower could respond, Marlowe cut in on the RT.

"Kruze, don't be a bloody fool. You've got plenty of height. Bail out now. Forget bringing the 163 in; that fuel will eat through you in a second if you get a serious leak in there."

Kruze could now see the tiny pinprick hole in the starboard tank where the fuel was spilling onto the floor of the cockpit. He watched, half fascinated, half in horror, as the hydrogen peroxide began to eat through the rubber cover at the base of the control column, sending noxious contrails spiraling up against the clear canopy. Even beneath goggles, his eyes began to run as the vapor worked its way through the tiny gaps between the glass and the frame.

He looked around for an extinguisher, but couldn't see one. It was quite useless, anyway. Once the chemicals started to eat their way into the aircraft, nothing could stop them except hundreds of gallons of water.

He estimated that he was about one mile downrange of the runway now, at an altitude of one thousand feet.

Fifty feet to his left, Marlowe could scarcely see the hunched figure of Kruze for the swirling fumes inside the cockpit. He yelled another warning.

Kruze heard but ignored the desperate pleas. He disconnected the lead that ran from his headset to the instrument panel. The silence enabled him to concentrate on his dials and his badly obscured view of the runway. He looked down quickly and saw the colorless liquid seeping in little spurts from the widening hole in the tank, like blood pumped from a severed vein. T-Stoff sloshed around the floor of the cockpit. It had completely dissolved the rubber where the joystick met the floor and Kruze imagined it eating through the linkages that ran from the bottom of the control column to the hydraulic lines, which led to the control surfaces. Once those were damaged he'd lose all control; the 163 would peel away and hit the ground. If that happens, may it be instantaneous, he thought. Anything but a slow death in the acid bath that surrounded him.

He was down to a few hundred feet. If he had wanted to bail out, now it was too late.

Concentrate. You're committed now, 100 percent. There's no going back.

He looked for the flap-selector lever, remembering that it was somewhere near his left leg. The flaps deployed, but the aircraft felt as if it had barely slowed. It was hurtling for the runway at over 200 MPH.

It was then that he saw the quick-dump lever for the fuel. How could he have been so bloody stupid? He pulled the handle hard and felt the aircraft buck as the remaining pounds of the lethal T-Stoff fell away harmlessly, evaporating over the Hampshire countryside. He kept his heels at the top of the rudder bars, avoiding the fuel that still glistened on the floor.

He crossed over the airfield perimeter fence at over 170 MPH. He couldn't get the bitch to slow down any more than that.

The Komet banged the runway hard, spraying the hydrogen peroxide all over the cockpit. Horrified, Kruze saw parts of the Plexiglas canopy begin to dissolve. Vapor hissed from his suit where the acid tried to eat through the asbestos. He prayed that the aircraft would not flip onto its back.

He pulled the emergency canopy-release cord while the Komet was still bumping along the runway. The slipstream tore the canopy off the fuselage and it skidded across the concrete, coming to rest on the grass perimeter, where the T-Stoff continued to gnaw great holes in the Plexiglas.

Kruze released his safety straps and sprang out of his seat. He rolled over the side of the cockpit, across the wing, and onto

173

the ground as the rocket fighter came to a halt. Then he was on his feet, desperately trying to tear the smoldering suit from his body. He pulled the hood off his head and took in great gulps of air. Then the fire trucks were around him, hosing him down with cool, clear water. It splashed over his face, bringing him out of the nightmare.

The 163 stood a few yards away. One crash truck filled the cockpit with water, while another sprayed down the wings and the fuselage.

Jeeps and trucks tore across the runway toward the aircraft. Kruze stepped out of his soaking asbestos suit and strode off in the opposite direction, toward the debrief room.

If Staverton wanted his report, he could give it to him right now. The Messerschmitt 163C was a killer.

4

Lavrenty Beria, head of the NKVD, watched the sun start to slip behind the dilapidated roof of the Art Theater, across the way from his small apartment on Kuznecki Most. It was going to be another crystal-clear evening, the ebbing, wintry sun casting golden spears of light onto the tops of the spires and domes that were scattered among the drab living blocks that remained on Moscow's decimated skyline.

Beria liked to escape to this, his "other" apartment, when his duties allowed. Surrounded by luxurious furnishings and an abundant supply of vodka, he would while away the small hours here, in a city where two-thirds of the population was on the brink of starvation.

Tonight, as always, he was not alone. The girl whom he had spotted the previous summer at the gymnastics competition during a morale-boosting Young Communist League festival was still his favorite, but the general's daughter who now lay in his bed in the next room came close, very close. His body ached at the thought of her, but first he had to work. It would increase his appetite for what would come later.

He flipped through the pages of the dossier. It was an exercise he pursued regularly. It not only helped him watch Stalin's back, but also his own.

As he did so, he was once more impressed by the breadth of his intelligence-gathering network. Information was power. It was also insurance. His NKVD men had furnished him with every detail he wanted to know about each senior officer in Frontal Command. If any one of them so much as played with himself at night, Beria knew about it.

He sensed a movement to his left. The girl was beside him, shielding her eyes from the glare of the lamp on his desk. She looked slightly ridiculous in the shirt that he had given her as a nightdress, but he patted her on the buttocks as if to tell her to run along back to bed. In a few more minutes he planned to be with her.

"Why, that's Uncle Nikolai," she said in a sleepy voice, pointing at the photograph in the file.

"I did not know Nikolai Ivanovich was your uncle, beloved."

"He's not really," she replied. "It's just that he used to come around and see Papa a lot. He was nice to me. He used to bring me cakes from his wife. I liked him, so I called him Uncle. He was nicer to me than the others."

"What others?" He eased her around and onto his lap, slipping a hand up under her shirt.

"The friends of Papa. They used to come to our apartment. I did not like them very much because they took Papa away from me."

"What do you mean, beloved?"

"They talked for hours and hours. They would not let me or Mama go near them. Then Papa went back to the war. Now my mother cries every day and I hear her at night, too. She thinks she will never see Papa again." She frowned.

"Who were these men?"

"I do not know their names. They never used to talk to me. Except for Uncle Nikolai. The old man scared me especially. There was something horrible in his eyes. I used to hate to look in his eyes. They gave me nightmares."

"What old man?" Beria asked. There was more than idle curiosity in his voice now.

"He was tall and thin, with gray hair and wrinkly skin. And cold, blue eyes. My father was scared of him, I think."

"But your father is a general, beloved. He should be scared of no man." Except for Stalin—and me, Beria thought.

"I think it is because the old man is senior that Papa was scared," she said defensively.

"Senior to your father? That would make him a marshal." He was thinking aloud. The girl began to inch away from him, sensing a change.

Beria stared at the book, unconsciously tugging at his lip. Clandestine meetings of army officers, one of whom was a marshal; what was this? Since the purges, even brothers over the rank of lieutenant would restrict their visits to each other. If Stalin ever got to hear about such gatherings he would want to know what was so interesting that groups of officers could not talk openly in the staff room or in the halls of the Kremlin. Comrade Stalin distrusted such men. They usually did not last very long.

He pulled the girl back to the book with such force that she yipped with pain.

"Nadia, look through these photographs until you see the man with the eyes. When you see him, you must tell me."

The girl was scared. She nodded at Beria, following his gaze down to the album on his desk. The pool of light from the lamp fell upon the photograph of a general she did not recognize. She shook her head. Beria flicked the pages over. He kept on turning them until the girl froze.

"That's him," she whispered.

"Are you sure?"

"Yes."

Beria pushed her aside, taking no notice of her whimpering as she ran into the bedroom, slamming the door behind her. He picked up the phone and dialed the number of his senior investigation department at the center. He was connected straightaway with Shlemov.

"I want to know the whereabouts of Shaposhnikov . . . shall we say over the last six months? That means who he's seen, where he's been, who he's sleeping with, women, men . . . got the picture?"

The clipped, unquestioning tones of NKVD Major Vladimir Filippovich Shlemov filtered through the static on the line.

"And while you're about it," Beria shouted, "do the same for that lapdog of his. Colonel Nikolai Ivanovich Krilov." The NKVD chief turned to the door of the bedroom, satisfying himself that it was closed and he could not be overheard. "Finally, get me the file on Army General Nerchenko, deputy commander in chief of the First Ukrainian front. But make it discreet, Comrade Major, discreet. I want that report on my desk by morning."

He hung up and walked toward the bedroom, unbuttoning his shirt as he went. The Nerchenko girl's disclosure had caused

177

the hairs on the back of his policeman's neck to bristle. It was a feeling he had learned to enjoy.

□

If anything, Fleming felt the Bunker had acquired a certain benevolence since the shock briefing on the Russian invasion plan for Europe, the plan called Archangel. Fifty feet beneath the pavements of Whitehall, with no natural light or sounds of everyday life to distract him, it was hard to believe that anything that nightmarish could exist on the outside.

Fleming knew that to have endorsed Operation Guardian Angel, the Cabinet advisers had to be desperate. For all Staverton's drive and determination, it stood little chance of success. Even the Germans, desperate as they were, had not cleared the Me 163C for operational use. And they still had to persuade Kruze to undertake the mission.

Staverton was bent over a large-scale map of southern Europe, drawing a hemispherical arc with his compass, when the phone rang. He picked up the receiver and listened intently for about a minute before replacing it. His lip quivered involuntarily beneath his clipped, gray moustache.

Fleming stopped his calculations. "What is it?"

"The 163's crashed." Staverton's head lolled into his hands. "It's all over."

Fleming was on his feet. "What about Kruze?"

"He's alive."

"What the hell happened?"

Staverton's voice was weak, almost inaudible. "The fuel tanks ruptured in midair and T-Stoff leaked into the cockpit, but Kruze stayed with the aircraft and brought it back in, the bloody fool. He was lucky." He paused. "What the hell am I going to tell Welland?"

"First things first. Is Kruze all right?"

"He's with the medical officer at Farnborough having the once-over. He'll live. You know Kruze." Staverton banged his fist on the table. "Why did this have to go and happen now?"

Fleming composed himself. "It was a rush operation, sir." And a damned stupid one, he thought. "What state's the 163 in?"

"Badly damaged. Mulvaney said something about a design fault."

"Then at least that's solved one of our problems," Fleming

said. "The Nazis can't exactly defend the Alpine Redoubt with a fighter that doesn't work."

"The Alpine Redoubt could have bloody well waited," Staverton snapped. "I don't have to tell you that."

Fleming paced the room for at least a minute before he spoke.

"The rocket fighter has served its purpose; it's persuaded the other Cabinet advisers that an air strike in a fast German fighter-bomber is the only way of getting through to Branodz."

"Don't waste your breath, laddie. The Komet had the speed, it had the range, and it had the punch. Now it's just a pile of useless junk, beyond repair. We've nothing else capable of doing the job."

Fleming smiled. "We haven't anything here at Farnborough, but the Germans have."

"What are you getting at?" Staverton asked.

Fleming lit a cigarette and looked Staverton in the eye. "With all due respect, sir, using the Komet for a deep interdiction mission would never have worked."

"Oh yes? And how would you have done it, Robert?" Staverton's tone was challenging.

"I would have resurrected Operation Talon, sent a team into Germany to steal a fighter-bomber from a Luftwaffe base. If it worked at Rostock, it can work again. This time, though, the team would be small, handpicked. We would need a pilot, a coordinator, and an able German speaker."

Staverton remained silent.

"I could fly that aircraft," Fleming added.

"No, Robert."

"I'm all right now," Fleming said simply.

Staverton shook his head. "It doesn't matter how fit you are; we don't have the resources to reactivate Operation Talon at such short notice. Apart from finding a pilot, we've got to lay our hands on a shepherd, someone who could guide our man to the airfield, get him safely through the Reich. They don't come two a penny, you know, not even in Special Operations."

"There must be something you can do. What about your friends in intelligence? Surely they must have trained operatives ready to drop into Germany at a moment's notice. We can't give up now."

When Fleming looked up at Staverton he noticed that he was sitting ramrod straight, his eyes gleaming.

"What is it?" Fleming asked.

"Something you said just now. Perhaps . . ."

Staverton got up and walked over to the solid, gray filing cabinet in the corner of the room. He twiddled the combination lock on the side and pulled open the second drawer from the top. Thirty seconds later he held the Operation Talon file in his hand. Fleming watched him expectantly.

"Perhaps we could find ourselves a shepherd after all," Staverton said. "What aircraft did you have in mind for this mission?"

"An Arado 234 from Oberammergau." Fleming went over to the map, picked up Staverton's compass, and drew an arc whose point lay deep in the brown and purple topography of the Bavarian Alps. "That's a 234's approximate range—enough to get into western Czechoslovakia and out again, even at low level. The rest would be up to the pilot."

"There definitely are 234s at Oberammergau?"

"Been deployed there for a few weeks now," Fleming said. "My men have had them under high-altitude surveillance since they got there. With our troops moving into Bavaria I wanted to see if Oberammergau was worth a diversion. I know that airfield like the back of my hand."

"We've never laid our hands on an airworthy Arado, though. We'd need time to familiarize a pilot on the type, and time we don't have."

"I don't think that's a problem," Fleming said. "From our calculations the 234 would not be that different from the Me 262 as far as its controls and flight characteristics go. Almost all the pilots at the EAEU flew the Messerschmitt at Farnborough before it was destroyed."

Staverton wasn't convinced. "I was too bloody clever for my own good believing that we could use the Komet for this mission. The PM will never buy a change in the plan now."

Fleming could see the fatigue behind the Old Man's eyes. "Not necessarily. Kruze is all right and the demo worked. If you hadn't staged something that exotic, Welland would still be racing off at half cock with notions about parachuting assassination squads into Czechoslovakia. As it is, they've recommended to the prime minister that the EAEU mount a mission against the Russians. You've won their confidence. Now all you have to do is prove that a new scheme based on an extraction operation from Oberammergau is watertight. We have to persuade them that it's just a matter of reactivating Talon."

"Perhaps you're right." Staverton opened a drawer in his desk and produced a half-empty bottle of whiskey. He poured himself a measure and offered some to Fleming. The younger man shook his head.

Staverton raised his glass. "It's good to have you back. I missed you." It was the first time Fleming had seen a crack in the Old Man's facade. Staverton took a sip of the whiskey and rolled it on his tongue. "It's got to be Kruze, Robert. He has the skill, a little of the language, and the experience. It has to be Kruze." He shook his head. "Otherwise it will be over to Welland and his SBS team, God help us."

"Does that mean you're going to put this to the Cabinet advisers?"

Staverton leaned forward, his face so close that Fleming could smell the whiskey on the AVM's breath. "No, Robert."

"What do you mean?"

"I am not going to tell the Cabinet advisers. They're reactionaries. A change of plan now would throw them into disarray."

"You're just going to go ahead without their approval? You'll never get away with it."

"They'll never know, until it's all over and either Shaposhnikov is dead or we are."

"You can't keep that crash a secret. Not from the other Cabinet advisers at least," Fleming said.

Staverton was already reaching for the phone. "Can't I?"

A few seconds later and the AVM was connected with Mulvaney.

"Paddy? I want you to throw a cordon around the crash so tight that no news of it leaks out. Have all incoming calls screened, all outgoing calls stopped, and all leave suspended. Nobody gets off the airfield. Have you got that? If anyone from Whitehall rings you for a progress report on the 163C, tell them the flight was a success and the aircraft's undergoing deep maintenance . . . anything except the truth. Is that understood?"

He put the phone down. Mulvaney would not question an order from Staverton.

"But we need to reactivate the network established for Talon. That's going to take high-level approval."

"There are people at intelligence who owe me," Staverton said, getting to his feet. "Meanwhile, find out if our man is still fit to fly and, if he is, get him to report here tonight." He picked up his coat. "I'm going to get us our shepherd."

Left alone, Fleming went back to his calculations, losing his fears in the 234's performance data, fuel consumption, time of flight between Oberammergau and Branodz, weapon loads. From Oberammergau—which was close to Munich—to Shaposhnikov at Branodz, it was only a matter of two hundred miles on the inbound leg, but since the whole trip had to be done at low level, fuel consumption would be high . . .

Fleming was so absorbed in double-checking the details of Operation Guardian Angel that he wasn't aware of the phone until the third ring. When he picked it up, he recognized General Deering's voice immediately.

"Whatever arrangements you still need to make to get the 163C over to Germany, Fleming, you'd better get a damned move on." The general's voice no longer maintained its steady, Sandhurst drawl. "We've just had word from our embassy in Moscow. Shaposhnikov left yesterday to, and I quote, 'boost the morale of the Red Army at the front.' He's due in Branodz tomorrow. Archangel's moving, and sooner than we thought. The PM wants you on your way by midday tomorrow."

□

The four-star general from Moscow's embassy liaison office stood to attention before the commander in chief of the Soviet armed forces. The commander was bending over maps of the front, seemingly absorbed by the minutiae of each projected troop movement that was recorded there in colored crayon.

Until a few weeks ago, Army General Semyon Sabak's place had been here, in Stalin's operations center in the Kremlin. He missed his strategic role, even though he knew that his new position allowed him to play out the most crucial role he was ever likely to face in his military career.

Stalin glanced up. The look of mild irritation on his face disappeared the moment he saw who it was.

"Ah, Sabak. You said you had news," Stalin said.

"I received a telephone call from the British military attaché, Brigadier Vereker." Sabak pronounced the *v* as a *w*.

"Ah yes, the 'attaché' . . ."

"He was inquiring as to the whereabouts of Comrade Marshal Shaposhnikov," Sabak said.

"Why did he want to know?" Stalin turned away from the map.

"The British mission wants a progress report on our front operations for onward transmission to London. I reminded him that such briefings are given through the liaison bureau and not the chief of the general staff, but he was most insistent. He wanted to meet with Shaposhnikov personally."

"I briefed the ambassador and his defense staff a few days ago," Stalin said. "The British know that nothing significant has changed. What did you tell him?"

"Exactly what we agreed, Comrade Stalin. Marshal Shaposhnikov left Moscow yesterday on his morale-boosting tour of the front. That he would be in Branodz, Czechoslovakia, tomorrow."

Stalin smiled. "Well? What are your conclusions?"

"The British have never requested a meeting with Marshal Shaposhnikov. Suddenly they are showing interest in him. I think they have it."

"So Paliev's message did get through after all," the generalissimo said, a gleam in his eyes. "When news came through of the ambush I thought we would have to make other arrangements."

"It is too early to be certain, Comrade Stalin, but it would seem so. We will monitor British and American troop movements just to be sure. We should know within the next few days."

Stalin nodded his satisfaction. "Keep me informed," he said.

□

Herries paced the room impatiently. He had spent the afternoon telling everything he knew about the area around Branodz and the dummy tank buildup at Chrudim. In return, he had been promised his freedom; a reward for his having opened the bidding, White-Smith had told him. The man from military intelligence, section 6, seemed happy with the level of detail Herries had given him and, having finished his copious notes, withdrew. The Freikorps debriefing would take place over the next few weeks in less austere surroundings. In other words, he was about to be paroled.

White-Smith reluctantly promised that the transfer papers would be produced by the evening, but six o'clock had come and gone and there was no sign. Herries took a step toward the door and smashed his fist against it. He called out for White-Smith, but there was no response, not a sound from the entire building.

He slumped on the floor, his back against the wall, rubbing his knuckles where the flesh was torn.

The footsteps made him start. The metal toe caps of the police guard clattered up the stairs. His heartbeat quickened and he had difficulty breathing. He was going home.

Once more the key scraped in the lock. Herries did not bother to get to his feet as the door swung open.

He was surprised when he didn't see White-Smith. Instead, a tall, aging RAF officer loomed over him. His iron-gray hair and precisely trimmed moustache made him look distinguished in a way White-Smith never could, but there was also a hardness about the face and eyes that made Herries clamber to his feet.

"Good. I don't like a man who spends his time around my ankles." The tone was unforgiving and betrayed a hint of the man's origins, somewhere in the north.

"Who are you?" Herries asked. "Where's White-Smith?"

"My name's Staverton, but don't bother memorizing it because we won't be meeting again after today. And as for White-Smith, shall we say, he has temporarily handed over the matter of your reeducation to me."

Staverton moved into the middle of the garret and waved the guard away. The door was closed once again.

"Where are my release papers?" Herries went on the offensive. "What's a bloody air force officer doing on my case? My business is with the army and military intelligence."

Staverton walked casually around the little attic room, occasionally pulling at a piece of loose plaster or peeling wallpaper. He seemed not to hear.

"I demand that you get me out of here before I utter another word; do you understand me?"

Staverton peered out of the window, minutely studying the rooftops and the budding trees. Beneath the composure, his mind worked fast. He prided himself on his ability to judge accurately on first impressions. In Herries' ruthless, aquiline features and deep-set eyes he saw a cornered animal. Afraid, yes, but dangerous. The very person he needed. The very person Kruze would need if he were going to penetrate the crumbling defenses of the Third Reich and steal the Arado jet bomber from Oberammergau.

He saw a sudden movement reflected in the window and whirled around to see Herries bearing down on him, his face contorted with rage. "I've delivered, now you owe me," he screamed, his hands raised to strike.

The momentum in Staverton's upper body gave him the advantage. He brought his fist up into Herries' jaw. Herries reeled, arms flailing for balance. He fell in a heap on the bed in the corner.

Staverton wanted to rub his knuckles, but did not. He looked down, revulsion for the man boiling up inside him. Herries knew it and lay still, his eyes narrowed.

"You'll get nothing from me unless you listen very carefully to what I have to say," Staverton said as evenly as possible. He delved into the breast pocket of his jacket and produced an envelope. "This is for you."

Herries, nursing his jaw with one hand, took the small brown envelope. He ripped it open and pulled out a single sheet of paper. He read it and then leaned back on the bed and laughed.

"So I'm to be pardoned," he said, "and by no lesser authority than the head of military intelligence. Couldn't you find the bloody king?"

Staverton took a step forward and whisked the paper away.

"This isn't yours quite yet." He paused. "You've got to do a little job for us first."

"If it means getting out of here, I'll do anything."

"Good." Staverton folded his arms and looked Herries straight in the eye. "You're going back into Germany."

The color drained from Herries' face. "Germany? Are you quite mad?"

"We want you to put the skills you have learned over the last three years to good use by helping us put an end to Archangel. We need to get a pilot into a Luftwaffe base in southern Germany. His German isn't quite fluent and he's not too familiar with the terrain. That's where you come in." Staverton realized he was starting to enjoy the other's discomfort. "Your papers are valid and you're in the SS, which should cut some ice with the guards at the airfield, and at any other obstruction you are likely to meet. So I put this scheme to the authorities here and as you see, after a little persuasion, they decided to give you the job."

"But a Freikorps officer—particularly a British one—is not accorded the same privileges as the regular SS within Germany. They'd no more let me into that base than they would you."

Staverton reached into his pocket and threw Herries another envelope. "Then you had better take a look at this."

Herries found himself staring at his own SS *soldbuch*. He opened the identity document, dog-eared and stained from years on the eastern front. Opposite the photograph of the führer was his *personalausweis:* name, rank, number, and regiment. But all references to the Freikorps had been carefully removed. He looked back to the cover again and flipped through it until he found the page with his photograph. It was his book, there was no mistaking that, but the forger who had made the deletions was a craftsman. There was no sign that a scalpel or new ink had gone near the document.

"SOE were able to do that in a few hours," Staverton said. "It's perfect."

"Yes, it is," Herries was forced to agree. He was now merely Obersturmführer Christian Herries, First Company, Third Battalion, Second SS Panzergrenadier Regiment, Das Reich Division.

"We'll supply you with a uniform, obviously. You have to ensure that our man gets new papers in Munich and then into Oberammergau. Do that and you're free. The rest is up to him."

"Why Munich? Why can't the pilot have his papers forged here?" He held up his *soldbuch.* "They don't come much better than this."

"Yours were relatively easy. His will take time. To do it here would mean two more days in London for him and I don't need to tell you that's just too long for us. SOE has a specialist in Munich. All he needs is the pilot's photograph and he can finish the job that we've already set in motion."

Herries said, "You know what you can do with your proposal, don't you? I made a deal with General Styles."

Staverton was unmoved. "Yes, they told me that you'd be difficult. But it's not a proposal, Herries; it's an ultimatum. The only choice you've got is between being tried for war crimes—and I don't think you would come out of it that well—or doing this and going free. Now, I'm a very busy man, so I'll leave you to think about it." Staverton allowed himself a smile. "Germany, Herries, or the gallows?"

"What about the Red Cross?" Herries' voice cracked. "If I die, you and Styles will be the war criminals."

Staverton shrugged and moved over to the door. "On balance," he said, "I'd say our record on atrocities is somewhat better than yours."

Staverton banged on the door and called for the policeman.

"No, wait." Herries was on his feet. "Look, if it's just for a few days, I'll do it."

"Good," the AVM said. "In that case, let me run over exactly what it is we want you to do. To start with, you will under no circumstances reveal your identity to the man you'll be taking in. I don't think he's going to be too thrilled by the idea of teaming up with a two-bit traitor." He looked at his watch. "Now listen carefully, because you'll be back inside your precious Reich by this time tomorrow night."

5

With little traffic on the roads between Farnborough and London, the staff car that Fleming had commissioned to bring Kruze to the Bunker made the journey in under two hours.

The Bunker hadn't wasted any time, Kruze thought, as he made his way along the maze of corridors in the ministry that led down to the subterranean nerve center of the EAEU.

He knocked on the Old Man's door and went in.

"Sitdown," Staverton said, rolling the two words into one. Fleming was sitting beside the AVM, behind the long desk. His presence made Kruze feel uneasy.

"How are you feeling?" Staverton asked. The Rhodesian looked distracted.

Kruze involuntarily rubbed his arm where it had received a crack when he rolled onto the runway to get away from the 163.

"I've been better."

"What happened?" Fleming asked.

Kruze said, "Well, you don't have to worry about the 163C being used to defend any Alpine fortress. It will never fly operationally."

"How do you know?" Fleming asked.

"When they removed the T-Stoff and C-Stoff tanks from the aircraft, they found that both were seriously flawed. The forward tank had only sprung a minor leak into the cockpit, but the rear one was so badly corroded that it was just about to blow apart. When they looked at the tanks a little closer, they discovered them to be made out of light steel alloy, the wrong metal. It's a flying acid bath."

"They?" Staverton asked.

"The Rostock experts."

"What are the tanks meant to be made out of?"

"Apparently aluminum is the only thing that will stand up to the T-Stoff. The German industrial belt must have been so badly flattened that the enemy doesn't have the ability to make high-grade aluminum any more. Messerschmitt must be making 163 tanks out of steel alloy instead, hoping that they'll stay the distance. And if that's true, it means that the Nazis are out of new rocket fighters."

The trace of a smile played across Staverton's lips. Kruze's old confidence had not been marred by the accident. He was fit to fly.

Kruze's expression hardened. "I've got to say I'm a little mystified about why you rushed the air test through so quickly. It should take weeks to set up something like that."

"We really didn't have any choice," the AVM said. "I regretted not being able to tell you the whole story at the time, but believe me, the role you played was vital."

"Role? You make it sound as if it was a stage performance."

"In a sense it was, I'm afraid."

Kruze's brow creased.

"Your 163 flight was a firework display to convince Churchill's other Cabinet advisers that using a single German jet airplane is the only way to penetrate almost two hundred miles of the densest troop concentrations and air defenses seen in mainland Europe since the war began."

"I don't believe it," Kruze whispered. "A circus sideshow. And I risked my neck to bring that death trap back to your experts . . ."

Staverton appeared not to hear the anger in his voice. "And it worked. They've agreed to do it my way."

"Don't think for a minute that your conclusions on the rocket fighter aren't useful to us," Fleming cut in. He wished Staverton would get straight to the point. "The Alpine Redoubt is a very real threat—"

"But it's as nothing to the problem we face now," Staverton said. "The real reason you're here tonight. The reason why I have to find a pilot to fly a German bomber two hundred miles and back through nightmare country—almost all of it Russian-controlled."

"I think you had better start from the beginning," Kruze said.

Staverton kept it simple. There was no need to tell the Rhodesian too much. He told Kruze about Archangel and its architect. He explained how Shaposhnikov might be a maverick, but then again he might not—that there was no way of checking if the marshal had the backing of Stalin and the *stavka*. He told him that they were on their own; American support had been vetoed because their allies' reaction might be wild and unpredictable. He said that it was imperative for Shaposhnikov to be removed, and that the instrument of his termination was to be a pilot, carefully chosen from the EAEU, who would fly a German aircraft at low level through Soviet-captured territory, and bomb Shaposhnikov at his HQ in Branodz, western Czechoslovakia. And finally he told Kruze that there was no other way, because not only was it the best means of penetrating the Russian defenses, but it would also make Stalin believe that the assassination of his chief of the general staff at the front was a last desperate act of revenge by the Nazis. Status quo restored. No repercussions.

"And you want me to fly the plane," Kruze said, without emotion. "What aircraft have you got in mind?"

"An Arado 234 Blitz jet bomber," Fleming replied. "We want you to take it from the Luftwaffe's base at Oberammergau, outside Munich, and fly it into Czechoslovakia."

"You would have excellent backup," Staverton added, before Kruze could say anything. "Robert would be your coordinator, going with you into Germany until you cross their lines. Thereafter, you'd be assisted by an able German speaker, someone with great knowledge of the Nazi military. You have some German yourself, don't you?"

"Some," Kruze said.

"SOE have lined up a safe house for you in Munich, owned by the Jewish underground. You'd make your way there, lie low for a day while papers are being prepared for you, and then move by night to the airfield. The shepherd, your German-speaking companion, would then get you into the base. The rest would be up to you."

Kruze said, "You make it sound simple."

"I'm not pretending it won't be dangerous, but you will have good support every step of the way."

"And this shepherd. How good's he?"

"The best," Staverton said simply. "He's English, but has infiltrated the German military before. Intelligence background." He managed to keep his voice even. "Robert, perhaps you would care to outline the plan in a little more depth."

"We have to move fast," Fleming said. "The latest intelligence is that Shaposhnikov has left Moscow for Branodz—a little earlier than we expected. It's possible that for reasons of security he has moved the plan forward. We're going to hit him hard before he's even had time to get his hands dirty at his field HQ. Your attack is set for dawn in two days' time. We just have to pray the Russians do not move before then."

"How do you know Shaposhnikov will be at his HQ when I go in?"

Fleming tapped the folder on his desk, which contained Shaposhnikov's translated text. "The Archangel battle plans state that following his arrival he will monitor the radio every morning at six-thirty for coded progress reports from his commanders in the field. He's keeping one channel free for half an hour to ensure that if they've got anything to say to him, they can get through. The only building with a transmitter powerful enough to reach his accomplices is the HQ. So, we've got him, as long as you hit him between oh-six-thirty and oh-seven-hundred."

Kruze listened, knowing that Fleming had once more become the man that Penny married. He could still detect the shadows of Fleming's ordeal around the eyes, but the shaken, haunted man he had captured in his gun cameras not so long ago was a rapidly fading memory.

"But first we have to get you to Germany," Fleming continued. "Stabitz airfield is ideal. Just been captured by our forces marching on Munich. I'll run over all the details there until you both know Guardian Angel by heart."

"It sounds like I'm going whether I like it or not."

"Not so," Staverton said. "You will be free to choose, but please hear us out first."

"You and the shepherd will then be dropped behind enemy lines by Auster the following dawn," Fleming said. "I remain at Stabitz to coordinate between you and London." It was not a part of the mission that he enjoyed dwelling on. "You're to make your way into Munich and contact a watchmaker named Schell, a member of the Jewish underground. He's been alerted of your arrival—but not the purpose of your visit—by SOE.

191

He's arranging all the papers you will need to get through the checkpoints on the road to Oberammergau. He will shelter and feed you until nightfall when you will leave the city and make for the airfield. It's not far."

"Maybe," Kruze said. "But papers or no papers, that place is going to be swarming with troops and my German isn't good enough to get me past the first checkpoint, let alone into Oberammergau."

Fleming held his hand up. "You've got to trust us," he said. "You will be given papers that prove you are a Romanian government official seeking transport out of Germany back to your country and that the shepherd, who will be masquerading as an obersturmführer in the Waffen SS, is your escort. The Wehrmacht is not going to brush with people like him, believe me."

"Why Romanian?"

"They're still allies of Hitler—"

"—and there aren't that many Germans who speak Romanian," Staverton said.

Kruze lit a cigarette. "What then?"

"Once at Oberammergau, the shepherd will get you through the gates. The rest, as they say, is up to you."

Kruze smiled and let out a stream of smoke. "For a moment there you almost talked me into this thing. But do you seriously think I can walk up to a 234, conveniently bombed up and ready to go, and take off into the blue? I wouldn't get within a hundred yards of one of their aircraft."

"This is no suicide mission," Staverton said. "There will be a diversion to enable you to take your airplane unchallenged."

Fleming put his notes down. "Yes, at first light, the RAF will mount a strike against the airfield. The pilots will be told to leave the aircraft, just go for buildings and personnel. In all the confusion, you'll be able to steal your Arado."

"Next stop, Branodz," Kruze said. "As simple as that. I think I prefer next stop Waterloo Station and a train back to Farnborough. You've got to be mad if you think that this is actually going to work."

"It can if you'll be the pilot," Staverton said.

Kruze banged his fist on the table. "This isn't just about flying an airplane, Air Vice Marshal. It's a fucking long way from gun cameras and cozy postmortems—"

"The shepherd can take care of the rest," Staverton said.

"What if I say no?"

"That will be your privilege."

"And a transfer to Coastal Command to wash seagull shit off Sunderlands for the rest of the war." Kruze breathed deeply. "I read you like a book, Staverton. You extract loyalty from people around you and then spit it back in their faces when it suits you. You're loving every minute of this, because it's a big game, except you've got real lives as the pieces on the board."

Kruze suddenly felt as if he were poised above the eye of the storm. He was looking down at a place at the center of the vortex where all was still, where Penny was calling his name but Fleming was answering. Chief Broyles, somewhere on the edge, was holding Billy's hand, and a long way away there was Staverton, the puppeteer, watching them and doing nothing.

And then he knew what he must do. He must go to Germany with Fleming, who stood between him and a happiness that he had tasted but could not have. A happiness that nonetheless would give him the sense of purpose to carry this through to the end.

Staverton was leaning forward. There was no fluctuation in his tone. "As I said, that would be your privilege. But Archangel is real and it's going to happen unless you help us. I won't beg you, Kruze, but I want you to think of this. When the war is over and you're back in Rhodesia, give a thought to the poor bastards in Paris, Marseilles, and Boulogne who are having their sons and daughters raped by those savages. Some night when you get yourself blind drunk in a bar in Salisbury you might even turn to the person next to you and stagger through some story about how you could have done something about it."

Kruze got to his feet and picked up his heavy gray overcoat.

"Where are you going?" Fleming asked. He gave Staverton a hostile look. Kruze had already had a bellyful that day and the Old Man has pushed too hard.

Kruze paused at the door and turned to face them. "I'm going to find some air that's fit to breathe. But I'll get Shaposhnikov for you, even if I have to find him in hell."

The AVM's face was set in granite, his hands clasped in front of him. He looked like a judge about to pass sentence. "Then be ready to leave from Farnborough by midday tomorrow. You'll get the rest of your orders in Germany."

Kruze pulled up the collar of his coat, took a last look at Staverton, and closed the door behind him.

"Did you have to do that?" Fleming asked. "He would have done it anyway."

Staverton said, "I know that, Robert, but I want Kruze angry, really angry. The trouble with our Rhodesian friend is that while he's the best technician we've got, where he's going that won't be enough. What he needs is fire in his belly if he's going to get to Branodz. Shaposhnikov is in hell all right, and Kruze is going to have to go all the way to find him."

"Who is the shepherd?" Fleming asked.

"The man who delivered us the secret of Archangel. Obersturmführer Christian Herries."

Fleming felt his blood run cold. "You can't do that, for God's sake . . ."

"There is no one else. Herries has been granted immunity from prosecution. At least this way he'll work for it."

"You have to tell Kruze. It's the least he deserves."

Staverton shook his head. "I'm afraid that's out of the question. I received permission to employ the traitor only as long as his true past and identity remained secret. Herries is an embarrassment to this country and there are people who would like to ensure his story never gets out—to anyone beyond these walls."

Fleming got up, disgust on his face. "Kruze was right, damn you. You really are enjoying this. I used to think that you watched over us, that the tests you set were for our own good. But you toy with people's lives when it suits your purposes, and you don't give a shit about what happens in the end. If I get back from the place you're sending Kruze to, you'll have my resignation, I swear it."

□

They met in a wood outside the village of Krazna Hora, some fifty kilometers from Branodz. Darkness had long descended on the dripping pine forests of western Czechoslovakia. The rendezvous had been set by Shaposhnikov and communicated to the Archangel activists in the field via Krilov's specially encrypted codes. The GAZ jeeps were ranged around the tiny clearing, the subdued beams of their blackout headlights cutting as far as they could into the forest before being overwhelmed by the density of the trees.

Shaposhnikov and Krilov were the last to arrive. As their jeep slowed to a halt, the generals got out of their vehicles and strode over to meet their leader. Krilov noticed that Branodz and Vorontin had brought their trusties with them as drivers.

Only Nerchenko had driven alone. It was a stark reminder of Paliev's fate.

Krilov and the trusties stood back as the four men greeted one another. There was no exchange of words until each had laid his right hand upon the other's. The eerie silence in the clearing and the intensity of feeling that radiated from the simple gesture made Krilov's pulse race. It would not now be long before these four men would lift Europe out of the chaos of the last five years, and unite the continent under one great socialist structure that would last until the end of time.

Shaposhnikov's face broke into a smile. He placed his hand on Vorontin's shoulder and embraced him warmly. "Arkady Matveevich, it is good to see you." Then to Badunov, "And you, Marius Fedorovich, a long way to come for such a short meeting." Lastly, it was Nerchenko's turn. "Even you seem a little happier now, Petr Pavlovich."

"The waiting is almost over, Comrade Marshal. That makes me happy."

"And the insurgents?" Shaposhnikov said.

Nerchenko looked sheepish. His last message to Shaposhnikov must have reeked of panic. "My men have swept the hills for survivors of the explosion that wiped out the SS camp, Comrade Marshal, but they found nothing. The officer in charge of the search, Major Malenkoy, thought there might have been others, but I think not. I am sure they are all dead. The area is clean and Archangel is safe."

"This Malenkoy has no reason to suspect, does he, Petr Pavlovich?"

"None, Comrade Marshal. He is only an engineer in charge of the *maskirovka* at Chrudim. Such men do not think; they merely work with their hands. It is why I chose him to head up the hunt for the SS terrorists." He remembered the day Malenkoy relayed the news of Paliev's recovered ID papers and the chill he had felt at the prospect of the SS finding the Archangel documents. "No one has cause to suspect at Branodz," he added firmly, partly to convince himself.

Shaposhnikov clapped his gloved hands together. "Then to business," he said. "The battle plan remains unaltered except for the change of date, which was, as you know, a precaution against the defection of the traitor, Paliev." His eyes left the group and probed the stark shadows of the forest. "May all traitors suffer the same fate."

Shaposhnikov conveyed the threat without even having to look at them. Nerchenko felt it more than the others, a sudden frisson running down his spine.

"In any case, this might be a blessing," the marshal said, lightening his tone again. "I am convinced that the Red Army's order of battle is at peak strength now, such has been the momentum behind our second-echelon forces in the past month. I have just seen the morale of our troops at Ostrava. They are pouring toward the front, and keen for the signal that will finish the fascists. They will need little persuasion to take on the British and Americans as well."

"Then we go in three days," Badunov said, unable to hide his impatience.

"As soon as we are all in position," the marshal said. "How long will it take you and Comrade General Vorontin to make your separate ways back to your headquarters at the First and Second Belorussian fronts?"

"Twelve hours," Badunov said.

"Eighteen at the most," Vorontin added.

"Then all is set for the tanks to roll at dawn in three days' time. Comrade Krilov and I will be with Comrade General Nerchenko in Branodz later tonight. Signal us at the allotted time once you are in place. Thereafter, keep your progress reports brief and strictly between the times we agreed."

The two generals clicked their heels. "I do not think I could have waited another week anyway," Badunov said. "The NKVD are everywhere. I feel their eyes boring into the back of my skull. It is time."

"Do not forget," Shaposhnikov said, "that the NKVD will have to be rounded up at exactly the same time as Zhukov, Rokossovsky, and their advisers. I don't want Beria's dogs interfering once everything is under way."

Each of them knew that the first hours were vital and relied on perfect synchronization between the conspirators on all fronts. Two hours before the forty-one thousand howitzers opened up and the T-34s began clanking their way across their front lines, Vorontin, at Second Belorussian, was to dispatch loyal guards to Marshal Rokossovsky's quarters and have him shot on Stalin's orders—forged orders, citing cowardice in the face of the enemy for slowing the pace of the Soviet advance. Vorontin would then have command of Soviet forces in the far north of the nine-hundred-sixty-kilometer front.

At First Belorussian, in the center, Badunov was to do the same with Marshal Zhukov. At First Ukrainian, Nerchenko would terminate Marshal Konev, allowing Shaposhnikov to step into his place. The marshal would supervise the spearhead assault west, as well as coordinate Archangel from Branodz. Nerchenko would then make his way to Second Ukrainian and take up command of Shaposhnikov's left flank. New orders would be relayed to commanders in the field. If any of them had reservations about attacking the Western Allies, none would show it.

"When you have control and the attack has begun, remember to signal me again, both of you," Shaposhnikov said. "When I have your transmissions I will relay the communiqué to Moscow that we, the free officers of the Red Army, have struck a blow for the October Revolution that will once and for all remove imperialism from our doorstep. Comrade Stalin will have no choice but to throw the weight and resources of the Motherland behind Archangel's iron fist."

Vorontin laughed. "I would love to see his face when he reads that signal."

Shaposhnikov did not seem to share the joke, but nodded. "He will have no choice but to join our victory parade in Paris in six weeks. By then we will be so strong that he will be in no position to move against us. Should he show signs of wavering, we have friends in Moscow who can take care of that, as you know."

The euphemism chilled Krilov. It was strange that even Shaposhnikov could not say the words outright.

Shaposhnikov moved on to the subject of the *maskirovkas*, the huge, carefully coordinated, military deceptions on all three Soviet fronts that had convinced the Germans—and the Western Allies, for that matter—that the Red Army was amassing resources for one last thrust that would squeeze the lifeblood from the Reich. "They have bought us valuable time. The confusion that will greet our actual assault plan should take our troops halfway to Paris before meeting serious resistance."

"And if it doesn't . . ."

Shaposhnikov looked from one to the other, and saw from their expressions that Vorontin had spoken for them all. "Yes, Comrades. If it doesn't, we will have no alternative but to use the Berezniki consignment. We should none of us dismiss the possibility that, even with the massive weight of resources behind Archangel, our troops may become bogged down. Should that be the case, I will have no hesitation in using the chemical weapons at our disposal. I want you to know that."

"Where is the consignment?" Badunov asked.

"Making its way to Branodz in an armored convoy under the command of Major Ryakhov, Military Chemical Forces. If the sector is clear of the enemy, as you suggest it is, Comrade General Nerchenko, then there really is nothing to fear while the munitions are in transit."

"Quite, Comrade Marshal," Nerchenko said, his heart in his throat. He thought of the trucks winding their way up the mountain tracks that led to Branodz, Ryakhov peering past the straining windshield wipers, down the tunnel beams of the headlights, looking for the slightest sign of trouble ahead. If they were attacked, if even one of the chemical shells were to rupture, the very breath he was taking now could be his last.

"Rest assured that the decision to use the hydrogen cyanide artillery shells will be mine, and mine alone." Shaposhnikov's words brought Nerchenko's attention back. "Given the prevailing wind conditions, I am satisfied that none of the gas can possibly reach as far north as your troops," he said, nodding to Vorontin, "but the rest of us will have to take the precautions we discussed, at all times."

Badunov, however, remained anxious. Even the troops at the very northern extreme of his First Belorussian front, about 150 kilometers from the impact point of the shells, would have to fight in gas masks if Shaposhnikov decided to resort to chemical attack.

But God help the enemy. Tens of thousands, perhaps hundreds of thousands, would die. And that didn't include the civilians.

"Do you think they will counterattack with chemicals?" Vorontin asked.

Shaposhnikov shook his head. "The Western Allies' command structure is already too fragmented for them to initiate a rapid response. By the time they are in a position to deploy their own chemical weapons we would be on our way to Paris. Their troops, unlike ours, are not trained to fight in such an environment, and they would never risk the slaughter of their French allies."

"What about the Germans?" Badunov asked.

"Not even Hitler would sanction the use of chemical warfare on German soil. No, believe me, if we have to use these weapons, the way is clear to do so. But given the readiness of our conventional forces I don't expect any serious hitches. The chemicals are just an insurance policy."

□

By the time he had paced the streets for an hour, Kruze had got most of the anger from his exchange with Staverton out of his system. He hailed a cab and asked the driver to take him to the station, then changed his mind and asked to go by the hospital first.

The taxi waited in front of its great gothic exterior, while Kruze made his way toward the main entrance. As he walked, he carefully removed the service ribbons from his chest and wrapped them in his handkerchief. They wouldn't make much of a memento for Billy, but they were all he had.

He approached the duty desk. The nurse was not the one who had spoken to him and Penny on their last visit. She looked up from her book and smiled.

"Can I help you?"

He put the hankerchief on the desk. "I wanted to leave this for one of your patients," he said. "A little boy by the name of Billy Simmons. He was brought in a few days ago following the Strand explosion."

"You're Squadron Leader Kruze, aren't you?" She turned the book over and stood up. Her expression had changed.

"That's right. How did you know?"

"We've been trying to get hold of you and Mrs. Fleming all afternoon," she said, then paused. "Billy died shortly after two o'clock. I'm terribly sorry."

He looked at her incredulously. "You must have got the wrong patient. Billy had broken his legs, that was all. He was getting better."

She tried to put a hand on his arm, but he shrugged her off.

"There was a complication," she said. "The doctors didn't see the blood clot. By the time it had entered his brain it was too late. There was nothing they could do." She paused again, watching the shock on his face. "We tried to contact you at your base, but they weren't accepting any calls."

Kruze did not need to hear any more. He turned on his heels and walked through the exit, leaving the tiny bundle of ribbons where he had placed it on the desk.

By the time the nurse was through the doors, the taxi was already pulling out of the gates.

6

"Comrade Beria," NKVD Major Shlemov said, "I think I have found something which is not as it should be." He coughed, awkwardly. "I need more guidance." He had rehearsed the opening words of his speech for the last half hour, but somehow it still came out wrong. The directive had been vague, so it was hard to know exactly what Beria was looking for.

"You've had the entire night to get answers. I want them now," Beria said from behind his immense desk.

Shlemov got out his notepad. "We pulled the Krilov woman in for questioning and—"

"You did what?" The NKVD chief slammed his fist down on the blotter. "I thought I told you to be discreet."

"There were many dead ends. No one knew anything about these three men—nothing concrete, anyway. We needed a break."

Beria waved his hand. His mood could change in an instant; Shlemov had learned that. "Continue then, but start from the beginning," the NKVD chief said.

Shlemov looked back to his pad. "I have had my men examine the records of Shaposhnikov, Nerchenko, and Krilov, but individually they're clean. Oddly, however, their paths crossed for the first time three years ago when they taught at the Voroshilov Military Academy. Were you trying to establish a particular link, Comrade Beria?"

"Maybe, maybe not," Beria growled. "Carry on."

"It was when Shaposhnikov was commandant and Krilov and Nerchenko were on his staff, teaching tactics and strategy. Apparently, they were rather friendly, although you would never have guessed it from the way they behaved at the academy. They almost crossed the street to avoid each other."

"How do you know this?"

"We interviewed some of the academy's 1942–1943 intake. Shaposhnikov was extremely popular—his particular brand of patriotism appealed to the young lions whose fields and cities had just been sacked by the fascist invaders."

"This jingoism, do you think it could be a blind? Would it be possible, for instance, that he was involved in pro-Western activities?"

"No, quite the opposite; that was the strange thing. These lecturers were so anti-Western that they made no distinction between Nazi, British, or American. I know the fascists had only just been driven back and feelings were riding high, but even so, their rhetoric was remarkable for people who were never seen with each other. To the students of Voroshilov, all five of them spoke with one tongue."

"Five? Who were the others? You have only mentioned Shaposhnikov, Krilov, and Nerchenko."

"Generals Badunov and Vorontin."

"Why do the students remember this rhetoric as particularly remarkable?" Beria asked. "Anti-Western doctrine is something that should be encouraged, albeit with some subtlety—don't you think?"

"Quite, Comrade. I merely recorded the students' observations."

Beria began to lose patience. "This is all very interesting, Comrade Shlemov, but how do you know that they were operating in unison if they were never seen together?"

Shlemov coughed. "Policeman's instinct, I suppose."

"But no evidence?"

"Not until we spoke to Valentina Krilova."

Beria appreciated the use of the word "spoke." Chances were they had beaten her half to death. "Why her, especially?"

The NKVD major mirrored his superior's thin smile. "I thought she was bound to know something, Krilov being the marshal's aide. He took up the post shortly after Shaposhnikov was called back from the academy as chief of general staff. I also thought it would draw less attention pulling a colonel's wife out of bed at three in the morning. Generals' wives can be a little more difficult."

Shlemov brought out his notepad again, skimming through the pages until he found the relevant section. "As for Shaposhnikov, he did have a family, but the records show they died shortly after the October Revolution. Nerchenko has a daughter, but we haven't had time to question her yet."

Beria looked levelly at Shlemov, trying to read the face for a sign that his relationship with Nadia Nerchenko had surfaced. He was satisfied that the policeman knew nothing.

"Remember what I said about discretion," Beria cautioned.

"Yes, Comrade Beria."

"Go on about the Krilov woman," the NKVD chief said. "Perhaps it was a good decision. It depends on what you found."

"She told us everything she knew, I'm sure of that. Shaposhnikov, Krilov, and Nerchenko had been meeting regularly for months in Krilov's apartment, even though they appeared to shun each other at the academy. That's odd for a start."

Beria nodded. Come on, Shlemov, he thought, tell me something I don't know.

"They never let her into the room where they talked. She thought they were probably reliving old campaigns—as old soldiers do over a bottle or two of vodka. That was when she told us about Operation Archangel—"

"What?"

"Archangel. It was about the only snippet she caught. She thought it was some battle they had fought together during the last war and that they were just reminiscing. She heard them mention it several times on different occasions. I think she only told us because she thought it wasn't of any importance."

"And when was this operation? I have to confess I've never heard of it."

"You won't have, Comrade Beria. We did a check. Neither our own side, nor the fascists for that matter, have ever staged a military operation by that name, in this war or the last."

"What did it suggest to you, then?" Beria liked the methodical way Shlemov worked. It was the reason he had picked him for the job. He just wished the man would speed things up.

Shlemov sucked the end of his pencil. "Nothing at the time, but there is more." He turned the pages of his notebook. "She broke down. Told us that her relationship with her husband had never been particularly strong, but when Krilov left her two days ago, she was convinced that they weren't going to meet again. There was something rather final about his good-bye that's had her worried ever since."

"Where has he gone?"

"On Shaposhnikov's morale tour of the front—hardly any cause for concern, I thought at first. I mean, they're unlikely to go anywhere near the fighting. But here's the interesting part: their first port of call, according to Shaposhnikov's itinerary, is Branodz, HQ of the First Ukrainian front. Nerchenko is second in command there, under Marshal Konev."

"So you think that Archangel is something in the future?"

Shlemov shrugged. "Perhaps it is the *stavka*'s given name for an action against the fascists."

Beria ran through the minutes of the last few sessions of the Supreme *Stavka* in his mind. There had never been mention of any operation by the name of Archangel. He remembered something else, however, that made his stomach knot with excitement. "What if I were to tell you that Badunov and Vorontin have also been meeting up with them, only at Nerchenko's apartment?" The eyes sparkled behind the wire frames of his glasses.

Shlemov forgot his place momentarily. "How can you know this?"

"I know it, Shlemov, never mind how."

The NKVD major felt the perspiration under his uniform. But Beria was racing toward the next link in the chain.

"And what if I were to tell you," the head of the NKVD said, "that one of Shaposhnikov's tasks as chief of the general staff, a duty he took up after Voroshilov, was placing commanders in the field—at the front?"

"Badunov and Vorontin at First and Second Belorussian sectors . . ."

"Yes, his fledglings on all three fronts. Too much power for one man. Too much power for Comrade Stalin's liking—and for mine. And they meet regularly in Moscow to discuss an operation called Archangel. Go, Shlemov. I don't care how you do it, but get to Branodz. Find out what is going on there. Do it now!"

Malenkoy was as surprised as the dozen or so other junior officers at the HQ for the First Ukrainian front in Brandoz when Marshal Boris Shaposhnikov, Hero of the Soviet Union and chief of general staff, walked into the operations room unannounced, escorted by General Nerchenko.

Marshal Ivan Konev, the commander in chief of the First Ukrainian front, snapped to attention, but tried not to wear the same startled expression as the other men in the small operations room.

Malenkoy pretended to carry on with his work, placing the finishing touches to the charts outlining the main components of his *maskirovka*, but he was too excited to concentrate. The starting gun for the race to Berlin was already raised; Shaposhnikov's sudden arrival meant that the firing hammer had just been cocked.

The marshals seemed to measure each other up before embracing.

"Welcome to Branodz, Comrade Shaposhnikov," Konev said. "From here you will witness the beginning of the destruction of the heart of the Third Reich."

"I aim to have a hand in it myself," Shaposhnikov said, loud enough for everyone to catch the remark. Malenkoy had heard of the man's charisma. Now he could feel it.

"It would be an honor to have our efforts on the First Ukrainian front guided by your hand," Konev said.

A sudden burst of radio traffic cut through the stilted exchange. The operator, a young lieutenant, moved to silence the screech of static that accompanied the words of the field commander, and to listen instead to the man's status report through the headset.

"Leave it," Shaposhnikov ordered over the noise. "It sounds better than any symphony to an old man who has heard nothing but the snow and leaves fall in Moscow these past months. I didn't know how much I had missed the battlefield until now."

General Nerchenko took a step forward. "Get on with your work," he barked, first at the lieutenant, then at the rest of them, sweeping the operations room with his gaze. "The Comrade marshal will not tolerate complacency in the hour of our victory."

Malenkoy redoubled his efforts at checking the *maskirovka*, even though there was nothing more to do. His part in the buildup was all but complete, and now he was left only with reporting its conclusion to Nerchenko, as soon as the opportunity presented itself.

Konev bristled momentarily at the way his second-in-command had undermined his authority, but said nothing. He was aware that there was some personal friendship between Shaposhnikov and his number two, and he did not want to suffer the ignominy of a rebuke from the marshal in front of his men. He just wanted Shaposhnikov out of there as quickly as possible so that he could attend to running the war in the sector he regarded very much as his own. The last thing he needed was interference from Moscow.

"I am afraid we have had no time to prepare a room for you, Comrade Marshal Shaposhnikov," Konev said.

Shaposhnikov waved him aside. "Do not concern yourself. I will share the quarters of my old friend, General Nerchenko. It is some time now since we taught together at Voroshilov. We have much to talk about."

"Perhaps you would like to begin your tour of the front? As soon as you have settled in, that is." Konev wanted elbow room.

"The comrade marshal is tired after the long journey, no doubt," Nerchenko cut in. "I will take him and his ADC, Colonel Krilov, to my quarters immediately."

"So be it." Konev gave a curt nod and clicked his heels.

A cry, muffled by the crackle of static electricity, burst from the radio. The field commander's bulletin had been interrupted by some sort of attack.

Konev shrugged it off. "It is just a probing mission by a German reconnaissance platoon; there have been several in the past week."

As all attention was drawn toward the exchange between the radio operator and the officer in the field, punctuated by sharp, whiplike cracks of background rifle fire, no one noticed Krilov appear at the doorway. He quickly surveyed the room, saw Shaposhnikov hunched over the radio, then beckoned Nerchenko.

"We will leave you now, Comrade Marshal," Nerchenko said to Konev. "I will be back as soon as I have settled our distinguished guest into my quarters."

Malenkoy sensed, rather than heard, Shaposhnikov and Nerchenko coming back toward him. When he looked up from his work, he stared straight into the general's face.

"Report to me outside in five minutes, Major," Nerchenko snapped. "I want to hear the status of the *maskirovka*."

Once they were a hundred meters from the entrance to the wooden, alpine villa that served as Konev's headquarters, Krilov spoke quickly, trying to keep his voice down.

"It's arrived, Comrade Marshal. The Berezniki consignment is here."

Krilov had not expected the convoy to make such rapid progress.

Shaposhnikov scanned the clearing, an area of several hundred square meters stripped of pine forest and now bustling with military vehicles. In the row of GAZ jeeps, trucks, and motorcycles lined up behind the checkpoint he saw the convoy he had last encountered at the Ostrava railhead.

The almost boyish excitement that had lit the marshal's eyes inside the HQ was gone. "A little earlier than we anticipated, but at least it is here, safe and sound."

He breathed the cold, crisp air appreciatively, a gesture that was not lost on either of the two men before him. Nerchenko, especially, had been able to think of little else in the last few hours. All it would have taken was one bullet to puncture a shell casing in one of the trucks . . . He realized his aggressiveness in the HQ had been a direct consequence of this nervousness, but he had been unable to control it.

"The documentation and packaging registers the consignment as sanitation equipment, but it should be stowed as quickly as possible," Krilov said. "Konev and the NKVD are too close for my liking."

"It is already taken care of," Nerchenko said.

As if on cue, the door of the HQ opened and Malenkoy appeared in the bright sunshine. He lifted his hand to shield his eyes from the glare and then dropped it the moment he spotted Nerchenko, with Marshal Shaposhnikov and a colonel by his side, in the midst of the clearing. He broke into his best parade-ground step and brought himself to attention a meter in front of Nerchenko.

"Comrade General, the *maskirovka* is complete."

"Good, Major," Nerchenko said. "All that remains is for you to start the radio transmissions and light the fires at Chrudim. First, however, I want you to assist in some administrative work here at Branodz."

"Yes, Comrade General." Malenkoy's gaze remained straight, despite his desire to look toward Shaposhnikov.

"You see that line of trucks over there? Take some men and get them marshaled immediately. Colonel Krilov here will show you where to put all the crates. We don't want Comrade Marshal Shaposhnikov to have to suffer the sight or smell of sanitation equipment on his illustrious visit to the front, do we?"

"No, Comrade General." He snapped to attention and turned to go, a hot flush of embarrassment rising to the roots of his hair.

"Major." Shaposhnikov's calm voice stopped Malenkoy in his tracks.

"Yes, Comrade Marshal."

"General Nerchenko has spoken to me of your efforts with the *maskirovka* at Chrudim. I myself would like to congratulate you for what you have done there."

Malenkoy mumbled his thanks and walked with Krilov toward the trucks. His humiliation at being asked to schlepp crates of sanitation equipment evaporated, and there was a new spring in his step.

7

Kruze looked at his watch. In just over an hour he would be in the Auster. The cocoonlike environment of the EAEU had often sheltered him from the real war, and sometimes he'd been grateful for it. Now, at Stabitz, its aircraft and buildings still smoldering from the fires set by the Luftwaffe as it retreated to the next bolt-hole a few miles down the road, he knew he was about to make amends.

Fleming's voice cut into his thoughts. Another briefing. He must have gone over Guardian Angel a hundred times. To Fleming, the perfectionist, it was not enough. There always had to be one more.

The man's eyes shone where only days before they had been gray and lackluster. But Kruze could not read them and that worried him. He still felt Penny's shadow across them both, and wasn't sure whether he regarded Robert as friend or foe.

The Rhodesian, dressed in the dark, civilian suit and reversible raincoat of his Romanian alias—Stefan Krazianu, emissary of the crumbling government in Bucharest—shifted uncomfortably in his chair and tried to concentrate on Fleming's instructions. Herries had told him it could save his life, as if he didn't bloody well know it. He didn't like the look of that nasty piece of work, either. It was an impression not eased by the fact that the man from military intelligence was sitting beside him in the full regalia of an obersturmführer in the Waffen SS, and the costume fitted him well.

"The Auster's going to land with us on a frozen lake?" The incredulity in Herries' voice brought Kruze back to the briefing. "It's damned near spring, man. Where is there ice thick enough to support an airplane this time of year?"

"In the Bavarian Alps," Fleming replied. "There's a large lake, south of Munich, close to the Austrian border, called the Achensee. The ice is still thick there; that's where you're going in."

"But it's about fifty miles from Munich! What happened to the original plan? I thought you were going to get us within walking distance of the city."

Again, Kruze tried to fathom the man behind the voice. Was there panic there? It didn't seem to gel with Staverton's picture of the shepherd.

"We were, but it's changed," Fleming said. "As you know, the Auster was to have dropped you closer, but the Americans have advanced more rapidly than we anticipated in the last twenty-four hours. They're almost at the suburbs and, with the Luftwaffe getting jumpy, an Allied aircraft is never going to be able to slip through without catching it in the neck. So we need to play safe. It was Staverton's idea, not mine, but I'm sure that a man of your talents, Herries, will be able to overcome such obstacles. You should be there by first light tomorrow morning."

"Is there anything else you haven't told us about?" Herries asked.

"Nothing. The rest of Guardian Angel is the same. Once in the city, make your way to the old center, just south of the Englische Garten—that's a long park that runs almost the length of Munich."

"I know Munich," Herries interrupted. "I spent some time there—before the war."

"Of course," Fleming said, "I should have remembered." Herries' training and indoctrination for the Britische Freikorps had taken place at the SS camp in Bad Tolz, just outside Munich. "I think quite a lot will have changed since your last visit."

He paused, then turned suddenly to Kruze. "What's the watchmaker's address?"

"Seventeen Piloty Strasse, ground floor. That's where we find Schell and his boy."

"What do you do there?"

"We bed down in the basement and wait for the watchmaker to finish our papers—the ones that will get us into Oberammergau."

"Right. And?"

"On no account are we to go out before we make the journey to Oberammergau."

"Why?"

Kruze paused. It was pretty damned obvious why they shouldn't leave the sanctity of the forger's safe house.

"*Kampfgruppen*," Herries interrupted. "SS battle groups. If we're spotted wandering aimlessly around the place we're liable to get shot as deserters, or rounded up to serve in a KG unit."

"What the hell are KG units?" Kruze asked.

"They're sort of ad hoc platoons, organized by the SS, drawing from any personnel source they can find to plug the gaps," Herries answered. "Once we get into one of those, who knows where we could get sent in the defense of the Reich."

"But I'm supposed to be a Romanian government official, a civilian," Kruze said.

"The SS don't care who you are," Herries said, ice cold. "You could be an old man, or a child, but when you get assigned to a KG squad you don't argue, believe me, fly-boy."

Kruze saw the lip curl into a smile. The more he saw of the man, the more he disliked him. He kept on having to tell himself that, given the importance of the mission, Staverton would not have risked sending him in with anyone but the best.

"Once Schell has forged your papers, what's your next move, Herries?" Fleming asked.

"We wait till midnight, take his car, and set off for Oberammergau. It should only take a couple of hours."

"Under normal circumstances, yes. But there will be refugees, more roadblocks than usual, American snipers maybe. And then?"

"We bluff our way onto the airfield."

"Your excuse?"

"Kruze—er, Krazianu—has to be flown out to join rebel Romanian Army units fighting the Russians outside Bucharest. I am his escort through Germany."

"Remember," Fleming said, "that you have to get to Oberammergau well before oh-six hundred hours."

"To leave me enough time to become Rolf Peiper," Kruze

nodded. "If I go down behind Russian lines, the Soviets then have conclusive proof that it was the Germans who did away with their precious Marshal Shaposhnikov." He leaned back in his chair. "Staverton's thought of everything."

"Only as long as they find you dead," Herries said, smiling. "Got your cyanide pills, fly-boy?"

"I don't need any," the Rhodesian said, patting the Luger in his pocket.

"It's not going to come to that," Fleming interrupted. "We'll get you back again, don't worry." He pressed on, conscious that he hadn't sounded too convincing. "Oh-six hundred is also significant because—"

"That's when the RAF attacks the airfield," Herries cut in. "Look, Fleming, we know all the details. So when do we get out of here?"

"Soon enough, Herries. And to you, I'm still Wing Commander."

Herries stared at his reflection in the gleaming surface of his polished jackboots and sneered. "Yes, sir."

"Let me get this part straight, once and for all," Kruze said. "The strike will happen at oh-six hundred and that's when I'm to take a bombed-up 234, preferably one with long-range tanks. What makes you think I can find one just waiting for me to take it?"

"The Germans are very consistent," Fleming said. "We've had Oberammergau under high-altitude surveillance for a long time. All the photographs have established a pattern. The 234s are readied for their dawn strikes throughout the night. There'll be plenty of aircraft. You'll have to exercise your own judgment as to which is the most suitable aircraft for the mission."

Kruze nodded. It would have to do. "And the Meteors will keep the Germans' heads down long enough for me to work out what the bloody hell I'm doing in an aircraft I've never flown before and then I take off."

Fleming nodded. "Not forgetting to—"

"Waggle my wings when I'm airborne to show the Meteors it's me. How are you explaining away a friendly pilot in the Luftwaffe's latest operational bomber? I thought this op was so secret no one was meant to know about it outside these four walls, give or take a few people on Downing Street."

"We'll think of something," Fleming said. "In the meantime, you're to fly a two-leg course to Branodz, low level all the way, using the maps sewn into your coat. The first leg will keep you in the mountains, your best chance for survival against Allied fighters, which are particularly active over southern Germany and Austria at the moment. You leave the mountains behind about thirty miles west of Salzburg and from then on you only have to worry about the Red Air Force."

"What sort of country is it?"

Fleming twisted the standard lamp around so it shone on the map pinned to the blackboard behind him. He pointed to the 120-mile second leg, tracing its path with a ruler.

"Mostly flat, as you can see, so you'll stand out like a sore thumb if you're not careful. But the 234's fast—it will give you an advantage, despite the concentration of their air defenses. About the only piece of intelligence we have for the area is that the Russians have moved some fighters into the old Luftwaffe base at Grafen, here, so keep it tight; you don't want to stray. It's a short flight, too, so the element of surprise will be very much on your side. The Soviets won't be expecting an attack on Branodz. It's well defended, it's almost impossible to find amongst those valleys unless you know what you're looking for, and they know that the Germans are going balls-out to stop the Americans in the south. So far, the Russians have had it damned easy in Czechoslovakia."

"What about the target itself? When am I going to see a model, study photographs?"

"We haven't got any."

Kruze shook his head in disbelief. "I can't go in there with no idea what it is I'm meant to be bombing, for Christ's sake."

"And we can't just send in a Mosquito two hundred miles behind Soviet lines on a photo jaunt. We do have eyewitness reports, though." He tried to make it sound casual. "Herries, over to you."

Herries cast his mind back to his fleeting recce of Brandoz. He repeated what he had already told his debriefers in London a dozen times.

"The building you're looking for is a large alpine villa, chalet style, of all-wooden construction," the traitor said. "It's situated on the edge of the town, in a clearing that doubles as a motor pool. It's easily the largest building in the village and has flags sticking out of every orifice. Even at the speed you'll be coming in at, you won't be able to miss it."

"Remember," Fleming added, "we know that Shaposhnikov will be manning the radio between oh-six-thirty and oh-seven-hundred." He paused. "We've also heard from Moscow that he's already at Branodz. If you time your attack for around oh-six-forty, you'll catch him in the operations room, just after his early morning shit. You might even get him while he's still got his trousers down."

Kruze laughed, purging the tension that had been building in his muscles and knotting his stomach. At first, Fleming's expression did not alter, then he allowed himself a smile. "You've worked with the Lotfe bombsight at Farnborough. At the height you'll drop from, you can't miss; you'll obliterate the entire area."

"I hate to break up the party," Herries said, "but what about our escape routes?"

"Once Kruze is on his way, get out of Oberammergau and lie low, wait for the Americans to advance, and surrender yourself to them. We'll get you out of their custody as soon as we can." He saw Herries move to protest and then realized that there was nothing he could say in front of Kruze. "You'll just have to trust us," Fleming said.

"As for you, Piet, once you've dropped your bombs on Sha-poshnikov you'll be low on fuel, so head west as fast as you can. Make as if you're going for the German lines, that's important, but as soon as you're in the clear, divert to any Allied airfield. We can't tell anyone to expect you, for obvious reasons, so make sure you land on your first approach. As soon as they see that you're surrendering an Ar 234 to them, they'll let you in. Then sit tight and don't say anything until the EAEU comes to get you."

Fleming wandered over to the window, pulled the tattered curtain aside and studied the night sky. There was a bright, three-quarter moon with intermittent cloud cover, light enough for the Auster pilot to see the landing area, but too dark for them to be picked up by night fighters . . . hopefully. He looked at his watch and then to Kruze. It was just past eleven.

"The Auster leaves at midnight. Try to snatch some rest. If you have any further questions, I'll tackle them on the way out to the aircraft."

As the two of them moved for the door, Fleming caught the traitor's eye. "Herries, I want to talk to you," he said.

Fleming waited until they were quite alone.

"It hasn't escaped our notice that you could quite easily shoot Kruze in the back and blame your German friends. But if you live and he doesn't, we're not going to believe you, it's as simple as that."

213

Herries said nothing.

"So, we've built in a little safeguard just to make sure you don't do anything rash," Fleming continued. "Although Kruze isn't allowed to know who you are, I'm going to give him a code word. He will pass it on to you when—and only when—you finally part company at Oberammergau. He'll think it's to let us know that he got to the aircraft in one piece."

Fleming looked into Herries' eyes and allowed himself to smile. "You, on the other hand, can look on it as the only way you'll dodge the gallows."

☐

After wrestling with his conscience in the solitude of the briefing room, Fleming sprang to his feet and strode outside, slamming the door behind him.

Kruze, about to risk his life, deserved better. He had resolved to tell the Rhodesian about Herries. The longer he spent with the traitor, the more he realized that Kruze needed to be forewarned, code word or not.

☐

Kruze was too wound up to rest. The room was cold and miserable, with only the muted glow of an old hurricane lamp to see by, and he suddenly ached for Penny.

There was a faint knock at the door. Fleming looked in hesitantly, then entered when he saw Kruze was awake.

"I thought I'd see how you were doing." He drew a chair up beside Kruze's bed. "Cigarette?" He offered the pack.

"No thanks," Kruze said, still staring at the ceiling. He sensed Fleming's awkwardness in the silence that hung between them.

"How did you feel before you went into Rostock?"

Fleming took a long pull on his cigarette and watched the blue smoke curl in the chill air. "Rostock . . . seems like a bloody lifetime ago. I remember . . . it felt like everything was down to me, just me. But it wasn't Staverton I didn't want to disappoint, it was myself."

Kruze nodded. "Staverton wouldn't have given a shit if you hadn't come back, as long as he'd got his precious 163C. Don't think I have any illusions about his intentions toward Rolf Peiper. He'd do anything, bend any rule, to get the job done."

Fleming tried to explain the other side of Staverton, the man who had helped push him toward recovery, but all he could think of was the AVM's refusal to tell the truth about Herries.

"That's balls, Robert. Stop kidding yourself. Why do you think he sent you into Rostock, for a miracle cure? You're one hell of a good intelligence officer, but Staverton seems to have owned you, body and soul, since Italy."

"Christ, you don't mince words, do you?" Fleming threw the cigarette to the floor and ground in the stub with his boot. "I didn't know my past was aired so openly around the EAEU."

Kruze took his eyes off the crumbling, yellowed paint above the bed and looked across at Fleming. There was none of the self-pity in his face that he had expected.

"No one knows who you really are, Robert, so no one talks about you, except for Mulvaney and you know what he's like; holds you in the highest admiration, old boy, and all that."

Fleming smiled, shaking his head. "Admiration from a pompous, stuffed shirt like Mulvaney. God, I must have been an even bigger prick than I thought.

"I've always thought of us as having quite a lot in common, you know, Piet. Does anyone know who you are?" Behind Fleming's eyes there was a serenity and a wisdom that disturbed Kruze. The words, delivered without any trace of malice, hit him hard.

"There was someone. I think she knew."

"Someone to go back to?"

"Right now I can only think of Shaposhnikov," Kruze answered, stiffly.

Fleming lit another cigarette. "I wish I shared your sense of professionalism."

"How do you mean?"

"You asked me about Rostock. To tell you the truth, it was Penny who kept me going. This past year has been pretty bad for us, and I realized then that it was my fault, that it was up to me to do something about it. A little late in the day."

Again, Kruze felt the cramp in his stomach. Fleming had stopped, was pulling on his cigarette. "What exactly happened to you in Italy?"

Fleming hesitated, then began. "I was on the tail of an FW 190. I remember feeling elated; he was slap in the middle of my sights, didn't have a clue I was there. I thought he must have been half-asleep, so I closed the range, just to make sure. Stupid. I was the dozy one. I must have been about a hundred feet behind him, when he lowered his undercarriage and flaps—just like you did with the Junkers the other day. I shot past him and the next thing I knew was his cannon thumping into

215

the wings and the fuselage. Then the instrument panel exploded and I blacked out."

Fleming took another drag from his cigarette.

"I came to with this bloody awful pain in my side. The aircraft was in an inverted spin and I reached up and tried to pull the hood back. But my Mae West dug into me and hurt like hell, so I reached down to untie it. It came as a bit of a bloody surprise when I found I had no Mae West and most of my tunic was missing and there was just this big hole in the left side of my body. Then I just started watching the ground spinning lazily overhead. I would have been quite happy to have carried on like that, except the shell that hit the instrument panel had also severed my oxygen pipe and I started to breathe in the flames which had eaten through the forward bulkhead. I gave the canopy a bloody good tug and then I must have been sucked out. God knows how I opened the 'chute, because I don't remember a thing between sitting in the cockpit and waking up in bed in a field hospital."

He dropped the cigarette next to the first stub. "So there you have it. Penny must have been by my side for every single hour of the day and night when they shipped me back to England. They told me afterward that when she wasn't in the operating theater watching bits of metal being removed from me, she was in that chair by my bed, holding my hand, worried sick. She thought I was going to die. I did die for a while—here, inside." He thumped his chest with his fist. "But not then. That came later."

"How long did it take for you to come to?" Half of Kruze wanted Fleming to stop, but the other was mesmerized.

"I was in a coma for about three months. It's funny, you know. No one could possibly have loved a woman more than I loved her on that morning in Tuscany. I suppose I thought that there wasn't a hope in hell she would want to stay with a man who couldn't change his own clothes, who had to be spoon-fed, pissed himself without even knowing it. So I shut her off, before she had the chance to leave me. There were violent moments too, when I couldn't even control my actions. God, I hated myself for that. Even so, I loved her all that time. I just bent over backward not to let her know . . ." His voice trailed away.

Suddenly he said, "I've never told a soul before."

"You've changed, Robert, that's why. You're no longer the prick of the EAEU."

216

Fleming stared at him for a second and then burst out laughing. "I suppose from you, Kruze, that's a compliment."

Kruze allowed himself a smile. "It was meant to be one." He took one of his own cigarettes from his pocket and lit it. "What are you going to do about your wife?"

"She wants a divorce, so it's probably too late for us. I have to start getting realistic. Still, I'd just like a chance to explain."

Kruze swung his feet off the bed and sat on the edge of the mattress.

"It's not too late, Robert." Kruze took a deep breath. "If you get out of this shithole alive, and there's every reason why you should, you must go to her as soon as you can."

Fleming laughed again. In the dim, half-light of the room, he looked ten years younger. "Piet, you've only met her once, you don't know her; she's a headstrong girl and—"

Kruze cut him off. "No, Robert, I bumped into her a few days ago. I was leaving the ministry and she was heading in to deliver the letter."

"The infamous letter. So, you knew we were getting divorced."

"Only later. She seemed upset, so I bought her a drink. That was when she told me."

"I see," Fleming said, his voice suddenly distant.

"She loves you, don't you see? The letter was a cry for help."

Fleming straightened. "How can you possibly know? Did she tell you all this?"

"She didn't have to. It was obvious. The girl is still in love with you."

"You really don't have to do this, Kruze. I've come to terms with it. Look at me, I've made a full recovery." He held his arms out. "But this is not the man she married. He never got out of that Spitfire over Monte Lupo."

Kruze felt an urge to shake him. "You look like the same guy to me."

Fleming shrugged. "You didn't know me then."

"I saw the photograph of you in the Spit . . ."

Fleming got to his feet. The look of bewilderment had changed to anger. "I only sent that picture to her a month ago, long after you came to the cottage."

"What are you talking about?" Kruze pushed himself off the bed.

"The shot of me in the Spitfire. I found it in the Bunker and sent it to her. Now you tell me you've seen it at the cottage. What the bloody hell were you doing there?"

Kruze shook his head. "It's nothing."

Fleming pushed the chair back. "I asked you what you were doing there."

Kruze dropped his cigarette. "I told you. We met quite by chance. It must have been the day before you were sent to Rostock. We saved a child from that V2 blast near the ministry. That night I had a long talk with her. Two days later we had a bite to eat in Padbury."

Fleming's face twisted in disbelief.

In the semi-darkness, Kruze saw the fist coming a little too late. He made no attempt to parry it, but tried to duck. The blow caught him on the side of the face and he fell backward against the thin wall of the hut. He shook his head and began pulling himself onto his feet, but Fleming's hands were already on him, dragging him up.

His breath was coming in deep, convulsing gasps. "You've got a fucking nerve, Kruze."

Even with his head ringing from the blow, Kruze easily wrenched the other man's grip from him. With all his might he pushed, ramming Fleming up against the far wall. The whole hut rocked.

"Listen, Robert, I didn't start telling you this so I can have a bloody good gloat. I'm trying to get it into your stupid skull that she may not know it, but she still loves you, and you're never going to discover that for yourself if you sit on your ass, thinking about the good times you could have had."

Fleming tried to push himself free, but Kruze had him pinned hard against the wall. Fleming rammed his face right up to the Rhodesian's.

"Did you touch her?"

"You said it yourself; we're two of a kind. She's lonely and afraid, but it's not me she wants. She wants you, needs you, but you have to make the move. Don't waste any time when you get back. Go to her."

Kruze felt Fleming's body relax, saw his eyes look away. He drew back, not sure what would happen next. Fleming's breath came more easily as he looked into the Rhodesian's face, straightening his tie and uniform as he did so.

"I need to get some air," Fleming said, simply. "The Auster leaves in fifteen minutes." And with that, he stepped out into the night.

Stalin looked at the two reports on his desk. He picked up the first and held it to his chest for a moment in the silence of his office. The news could not have been better. All across the front, the great nine-hundred-fifty-kilometer front, the British had halted their eastward advance and were digging in.

All the signs were clear. Archangel was in London. In a short time it would be in Washington too.

Sabak could feel his master's elation.

"What about the other matter?" Stalin asked.

"The problem is solved," Sabak said. "We have obtained the Nerchenko girl's complete cooperation. It seems the prospect of her father being informed of her little performances for Comrade Beria terrified her more than the chief of internal security himself."

"But has she served her purpose?" Stalin asked.

Sabak smiled. "We need make no other arrangements, Comrade Stalin. She was going to give the game away sooner or later, but as it happened, she tripped the wire sooner than we expected. It's all in the report."

Stalin opened the second file and read the dispatch. With scant clues available to him, Beria had nonetheless picked up the trail.

He read on. Shlemov had been sent to Branodz. Stalin knew the diligence of Beria's most tenacious investigator; he would now be roaming the First Ukrainian front, pulling in the missing strands.

On the other hand, Shlemov was a loose cannon, Stalin thought to himself. A little knowledge in his hands was certainly a dangerous thing. Something had to be done.

He closed the file and started drafting the note. Sabak could ensure that it was typed up, with no clue to its origins, and delivered anonymously to Beria's love-nest on Kuznecki Most.

Beria and Shlemov would take it from there.

□

Herries had taken his cap off and thrown an RAF greatcoat over his shoulders to shield his uniform from the USAAF groundcrew who worked through the night to get their battle-weary Mustangs ready for operations the following morning. Despite their proximity to the front line, there was hardly any gunfire to be heard, the wind carrying most of the sound back inside the retreating borders of the Reich, but every now and again the horizon lit up as another Allied artillery barrage began to pummel the Wehrmacht's positions around the Bavarian capital, a mere 20 kilometres away.

They jumped into the jeep. Fleming drove, while Kruze peered through the night trying to avoid any source of light, the distant gunfire, the glow of an arc-welder's torch, or the sparks belching from the exhaust of a night fighter taxying by. Although the moon would allow the Auster pilot good visibility for their short journey to the Achensee, he would need the help of an extra pair of eyes to spot for any Luftwaffe night stalkers that might latch onto their scent.

As they journeyed in silence to the far end of the airfield where the Auster was waiting, Kruze's urge to speak to Fleming intensified until it became almost agonizing. But there was nothing he could say in front of Herries, who was hunched, animal-like on the back seat, shielding himself against the cold slipstream as the jeep bounced across the frozen, pitted ground.

They passed a row of sleek aircraft tucked away in their dispersal pens. Kruze strained for a better look, his eyes tracing their forms: the graceful lines, the curious bulge in the middle of each wing where the powerplants were grafted to the airframe, and the short nose, from which four lethal-looking twenty-millimeter cannon protruded.

"The Meteors that are going to give us a hand at Oberammergau?"

Fleming nodded, but said nothing.

They left the RAF jets behind and drove on for another half minute in silence. Fleming seemed agitated. He took a wrong turn behind a hangar, cursed, and set off on the right course again. Then, Kruze caught a glimpse of the Auster a few hundred yards ahead of them, its distinctive high-set wings shimmering in the blinkered headlights of the jeep.

They pulled up alongside it. The pilot was in the cockpit doing his last instrument checks, the motor was idling. Herries shed the blue-gray greatcoat, donned his peaked cap, and jumped from the back of the jeep and pulled himself on board, settling himself in the rear of the cabin, which was just big enough for three.

Kruze, still in his seat, turned to Fleming, who was gripping the steering wheel, staring straight ahead. Kruze looked to the aircraft. The pilot was beckoning him toward the passenger door.

Fleming turned to face him. When the words came they were fast, urgent.

"Whatever you do, don't look up at the aircraft," he said. "Herries is a traitor who served in some sort of British legion in the SS on the eastern front. Staverton made a bargain with him: his amnesty in exchange for getting you into Oberammergau. I had to tell you—you had a right to know."

A thousand questions churned inside the Rhodesian. Fleming carried on before Kruze had a chance to ask any of them.

"Herries has to get a code word off you before he leaves you at Oberammergau. The word itself isn't important, and as far as you're concerned it's to signal us that you made it to the base. But Herries knows that if anything happens to you and he doesn't get the word, he swings.

"Piet, watch him like a hawk. If he gives any trouble, shoot him. No questions, no mercy. Which is what you'll get if you fall inside Russian territory. I'm sorry . . . Have you got that? About Herries, I mean."

"What's the code word?"

"How about 'traitor's gate'? Should be easy to remember. But for God's sake don't give it to him until you're about to take the aircraft."

Fleming could see the pilot beckoning. "About the other matter," he said. He looked up as a cloud scudded across the face of the moon. "It hasn't been a waste; at least, I don't think so." He hesitated. "Good luck."

Kruze pulled up the collar of his coat and jumped into the passenger seat beside the pilot, who opened up the throttles and eased the Auster onto the runway. With its hybrid wheel and skid assembly it rolled down the concrete, fighting for airspeed. Then it disappeared from Fleming's view into the night. He listened to the fading sound of its engine long after it had lifted off and turned southeast toward the Alps.

BOOK THREE

1

Malenkoy was still too excited to sleep. The chief of the general staff had congratulated him on his *maskirovka* and that was all he could think about. Now he patrolled his way around Chrudim, looking over his dummy tanks, vehicles, and gun emplacements with a new sense of pride.

During this moment, even the chaos and the fear that the SS had brought into his sector had receded to the very back of his mind.

Even close up, his mock-ups seemed alive. The fires and lamps flickered around them, and shadows moved, like men scurrying around their tanks, making final preparations. From the air it would look just like the camp of an army that was poised to rout the enemy. A liberating army, confident that this was the last push, an army that knew victory was close at hand.

Soon the Luftwaffe pilots would come again. This time they would bring listening equipment and hear the radio transmissions—orders from generals to men in the field, requisitions for more equipment to be sent up to the front, signals to start the engines of the T-34s.

The intelligence would fly back to Berlin. The Wehrmacht would be mobilized to meet the threat of his ghost army.

Meanwhile in the next valley over, stealthy preparations continued to build up Marshal Konev's very real divisions to assault-strength, preparations that would go unseen now, thanks to him.

He looked down at his chest and saw the Order of Lenin, which was surely his just reward now, swinging from his tunic. To Malenkoy, the vision was as real as the *maskirovka* would be to the Luftwaffe when they arrived at dawn.

□

The moonlit lake at Achensee was iced over from shore to shore, just as Fleming had said it would be. Kruze looked down and saw a sparkling, frosted pane of glass lying unbroken in a basin between the mountain peaks, some twenty-five hundred meters above sea-level. As they flew around it, the pilot chopping the Auster's engine right back, he was relieved to see that there was no sign of habitation on the lake's banks, but beyond the banks it was hard to tell. Below the tree line, the landscape was covered by an immense blanket of thick pine forest, a light layer of snow on the tops of its trees.

A thousand feet above the ground, the pilot picked out an imaginary runway on the ice and banked the Auster around a pinnacle of rock at the far end of the three-sided valley to line himself up for the approach. Throughout the half-hour journey no one had spoken, but Kruze did not have to question the young flight lieutenant to know that this was by no means his first trip behind enemy lines.

With jagged rocks behind them and more peaks stretching up into the night sky on either side of the Auster's wingtips, the pilot cut the engine and began sideslipping the little airplane, losing height in careful, measured steps, until they soared silently below the treetops and out over the lake.

It crossed Kruze's mind that the ice might not be able to sustain the weight of the aircraft. If the ice began to crack up below the Auster's skids—and with the option to put on power closed to them—it would all be over in a second.

They came in to a dead-stick landing, the skids brushing the frozen surface in a perfect three-pointer. Over the diminishing noise of the slipstream and the swish of the skids, Kruze asked the pilot to try to position them at the far end of the lake where, a few moments before, he and Herries had spotted the white water of the mountain stream trickling down toward the valley below. There, they would pick up the road that would eventually lead them into Munich—provided Herries could get transport.

The Auster slid to a stop a hundred yards from the shoreline. Kruze moved fast, scrabbling out of the front seat, Herries seconds behind him. They sprinted for the trees, slipping and sliding on the ice, the Rhodesian looking back only once across the luminous silence to catch the wave of the pilot, whose name he had never known. In a few minutes, after they had had time to slip into the vast expanse of the forest, the Auster's Lycoming would be gunned into life and the pilot would coax the aircraft into the night sky, back to the safety of the Allied lines.

They found the stream, neither of them speaking, for every step, every movement seemed to crash in their ears beside the lightly burbling waters that rippled the silence of the night. Kruze kept on telling himself that his mind exaggerated the sound, that his imagination had conjured up the whispers, the snapping twigs, and the crunch of snow under boots that seemed to emanate from every corner of the forest.

Herries led the way down the slope, always keeping the brook just a little way to his left. Kruze looked at the new SOE-issue Swiss watch given to him by Fleming earlier that afternoon. The luminous face told him they had only been on Reich soil for a few minutes, but already it seemed like a lifetime. Even the slow-motion world of aerial combat, in which a pilot might have engaged a score of enemy fighters in a tenth of that time, seemed like sanctuary to him at that moment. Here he was a stranger, vulnerable, out of his element, with only Herries to help him.

It was already nearly half-past one. Taking his eyes off Herries for a split second, he sought out the star-speckled inkiness of the night sky between the trees. In just under five hours dawn would be upon them. They had to be out of the wood long before then for Herries to find the means to get them into the city. He remembered the vast area of trees he had seen from the aircraft and began to doubt that they would ever make the valley floor in time.

As Kruze bounded down the mountainside, the cold stung his throat each time he drew in gulps of air to feed his aching limbs. Herries was like a mountain goat; it was all he could do to keep his eyes on the stark outline of the obersturmführer's uniform, silhouetted against the snow. He stumbled on a tree root that lurked unseen beneath the white carpet, and fell headlong at Herries' heels.

He lay there gasping for breath, his cheek smarting from the thousands of razor-sharp ice particles that pierced his skin. Further movement seemed impossible.

Then a new sound, a new smell. Herries' breath close to his face, the condensation mingling with his own. The voice, when it came, was a hoarse whisper in his ear.

"Get up, fly-boy. This is no moment to rest."

"No, we stay here for a minute," he panted.

Herries grabbed his shoulder and rolled him over. "In the forest, I'm king," he said. "Now move."

A sudden noise, like a buzz saw, split the night. Kruze saw Herries go into a tense crouch, his fingers clawing at his holster; a moment later, the Luger was in his hand.

"It's only the Auster taking off," Kruze said.

"All the more reason to put a bit of distance between us and the lake," the traitor hissed. "If there are any troops in the area, they'll find the landing point and our trail in no time. We've got to get lower down, below the snow line; that way, we're virtually impossible to track."

Herries' thin face seemed to glow green in the moonlight that filtered between the branches as the Auster droned off into the distance. He prodded Kruze in the ribs with the barrel of the gun. "You heard me; let's go."

In a sudden, fluid motion Kruze was on his feet and Herries was without his gun.

"I don't know who you are, or where you've come from," the Rhodesian snarled, "but never, ever pull your gun on me again, do you understand?"

"So you can move fast," Herries smiled. "I'm impressed."

Herries snatched the weapon back and slipped it into his holster, his eyes remaining fixed on Kruze's face. For a moment, they stood there, two dark shadows in the vastness of the forest, shoulders square to each other, scarcely a foot between them, then Herries moved off, twisting between the trees down the mountainside.

Kruze loped after him, settling into a mechanical rhythm after a while, enabling him to think about the man in front. Fleming's hasty warning had confirmed his own suspicions about Herries and in a strange way, it made him feel better.

They carried on at an unrelenting pace down the steep slope, pausing to rest one minute in every fifteen, until the snow began to give way to a rocky, stick-strewn, forest floor. Ahead, Herries appeared to relax. They had been going for about three hours; the mountain had to bottom out soon.

Herries had stopped running and was moving toward the stream. Kruze joined him by the bubbling water. The rushing filled his ears. It sounded good, invigorating, a long way from the war.

"Drink," Herries said, "even if you're not thirsty."

To Kruze, the order was superfluous. He took long, deep gulps of the crisp mountain water cupped in his hands and then splashed more over his face and neck, allowing the cold rivulets to run down his chest and back, cooling his sweat-stained body.

He looked over to the obersturmführer, who was on his haunches, leaning against a rock. Every now and then he sipped water, birdlike, and then threw some onto the back of his neck.

"Where did you learn to do all this?" Kruze asked. He couldn't resist it.

Herries' eyes swiveled around the forest briefly as if to warn Kruze that they might be overheard, but he realized that the sound of the stream would have drowned their conversation to anyone standing more than a few yards away.

"I served in a commando unit," he said.

"It couldn't have been just any mob." Herries seemed to flinch. "You must have done a lot of covert stuff behind the lines to have been selected for this. I suppose you'll be returning to your old unit when it's over—if we get out, that is."

"Unlikely," Herries said. "They're dead. The unit's been disbanded, you might say." He was back in the clearing above Chrudim, standing over Dyer, Gunnersby, McCowan . . . all of them, very, very dead. He splashed more water over his face. "And you ask too many questions, fly-boy. Save your breath for the rest of the journey. We leave here in five minutes."

Kruze suddenly wanted to get away from him. The forest seemed to call as the bush below the Mateke had, a long time ago.

"Don't go far," Herries said, as the Rhodesian moved off.

Kruze walked a little way from the stream, his hands thrust deep into the pockets of his raincoat. He found the ersatz cigarettes that had been provided for him at the airfield: cheap, German, military-issue tobacco, rolled in tatty paper that was too thick, so it kept going out. Herries would have told him not to smoke, the smell and the glow of the tip being obvious intrusions in the primeval world of the forest.

Kruze saw an outcrop of rock, rising up through the gloom ahead; there would be crags and nooks enough there for him to hide the flare of a match, and to hell with the smoke.

Then he saw the movement and froze.

At first he thought it was Herries, but almost as soon as the idea crossed his mind he knew that was impossible. In the fifty yards he had walked from the stream, Herries would not have been able to work his way around to his front, to be standing where this figure was, to the right of the outcrop.

Kruze had never felt so vulnerable. A patch of moonlight illuminated the ground between him and the rock and played delicately over the man standing not more than thirty yards away. He could see a peaked cap, a long coat and a rifle slung over the shoulder. The figure's back was turned three-quarters from him, but was moving as if surveying the forest.

A sentry. Turning toward him.

Kruze began lowering his body, pulling his arms in, hunching his shoulders, so slowly that he knew he would not be able to get to the ground before the sentry's eyes swept his position. Shooting him was the only other option but, his mind screamed over the fear, there would be others.

He was bent almost double, with the soldier's line of vision perpendicular to his own, when a cloud covered the moon and the spotlight above him went out. It was his only chance. Kruze pitched forward, his arms sinking into the deep, wet, pine carpet lining the forest floor, muffling his fall. He felt the stick caught between his right hand and the damp earth below, felt it bend beneath his weight. He held his breath.

The twig snapped.

The sentry did not utter a sound, but Kruze heard him unsling the rifle and take a step forward. Then another. He was coming his way. The Rhodesian's eyes were wide open, but he dared not move his head, which pointed toward the advancing sentry, making it impossible for him to see what was going on. All he knew was that the moon was still behind the cloud. But for how long?

The steps stopped. The cloud held. And a new fear gripped him. Herries would bound out from the small ravine and be spotted in an instant. He cursed his stupidity.

The sentry was almost on him. Above the noise of his pounding heart he heard the man's breathing, the creak of his leather boots. The patch of ground before his face began to glow, its luminescence increasing as the veil slipped from the face of the moon. There was a sudden rush of movement, a muffled cry of animal surprise, then the hands were on him, rolling him over.

Herries looked down on him, a knife between his teeth. Kruze, eyes wide in amazement, drew breath to speak, but Herries silenced him with a hand across his mouth. The traitor jabbed a thumb in the direction of the rock and Kruze slowly got to his feet.

The sentry lay in the middle of the pool of light, an obscene red mouth stretching from ear to ear beneath his jawbone.

Herries sheathed the knife and slipped down toward the rock, gesturing for him to follow. Kruze's legs wanted to buckle, but he forced them on.

They worked their way around the outcrop, Herries stopping to listen and sniff every few steps, before he disappeared behind the crag. When he, too, rounded the rock, Kruze saw what it was that Herries had smelled, even though to him there had been nothing unusual in the air. Herries had told him that in the forest he was king; now the Rhodesian believed it.

Five sleeping men were huddled around the smoldering remains of a camp fire. There was no movement, the brief struggle that had just taken place having been shielded by the monolith jutting from the ground between them and the sentry's station. Herries let out a low, almost imperceptible, moan and rolled back against the rock, his face like a death mask. Kruze followed him back to the body of the sentry, by this time wanting answers.

"What is it?" he hissed in the traitor's ear.

"We've got to move fast," Herries whispered, his eyes as wide as the thin slits would allow. "We've got to get away from this place." He found what he was looking for beneath the body of the German; a peaked forage cap.

"They're asleep, Herries. Calm down, for God's sake." Kruze had mastered his nerves. He felt elated that he had been allowed to live, to be free, granted a reprieve to carry on with the mission.

Herries waved the cap in front of Kruze's face. "These aren't ordinary soldiers. They're Gebirgsjäger—crack mountain troops of the Thirteenth SS Gebirgsjäger Battalion. They could find a pin in this forest with their eyes shut." He pointed to the body. "When they find him . . ."

Kruze felt his blood go cold. He slid after Herries, putting new care into his every stride, as they slipped down toward the valley. It wasn't merely the troops he had just seen that worried him; somewhere on that mountain there would be a whole battalion of Gebirgsjäger.

□

It took them another two hours of stealing through the Ge-birgsjäger positions to get to the valley floor. Herries was so good, Kruze thought, that they only saw one other patrol on the mountainside, one that they easily avoided thanks to the traitor's well-developed senses of sight, sound, and smell.

They were poised behind a rock, watching the traffic on the road a hundred yards below. Every now and then Herries, seeing more headlights through his Zeisses, swore under his breath. There was transport galore, hundreds of *kampfwagen* jeeps, armored personnel carriers, and trucks on the road, but all of them were going the wrong way, fleeing Munich for the mountains. To Kruze, Staverton's theory about the Alpine Redoubt now looked horribly real.

"So what happens next?" Kruze asked.

"We have to take one of those vehicles," Herries said, still looking through the binoculars. "And that isn't going to be easy."

"Make your plan soon, Herries, because when that body is found, this place is going to go up and us with it."

Herries let his binoculars swing from their strap. "What do you suggest we do, pilot, just go down there and thumb a ride? If we are searched they will find you without papers. They will shoot you, and me with you, for desertion, or espionage—take your pick—no questions asked."

"You have papers?"

"Provisional ones, yes. Not good enough to get us into the airfield, just basic identification documents."

That devious shit Staverton had let him keep his Reich service papers, Kruze thought.

"Then go down there and requisition a vehicle for your very own KG unit," Kruze said, the urgency in his voice steel-hard.

"What are you talking about, fly-boy?"

"If this place is as chaotic as you said it was, no one's going to think twice about you stopping a truck and forming your own KG squad—only in this case it will just be you, me, and the troops in the vehicle."

"You think they will obey me, one man against all of them? When I said Germany was the closest thing you would find to chaos, I meant chaos with a capital *C*. They would just shoot us and carry on their way."

"Not if you stay authoritative, leave them no other choice."
He saw Herries thinking hard. "The alternative is to stay here
until those mountain troops hunt us down like dogs."

Herries suddenly seemed to stir himself into action. "Then
we wait for a Wehrmacht truck and pray that it hasn't been
requisitioned by the SS."

They slid down the last stretch of scree to some foliage beside
the road. A heavy six-axle truck rumbled past them every thirty
seconds, to their desperate dismay each one bearing the emblem of the Twelfth SS Panzer Grenadiers. Herries bit his lip
impatiently, throwing glances alternately between the vehicles
and the mountain behind them. They needed a regular army
unit, one that would quake at a bit of typical SS bullying, but
they needed it before the Gebirgsjäger came for them.

After half an hour, the Panzer Grenadiers gave way to trucks
from the Second SS Das Reich Division. Kruze battled to keep
his eyes open, but the fatigue of the last few hours began to
spread from his limbs to his head, numbing his mind even to
the drone and vibration of the vehicles grinding their way along
the roadside a few feet from where he lay. He closed his eyes,
no longer caring about the Gebirgsjäger, or the rendezvous they
had to keep with the watchmaker.

He saw Herries leave the ditch by the road and wave down
a truck. He watched, biting his knuckles, as the traitor remonstrated with the driver, but he could not hear their words. At
last, the driver nodded, Herries smiled, and then the tailgate
fell away and the mountain troops dropped to the road, their
machine pistols unslung, pointing at him. Rough hands pulled
at him, while he struggled to find his automatic so as to put
one bullet through the laughing face of Herries and a second
through his own temple.

The hands shook him until he woke up. Herries' face was not
full of mirth as it had been in the dream, but desperation.

"For God's sake, wake up; this is it."

He pulled Kruze from the ditch and into the road. Down the
valley, Kruze saw the two slit beams of light approaching.

"The last two trucks have been from the Fourth Panzer Training Division—regular army—it couldn't be better," Herries
said.

Kruze shook the bitter taste of the dream from his head. "As
long as they weren't strays, sandwiched between more SS
units."

But Herries wasn't listening. "Shut up. Don't say another word till we get to Munich. If anyone asks about you, or talks to you, leave the explanations to me."

Herries stepped into the middle of the road and held out his arms. The brakes squealed and the gears crunched as the vehicle slowed. Kruze looked sidelong at the motif on the cabin door, his heart in his mouth: he could make out a crude stencil of a tank and the number four. Herries' gamble had paid off.

The driver, a gefreiter, could not have been a day over seventeen. He blinked every time Herries barked at him and once tried to step down from the cab to verify something with a superior in the back, but Herries was not having any of it. Herries' was an awe-inspiring performance, his ranting punctuated with words that Kruze could understand, such as "urgent," "orders," "disobedience," and "reprisals." He was pure Aryan bully, arrogance itself, and utterly convincing.

Herries waved Kruze aboard. The Rhodesian slid up into the cab, next to the driver, while Herries went around to the back of the truck. He saw the youth's hands tremble as Herries' orders to whoever was behind them boomed in their ears. No one dissented.

Herries clambered in beside Kruze and hit the dashboard. The driver pushed the gear stick forward and they began the slow turn that would take them into Munich.

2

There was a lightness in Malenkoy's step as he walked from the site of his regular morning ablutions—a backwater of the mountain stream that ran through Chrudim—to his tent, pitched between the sides of two bogus T-34s. As he traced the path through the center of the town, past the tanks of his phantom army, he kept one eye on the lightening skies and one ear cocked for Luftwaffe reconnaissance aircraft.

In the silence of the pre-dawn and the unnatural tranquility of the *maskirovka* encampment, the major's mood drifted into despondency: there was not an airplane engine to be heard; nor was there the buzz of anticipation that usually preceded a new offensive, because his armored regiments were manned, not by troops charged with adrenaline, but a skeleton crew waiting to offer a realistic response when the Luftwaffe came sniffing.

He fumbled his way past the T-34s that stood like leviathan sentries on either side of his tent, tripped on the guy ropes and groped for the flap. When he pulled it back, the familiar, sweat-soaked smells of the interior mingled with something that had not been there when he had left a half hour ago.

The match flared and illuminated the stubbled face of a man he had never seen before. Malenkoy reached for his pistol.

"There won't be any need for the gun, Major."

The voice carried an authority that Malenkoy responded to instinctively.

"Who are you?" he stammered.

"The name's Shlemov. I've come from Moscow." He lit the lamp and threw the match to the ground. "I've been looking for you all night."

"What do you want with me?" Malenkoy asked, suddenly afraid. Shlemov didn't have to say what unit he was attached to, Malenkoy just knew; he reeked of NKVD.

"I just want to ask some questions—routine questions. And Comrade Major, there is no need to stand, we are of equal rank."

Malenkoy sat at the opposite end of the blanket that had kept some of the ground's stored coldness off his back during the night, realizing how preposterous it was that an NKVD major should come all the way from Moscow to ask "routine questions." Fear clogged his mind. He could only think it was something to do with his parents—perhaps they had been caught uttering anti-Soviet sentiments and now the NKVD were coming to take him away for their sins against the state.

Shlemov put his hands up to the lamp and rubbed them gently. It had been a long night, indeed, especially after the grueling journey of the day before. Having flown from Moscow to Ostrava in a large twin-engined transport, he had been able to persuade a liaison pilot to take him from Ostrava to a forward airstrip close to the front lines only by showing the man Beria's warrant.

Upon his arrival at Branodz, late the previous evening, he checked in with the local NKVD detachment and, without divulging the nature of his mission, had found out that Malenkoy was the only local officer, outside his own little group of suspects, with whom Shaposhnikov was known to have made contact. The major of tanks had been spotted with the marshal deep in conversation outside the HQ. It was an encounter that had not gone unremarked among the thousands of troops—and NKVD infiltrators—milling the square outside Konev's headquarters. For Shlemov, that was a good enough place to start, but it had taken him the rest of the night to make his way to Chrudim and find Malenkoy's hovel in the maze of dummy tanks.

Having established that Malenkoy was a simple Georgian, no more interested in overthrowing the state than Shlemov was in getting a transfer from Moscow to the front, the NKVD major decided to unfurl part of the truth. If it became necessary to cover his tracks later, Malenkoy could simply be removed.

"I'll be candid with you, Comrade," he began. "General Nerchenko is under suspicion of anti-Soviet behavior." He let the words hang for a moment, long enough for their significance to permeate Malenkoy's consciousness. "Well, Comrade Major, what do you have to tell me?"

Malenkoy looked up from the ground and into the hard features of the NKVD investigator. The import of Shlemov's statement was still masked by fears for his own safety. "Then this is nothing to do with me?" he asked.

"No, it is purely a security matter regarding your superiors," Shlemov smiled. "Comrade Stalin wants nothing to darken the efforts of the Red Army in this, the moment of our triumph."

"Comrade General Nerchenko, you say? There has been nothing, Comrade . . . I'm sorry, your name, it escapes me."

"Major Shlemov," he added softly.

Malenkoy seemed to relax. "There has been nothing unusual here, Comrade Major."

"But you have had dealings with Nerchenko, have you not?"

"Yes, but—"

"Then I fail to see why you hesitate," Shlemov cut in quickly. "I am telling you that the general is under strong suspicion in Moscow; you tell me that you have had day-to-day dealings with him—but you have neither seen nor heard anything unusual. I find that hard to believe." His voice had suddenly become that of an interrogator. "What duties have you performed for the general since your transfer here?"

"This *maskirovka*," Malenkoy stuttered, suddenly thrown off-balance by the major's soft and hard approach. "I built it on the comrade general's orders."

Shlemov held his hands up before the lamp once more. "Then at last we are getting somewhere," he said. "So you have simply been engaged in fabricating these . . . ghosts all that time, nothing else?"

"No, nothing else, Comrade, that is the truth." He racked his brains and thought of something and it chilled him.

"Not quite the whole truth, perhaps?" Shlemov prompted.

"Something very small, hardly worth mentioning. The sector was infiltrated by fascist commandos, a small band, but they threatened the *maskirovka*. Comrade General Nerchenko asked me to lead a clean-up operation, which took just a few hours. That is all."

"I see," Shlemov said. He had hoped for more, somehow.

237

Malenkoy remembered the counterinsurgency operation, the carnage of the SS camp, the headless corpse and the bloodied papers of his friend, Yuri Petrovich Paliev, that he had found there. He nearly sat on the information, knowing that there was no way Shlemov need ever find out the details of the conversation he had had afterward with Sergeant Sheverev at the motor pool. Yet he felt as if he was under suspicion, too, and the unsolicited offer might be a way of ingratiating himself with this NKVD major.

"The comrade general sent a squad of Siberians to hunt down an officer by the name of Paliev—it happened almost a fortnight ago," he said in a small voice.

Shlemov sat up, realizing that Malenkoy was trying to tell him something that he thought was significant. "Go on."

"The general claimed that Paliev was a deserter—that was why he put the Siberians onto his trail, but they never caught him; the fascists did instead, the ones who threatened the *maskirovka*. I showed the general Paliev's papers, which we found on the body of one of the SS commandos, not knowing that he had already put a price on Yuri Petrovich's head." He stopped, searching for the right words.

"And?"

"He was shocked—I mean, really shocked—when I told him that the fascists must have killed him. I found out later about the Siberians and what the comrade general had asked them to do, but it did not tally with his reaction that day . . . it was as if he was really scared of something, something that I had uncovered. Something to do with Paliev's defection." He screwed up his eyes and pinched the top of his nose. "He was particularly anxious to know whether we had found anything else of Paliev's on the fascists."

"What? Anything particular?"

"Yes, papers and plans, he said."

"Who was this Paliev, exactly?"

"A major of signals—also the general's aide. He was no deserter, Comrade Major. He was the most loyal officer the Red Army could have—a real patriot. And the general wanted him dead. It just doesn't add up."

"And I thought I had been sent here on a wild-goose chase," Shlemov whispered to himself. The scent had suddenly become strong enough to choke him.

"I'm sorry, Comrade Major?"

"Nothing," Shlemov said suddenly. "You've been most help-ful. Incidentally, what were you talking about to our illustrious chief of the general staff, Comrade Shaposhnikov, last night?"

"He was congratulating me on the *maskirovka*. It is complete now, ready for the final phase."

"And Nerchenko spoke to you at the same time, did he not?"

"Yes, but . . ."

"Relax, Comrade, I am not trying to implicate you in any-thing here. It is purely General Nerchenko that I am interested in."

"He asked me to get some men and help off-load equipment that had just arrived at the front, that was all. Hauling crate-loads of sanitation fluid is not my usual line of work, Comrade Major," Malenkoy said.

Shlemov's eyes narrowed. "What did you say?"

"I'm a major of tanks," he said. "I don't perform those sort of duties."

"No, before that. Something about Nerchenko asking you to off-load sanitation fluid. How much of this stuff was there?"

"Twenty trucks' worth," Malenkoy said, indignantly. "Me, a major, having to supervise the removal of almost one hundred tonnes of delousing liquid for the general, with that smug Colo-nel Krilov just standing there, looking on." He laughed, shaking his head.

Shlemov's ice-cool facade cracked. He grabbed Malenkoy by his uniform and pulled him out into the crisp, dawn air.

"Have you got transport?"

Malenkoy nodded.

"Then you're going to take me to see this sanitation fluid, right now."

"But what about my *maskirovka*? I'm needed here."

"Your damned *maskirovka* can wait," Shlemov shouted.

□

As the Focke Wulf lifted off from Altenburg and headed south-east, Hauptmann Rudi Menzel had a strong feeling that it was the last mission he would ever fly. It was not a sentiment that came to him as any great surprise. He had been resigned to dying or capture—in Russian hands, the two were synony-mous—for weeks.

There were only two FW 189 Uhus still left in the squadron, their last mount having been shot from under their asses a few days before. Lutz, the gunner, had died in the forced landing and their pilot, Klepper, had been so badly wounded that he was now languishing in the field hospital at Altenburg.

As for the airfield itself, he didn't have to be a master tactician to appreciate that it was thirty-six hours away, at best, from being overrun by the Russians. His own promotion from oberleutnant the previous day had only served to heighten his utter misery, for the sole responsibility of running the staffel, or what was left of it, had been given to him.

And he wasn't even a pilot; he was just the most experienced airman alive on the staffel—but in the Luftwaffe of spring 1945 that was enough. He glanced back from his position in the nose of the Uhu at the pilot, a blond, spotty leutnant called Ritter, who sported a wispy moustache to make him seem a little older to the ground crew. He had arrived on the staffel three days before straight from C-Schule, where they rushed multi-engine pilots through training in a few weeks in a pathetic attempt to keep up with losses on both fronts.

Their own FW 189 had to be the last SIGINT variant left to the Luftwaffe's Tactical Reconnaissance Command, which was particularly bad luck for them, since orders had come down from the Aufklärungsgruppe HQ in the early hours of the morning for an Uhu to be sent over Ivan's First Ukrainian front on a signal intelligence mission of the utmost importance. Ivan's radio traffic was building up, a sure sign that a new offensive was imminent.

Menzel had also been told to get pictures since, on his previous mission to the target, none of the photographs had come out. Some stupid technician in the photography lab had overexposed the film. Menzel had been tempted to draft the idiot as one of his crewmembers for the return flight, to teach him a lesson he would never forget.

Their gunner, a gefreiter recruited from the almost redundant flight maintenance shop on the airfield, uttered bullish oaths every few minutes about how many Yaks he would cut down under his twin MG 81 machine guns. Menzel had not moved to silence him even though he knew the teenager would be lucky to spot a Russian fighter, let alone hit one, before the Uhu went down in flames.

Because Menzel knew where they were going. Worse than that, he had been there only six days before.

He flicked the powerful eavesdropping radio to test, thumped it once, and marveled as his headset burst into life.

Then he looked back up to the pilot's and gunner's positions. Chrudim was a rotten mission for these kids' first—and very probably, last—flight, but then perhaps they were the lucky ones. At least they didn't know they were heading for one of the biggest concentrations of Soviet armor, troops, and flak on the eastern front.

□

"Turn left," Herries said, "onto Martin Luther."

The driver nodded and swung the truck off the wide and straight Grunwalder Strasse that had brought them into Munich. The journey had been much shorter than Kruze anticipated, but that was only because the road into Munich was almost devoid of traffic. The same could not be said of the highway leading south, toward the mountains. It was an unrelenting, slow-moving stream of military vehicles, horse-drawn refugee carts, and stumbling humanity, trying to escape the American advance pressing toward the city from the other side.

The few checkpoints they had encountered on the way to Munich had not been concerned with a single KG squad heading back into the teeth of the fighting in defense of the Reich. They were looking for deserters heading the other way. Kruze had caught the meaningful glances between the Wehrmacht guards and the driver as papers were exchanged: thanks to the pig of an obersturmführer sitting in the cabin, they were now going back to an almost-certain death.

Yet no one in the truck had dared oppose Herries, mainly because the average age of the dozen or so troops in the back was about the same as their teenage driver.

They slowly drove northward along Eduard Schmid Strasse, Herries throwing quick glances past the driver at the river Isar. Kruze knew exactly what was going through the traitor's mind. They had to get across to reach the old town, yet so far one bridge was down, a massive center section lying broken and twisted in the swirling brown water, and the next bridge was manned on both ends of its span by a particularly officious-looking SS detachment, whose soldiers were examining the papers of all and sundry.

The driver was too busy avoiding bomb holes, negotiating a path around makeshift street barricades, and hustling civilians out of the way, to notice his travelers' agitation.

Kruze was horrified by the devastation. Houses still burned

from a raid the night before; shocked civilians wandered aimlessly around them, clutching their last few possessions. Others darted to and from the shadows of shell-like buildings, teetering over the rubble as they tried not to spill pans filled to the brim with precious water, collected from broken mains in the street.

Only once was their way blocked. A dead workhorse, killed from a nearby bomb blast during the raid, was having strips of flesh torn from its carcass by a mob of hungry citizens, their eyes gleaming in blackened sockets at the sight of meat, whose taste was a far-off memory. They ignored the driver's frustrated attempts to dispel them with bursts on the horn, so he simply slipped the truck into gear and drove over the horse, ignoring the angry shrieks of the women who witnessed next week's meal ground into the mud of the street.

The gefreiter, clearly upset at what he had had to do and with no indication from Herries as to their final destination, could no longer contain himself.

"Where are we going, exactly, Herr Obersturmführer?" He asked, wiping the sweat from his brow.

"Gestapo headquarters, Thiersch Platz," Herries said, as nonchalantly as he could.

Kruze's muscles tensed. What was he playing at now? His fingers inched around the solid butt of his Luger, deep inside his raincoat pocket, just as Herries gave him an almost imperceptible nudge and held his hand out flat, as if to say he had things under control. Like the driver, however, Kruze was sweating profusely, beads of perspiration running down his face and under his collar. Whatever Herries was up to, he did not like it one little bit.

"We need to cross the river soon, Herr Obersturmführer," the gefreiter mumbled nervously.

"I know the way," Herries snapped. "We're going over the Cornelius Bridge, if it's still standing." He only hoped that it was and, just as important, that it was not guarded by the SS.

Through the smoke of the smoldering city and the early-morning mist that rose from the Isar, the dim outline of the Cornelius Bridge heaved into view. On the far bank, Kruze could just make out the silhouette of the ancient, rickety Bavarian houses of the old town, within which they would find the watchmaker, if Herries was not aiming to turn him over to the gestapo first.

The driver joined a short line of vehicles that had lined up to cross the bridge. Kruze looked at his watch, hesitantly, as if even this innocent action was likely to give him away. It was nearly seven o'clock, the hour of their rendezvous with Schell on Piloty Strasse. It was not worth fretting about whether the man was there or not; first, they had to get over the Cornelius Bridge.

The high-sided trucks in front still occluded their view of the guards. It was not until they pulled up onto the bridge itself, that Kruze caught a glimpse of one, a stooped man of about sixty, wearing a uniform that looked at least two sizes too big. He almost let out a sigh of relief, for this had to be a *volkssturm*, a member of the Reich's home guard, about which he had been briefed prior to his departure from Stabitz.

It was not until the guard moved toward the cabin of their truck that he saw the SS flashes on the collar and realized that the sentry was a young man in an old man's body.

The man slammed his fist on the driver's cabin door and asked for papers. The gefreiter stabbed his finger toward the passenger seat and the untersturmführer shuffled around to the other side, where he stared straight into the unforgiving face of Herries.

The officer did his best to straighten in front of his superior.

"Do you call that a salute?" Herries shouted.

The man thrust his right arm out, his gloved hand pointing to the sky. "Heil Hitler, Herr Obersturmführer," he croaked.

Herries flashed his ID quickly, looking over the man's head to the old town. "Is the road still open to Thiersch Platz?" he asked, before the officer could ask him where he was going. There was no need to spell out his precise destination; the untersturmführer would know there was only one place in the square an officer of Herries' caliber would be going.

"There are a few barricades, Herr Obersturmführer. You may have to go some of the way on foot. Perhaps it would be better to leave the truck here," the soldier offered.

"And risk losing my transport to some fucking deserter? You must be out of your mind, man."

The untersturmführer craned his head above the level of the window. "Who is he, Herr Obersturmführer?" He asked, pointing at Kruze, the only civilian in their midst.

"Mind your own damned business," Herries barked. "Put it this way; if I don't get him to gestapo headquarters in the next fifteen minutes, you're going to pay for it. This man is here on the orders of the reichsführer himself.''

Hearing the name of Himmler, Reichsführer SS, invoked, Kruze thought that Herries had played his highest card too soon. Gestapo HQ was one quick telephone call away, or the time it took a dispatch rider to get to Thiersch Platz and back. It would take but a few moments to expose the emptiness of Herries' bluff.

The untersturmführer seemed to shrug. Threats were no longer of any deep significance; he just wanted to get this arrogant bastard on his way, before the Americans reached them. "You'd better move fast, Herr Obersturmführer,'' he said. "They're burning papers in there at the moment, I heard, in preparation for the withdrawal.''

Herries hit the dashboard, muttering oaths about treason and defeatism. The gefreiter eased the truck forward across the bridge while behind them the SS officer waved to his comrade at the other end to let them through. Kruze removed his thumbnail from the palm of his other hand and noticed the pain for the first time. He thought they were never going to get across.

The truck bumped along the cobbled streets, Herries skillfully directing the gefreiter down side roads until they emerged in the square itself. An imposing red flag, bearing the jagged emblem of the swastika, hung listlessly from a large building with a colonnade facade on the other side. Sure enough, black smoke was pouring from almost every window as the clerks threw file after file into hastily constructed incinerators. Soldiers of every rank swarmed in and out of the front like ants.

Kruze looked sidelong at Herries, his eyes narrowed to slits. Make your move, you bastard, he thought.

"You can go,'' Herries said simply to the astounded gefreiter.

"Herr Obersturmführer?''

"I said you can go, you stupid shits,'' Herries shouted. "You've done your duty, you've provided escort for us to our destination, so, unless you want to wait here long enough for me to change my mind, you had better get going.'' He hopped down from the cab and Kruze followed him.

The gefreiter did not need another second for the reprieve to sink in. The truck tore around the square and headed off back in the direction of the bridge.

Kruze followed Herries down an alley leading off the square. They marched briskly, but did not run; it would only have drawn attention.

"How did you know gestapo headquarters was here?" The Rhodesian whispered.

"You ask too many questions, fly-boy," Herries gasped. "Save your breath till we get to the watchmaker's. It's only a short way from here."

"This close to the gestapo?"

Herries smiled. "Why not? They're always too busy to look under their own noses."

In a few more minutes they were standing before 17 Piloty Strasse. Unlike other districts of the city, parts of the old quarter were comparatively undamaged. Except for one flattened block at the end of the narrow street, the other townhouses stood firm, with only a few broken panes of glass in their small Bavarian window frames to show for the Allied bombing. There appeared to be no one else around.

It was a moment of strange and unnerving tranquility, as if they were in the eye of the storm.

"I'm going in," Kruze said. "You'll only scare them looking like that. I doubt whether London told the watchmaker and his father they were sending a bloody obersturmführer of the SS as my escort."

While Herries watched from a discreet distance, Kruze walked over to the door and knocked. There was an interminable pause, then a slight rustle from within. Locks and chains rattled, the door opened a crack and Kruze's heart leapt when he saw a man, bent and old, with wisps of gray hair and glasses.

"Guardian Angel," Kruze said, his pulse racing.

"Come in, quickly," the old man replied in German. He pulled Kruze into the hallway, shutting the door behind him. Kruze followed him toward the back of the house.

A young man with a mop of full, dark hair and piercing brown eyes stepped forward from the shadows. "You've got the wrong person," he said in perfect, but heavily accented English. "I am Schell, the watchmaker, the one you are looking for. He is my father." He pointed to the old man.

They stood looking at each other for a moment, then Kruze crossed the corridor and shook his hand warmly. "Thank God," he said, suddenly feeling the strength in his legs crumbling to nothing.

"Where is the other one?" Young Schell asked urgently.

"Across the street," the Rhodesian replied.

"Father," the younger Schell rasped, gesturing him toward

the door. Too late, Kruze realised he had forgotten to warn them about Herries' appearance.

The old man looked out nervously and pulled his head back inside in almost the same instant. "There's an SS officer watching us," he said, his eyes wide with fear.

"It's all right," Kruze said. "That's Christian Herries, my bloody guardian angel. I'd better call him in."

3

They parked the GAZ on the outskirts of Branodz and battled their way on foot through the thousands of mobilized troops who jostled and collided with them in the confusion of the early morning mist. Malenkoy led the way into town, while Shlemov hissed for him to make more speed. Malenkoy's legs propelled him as best they could, but it was hard to walk at all when his limbs seemed to have the consistency of watery broth.

On the forty-kilometer journey from Chrudim the NKVD man had given nothing away, despite Malenkoy's questions as they wound their way up the mountain track, leaving the major of tanks to suppose the worst. Whatever Shlemov was after, his own role in off-loading the crates was unlikely to be forgotten by the NKVD. He could only hope to reduce his crime in the eyes of the man from Moscow by lending him as much assistance as possible. He had started by furnishing all the details he could remember of the place where the crates were located.

"The mist will help us," Shlemov growled, "if we can get there before it lifts."

"How are you going to take a look? Krilov is bound to have posted guards; there is much pilfering here, even for something as worthless as delousing fluid."

"Then you are just going to have to distract them long enough for me to get into the corral," Shlemov said. "How much farther

247

is it? This damned mountain mist makes the place unrecognizable."

"We're almost there. Any moment now we should be able to make out the buildings. They will be visible just beyond the next checkpoint."

The red and white barrier suddenly cut through the fog like a beacon. Shlemov elbowed his way in front of Malenkoy, flashed his ID papers at the sentry, and slipped through into the square, the main marshaling point for all vehicles and supplies passing through the town.

"Now where?"

"Over there," Malenkoy said, pointing at a group of low buildings just visible at the far corner of the square. "It was used as a cattle enclosure until the First Ukrainian arrived. The milking sheds border three sides. Access is only possible through that gate straight ahead."

At that point a light breeze rippled the gray curtain and they saw a guard lounging against the rough wooden planks that some peasant farmer had carelessly fashioned into a barrier for keeping cows in at night. Shlemov caught a glimpse of an immense wooden blockhouse beyond the gate, at least twice the height of the two-meter stone walls of the surrounding sheds. It was only after the wind died and the veil was drawn shut once more that he realized the wooden fortification was the focal point of his quest.

There could be three hundred crates or more in there.

"Give me a minute, then do something to get that guard's attention," Shlemov said. "If that cattle yard contains what I think it does, I don't want Comrade General Nerchenko to know that the net is drawing in around him."

Malenkoy wanted to ask how he should go about the task of diverting the guard, but Shlemov had already slipped away, positioning himself on the corner of the corral, out of the sentry's line of sight. He counted the seconds down, trying to suppress the questions that kept bubbling up in his mind, until it was time to make his move. He adjusted his cap and marched purposefully over to the private.

The gate creaked as the soldier pushed himself away from his leaning post and stiffened to attention.

"Open up," Malenkoy said, "I need to go in there."

"I'm sorry, Comrade Major, that is not possible. The colonel gave orders that no one is to be allowed in."

"And which colonel would that be?" Malenkoy asked.

"Marshal Shaposhnikov's aide, Colonel Krilov," the guard said, resolutely.

Just as Malenkoy felt his own resolve flag, he saw the movement out of the corner of his eye, a shadowy form stealing between the bars of the gate, as stealthily as a poacher after chickens on a peasant's smallholding.

"I have to go in," Malenkoy pressed. "I believe I dropped my papers here yesterday while those crates were being unloaded. I supervised that operation myself, Comrade."

The guard seemed unimpressed.

To his immense relief, Malenkoy saw the form dart behind the nearest of the crates. Somehow he had to keep this oaf talking long enough for Shlemov to find what he was looking for and then get out the way he had gone in.

Inside the corral, Shlemov heard Malenkoy continuing to badger the sentry. For a moment he was worried that the private would relent and escort him in, only to find an intruder there as well. But Shlemov knew what was in the crates; he felt it in his bones, and with it came the realization that there was no possibility of anyone receiving access to the cattle yard, other than Shaposhnikov, Nerchenko, and Krilov, and perhaps some of their cronies who had delivered the stuff.

He worked his way around to the rear of the boxes. In places, he had to squeeze between them and the walls of the shed, because there were so many it left little room for maneuvering. He looked up and noticed that for the most part the crates had been stacked five high, or roughly five meters from the ground to the camouflage netting that had been thrown casually over the top. The entire collection looked innocent enough. Stencils had been applied to each crate, marking them as "sanitation fluid," so Shlemov knew that it did not matter which one he pried open—they would all yield the same result.

He took his knife and carefully levered out the tacks that had been hammered into the lid of a box lying on the ground beside him. A dozen meters away, he heard Malenkoy telling the guard that he was going to have to report his insubordination to General Nerchenko, a threat that appeared to cut little ice. Shlemov knew that he only had about two minutes left to find what he was looking for. Malenkoy could not hold out much longer.

The last tack pinged out of the top of the box, making a noise that sounded like a ricocheting bullet. He paused for a second, listening for a change in the tempo of Malenkoy's monologue, but there was none. He carefully lifted the lid off the box and plunged his hand down into the layer of straw that packed the case.

He felt something metallic and cylindrical. His fingers darted left and right with the dexterity of a blind man's, until he felt another and then one more. He brought his right hand up slowly from the base of the box, parting the straw with his left.

The leaden nose of the shell seemed to thrust from the crate like a spire rising from the rooftops of the Kremlin palace. He pulled more packing away until he could see at least ten of the specialized munitions, each one longer than his arm from its flat base to the fuse in the tip. He didn't really need to see more, but he peered in, searching for the lettering he knew to be stenciled on the side of each round.

The initials VKhV swam before his eyes. He remained transfixed for a moment, then broke himself out of the trance and replaced the lid of the box, pushing as many tacks as he could find back into the holes with his thumb.

Then he stole back toward the gate.

Malenkoy was still berating the private for obstructing his access into the crate compound, when he felt a tap at his shoulder and turned to find himself staring straight into the face of Shlemov.

"Come with me, Comrade," the NKVD man said, before Malenkoy could show any surprise at his escape from the corral.

Shlemov tugged Malenkoy back toward the checkpoint where they had entered the square.

"What is it?" Malenkoy asked, frightened at the expression on the investigator's face. "What the hell did you find in there?"

They passed by the checkpoint. Already the mist was beginning to lift.

"Have you got access to a transmitter?" Shlemov asked him, ignoring the questions.

"There's a field radio in the tent."

"I need range, you fool, something with power."

Malenkoy racked his brains. The obvious place for transmitting and receiving all long-range signals was only meters away from them, there in Branodz, within the HQ of the First Ukrainian front, but that was clearly something Shlemov wanted to avoid. Any signal sent from the HQ would be witnessed by at least a half-dozen people.

There was one other place, manned by soldiers he could trust to keep their mouths shut.

"My *maskirovka* has all the Morse and encryption facilities you would need. We use them for sending false signals into Germany."

"There's no time for coding; I'm just going to have to risk using the radiotelephone. Can you connect me with Moscow on a frequency that would not be monitored at front HQ?"

"I can put you through to Vladivostok with the equipment we've got back there," Malenkoy said proudly. "Frontal headquarters is too busy talking with commanders at First and Second Belorussian to listen to what we're doing at Chrudim. As far as they're concerned we are just a deception and disinformation unit whose job is to keep the fascists from pinpointing the main thrust of the final attack."

They arrived at the parked GAZ and Shlemov motioned for Malenkoy to get in and drive. The major of tanks gunned the engine into life.

"Chrudim and fast," Shlemov said. "I believe there is no time to lose."

"For what, Comrade?"

"For whatever it is that Shaposhnikov and Nerchenko have planned in their nightmare scheme." He held on tightly as Malenkoy threw the jeep into a bend in the track.

"The marshal is involved?" Malenkoy's eyes widened.

"Yes."

"What would a man such as he want with sanitation fluid?"

Shlemov gritted his teeth as Malenkoy tried to edge past a slow-moving troop truck, then swerved suddenly to avoid an oncoming vehicle.

"Do you really think I would have come all this way on the express orders of Comrade Beria to investigate these men for improper conduct over a few damned delousing baths? Those crates contain enough shells to wipe out every man, woman, and child within a radius of one hundred fifty kilometers. I saw what was in there with my own eyes, Malenkoy. I touched those damned things with my bare hands." He was shouting over the slipstream.

Malenkoy stared at him as if he were an inmate in a mental

institution. "But there couldn't have been more than a few thousand shells in the corral, hardly enough for one artillery barrage along a ten-kilometer stretch of front," he said cautiously.

"Shut up and concentrate on the road," Shlemov yelled. The jeep veered wildly about the track, trees whistling past on the left, a steep ravine falling away to the right. Shlemov paused, running over the facts once more, trying to find a hidden flaw in his argument. It would help to talk it through.

"A few weeks ago, we received information that a consignment of shells had come up missing from a weapons production facility at a place called Berezniki, in the lee of the Urals. Although an immediate inquiry was launched, neither the munitions, nor a plausible explanation for their disappearance from Factory 497, were ever produced. It was presumed that there had been some incompetence in the filing of the manifest, so the individual responsible was punished. Incident closed, or so we thought."

"And it is those shells which have turned up here?"

"Undoubtedly."

"How can you be sure? One shell is identical to another, is it not?"

Shlemov looked at Malenkoy in a pitying way. "Berezniki is our country's principal center for the manufacture of chemical weapons. In the twenty-five years we have been producing them, there has never once been an instance where a kilo of the stuff has been missing, let alone a hundred tonnes of it. I'm telling you that what I just saw was part of the missing Berezniki consignment and that it was brought here on the orders of Marshal Boris Shaposhnikov. I believe that he, Nerchenko, and Krilov have formed some plan to unleash hydrogen cyanide on this front as part of a hideous scheme they have dubbed Archangel."

Malenkoy almost put the GAZ into the ravine. "Every man, woman, and child within a radius of one hundred fifty kilometers," he whispered. "It's not possible."

□

Ritter held the FW 189 in a figure-eight pattern over Chrudim a few hundred feet above the intermittent cloud cover. Menzel divided his time between monitoring the signals that poured from the massed tank regiments below and working the Hasselblads when a gap in the clouds allowed his cameras to take pictures of the olive-brown mass of armor in and around the town.

In the brief moments that he was not occupied, he glanced up nervously, looking past Ritter and their fanatical gunner, Julend, who was still muttering do-or-die oaths over the intercom for the Yaks that must surely be coming for them at any moment. Much to their relief and amazement, the only Russian fighter patrol they had seen either failed to spot them, or for reasons which eluded Menzel—seeing as they were a tactical reconnaissance aircraft much prized by Yak pilots—left them alone in pursuit of bigger fish farther to the west. As for ground fire, Ivan had to be blind, or out of ammunition. So far, everything had been much too easy for his liking.

He forced himself to concentrate on their primary SIGINT mission. Although Menzel spoke Russian, there was little use for the skill in the Aufklärungsgruppe since most of the radio traffic was in code. He merely recorded the signals and left it to others back at HQ to decipher them, a task of almost childlike simplicity, he had been told; the Oberkommando der Luftwaffe had long since possessed the means of unraveling Ivan's principal code networks.

"How much fuel have we left?" he asked Ritter.

The pilot stared at the gauges, then tapped them with his forefinger, a gesture that summed up the Luftwaffe's confidence in its equipment over the last few months, Menzel thought bitterly.

"Enough for another thirty minutes over the target area before returning to base," Ritter said matter-of-factly. "Where are all the fighters you told us about, Herr Hauptmann?"

Menzel was on the point of voicing his misgivings about the unnerving lull that existed on the eastern front above Chrudim when a transmission of such energy screeched in his headphones that he cried out with pain. He instinctively grabbed the scratch pad and held his pencil poised above the paper for the dots and dashes that would begin flitting at lightning speed through his receiver. He was still joggling the handle that adjusted the direction-finding loop beneath the aircraft for the optimum fix on the signal, when the clear tones of the radio operator burst through his headset. For a moment his pencil hovered above the paper as he recovered from the shock of hearing an open voice channel over his equipment, then he began writing.

When he stopped two minutes later, his whole body numbed

by what he had just heard, he turned to Ritter and, in a voice that he tried to control, ordered him to swing the Uhu around to the west and hold the vector for forty kilometers.

□

Had the FW 189 stayed over Chrudim a few minutes longer, Menzel would have had much more to write down on his scratch pad than the signal that had flashed from Shlemov to Beria's headquarters in Moscow. Within moments of the Uhu banking off toward Branodz, the DF loop—the "ears" of Menzel's SIGINT equipment—lost all further transmissions because of the temporary masking effects of the mountains over which they sped as low and fast as the aircraft's two Argus engines would propel them.

In the darkness of the Chrudim radio hut, Shlemov remained by the radio as Beria had instructed, waiting for the callback signal. He had rattled off his findings as quickly as possible, fully aware that the longer he spoke, the greater the risk of his transmission being picked up by an eager sparks operator at Konev's HQ in Branodz. Apart from the danger of Nerchenko or Shaposhnikov learning that the plan they called Archangel had been compromised, Shlemov had received explicit orders before leaving Moscow that the NKVD was to take the lead and wrap up the investigation into Shaposhnikov's conspiracy, if that's what it was. It would be a bitter end to all their work if Konev moved to arrest the plotters and received all the kudos from Stalin—glory that rightfully belonged to the NKVD.

There was a faint crackle over the headset as the connection between Beria's radiotelephone was reestablished between Moscow and Chrudim. Beria's voice was instantly recognizable to Shlemov, despite the atmospheric distortions through which the signal had battled for hundreds of kilometers before reaching its final destination.

"Shlemov?"

"Yes, Comrade."

"Make your arrest, extract a full confession, and dispose of them with extreme prejudice."

"It will be done, Comrade." He was about to shut down the equipment, but something told him that Beria was not yet finished.

"I know why he has done it," Beria said, his voice an eerie mixture of hiss and static. "Write this down. It may help you when you deliver the *coup de grace*."

A moment later, Shlemov had all the evidence he needed to put the Archangel conspirators in a shallow grave somewhere in the woods on the edges of Branodz.

□

The Uhu roared down the valley, dodging and weaving to avoid sporadic bursts of light-arms fire from the forest below. Menzel was too busy navigating to use his machine gun in the nose, and left the job of suppressive fire to Julend, whose MG 81s chattered with an intensity that was matched only by his howls of delight each time an Ivan patrol scattered from a clearing under a hail of his bullets.

"My God!" Menzel looked up from his calculations as the full impact of the radio transmission sank into his soul. "Those barbarians are going to kill us all with the stuff they've got stored down there."

Ritter glanced at the crazed face of the hauptmann for a second longer than he should have. The mountain ridge leapt toward the Focke Wulf at a sickening speed, leaving Menzel with a sudden vision of trees and gray, jagged rock that filled from frame to frame the Plexiglas dome in front of him. He felt the force of three times gravity come on as Ritter pulled back on the stick in a desperate bid to haul them over the valley wall. Then, while his eyes were still bulging in their sockets from the gravity, he heard the wump on the Uhu's belly as it brushed the tops of the trees and was clear, now plunging down toward the floor of the next valley, in whose midst lay the town he was looking for.

"There it is," Menzel said. "Straight ahead and hold her steady."

Ritter, still shaking from their narrow escape, saw the outline of the buildings and the little alpine cow sheds.

"It looks innocent enough to me," the pilot said.

Menzel tried to think of words to convince the pilot to stay on their present heading, but rational speech eluded him.

A thin beam of tracer arced its way toward them from the center of the town. Menzel ducked as the bullets found their mark, punching holes in the Uhu's wings. A ranging shot? The town and the forest around it answered a second later as a hundred guns opened up on them.

"Jesus," Ritter yelled, as the aircraft almost bucked the control column out of his hands.

255

"That's no ordinary town," Menzel said. "Get lower, or they'll have us."

Ritter didn't need to be told twice. Despite his inexperience, he coaxed the Uhu down to tree level, but the defensive fire followed them. Just as it seemed the heavy-caliber weapons would find their range, a small valley opened up before them. Ritter darted into it, bringing the aircraft below the tops of the pines.

It was then that Menzel saw the T-34s, camouflaged, but unmistakable. The single, snatched glimpse unleashed the doubts he had harbored about Chrudim in the same instant.

"Chrudim's a *maskirovka*—Ivan's name for a huge military deception to make us look in the wrong place. This is where they intend to start their final assault on Berlin, here at Branodz, safe in the knowledge that we're always looking at something else a few valleys away."

Their cover started to give way as the hills on either side of them leveled out.

"Then let's get out of here," Ritter choked into his intercom. "We've done all we can do in this place."

"No, I need pictures, proof," Menzel said, fumbling for the switch on the end of the cable that led to the twin Hasselblads under the nose of the aircraft.

"Proof of what?"

"Of the stuff they've got stored in this place," the hauptmann muttered, too low for the pilot to hear over the exploding shells that had now started to find the range of the Uhu. "Take me right over the center of the town," Menzel added as forcefully as he could. "We'll be lucky if we even get one stab at this."

Ritter lined the nose up on a large alpine villa, a red flag fluttering from its balcony, situated beside an immense clearing in the middle of the town. The square was suddenly full of vehicles and men, who darted for cover like field mice as the Uhu swept down, emulating the nocturnal bird of prey from which it took its name.

"There!" Menzel shouted, suddenly spotting his quarry. "Left a bit, just a fraction. That farmyard beside the villa. See it?" Ritter nodded. "Head for that—and get lower!"

The Focke Wulf rocked from a near miss, but Ritter kept it steady. The corral grew in the Plexiglas until Menzel could make out what was stored in its midst. Despite the camouflaged netting, he saw the boxes—couldn't miss them, they were stacked so high.

He pressed the switch and the cameras started clicking.

In the rear of the aircraft, Julend whooped with delight. "There's a fat Ivan down there just staring at us from the balcony of that villa. Looks like a general or something. Stupid bastard's going to catch it right up the asshole when I get these guns on him."

"For God's sake don't shoot," Menzel yelled. "Wait until we're clear of the town before you touch those things again."

"Why the hell, Herr Hauptmann?"

"Because I've given you an order, that's why." Menzel wiped the sweat off his brow.

They swooped over the corral, the Hasselblads continuing to take pictures until the film ran out. Then they were out over the vastness of the forest, clear of the town and the flak, but not the fighters. And this time the Yaks would come for them; he knew that.

He also understood what he had to do next, for he had heard the radio signal about the weapons stored in the corral at the center of Branodz and that had placed a burden on his shoulders far heavier than the responsibility of running his decaying squadron. He had translated the words, had written them down even. As if to reassure himself, he found the scratch pad and read once more.

Hydrogen cyanide sounded the same in any damned language.

In that instant, he realized that the main reason for his impending action was that he was running scared, hoping to put as much distance as possible between himself and Branodz.

Hauptmann Rudi Menzel had had enough.

"Hug the trees and steer two-two-zero," he said.

Ritter stared at him in amazement. "That's about ninety degrees off course."

"We aren't going back to Altenburg," Menzel said calmly.

"Where are we going, Herr Hauptmann?" Julend piped up from the back.

"We're making for the nearest Allied airfield," Menzel replied. "Ivan has got a hundred tonnes of hydrogen cyanide stored down there and I, for one, don't want to be on the receiving end when they start using it."

"That's cowardice," Julend said, unstrapping his harness. "You could be shot for what you're saying."

"Who is going to know?" Menzel looked at the two faces, gauging each for their response. Ritter stared at him like a frightened child. At least he knows what hydrogen cyanide does to you, Menzel thought.

Julend's expression was twisted in hatred. "You're going to hand us over to the enemy just because Ivan's got a bit of mustard gas down there."

"We're not talking about mustard gas, you idiot," Menzel shouted angrily. "That stuff is like pure oxygen in comparison with hydrogen cyanide."

"Whatever it is," Julend said, reaching for his holster, "it's my duty to stop you. Turn the aircraft back on a heading for Altenburg, Herr Leutnant."

Ritter shook his head. "I'm not going back," he said. "I'm with you, Herr Hauptmann."

Julend never managed to put the gun barrel against Ritter's temple. One shot from Menzel's Walther and he slumped over the breeches of his twin MG 81s, a red stain spreading on the left-hand breast pocket of his uniform.

"The Yaks got him," Menzel said to his terrified pilot. "And they'll get us, unless you fly this crate like you've never flown before, toward the Allied lines. And for the last time, get down amongst the trees."

"They never taught us low level at C-Schule," Ritter mumbled, apologetically.

"Then look on this as a bit of post-graduate training free of charge. But don't fuck up, Ritter, because without anyone manning those pop guns in the back, staying low is all the protection from Ivan we've got left."

Ritter smiled hesitantly and pushed the Uhu's nose lower, lower as they sped westward toward Bavaria.

4

When Kruze hauled himself off the mattress after a fitful five hours' sleep, every muscle in his body seemed to burn from his descent of the mountain at Achensee. Despite the desire to rest his aching limbs, he knew that to sink back onto the bed on the basement floor would be to invite his mind to run over the task ahead for the hundredth time since going behind the lines.

There was nothing more to rehearse.

He could see Schell in the next room quietly going about the task of fabricating the documents. He was grateful for the mild intrusion; it provided something to keep his mind off Oberammergau and Branodz.

He stepped over the sleeping form of Herries and walked into the adjoining room. It was dark but for a pool of light from a lamp in the corner, where Joseph Schell worked on the papers that would get him into the airfield. The whole basement was given over to the legitimate trade of a watchmaker; but it was an easy matter turning those same tools to forgery. Perfect cover.

The Rhodesian leaned against the wall and watched the young man at work. His father appeared to have taught him well. A strange skill for one so young.

The boy turned to him. "These are good papers," he said, waving Herries' ID documents in the air, the ones that had got them over the Cornelius Bridge. "In fact, they're the best I've seen. SOE's improving." He grinned at Kruze. "Your papers have been a little more difficult; I've never done Romanian stuff before. Don't worry; they'll still get you inside."

"They'd better," Kruze said, attempting to smile. He wondered how the young watchmaker would react if he were to tell him that Herries' papers were good because they were real.

"You're going to take an aircraft, aren't you?"

Kruze tried not to show his surprise. "What makes you think that?"

The boy shrugged. "First they ask me to turn you into a Romanian, then they say you will need the service papers of a Luftwaffe major. I think—"

"It is best not to think too much."

"Perhaps." He smiled and turned back to his work.

"Where did you learn your English?" Kruze asked, moving the conversation away from Oberammergau. The air force uniform that he had worn under his loose, civilian clothes since before his last briefing suddenly seemed to constrict him.

"London. My mother took me there when things started to go bad before the war. It is from her that I get my Jewish blood. My father is German, but too good a man ever to have sympathized with the Nazis."

"When did you come back?"

"About six months ago a man came to my aunt's house in Streatham and asked whether I would be prepared to go back into Germany. My father had been working for SOE for some years, at first supplying information on troop movements, then moving into the forgery business." He held up one of his documents to the light and grunted his satisfaction. "But his eyesight has gone and they needed someone to do the work for him. That's when they thought of me," he said proudly.

"But you're only a kid. You can't be a day over seventeen."

"I'm eighteen and a half, old enough to fight. Only what I do is more effective, I think." He passed Kruze's documents to him. "There, how do they look?"

Kruze peered hard at the papers. He didn't know whether they contained all the right information to get him into the airfield or not, but they looked authentic, right down to the weathering effect on the carnet, which made it appear as if it had been well-thumbed.

"SOE taught you to do this?"

"And much more besides. Now I can take apart a Sten and

reassemble it blindfolded, I know about explosives, how to operate a transmitter-receiver, listen for the codes on the BBC, and parachuting—"

"Which is how you got back in."

"Of course. I made the jump two months ago."

"And in all that time you have not left the house? What if the Germans were to conduct a search?"

"There is a hidden compartment, like the priest hole in English mansions. One of the blessings of these old Bavarian buildings is that you can always find somewhere to hide a man if you try." He laughed softly. "Sometimes the Nazis come to my father to have their clocks or watches mended. Little do they suspect their every word can be heard by a Jew from behind the baseboard."

He began to pack up his equipment. "The papers are ready," he said. "You can give these to your friend when he wakes up. Perhaps you should get some sleep also."

"I've done all the sleeping I'm going to do."

"Do you think you can complete your mission, pilot?"

"I have to. There can be no room for doubt."

Schell stood up and clapped him on the back. "Come, it is time for the BBC news. I have to listen in case it mentions us."

"Us? How do you know?"

The boy's face lit up. "SOE gave me a call sign all of my own. If I hear it on the news bulletin then I know I must radio London and await instructions. How do you think I prepared for your visit at such short notice?"

Schell led the way up the narrow, darkened stairwell to the small back room, where two armchairs pointed forlornly at an empty fire grate. He moved over to the table in the corner and turned the knob on the large radio. "Whatever you do," he whispered, "stay away from the windows in the front of the house. Only my father should be seen there."

The valves in the back of the radio began to hum into life. "Now," Schell said, "let's see if Nazareth made the news today."

□

For the umpteenth time since his arrest, Malenkoy asked himself why. How had he got involved in this terrible mess? All he had ever done was obey orders. He drew his knees up against his chin in an attempt to ward off the bitter cold in the basement of Branodz headquarters, which was now his cell.

He heard footsteps. Then the key rattled in the lock. The door swung open and the nameless NKVD officer who had arrested him marched in.

"You will smarten yourself and come with me," he said.

"Smarten myself? After half a day in this pigsty and with this around my wrists?" He held his hands up to show the rough hemp that bound them. "Where is Major Shlemov? There's been some mistake; you'll see."

"The major is outside and it was he, Comrade, who issued the orders," the lieutenant said with obvious pleasure. He prodded Malenkoy in the back with his revolver to get him up the stairs.

Malenkoy blinked as they stepped outside into the dwindling sunlight. The complete shame of his incarceration hit him like a hammer blow as he took in his surroundings. A hundred pairs of eyes looked him over furtively, then went back to overseeing their work as preparation for the final battle continued around the headquarters at Branodz.

A short time after his incarceration, left alone with his thoughts in the basement, he had been roused by the noise of antiaircraft guns. Then he had heard the aircraft roar over the HQ. Even though his own situation could hardly have been worse, Malenkoy felt bitter disappointment when the sound of the aircraft had faded and Branodz went quiet again. Despite his efforts at Chrudim, it sounded as if the Germans had found the real focus of the assault after all.

He looked over his shoulder at the alpine villa, where only the day before he had proudly reported in to announce the completion of the *maskirovka*. From the balcony, the imposing figure of Marshal Konev looked down on him, a mixture of rage and disgust on his face. Then he turned his thick bull neck and disappeared back into the operations room.

Malenkoy bowed his head. Things had happened so fast in the last few hours. He had been arrested at Chrudim, shortly after he had taken Shlemov to the radio tent. No explanations, just the sudden appearance of the lynching party: a pair of guards wielding their Sudayevs, which they pointed at his chest, and an automaton of a lieutenant. The lieutenant remained impassive to his pleas on the now all-too-familiar road between Chrudim and Branodz, where he was finally thrown into the basement beneath Konev's HQ and left to think about his fate.

The moment he saw the truck, he was left in little doubt as to what it would be.

Two guards dropped the tailgate and ordered him to get in. So this is it, Malenkoy thought, a bullet in the base of the head, and a shallow grave somewhere in the forest.

As his eyes grew accustomed to the gloom under the canvas awning, Malenkoy saw he was not alone. Bundled up against the cabin of the truck, he recognized the faces of Shaposhnikov, Nerchenko, and Krilov. Nerchenko, his face bruised and swollen, groaned in obvious pain. It looked as if he, at least, had been doing some talking to the NKVD.

The guards and the lieutenant hopped in the back and trained their Sudayevs on the four of them. Then the engine coughed into life and the truck began to move. Malenkoy's fears were confirmed as soon as the truck took the forest route up into the mountains. After about fifteen minutes, the driver turned off the track and drove a little way into the woods until he stopped in the middle of a clearing. The guards motioned, with sharp gestures of their submachine guns, for the small party to get out.

Malenkoy was suddenly no longer afraid. It was a beautiful, peaceful place and if he were to die, better here than in some stinking effluence pipe on the outskirts of Berlin. The NKVD lieutenant ushered him around the side of the truck where he saw a large staff car. The door opened and out stepped Shlemov, his new, swaggering transport mirroring the look of triumph in his eyes. To Malenkoy's left, Nerchenko dropped to his knees, his face in his hands.

"Get up, Nerchenko," Krilov hissed.

Malenkoy felt his head swim, but he checked his swaying in time to stop himself from falling over.

"So you thought we wouldn't find out," Shlemov said to them all, even giving Malenkoy a swift, disdainful glance. He strutted in front of the small, bedraggled line of men like a game bird on a mating ritual. Shaposhnikov stared brazenly at the investigator. "Well, you were wrong; we know everything. Partly because you are all amateurs." He looked with disgust at Nerchenko.

He nodded to the lieutenant who, in turn, snapped his fingers. Two more NKVD soldiers appeared from the cabin of the truck and went over to Nerchenko, picked him off the ground, and dragged him to the far end of the clearing.

"And partly," the investigator continued, "because you have an informer in your midst." He paused, reveling in their confusion.

"Comrade Beria was tipped off about Archangel," Shlemov continued, registering the startled look on Krilov's face. The investigator thought back to his radio conversation with Beria that had produced the last piece of the jigsaw. The NKVD was always grateful for anonymous information. This time they had been able to act on it fast.

"Doubtless, it was one of your 'friends' back in Moscow. We are still tracing them, but thanks to Nerchenko's confession, I don't think we should have too much trouble.

"Comrade Stalin does not like men who show . . . initiative," Shlemov said. "But then, your plan Archangel wasn't just for the good of the state, was it, Comrade Marshal? What would you have done when Comrade Stalin failed to support your plan?"

"We would have had him killed," Krilov said.

"Thank you, Krilov. I didn't think you of all people would be so cooperative," he said sarcastically. "I always find a forced confession a most unattractive procedure, most unattractive." He let his gaze fall on Nerchenko for a moment. "So what this all amounts to is a *coup d'état*, even if it is one that has been hatched by amateurs. Did you ever seriously think it would work?"

"The attack was scheduled for dawn tomorrow. Thousands of tanks, artillery, and aircraft, not to mention millions of men, would have pushed Russia's enemies off the face of this continent. Do you call that amateur?" There were tears of frustration in Krilov's eyes.

"Kolya, do not give him the pleasure," Shaposhnikov said softly.

Shlemov's eyes lit up. "Comrade Marshal, it is so good of you to contribute to our little conversation. I was just coming to your true motives for hatching up this plan."

"I was doing my duty."

"So, you took it upon yourself to undertake this crusade, a full-scale attack on the British and the Americans as well as the fascists."

"Yes."

"Why?"

"Because Comrade Stalin in the Kremlin has gone soft on us," Krilov interrupted. He pronounced the word "comrade" with real disdain. "He negotiates with Roosevelt and Churchill; it is he who is the traitor to the ideals of the Revolution, not us. We would have been doing him and Russia a favor."

"I see," Shlemov said. "And I suppose Churchill and Roosevelt would have just sat on their fat behinds while your hydrogen cyanide rained down on their troops in Germany. I presume you gave some thought to their reactions the moment you were to unleash what you have stored at Branodz."

"The chemicals were a contingency plan," Shaposhnikov said, simply. "They were a weapon of last resort."

"But if we had used them," Krilov shouted, "the Allies would have spent days arguing about a response; such are the divisions in their command structure. And by that time we would have been on our way to victory."

Shlemov finally lost his temper. "If you had fired just one of those shells, you would have started a chemical weapons exchange that would have turned Europe into a desert. Is that what we have fought so hard to achieve these last four years? Victory will come, but it will take time. The difference between us is that I will live to see it."

Shaposhnikov took a step forward. "I doubt it, Shlemov. Archangel was Russia's last chance for a united continent. You and your kind have ruined the best opportunity we shall ever have of achieving this goal."

"Really," the investigator said dismissively. He was fighting for the upper hand, but Shaposhnikov had stolen the initiative. Shlemov was tempted to play his trump card.

"Yes, really." Shaposhnikov was cool, full of menace, even when faced with death. "After the war, the Americans will strengthen their position in Europe; you can be sure of that. By the time they are ensconced on the continent, there will be little we can do through military action to remove them."

"And what do you think the Americans and the British would have done if you ever made it to the Channel ports? Just sit there and wait for you to go away? They would have come back in force."

Shaposhnikov shook his head. "The stupidity of the NKVD," he said slowly. "Just because we are not politicians do you think we had not thought the whole thing through? We had plans to negotiate a buffer zone. Our forces would have moved back to the Rhine, the Red Army remaining behind the river so long as no British and American troops ever crossed the Channel. We would have let communism take its natural course in France and the Low Countries. If the Allies behaved themselves we would have even released their POWs on a piecemeal basis to let them finish off the Japanese."

Malenkoy saw the logic of Archangel strike home with Shlemov, despite the investigator's attempts to hide it.

Across the clearing, Nerchenko's groaning reached a crescendo. A momentary twitch of irritation appeared at the corner of the investigator's left eye, then he cut the air with his hand, a swift and final gesture.

Malenkoy tried not to watch, but he could not tear himself away from the awful spectacle of Nerchenko stretched out on his stomach, with one soldier standing on his hands, while the other dug a foot into the small of his back. As Nerchenko wriggled in desperation, the soldier applied more pressure to his back. Then he drew back the bolt of his Sudayev, flicked the switch to single-fire and shot Nerchenko through the back of the head.

"Thus ended the lives of Badunov and Vorontin, also," Shlemov said dramatically, the shot still echoing through the forest.

Krilov lunged for the investigator, but took no more than a pace before a guard crashed a rifle butt down on his head, sending him sprawling at Shlemov's feet.

"Archangel would have given Russia everything she could have wanted," Krilov muttered defiantly, as he struggled back to his feet. "An impregnable divide between us and the capitalists, without bartering anything. But Stalin had to do worthless deals and betray us all. Comrade Shaposhnikov would have made him pay with our plan."

"Is that what you believe, Comrade Marshal?" Shlemov asked.

Shaposhnikov said nothing. He stared impassively at the investigator.

"Shame on you," Shlemov said to him, "for leading these idealists astray."

Krilov turned to Shaposhnikov and caught his eye. He looked imploringly at the chief of the general staff.

"Perhaps I can speak for him," Shlemov said softly. "I know enough to surprise even you, Krilov," Shlemov added, pulling his notepad from his greatcoat. He began to read the jottings of his radio communication with Beria.

"In the early part of 1918, Shaposhnikov was a young militiaman fighting the czarists in the Pomoroskiy marshlands, to the north of St. Petersburg. He was encouraged in his endeavors, no doubt, because he was not just defending the region against the enemy. Is that not right, Comrade?" Shlemov turned to the marshal.

Shaposhnikov said nothing.

"Prior to the Revolution, before the last war in fact, Shaposhnikov had worked hard on the land around the hamlet where he had been brought up, a few scattered houses made of mud and straw on the banks of the Onega estuary.

"It's a desolate sort of place. The swift waters of the river keep the White Sea open for most of the year, but when winter really bites, even the ocean freezes and then the place becomes truly inaccessible, by land or sea. But to Comrade Shaposhnikov, it was home. And just before the outbreak of the kaiser's war, he had saved enough money to buy his plot of land and build a house for his bride-to-be.

"He finished it just before he was pulled away to the battlefields of Europe, where he fought against the Prussians and achieved distinction for three long years. When the October Revolution broke, Shaposhnikov marched back to the mouth of the Onega and was reunited with his wife and three-year-old son. By all accounts, they were a rather happy little family."

"What has all this to do with now?" Krilov asked.

Shlemov ignored him. He was in full flow.

"In the spring of 1918, the czarists attacked the Pomoroskiy sector, but were rallied in the west by a militia force, which had been honed into a highly effective fighting unit by Shaposhnikov. Your mentor, as you are undoubtedly aware, Krilov, routed the infinitely superior forces of the czar and pushed them back to the Urals. But in the meantime, the British Expeditionary Force in support of the czar, which had landed earlier in the year, mainly at the instigation of one Winston Churchill, was fighting its way back to the northern ports. Our revolutionary forces, skilled in the ways of fighting a winter war, made short work of the British who, by the time they clawed their way to the little hamlet on the banks of the Onega, cold and hungry to a man, mutinied against their commander, General Ironside."

Shlemov seemed to relish the confusion on Krilov's face for a moment, before continuing.

"Militiaman Shaposhnikov, returning home after his triumphant push to the Urals, found a mutinous enemy occupying his beloved district. His forces attacked and the British retreated, but not before they had raped every woman and girl in the hamlet. It was unfortunate for Shaposhnikov that he arrived at his house too late to save his wife and child. In retaliation for Shaposhnikov's counterattack the British burned every building in the village; they found his family days later charred to a crisp in the smoldering ruins of his house. In the meantime, the British renegades retreated to their home port, where they turned themselves in to the authorities. The name of that port should be familiar to you Krilov; it, too, was called Archangel."

Krilov looked over to Shaposhnikov. "Tell me it's not true," he said.

Shlemov smiled slowly and gestured to the man standing silently before him.

"Look at your marshal. Yesterday he was the great leader; now he is nothing. That is what revenge does to you, Krilov; it drives you for so long—and then it burns you out."

Shlemov turned to the guards and gestured. The guards pushed the marshal and his aide to the edge of the clearing, Shlemov strolling after them.

Malenkoy saw Krilov turn to Shaposhnikov as the Sudayevs were leveled at their bodies. Shlemov raised his hand.

"Who informed on us?" the colonel asked, his voice cracking.

Shaposhnikov dropped his head. "I know who did it," he murmured. "I see it all now."

Malenkoy saw the puzzlement cross Shlemov's face, but then the investigator brought his arm down, the guns barked, and the two bodies fell as one onto the soft carpet of pine needles.

When the ringing echo had subsided, Shlemov wandered over to Krilov's body and flicked it over with his foot. There was no movement.

The marshal let out an almost imperceptible groan and opened his eyes.

"What did you mean?" the investigator asked casually.

"He is nothing to do with us," Shaposhnikov whispered, the pain carving deep lines into his face. He turned his gaze to Malenkoy with a supreme effort.

Shlemov followed suit. "I know," he said. "But it is important to Russia that no one ever finds out what happened here today, you know that. The NKVD can be trusted to keep the secret of Archangel, but he . . . well, he is just a major of tanks. He knows nothing about codes of silence."

"He won't talk. Look at him." There was a rattle in Shaposhnikov's throat.

"Forget him! I'm curious to know—" But when he looked down, Shaposhnikov's eyes had rolled into his forehead. Shlemov shook his head and walked away from the body.

"Bury them in the woods," he said to the senior NCO of the party. Then he gestured toward Malenkoy and spoke softly to the NKVD lieutenant. "Put him in the back of the truck and go back to Branodz. The killing is over."

□

The hum of the air-conditioning vents sounded loudly over the silence that fell on the underground room.

"We all believe in the effectiveness of the EAEU," Welland said, somewhat patronizingly, "but there is still the possibility that your man in Reisen has put too much faith in this Luftwaffe transmission interception."

Staverton rubbed his eyes. "Cochrane's a good man. We were damned lucky he was there when the FW 189 came in. The German was scared out of his wits. He literally fell into Cochrane's arms and said he was turning himself in because the Soviets had deployed chemicals at a place in western Czechoslovakia called Branodz. By the time Cochrane had developed the Uhu's film and had conducted a thorough debrief, he believed him. Only then did he put a call through to the Bunker."

"But these crates next to the HQ, how can you be sure that they contain the hydrogen cyanide?" Deering asked.

"We can't be, 100 percent. But we know what Shaposhnikov is planning at Branodz and we know that he's capable of anything. Then some Luftwaffe reconnaissance aircraft makes an emergency landing at one of our airfields in southern Germany with its crew babbling about Russian chemical weapons being stored in the very same place. Why should they make it up? We have to believe it—we can't afford not to.

"The worst thing is Shaposhnikov has located the dump right next to his headquarters, the very place my man is programed to bomb tomorrow morning."

"Kruze has been stopped, I take it," Deering said.

"Don't worry, George, we're taking care of that right now. Our concern is what we do next."

"I've already spoken to the PM about mobilizing our own chemical weapons in retaliation," Welland said. "He wants to hold off until there is more conclusive news about Branodz."

"Where's that going to come from? We can't just sit and wait," Staverton said.

"Perhaps now he has told the Americans . . ." Deering said.

"In my opinion, they should have been told the moment news of this first broke," Welland said.

Staverton thumped the table with his fist. "Guardian Angel would have worked."

"Are you convinced it would still not be possible to go ahead with the attack?" Deering said. "You told us yourself that this pilot of yours could drop a bomb down a chimney if he was called to do so."

"The crates are too close to the HQ, George," Staverton said. "I don't think any of us has the right to take that risk. With the prevailing wind coming from the northeast at this time of year, a few fractured shell casings could kill thousands of our men and countless more civilians. A hundred shells . . . well, I don't have to tell you gentlemen what that would do."

"So what next?" Deering asked, his voice weary.

"The PM wants to hear what the Americans suggest before we move again," Welland said.

"But time is running out, Admiral," Staverton said. "According to the Archangel document that attack is scheduled to happen within the week. For all we know it might even have been brought forward."

"Then we're just going to have to pray to God that it hasn't been."

"In the meantime," Deering added, "I'll see to it that all men in the field within a hundred-mile radius of Branodz are drilled in the use of gas masks and, where appropriate, new ones are issued."

"Without arousing any suspicion, George—routine exercise and all that," the admiral interjected. "We don't want mass panic at the front."

"Quite, Admiral," Deering said, a trace of irony in his voice. He was old enough to remember the piercing whistle blasts that signified the onslaught of chemical attack, the rush to don his gas mask, and the first sweet smell of the mustard gas as it swept over his position in the trenches.

"The general staff's order to commanders in the field to stop their advance eastward is still being implemented in some isolated parts of the front, but to all intents and purposes the drive for Berlin has halted," Deering anounced, his face somber. "We are now digging in to meet the Russians, although our men don't know that," he added.

"And the Americans?" Welland asked.

"It can only be a matter of hours before they do the same thing," Deering replied.

The meeting adjourned.

A few minutes later, Staverton scurried along Whitehall's slippery pavements toward the Bunker. As he crossed the road avoiding the traffic that crept cautiously through London's blackout, Big Ben chimed half-past six. Another thirty minutes until the next news broadcast. Thirty minutes in which to warn Kruze that Guardian Angel had been terminated.

5

Malenkoy came to in the cool ward of the military hospital in Branodz, his head hurting like hell and the rest of his body limp from the nightmare.

An orderly saw him stir and moved over to his bedside. He took Malenkoy's wrist, fumbled for his pulse and, apparently satisfied that the rate was not unusual, plunged a thermometer under his tongue. Malenkoy spat it out, ignoring his protestations.

"What happened to me?" he asked.

"We were hoping you would tell us, Comrade Major," the orderly said with reverence. "Some troops brought you in several hours ago, said you were a hero, that you were to be given the best treatment. Then they left, just like that, without another word. May I ask what it was that you did?"

"I don't know," he said softly.

"Such modesty, Comrade Major. Let me just tell you that it is an honor to have you here." The orderly began to pull him upright to a seated position.

"What are you doing?" Malenkoy asked with some irritation.

"I must make you presentable for the official visit." The orderly looked anxiously toward the door. "The delegation will be here in no time. You must be ready to receive it."

"What delegation—" Malenkoy had no time to finish. The double doors of the ward swung open, admitting a cluster of senior personnel. They were some way off and Malenkoy had difficulty focusing on the individuals in the group. He looked up at the orderly and was about to ask who was paying the visit, but the man had stopped fussing over the appearance of his bed and was standing rigidly to attention, his gaze fixed on the opposite wall.

The olive-green curtain of greatcoats parted for a moment and Marshal Konev swept down the central aisle, NKVD Major Shlemov by his side. As they did so Malenkoy's mind was flooded with images of the woodland execution. The delegation, Konev now at its head, stopped at the end of his bed. Malenkoy clamped his hands to his legs underneath the sheets to try and stop them from shaking.

"Is this Major Malenkoy?" Konev asked the gaggle of officers around him. There were several curt nods.

Konev took three paces forward. Malenkoy watched wide-eyed as he bent down, grasped him by the shoulders and kissed him on both cheeks. Then the marshal stood straight, a thin smile on his lips, and clicked his fingers. A lieutenant marched up, handed over a box, and withdrew.

"Major Malenkoy," Konev began, "thanks to your *maskirovka*, the enemy will be taken by surprise when our final assault is launched a few hours from now. The fascists have mustered almost all their forces in the sector against your ghost army, clearing a path for our divisions here in Branodz to assault Berlin from the south. A last-minute overflight by one of their aircraft has not prevented the deception from working to the full. In recognition of your work, I present you with a token of the esteem in which you will shortly be held by the Soviet people when they learn of the part you have played in our total victory."

Konev took the Order of Lenin from the box and pinned it to Malenkoy's shirt. He stepped back to the end of the bed and saluted.

Malenkoy didn't see Konev. His gaze rested instead on Shlemov, who was standing a few paces behind the marshal's left shoulder. The NKVD major held Malenkoy's stare for a few seconds and then nodded, a gesture so slight that it was missed by everyone else in the room. To Malenkoy the significance of that moment was crystal clear. His silence had just been bought by the state.

Konev turned to the delegation, which parted to admit him; he swept through the middle and was gone through the double doors. When Malenkoy looked again, the party had left, leaving an unnatural silence in the ward, as if the whole thing had never happened.

Malenkoy stared down at the glittering disk for several seconds. Then the cheers of the other patients began to ring out. He brought a trembling hand from beneath the bedclothes and fingered the Soviet soldier's most valued prize. He thought of his father back home, of how proud he would be.

But his thoughts returned to the clearing. A few spent cartridges scattered on the grass would be the only sign of the demise of Shaposhnikov, Nerchenko, and Krilov. He looked down at the medal again and its luster had dulled.

Malenkoy threw back the bedclothes and jumped out of bed. He pulled his trousers and jacket on and was just squeezing into his boots when the orderly appeared.

"Major, this is most irregular—"

"I am fit and well and wish to return to my unit," Malenkoy said, waving him aside. He marched from the ward, ignoring the looks of envy from the other inmates as he swept past them.

When he got outside, he commandeered a jeep and ordered the driver to take him to the motor pool at Chrudim. He felt the need for a drink with Sheverev as he never had before.

☐

Kruze and Herries had been sitting silently on their mattresses in the basement, smoking the Rhodesian's last two ersatz cigarettes, when the old man came down the stairs.

"You must go now," he said, his face taut. "The car is in the garage at the back of the house." He held his hand out. "Here is the key. Now go!"

Herries held up his hand. "Simmer down, you old fool; we're not due to leave for another five hours."

Schell was too nervous for the insult to register. He sensed only that Herries was trying to obstruct him. "No, there is not a moment to lose. If you stay here any longer you will be caught."

Kruze was on his feet. "What's happened? Why the change of plan?"

"Relax," Herries said, blowing cigarette smoke lazily from his nostrils, "we're not going anywhere."

"Keep your mouth shut, Herries," Kruze said. He touched the old man gently on the shoulder and felt that he was shaking. "What is it?" he asked softly.

"There is a KG squad at the end of the street, coming this way. The SS are turning everyone out of the houses to form work parties. They want us to build the street barricades that they believe will halt the Americans."

"Where are the Americans?"

"They say their tanks have entered the northern suburbs and that we are to fight to the finish. I have been in the presence of death too long to care for myself anymore. But Joseph, he must live to see his mother again and build a new life when this is all over. I don't know what it is you have come here to do, but if you stay, the Nazis will find him and he will die for nothing."

"Where is he now?"

"In the special hiding place. They will not find him there— not if you leave now." He looked imploringly into the Rhodesian's eyes.

Kruze did not need to hear any more. "We're on our way," he said, taking the key from the old man's quaking hand. "The car, does it work?"

"I have turned the engine over every week for the past year. And there is enough gas to get you to your destination."

"You're not actually going to do what this old coward wants, are you?" The Rhodesian whipped around at the sound of Herries' voice; he was still sitting on the mattress, puffing on his cigarette. "Why can't we share the Jew boy's hidey-hole until the danger's over? As unpleasant as that sounds, it would be much better than setting off for Oberammergau now."

Kruze's hands were on Herries in an instant, pulling him to his feet. The Rhodesian's words were fueled by hours of pent-up frustration and revulsion. "Has it become just a little too hot for you, Herries, is that it? Do you want to switch sides again, rejoin your old friends out there?" He saw the amazement spread across the traitor's face. "Oh yes, I know about you and the deal, but you're not working for Staverton now, you're working for me. The plan's changed and we're moving out." He pulled him toward the foot of the stairs.

"Not that way," Schell stammered. "There is a basement exit that leads to the garage at the back of the house." He ushered them through to another room and unlocked the solid, wooden door that was set in the far wall.

The cold, dark night, filled with the sounds of a dying city, forced the last traces of fatigue from Kruze's body. He could see another door across the little courtyard and pushed Herries toward it.

"The garage opens up onto Seitz Strasse," Schell said. "From there, it is only a short drive back to the Cornelius Bridge. If you are in luck, there will be no barricades up yet."

Kruze started for the garage, but Schell held him back, gesturing toward the dim figure of Herries across the yard. "I have lived among Nazis long enough for them all to look very much alike," he whispered. "But with him, it is not just the uniform he wears; there is evil deep within him too. I do not know exactly what passed between you just now, but take care of yourself. He is out to do you harm; I felt it."

"You and Joseph must come through this," Kruze said. "Thank you for everything." He did not know what else to say, so he turned and ran for the garage.

The air inside was so thick with dust it almost choked him. For a moment, Kruze felt dangerously exposed, for he could sense Herries close by, causing the hairs on the back of his neck to rise. Then the traitor lit a match, the sulphurous flare catching the anger and bitterness on the gaunt face beneath the black peaked cap. They stood for a moment beside the Mercedes, eyeing each other cautiously, before Kruze moved toward the double doors.

"Kill the light and drive," the Rhodesian said, maintaining the authority in his voice. The one thing he did know about Herries was that he seemed to respond to orders.

He threw open the doors of the garage and cast a quick look down the street. Some troops were attending to a fire that was raging in a house fifty yards away. He jumped in beside Herries, handed him the key, and held his breath as the man's finger pressed the ignition button.

The Mercedes started on the first try.

"Get us to Oberammergau," Kruze shouted over the surging engine.

Herries maintained the revs, but made no move to engage first gear.

"I should kill you, fly-boy," he said, a wild look in his eyes. "How long have you known about me?"

"If you want to talk, then let's do it on the road. Or do I have to use this?" He brought the Luger out from his coat pocket and cradled it in his lap. "Now drive!"

Herries swung the big car onto the cobbles and picked his way cautiously through the craters, fallen masonry, and broken water mains that had marked their drive into the center of the old city that morning. To Kruze's horror, he realized that dawn had seen Munich merely whimpering from the wounds it had received during the night; now it was crying out in agony. Citizens of every age rushed around with hoses, or buckets, doing what they could to keep their city alive, but the fires seemed inextinguishable as the Mercedes swung around every twist and turn of the old town.

They crossed back over the Cornelius Bridge with none of the fuss of the morning. Young troops ushered them along, glancing quickly from the car and the man at the wheel, to somewhere beyond the smoke and the flames, their eyes focused on the night sky. It was only when they were some way from the bridge and Kruze stole a glance at a nearby thirty-seven-millimeter flak gun, its barrels patrolling the heavens, that he realized they had come through the worst part of the city unchallenged.

When the RAF was coming from the night sky, what was there to fear from the Americans on the ground?

Herries coaxed the car into the middle of Grunwalder Strasse, maneuvering his way between the streams of refugees pouring from the city and the truckloads of reinforcements coming in. He put his foot down on the accelerator and the Mercedes leapt forward, its tires spraying the exhausted and bedraggled citizens with foul-smelling water that bubbled up from the shaken foundations of the city.

The Rhodesian looked at his watch in the receding glow of the fires. It was almost eight o'clock. Only ten hours to go until the Meteors swept over the tarmac at Oberammergau.

□

After telling the Meteor pilots to stand down, Fleming was left to himself in the ops room. Stabitz suddenly seemed a very quiet, lonely place.

The callback signal from Staverton was due at any moment. It sounded as if the Archangel emergency was finally over. A coded message to say their mission had been terminated was all that he had received, but he took that as good news.

The phone was on its third ring when he picked up the handset.

"Robert?" The voice at the other end was faint but unmistakable.

"Yes."

"Thank God."

There was an interminable pause. Fleming thought the line had gone dead. When the AVM spoke again, the words came rapidly.

"Guardian Angel, Robert; it's gone horribly wrong."

"This is an open line, sir, don't you think—"

"There's no time for security precautions. He's got to be stopped."

"Who?"

"Kruze. We've been trying to raise Nazareth for the past three hours to tell our man it's off. Shaposhnikov has got chemical weapons beside his HQ in Branodz. And Kruze has not acknowledged the termination signal."

"Chemical weapons—"

"As you said, Robert, this is an open line. Think about it afterwards, work out the permutations. I'm telling you we can't take any chances. We've got to stop Kruze in his tracks."

"Isn't it possible he might still call in?"

"SOE is monitoring all channels, just in case. But if there is no word—and we should have heard by now—I want the Meteors to go in as planned. Is there any chance of pulling it forward, destroying all—and I mean all—the aircraft on the ground before oh-six hundred hours?"

"The strike was timed to coincide with first light. It would be immensely risky sending the Meteors in any earlier."

"See that it's done." A pause, then, "You'll be going with them, Robert."

"What?"

"You're the only one who knows just how important it is that Kruze does not get through. You've flown the Meteor, haven't you?"

"A couple of sorties at Farnborough, but—"

"Good, then lead them in. I want no aircraft left on the ground at Oberammergau for Kruze when he arrives there at dawn tomorrow."

"He might already be dead, or captured. If he hasn't called in . . ."

The seconds ticked by before the static was broken and Staverton gave his reply.

"I have to brief the special advisers in an hour. Robert, Kruze is still out there, I know it. He must be stopped, at all costs. That's an order."

With that, he hung up.

□

"I wouldn't give much for your chances of concluding this deal," Kruze said, breaking the silence that had hung between them since Herries turned the Mercedes into the wood and switched off the engine.

"Is that some sort of threat?" Herries' tone was mocking. "Do you have orders to kill me, fly-boy, is that it?"

"Not me," he said. "But if you make it back to England, you'll have to look over your shoulder for the rest of your life. I wouldn't count on that being a very long time."

"It's a distinct possibility, but look at my options. I never amassed the sort of wealth my ex-colleagues did by pilfering from the vaults and art galleries of Europe. The only money I've got is locked up in my father's estates. When you're cash-less, dear boy, South America is an awfully hot, sticky, and unpleasant place. It had to be England. Archangel gave me the excuse to come back and claim what was rightfully mine."

"There was I thinking that you'd just got sentimental about a warm pint of English beer the last time you were in Berlin," Kruze said.

"Go fuck yourself, fly-boy. From what I heard you're no angel either. Fancy knocking off Fleming's wife. He seemed like such a nice man, too."

Herries knew he'd caught him off guard and moved in for another jab.

"Luftwaffe accommodation is so cheap, such thin walls." He smiled. "It's remarkable what you overhear sometimes."

"Don't push me, Herries."

"Oh, I'm not trying to unsettle you, old boy. I want you in tip-top condition when we go into Oberammergau. You're the one who signs my end-of-term report, remember? I do hope you haven't forgotten the code word." He rubbed his legs, mas-saging some feeling back into them after the long drive from Munich. "And you and I will be heroes when we return—not perhaps the sort that make the newspapers, but heroes none-theless. You're Whitehall's last hope, the only man who can stop the Red Army from marching across Europe. And when you pull it off, with my help, they'll be kissing the ground we walk on. I think that my past misdemeanors will soon be for-gotten in all the excitement."

"You seem very confident in my abilities."

"They tell me that you are the best. Why should I disbelieve

279

them? The difficult part will be getting into the airfield, but I know I can do it. After that it'll be downhill all the way. Shaposhnikov will be dead in under four hours and Archangel with him."

Kruze swung round to face him.

"Then let me inject a little realism into this conversation. I'm to take an Arado jet bomber, the only aircraft in the world that stands a chance of getting through the Russians' air defenses—so I have got that going for me. But there are just one or two minor problems to overcome first." He let the words hang between them for a moment. "I've never flown the Arado 234, so even if I make it to the aircraft, I still have to familiarize myself with the controls before some observant Kraut realizes that I'm not the bloke who's meant to be in the cockpit. Then there's the matter of the engines. German turbojets have a nasty habit of blowing up—shedding their turbine blades, if you want to get technical. I know, because it happened to me once at Farnborough when I was flying a Messerschmitt 262. Then, even if I manage not to get blown up on the ground by one of the Meteors, I still have to contend with Allied and Soviet aircraft trying to shoot me out of the sky all the way to the target. Finally, when I'm over Branodz, I've got to find Shaposhnikov's HQ on the first run-in, because that's the only way I'm going to catch him with his trousers down."

He studied Herries carefully in the moonlight and saw a thin bead of sweat trickle from his hairline down his forehead. "Still think I can do it?" he asked.

"Perhaps I'd better hand you over to the Luftwaffe at Oberammergau," Herries whispered.

"You'd have a hell of a lot of explaining to do," Kruze said.

"So would you."

Kruze reached over slowly and gripped the coarse material of Herries' jacket. "If you show any sign of putting this mission in jeopardy by pulling a stunt like that, I'll kill you with my bare hands."

"Fighting talk, fly-boy. Keep that spirit up and I'm home and dry." Herries pulled away and looked at his watch. It was oh-three-thirty. He turned the ignition and gunned the engine into life.

"We'd better be on our way," he said.

6

The Mercedes bumped along the tree-lined approach road, its blackout lights picking up nothing to indicate the presence of the airfield, even though their map told them they were there. The next moment a tower rose up out of the pre-dawn mist, its legs throwing eerie shadows as the car head-lights played over its crisscrossed supporting structure.

In almost the same instant, night turned into day.

Herries swore, shielding his eyes with one hand from the searchlight beam that illuminated them from the watchtower.

The light went out, leaving spots that danced before Kruze's eyes. The next thing he saw was the red-and-white-striped bar-rier at the foot of the tower. Herries began to slow the car.

"Remember," the traitor said, "not a word unless you're spo-ken to and even then, keep it simple. If they're regular army or a Luftwaffe field regiment, this will be a piece of cake. If they're neither, that leaves the SS . . . ."

"God, you're enjoying this, aren't you?"

Herries shrugged. "There's no choice, fly-boy. As you were kind enough to point out, I've nowhere to go."

A soldier stepped out into the road, an MP 40 at the ready in one hand, a flashlight in the other. Herries stopped the car a few yards short of him and left the engine running. Out of the corner of his eye Kruze saw him scan the guard for iden-tification, but the camouflaged smock he wore over his uniform

281

and the netting that covered his helmet obscured his rank and service affiliation. Beyond the barrier Kruze could see a machine gun emplacement ringed with sandbags and two pairs of eyes shining beneath dark, coal-scuttle helmets in the glare of their headlights.

Kruze tried to take all the details in slowly, as if he were used to passing through high-security checkpoints every day of the week, but the images flashed before him like film shown on a projector running out of control.

A dog barked close by. The Rhodesian turned his head. The Alsatian seemed to leap from nowhere, growling ferociously. It pressed its nose against his rolled-up window, the breath that steamed through its slavering jaws mingling with the mist around them. A second soldier appeared from behind and pulled the dog away from the car, slipping a leash around its collar as he did so. Harsh, guttural commands quelled the dog into silent obedience.

That's two in the road, two in the gun emplacement, and probably two more in the tower, Kruze thought. And a dog. Hardly what he had anticipated for a top operations squadron so close to the front lines. Then it crossed his mind that the 234s might have moved on to a new location . . .

Herries rolled down his window. The first soldier flashed his light at the front of the car, his expression hardening the moment he saw the civilian number plates.

"Was ist los?" The soldier shouted, waving his flashlight at the driver and his passenger.

The beam swept across the two occupants and then fell back with unshaking precision onto the gleaming obersturmführer's flashes on Herries' lapels. The soldier doused the light and walked over to Herries' door. In the dull glow from the instrument panel Kruze saw the faded eagle stitched on the tunic and had to stifle a sigh of relief. Oberammergau was defended by Luftwaffe troops and not the Waffen SS.

"We have been told American commandos are in the area, Herr Obersturmführer," the guard stammered, "and when I saw the plates—"

"Requisitioned transport," Herries interrupted. "I didn't catch your own identification, soldier."

"Senior Lance Corporal Giesecke, sir, Molders Regiment, Fifth Luftwaffe Field Division." He snapped to attention.

"Open the gate, Giesecke. If you keep us waiting much longer the Americans will be here to do it for you."

"No one enters without the right authorization, not even the SS." Lest the officer take his remark as impertinence, he added, "Orders from the OKL."

"If it weren't for the Oberkommando der Luftwaffe I wouldn't be in this god-forsaken hole at all," Herries spat, passing across his documents.

Kruze kept out of the guard's line of sight, taking the opportunity for one last look around him before the moment when he would be asked for the transit papers that Schell had prepared. He peered ahead, taking in the guardroom beyond the barrier, the barbed wire surrounding it, the road that led from their present position into the heart of the base.

"What brings you to Oberammergau?" the guard asked. Kruze felt his muscles stiffen.

"Herr Krazianu needs air transport," Herries said, jabbing a thumb toward Kruze. "I am his escort. Oberammergau is one of the few air bases left open in this damned country. And that's all I am allowed to tell you." He looked the guard straight in the eye. "It's in the documents."

Herries snapped his fingers at Kruze and barked something the Rhodesian did not understand. For a second he froze, disoriented, then he realized that Herries was asking him for his papers.

"Romanian," Herries said disparagingly to the guard.

Giesecke tried to look sympathetic, but he distrusted the SS as a rule and especially disliked the look of the one in the car. He leafed through Kruze's documents, shining his flashlight from the photograph on the carnet to the Rhodesian's face and back again.

"I have not been told about any Romanian," he said.

"Is that so? Security here must be worse than I thought," Herries snapped. "If you look carefully, you will see that this man's passage through the Reich has been authorized by the Air Ministry in Berlin and countersigned by General Riegl at the OKL. Now I suggest you let us through, or he will miss his aircraft and you will be answerable to the general personally."

The guard hesitated, looking around for someone with whom he could confer, but the other soldier had disappeared into the warmth of the hut, taking the dog with him. Kruze looked anxiously at his watch. The Meteors would be coming in a little over an hour.

The obergefreiter shook his head. "I will have to put a call through to the kommandant; I have no choice. Switch off the engine and come with me please, Herr Obersturmführer, and bring your passenger with you."

Kruze understood enough to open the door and step out onto the road. There was something reassuringly familiar about the place, something he could not immediately identify, but it lifted his spirits. He followed the obergefreiter and Herries to the guardroom.

Giesecke pushed the door open. The second guard, a boyish soldier who would not have looked out of place on the sports field of a junior high school, was playing happily with the dog. He looked up and smiled at his corporal. The dog let out a low growl as soon as it saw the two strangers in the shadows.

"Leave that damned dog alone and move the car to the secure compound," Giesecke ordered. "I'm taking them down over to the command post."

"What command post?" Herries asked, pulling Giesecke around to face him. "What's wrong with the phone in the guardroom?"

"It does not work, Herr Obersturmführer. You know how it is these days; nothing works anymore."

"Careful, Giesecke," Herries warned.

The obergefreiter led the way toward a long bank topped with small pines that was positioned between the guardroom and the perimeter fence. It was only when they got close to it that Kruze realized that the command post was a huge semi-submerged blockhouse covered with turf and vegetation to make it seem part of the landscape. Giesecke ran down a small flight of steps and tugged at an immense iron door, which opened slowly, its hinges groaning in protest. The smell of paraffin and the sweat of frightened men seeped into the night. A low-wattage bulb dangled from the ceiling near the entrance.

Giesecke ushered them inside. Bunks, stacked four high from the floor to the concrete ceiling of the immense room, overflowed with men. Some slept with their rifles, panzerfausts, and grenades held tightly to their bodies, others stared back at the intruders with eyes filled with terror at the prospect of the fight that lay before them.

"We have been ordered by the OKL to hold Oberammergau to the last man," the obergefreiter said. "They say it is worth the sacrifice."

"And so it is," Herries said, pulling himself together. "But unless you get me authorization to enter the base this minute, you, for one, will not live to see the first American soldier come down that road."

Giesecke's face twitched. He walked through the makeshift dormitory, stepping over the exhausted, filthy bodies that made up Oberammergau's garrison. He entered a corridor that led off the main room of the blockhouse, paused by a door halfway along, knocked, listened, and walked in. Herries and Kruze followed.

Kruze knew the name of the man who raised his head from the table in the middle of the room, because he had read the plate on the door. Hauptmann Klaus Philipp looked up at Giesecke, his eyes bloodshot from lack of sleep and from ingesting most of the contents of the bottle by his elbow. He glanced across to Kruze and Herries. The latter's uniform prompted him to raise an eyebrow, but nothing more. The hauptmann's blond hair fell forlornly over his forehead and there was at least three days' stubble on his face. Once, Philipp had been a great man, Kruze could tell. The Knight's Cross with Oak Leaves showed above the frayed collar of his gray Luftwaffe tunic.

There was the chink of bottle on glass as Philipp took a refill from the brandy bottle. When he looked back to Giesecke, the corporal was standing rigidly to attention, his eyes focused on the crooked picture of the führer behind the garrison commander's back. Philipp waved a hand theatrically and Giesecke stood at ease.

"This is either an American's idea of disguise, or the gestapo come to get me," Philipp laughed manically, pointing a shaking finger at Kruze. "Why else would you bring him here, Giesecke?" he asked, slurring the corporal's name. The Rhodesian suddenly felt sticky under his two layers of clothing, but he stared back at the captain, willing Herries to take the upper hand.

"He's a Romanian," Giesecke said, embarrassed at his officer's behavior in front of the SS. "And this is his escort, SS-Obersturmführer Herries."

"So what do they want here?"

"They say they are authorized to enter the base. I need to use your phone to obtain clearance from the station kommandant, Herr Hauptmann. We have nothing on them."

Kruze saw Herries look rapidly from the telephone on the table to the husk of a man behind it and saw what was going through his mind. Before the hauptmann could react, Herries made his move, pushing the corporal out of the way as he moved across the room. In one fluid move he pulled the hauptmann out of his chair, sending the table flying, the bottle and the telephone with it. If Philipp wanted to put a call through to the base commander, he would not be using the telephone in his office any more, Kruze thought. It lay in pieces on the floor, its wires covered with broken glass and alcohol.

"I have orders to get this man, an important emissary of the Romanian government, on a flight to Bucharest, and from this base." Herries grabbed the papers from Giesecke and shoved them under the Philipp's nose. "So far, I have had nothing but sloppy excuses. I take one look at you, Philipp, and I know why."

The hauptmann tried to shake the drowsiness from his head. "There has been no authorization from Berlin . . ."

Herries pressed the forged documents up against the man's face. "This order has come direct from Abteilung 13, which I should not have to remind you is the special operations department of the OKL. If you were not informed about this development, then I suggest it is because they could not trust you with the information."

"But this is a fighter-bomber station," Philipp protested.

"I don't care if it's a three-ring circus," Herries shouted. "In under an hour a Junkers transport is due to land here. Five minutes later it will leave with him on it—or you face the consequences."

Philipp looked down at the remains of his telephone and the shards of glass surrounding it and sighed. "Take them over to flight operations," he said to Giesecke.

"That won't be necessary," Herries said, trying to hide his elation. "We will find our own way. I am sure you need all the help you can get when the Americans arrive and that Giesecke, here, will be only too happy to lead the counterattack that will repel the enemy from the airfield."

"So be it," Philipp murmured. "Now just get out of here."

Herries and Kruze left Giesecke staring into the dazed, drunken face of the field regiment officer. They picked their way carefully through the dormitory, trying not to hurry. They reached the reinforced door, put their weight against it, and stepped out into what was left of the night.

□

Klaus Philipp sat back in his chair and lit a cigarette, taking the smoke down deep into his lungs to try to eradicate the pang he felt at the loss of the precious bottle. When he looked up, Giesecke was gone. The spot he had vacated was filled instead by the tall man with the steel-rimmed glasses who had been waiting since the previous evening in the room across the corridor for the staff car that was due to take him back to Berlin.

"I am sure that your car will be here at any moment, Herr Hartmann," the Luftwaffe captain said in a voice that showed he didn't really care about anything much any more.

"Never mind that," the other man said. "What was the name of that SS officer in this room just now?"

Philipp went through a pretense of racking his booze-filled brains, watching the smoke of his cigarette curl lazily upward the ceiling of his office. If it wasn't the SS who were giving him a difficult time at Oberammergau, it was the gestapo. Neither caused him fear any more. How could they when the Americans were so close?

"It was Herries, I think," he said.

"As I thought," the gestapo man nodded, satisifed. "An unusual name, too, don't you think? And yet I know it from somewhere. Now why should that be?"

"I can't think, Herr Hartmann," Philipp said.

"Herries . . . Herries," Hartmann mused softly. "It is a name I heard recently, two days ago, when I was in Berlin." He moved over to the table. "He is wanted for something; I am sure of it. Art theft, perhaps. No, something else. Damn it! I can't remember. Where's your phone? I must try to get through to Berlin."

The hauptmann pointed to the floor. "Broken. He did it, too, the son of a bitch. There's another one down the corridor, though, in the storeroom. Perhaps . . ."

But Hartmann had already gone, stumbling across the bodies that filled every piece of available floor space in the blockhouse. He ignored the curses of the men, whose fingers he crushed underfoot, not resting until he found the storeroom. It was pitifully empty of weapons and provisions, but it did still have a telephone on the far wall.

He had come to Bavaria on the special orders of the Reichsführer SS to make a whistle-stop inspection of the frontline forces under Field Marshal Schörner, paying particular attention to the morale of the troops. He would shortly convey the results to Himmler, confirming that the spirit of the troops had never been better and that the Americans would surely be repulsed. There was, after all, no point in telling him the truth.

Herries had him intrigued, though. He knew that name. For the life of him, he could not remember what offense it was the man had committed. There were so many things to take care of these days and his memory wasn't what it used to be.

He picked up the phone and fought for a connection to Berlin. Five minutes later and he was through to the headquarters of the Sicherheitsdienst, the intelligence wing of the SS, and asked to be put in touch with the records office if it hadn't been flattened by the Allied bombing.

□

They slipped through the trees surrounding the blockhouse and onto the road that led from the gate into the heart of the base. The Rhodesian looked at his watch. It had taken them half an hour to get through security and yet Herries, despite his bravado, seemed to have aged ten years. He wondered what it would take for the man to crack.

Kruze's sense of familiarity with the place returned. It was something carried to him on the wind. And then he had it: the tang of aviation spirit injected into a combustion chamber and blown out through a jet engine as hot, powerful thrust.

"They're here," he whispered.

"Who, fly-boy?"

"Not who, what. Smell the air."

Herries raised his nose to the wind.

"That's burned jet fuel," Kruze said. "It means the Arados are here—"

Before he had finished, they heard it. Almost imperceptible at first, the sound reached Herries' ears as the cry of a creature from the surrounding forest. Then it became a high-pitched, endless scream. Kruze grinned at him, but saw only fear on the traitor's face.

"Jet engine," Kruze said, his own fears forgotten. "We're in business."

"That is the jet sound?" Herries asked. His face showed white against the darkness and the dryness of his mouth meant the words did not come easily.

"They're testing their engines."

"You sound very sure, fly-boy."

"I am. The Luftwaffe uses its Arados in ones and twos, rarely for concerted strikes as we would. Fleming's lot have been watching this base for some time and they've seen the pattern. Sometimes they operate by night, but things really start to happen at dawn." He gestured toward the runway. "That means they're warming up for the day. Now all I need is some top cover from those Meteors, some chaos to allow me to get onto the apron and slip into an aircraft undetected." He paused before adding ruefully, "And some time to sit in the cockpit and find out how the bloody thing works."

They reached a junction in the road. At first Kruze thought that the expanse of concrete running left to right in front of him was another track leading into the base complex, but it was too wide. It had to be the taxiing strip, parallel to the main runway.

There was a sudden crunch of gears behind them and a truck lumbered out of the mist. Kruze's instinct was to run for cover, but Herries grabbed his arm and ushered him toward a group of low buildings just visible away to their left.

"It's too late to hide. We have to look like we know where we're heading, like we belong here. So move this way—and don't run."

The truck ground past, the driver hardly giving them a second glance.

"Where now?" Herries asked. He had to speak up to be heard over the engine noise as more Jumo turbojets tuned in across the other side of the airfield.

Kruze gestured to his civilian clothes. "I've got to find a place where I can get out of these and lie low till the Meteors do their stuff." He looked up at the rapidly lightening sky to the east. "Before long I'm going to stand out like a beacon. I need to blend in with the Luftwaffe. How long do you think we've got before someone raises the alarm?"

"If that drunken idiot in the bunker can find another bottle, you may just get away with it. If he sobers up, has second thoughts, and sends someone over to flight operations to look for us . . . well, your guess is as good as mine, fly-boy. It could happen any time."

They reached the corner of a long hut, which looked as if it could be a barracks. Kruze imagined he could hear the sound of pilots inside stirring for another day bombing the American forward positions. He pulled Herries around to the back of the building and crouched down beneath one of the windows, dropping his voice to a hoarse whisper.

"It's time for you to make your move, Herries. There's nothing more you can do here."

Herries's eyes shone in the half-light. "The word," he whispered. "Give me the code word."

For a moment, Kruze was tempted to make Herries stew. "Traitor's gate," he said. "I don't know why."

Herries cocked his head, looking for signs of deception.

"That's it. Now go!"

"Perhaps I should stay to guard my investment, after all . . ."

"In the forest you were king." The Rhodesian paused to look around him. "But this is where I take over. So, run, curl up in your hiding place and wait for—"

There was a sudden movement at the window above their heads. The blackout curtain parted and Herries saw the blurred face, heard the squeak of finger against glass as condensation was rubbed from the pane, then the curse as the bitter cold worked its way into the Arado pilot's flesh. Herries flattened himself against the wall, frozen still, until the curtain closed and the danger was past.

When he turned around, the Rhodesian was gone.

□

Herries moved back toward the gate, irritation with Kruze turning swiftly to anger. Somehow he felt cheated. The show was over for him, the curtain had come down too soon. He had wanted more, a bigger part to play, a more testing role.

As he skirted the bunker and approached the guardroom, he saw the Mercedes parked between two *kubelwagens* in the compound. He peered into the car and cursed when he saw the keys missing. Then he remembered Giesecke's order to the young private with the Alsatian. The keys were probably hanging on a wall in the warmth of the guardroom.

He pushed the door open, letting it swing slowly on its hinges. The private looked up, anxiety, perhaps even fear, in his eyes; the dog snarled a low warning from its place by the cast-iron stove in the corner.

"Do I look like the enemy to you, boy?" The tone was relaxed, but the private sprang to his feet.

"No, sir. I mean, I'm sorry, sir," he stammered. His voice had barely broken and, to Herries, it sounded almost angelic.

"Where's Giesecke?"

"I don't know, sir." A blond forelock fell across the private's eyes; he brushed it away, self-consciously, still standing to attention.

Herries kicked the door shut and moved over to the stove, then looked slowly around him. The private's rifle was propped up against the far wall, next to a panzerfaust. A tin mug of ersatz coffee steamed away on top of the stove, its pungent aroma filling the room. The soldier watched Herries cautiously out of the corner of his eye, his gaze darting from the sharp, aquiline features of the officer's face, to the SS flashes on his lapel and the death's head badge on the peak of his cap.

"Sit down," Herries said, motioning to the chair. "Tell me, do I frighten you?"

The private's face twisted in confusion. He did not know what it was that the officer wanted to hear.

"Or is it merely the proximity of the Americans that is making you feel uneasy?"

"They do not scare me," the private said. It was then that Herries noticed he was shivering.

He moved from the stove and stood in front of the private. A tingling sensation spread across his back and shoulders. He felt strangely excited, dominant, alive. He reached out and touched the soldier's cheek. The boy flinched, but held his gaze.

"I need a driver," Herries said, smiling. "I could ensure that you are many kilometers from here by the time the Americans arrive. No one here will question my order."

The boy tried to get up, but Herries moved closer, pinning him to the chair. The dog's lip curled in a low growl.

Herries heard the footsteps outside a moment too late. By the time he could react, the door had already swung wide open. A tall, bespectacled man in a raincoat stood in the frame, with Giesecke and two other field regiment troops behind him.

Hartmann pointed his Walther P38 at Herries' chest.

For an instant Herries was too stunned to move, but then pulled himself together. "What is this insubordination? Who are you and why the hell are you pointing that weapon at me? When I get back to Berlin—"

"You will be shot there as a deserter and a traitor," Hartmann said, slipping from the doorway, the movement covered by the three soldiers behind him, his Walther leveled now at Herries' head.

"This is no time for pathetic jokes," Herries said. "I asked you for your name."

"My name's Hartmann, Herries," the gestapo investigator said, exposing a row of jagged, yellowing teeth. "Oh, how careless of me, I should really have addressed you by your full title, Obersturmführer Christian Herries, late of the Britische Freikorps."

Herries felt the bile rising in the back of his throat, but he managed a harsh, guttural laugh. "Britische Freikorps? It sounds like a gestapo fantasy to me. I take it you are gestapo, Hartmann."

"Your accent is flawless and your papers are good, Giesecke tells me, but SD records in Berlin tell a different story." He clicked his finers. "Obergefreiter, disarm this man and take him to the blockhouse."

Hartmann took his eyes off his captive for only a moment, but it was enough for Herries to pull his automatic from his holster and point it unerringly at the spot where Hartmann's thick, greasy eyebrows joined on his forehead.

Even though four firearms were bearing down on him, Herries liked the feel of the rough stock in his hand; it gave him the authority he needed.

"This is all an outrageous lie," he stormed.

Hartmann glanced easily from the barrel of Herries' gun and into the eyes of its owner.

"The SD in Berlin has a file as long as my arm on you, Herries. It reads well . . . an easy assimilation into the Waffen SS, a model foreign-service recruit at Bad Tolz, and a good record in combat on the eastern front. Then you disappear and show up here. You are the same Christian Herries, are you not?"

Herries held the gun steady. They had him, knew exactly who he was, but there was not a ghost of a chance that they could have unraveled what had happened in Czechoslovakia, learned of the massacre of his unit in the forests above Chrudim or his trip to Britain.

"Yes, I am he," he said.

Hartmann gave a disarming smile. "Good, we're getting somewhere. Why all the fuss, then?" He lowered his Walther and motioned for the three soldiers behind him to do the same.

"I don't take kindly to having accusations of treachery leveled at me, let alone guns."

"A little hastiness on our part, I assure you. I have to say, though, that I am still curious as to why you doctored your papers and denied all knowledge of the Britische Freikorps."

"That's simple," Herries said. "Since I returned from the

front, I've found that the British aren't too popular here, not after what the RAF did to Dresden and Berlin. I found it was . . . easier if my nationality was conveniently erased from my service papers."

"I see," Hartmann said, "that sounds plausible enough, if a little irregular."

Herries brought his arm down slowly and holstered his automatic. He moved over to the stove and took a swig of coffee from the private's mug. His eyes flickered around the hut, looking for something with which to retaliate if things started to turn nasty again. They rested for a second on the panzerfaust leaning against the wall, then moved on around the room, finally falling on Hartmann's face.

"If you would allow me to go on my way now I will forget about this outrage," he said.

"You're good at forgetting, aren't you, Herries?" It was said casually, but there was enough menace there to raise the short hairs on the traitor's neck.

"What do you mean, Hartmann?" The panzerfaust was close now. If he could squeeze off the round, the detonation in that confined space might just give him a chance.

"Your unit, the men you fought with, for instance. Have you forgotten them, too?"

"They're all dead, unfortunately."

"Not all. There was one survivor."

Herries froze. "Tell me about it, Hartmann. Were you there?"

The gestapo man laughed. "No, I had better luck than to serve on the eastern front. But a certain sergeant by the name of Dietz did not. He made it back to our lines and lived long enough to make a full deposition to the authorities: that you killed your platoon on a mountainside in Czechoslovakia and were last seen heading for Allied lines. In my book, that's treachery and desertion—and murder."

Hartmann watched as the blood drained from Herries' face. "Dietz, it's not possible . . ." he mouthed in English.

Hartmann moved in for the kill, keeping his eyes all the time on Herries' face. He did not notice the traitor take a small step backward toward the wall.

"You have become quite a celebrity in Berlin," Hartmann said. "A very thorough description of you, based on your sergeant's report, is curently circulating around headquarters. The SS don't like to leave these loose ends untied, much like the gestapo." His eyes went cold. "When you altered your papers, Obersturmführer Christian Herries, you should have changed your name, too."

Herries whipped around and pulled the panzerfaust away from the wall before Hartmann or the guards could react. He pointed it roughly in the middle of the group, briefly registered the horror on their faces, and squeezed the trigger, preparing himself for the detonation of the antitank round as it rocketed toward its target.

In the frozen silence of the moment, everyone heard the soft click. The round never left the tube.

In the same instant that Herries realized the panzerfaust was a dud, the private leapt from this chair and knocked it to the ground. Then the others were on him, pinning him against the wall. Herries disintegrated, the sobs racking his body, drowning the savage cries of the soldiers who had cheated death by the miracle of a worker's carelessness in a munitions factory hundreds of kilometers away.

Hartmann clicked his fingers. Giesecke and the two guards disarmed and dragged Herries to the stove. Hartmann opened the lid, grabbed Herries by his short, blond hair and pushed his face close to the glowing, red and white coals.

"Now tell us," he said, "why make your way back from Czechoslovakia to this place? And who the hell is Stefan Krazianu?" He pushed his head further into the furnace until Herries' skin drew taut and his eyebrows began to singe.

Herries screamed out. "First we do a deal," he babbled in English. "You and I. I'll tell you everything about Archangel. Just let me go." His voice had risen an octave.

"I don't care about anything called Archangel," Hartmann said, pulling him away from the furnace. "I want to know about Krazianu."

"That's what I'm trying to tell you. But it's good information, the best. It does not come cheap." Herries fell on his knees, clutching at the hem of Hartmann's coat. The gestapo officer brought the barrel of his P38 across Herries' face, cutting his cheek. He cried out with the pain. "No deals," Hartmann said. "Talk, or your face goes back into the furnace."

"All right. Krazianu's no Romanian, he's a Royal Air Force officer, real name Squadron Leader Kruze. He's going to steal an aircraft from this base."

"What?" Hartmann roared. "Where is he now?"

"I could find him . . ."

"Then do!" Hartmann pulled him from the guardroom into

the half-light of dawn. Herries stumbled in the direction of the hangars, now clearly visible several hundred yards away, beyond the flight operations complex where he had last seen Kruze. The gestapo policeman and his escort were a few short paces behind him.

"But why?" Hartmann shouted after him. "Why is an RAF officer here? Why docs he want one of our aircraft?"

"He's after Archangel," Herries spluttered, nursing the cut on his cheek with his hand.

"And who is this Archangel?"

Herries turned to face him. "No," Hartmann barked, "you talk while you walk."

7

Kruze hid the last earthly remains of Stefan Krazianu—
trousers, jacket, tie, and documents—under the raised floor of
the barrack hut. He stepped out from the narrow gap between
the two sleeping blocks, where he had effected his change of
persona, as Major Rolf Peiper of 10/KG 77, one of the resident
Arado *kampfgeschwader* units operating from Oberammergau.

Fleming had told him bluntly at Stabitz that, if he did go
down behind Russian lines, Peiper's identification would be a
perfect alias—perfect for their purposes, that was, not his. Peiper had been posted missing by the Luftwaffe following a reconnaissance mission over southeast England in October 1944.
The Luftwaffe never found any trace of his aircraft, an early
model Ar 234B-1, nor did it receive word of his death or capture
through the Red Cross. The fatal crash landing in the Romney
marshes on that October morning provided the EAEU with its
first look at the radical new Arado machine. The Luftwaffe
believed that Peiper and his aircraft had sunk to the bottom of
the English Channel.

Kruze tucked into his boots the pilot's breeches that he had
worn under his civilian trousers, and reversed Krazianu's coat
to expose the plain gray which, he had been assured, would go
unremarked among the proliferation of dress styles sported by
the Luftwaffe. The coat hid the fact that he was not wearing
the *fliegerbluse* used by German fliers—there had simply not

been room under the civilian clothes. He wrapped the coat tightly around himself and adjusted the Iron Cross so that it hung neatly over the top button of his shirt. He looked himself over. It was not perfect, but it would have to do.

With just under an hour before the Meteors came over, he knew he had to find a vantage point, somewhere that would allow him an unrestricted view of the flight line. There was nothing else for it but to head resolutely toward the noise of the turbojets.

As the sky grew lighter, the mist started to clear and Oberammergau seemed to come alive. He moved around the low buildings, heading for the hangars that lay beyond, their outlines just visible above the barrack rooftops.

Mechanics, distinguishable by their black-cotton drill uniforms, began to emerge from the huts around him, rubbing eyes and yawning after too little sleep as they headed for the flight line. None of them paused to give him a second look. He tagged along behind a group of NCOs who trudged in the direction of the hangars, trying to look as if he knew the place intimately.

He had not seen any other flying crew, but then this was the hour of briefings that preceded the day's operations.

Suddenly he was out of the maze, with the airfield stretched before him. He kept walking, conscious of the sudden lack of cover.

The runway ran from left to right, a strip of gray that glistened in the half-light, its edge seeming to disappear into the foot of the Alps beyond. A few hundred yards from him were the two enormous hangars that he had seen from the barracks compound, their doors closed against the chill wind that had started to whip down off the mountains. The whine of the turbojets was louder now, but he still could not see the Arados, only a few Heinkel 111s and a Ju 52 transport parked haphazardly on the apron.

He walked faster, toward the hangars, pulled there by the sound of the engines. He had to see the aircraft that would take him into Czechoslovakia. Then he would worry about finding a place to hide.

He drew closer to the first hangar and stopped dead in his tracks. Across the other side of the runway there were three Arados, their silhouettes just visible against the mountains. As he focused on them, he detected others through the haze on the periphery of his vision and when he switched his gaze to them, more black crosses leapt at him out of the corner of his eye, this time from farther along the runway's edge. He became aware of the small, dark shapes of the ground crew scurrying around the aircraft. He strained for a better look and thought he could make out the bulbous shape of bombs and jettisonable tanks hanging from the pylons beneath the wings, like fat, blood-filled ticks clinging to the soft underfeathers of a bird of prey.

The aircraft appeared so ready to go that they seemed to be pushing against their wheel chocks. Soon their pilots would launch them from their alpine lair, on the dawn forage for enemy ammunition dumps, bridges, and other high-value targets. Kruze swore quietly. He was on the wrong side of the runway. Somehow he had to get across the clear expanse of ground between the hangars and the dispersal area on the other side. He had no choice. He scoured the area in the immediate vicinity of the Arados for a place to go to ground. There was only one, an immense graveyard of aircraft wrecks, filled with an assortment of twisted fuselages and broken wings. He knew that if he could make his way there and lie low until the Meteors arrived, he would only have to sprint a hundred yards to the nearest of the Arados.

There were still fifty minutes to go. He wondered if he could get into a plane without depending on the Meteors' diversion. He turned around cautiously and looked back at the barracks and flight operations compounds. There were no pilots in sight yet, only a few mechanics, still making their way to and from the hangars, but he felt that the appearance of the flyers was imminent. It was time to make his move.

Kruze was level with the second hangar, striding toward the runway, when he heard a cavernous groan, a low, metallic rumble that he felt even through the concrete beneath his feet. The forty-foot doors of the hangar parted, allowing a ray of light to spill across the ground, blinding him with the intensity of the arc lights within. He stood in awe as the doors were winched back.

The nose of the Arado that sat in the center of the hangar, facing him head-on, seemed to be on fire as the arc lights reflected off its Plexiglas canopy. He felt himself walking toward it, part of him mesmerized, part of him knowing that what he was doing was wrong. This was the aircraft that had filled his thoughts for the last two days.

He stepped into the hangar, nodding casually to the rigger

who was operating the electric motors that hauled the doors open. The corporal's wave turned to a salute when he spotted the prized Iron Cross at Kruze's throat. The other mechanics were too busy with their last-minute checks to pay any attention to the major taking an interest in their work. The bastard probably did not know that they had been up all night repairing the flak damage that the aircraft had sustained during the previous day's operations. They were all the same.

Kruze stood a little way from the mottled, gray and green bomber. It was a late production model Ar 234B-2. The long, smooth, tubular fuselage tapered away from the glazed nose, culminating in a tall, graceful fin. The wings were high and straight, attached to the shoulder of the fuselage to give plenty of clearance to the two turbojets they held underneath. He noticed the bombs slung beneath the engine nacelles and the drop tanks that were attached to the wings between the turbojets and the Rocket-Assisted Take-Off bottles. He reminded himself that for an aircraft operating at such a heavy all-up weight from an airfield as high as Oberammergau, RATO assistance would be essential for getting off the ground.

He moved closer to the cockpit. The Arado was different from almost all aircraft he had come across in that there was no raised canopy. The pilot sat out in the pressurized nose surrounded by a wraparound sheet of stiffened Plexiglas, which afforded him almost perfect visibility. He peered inside, casually, noting the ejection seat, and wondered whether it actually worked. It was a startling concept. Despite attempts at Farnborough and the Martin-Baker company, the British were hard-pressed to come up with a device that could get a pilot clear of a stricken aircraft automatically.

His eye caught the periscope that jutted out from the canopy roof. At first he thought it had to be something to do with the Lotfe bombsight, but then he realized that the optics pointed backward as well as forward. Intrigued, the Rhodesian stepped back and ran his eye along the fuselage until he spotted what he was looking for. Just forward of the tail, in the belly of the aircraft, was a smoke-blackened port, pointing aft. The EAEU knew that the Germans had developed rearward-firing cannon for some aircraft, but it was unaware that the device had been extended to the Arado. He hoped he would not need it to get him out of trouble; he was relying on the Arado's speed to do that.

An engine sound, like the rough cough of a motorbike starting up, made him whip around. The three-wheeled tractor, a rigger at the wheel, was backing up to the nosewheel of the aircraft. Kruze watched as the tow bar of the *scheuschlepper* was attached to a torsion point and locked in place. With a thumbs-up signal from two ground crew who checked the connection between the tow bar and the Arado's undercarriage, the driver gunned the tractor's engine and the Arado inched toward the hangar door.

The idea formed in a second. Kruze knew that to delay, to think it through, would cause him to miss the opportunity: he had been given his passport across the runway. Provided the driver chose not to strike up a conversation, which would be difficult above the noise of the little tractor's engine, he could get all the way to the dispersal point. He ducked as the Arado's wingtip moved over his head, then ran around to the front of the aircraft, nodding curtly to the ground crew who watched in bemusement as the officer chased the *scheuschlepper* out of the hangar. The driver started as Kruze jumped onto the seat beside him, but before he could say anything, the Rhodesian pointed to the engine, shrugged, and blocked his ears. The NCO shook his head, as he always did at eccentric officer behavior, and turned slowly toward the taxiway that bisected the runway and led to the gaggle of Arados on the far side of the airfield.

They were swinging around the corner of the hangar when he saw the small group of people not a hundred yards away from him, a mixed bunch of soldiers and, he thought, a civilian, marching into the first hangar. The goose-flesh was still rippling his scalp as the *scheuschlepper* rounded the building, preventing the opportunity for another look, a chance to tell himself that what he had just seen could not possibly be.

Except that it was. Herries had a face he could never forget.

He was still asking himself why when the third Arado in the dispersal line directly across the runway from him exploded in a sheet of orange flame, the ignited fuel from its full tanks shooting into the sky.

The driver stopped, dumbstruck. A black pall of smoke billowed above the broken, burning aircraft. Kruze glanced at his watch. Forty minutes to go, there were forty fucking minutes to go!

He was still shouting his fury as the first of the Meteors screamed over the hangar, missing its roof by ten feet.

The driver wrenched his gaze from the explosion, aware that his passenger was yelling over the din of the *scheuschlepper*'s engine and the eruption across the runway. Kruze felt a rough grip on his shoulder and remembered, too late, the presence of the NCO. The driver was staring into his face, a mixture of fear and bewilderment in his eyes, when the Rhodesian brought the butt of his automatic across the man's head, leaving his body to slump over the wheel.

He leapt off the tractor in the same instant that another Arado blew up on the other side of the airfield, its attacker flying directly through the explosion, so low was its altitude. The idiots were destroying the aircraft they had been specifically told to avoid. There was no time to think.

His fingers bled as he wrestled to detach the tow bar from the nosewheel of the bomber. At first, the nut holding it in place would not move, then it gave a fraction, enough for him to double his efforts. He felt no pain as he twiddled the fastener, not letting up until he heard the clunk of the bar as it hit the concrete.

He ran to the driver's side of the tractor, aware that people were sprinting for the shelters around him. He engaged the single gear of the *scheuschlepper* and rammed the unconscious driver's foot against the pedal. The machine jumped forward and headed off at high speed, relieved of the weight of the plane, across the grassland that lay between the taxiing strip and the runway.

Kruze had already discarded his coat and had one foot in the spring-loaded step on the Arado's nose by the time the tractor was clear of the aircraft. Then he was on top of the fuselage, pulling at the pilot entry hatch. It gave with a lurch and flopped open on its hinge. He took one more look around him, spotted a Meteor, sweeping low across the runway and shooting a sustained burst of 20-millimeter fire into another row of Ar 234s, and wondered how long it would be before they found his aircraft, tucked away in the shade of the hangar, while the world seemed to be exploding around him.

Then he swung his body into the cockpit and pulled down the clear cover, locking it shut over his head.

As he let his eyes race over the instrument panel, wondering where the hell he was going to begin, he heard the sound of shrapnel raining down from the sky onto the aircraft's skin.

□

Herries and Hartmann were the last to step inside the hangar. No sooner had the access hatch swung shut behind them than the shockwaves from the exploding Arado and the scream of Meteor engines buffeted the building.

The gestapo officer's face flushed with anger.

Then, over the noise of turbojets and cannon fire outside, he heard the wailing behind him.

Herries was on his knees, hands clamped over his ears, his face like a death mask.

A burst of cannon fire punctured the corrugated iron side of the hangar as if it was paper, destroying two aircraft that had been in there for maintenance. When Hartmann looked back he saw that Giesecke and the other two soldiers lay dead.

He pulled himself to his feet and only then felt the searing pain from the hot shrapnel that had cut a swathe through his thigh. He dismissed it as he dragged Herries toward the door.

"We must get out," he shouted over the infernal din of aircraft exploding outside. "Your RAF pilot is not in here. We must look for him in the next hangar and to hell with those buzzards up there."

Herries' arms flailed so wildly that Hartmann thought he would have to lash out to bring him under control. "Don't you see, Hartmann? This is the attack, the diversion, that has been laid on for him. You've left it too late. We have to get to the shelters, or those things will destroy us all."

Hartmann battled to control his rage. The man that Herries called Kruze was still within reach. But where?

He pushed Herries through the little access doorway onto the concrete apron. Buildings burned in the distance, mechanics lay dead in front of them, cut down by 20-millimeter fire as they ran to the shelters. One of the two Heinkels that had been left outside the hangars smoldered away, its back broken. The other by some miracle had escaped untouched, but Hartmann knew that it would present an inviting target for the RAF aircraft on their next pass.

Across the runway, some of the bombers of the resident *kampfgeschwader* blazed ferociously, their fuel tanks split by gunfire, while others were in the midst of their death throes, sending incandescent showers of exploding ammunition into the air, or launching brilliant, multicolored fireballs up against the dawn sky as their RATO bottles blew up.

Herries was jangling with anxiety and confusion. The jet sound. The bombs. The gestapo gunman at his side—it all bathed him in sweat and left him feeling weak and sick.

Hartmann's mind raced, shutting off the pain. The intruder

302

pilot, if he was of the mettle Herries had described, would be searching out an aircraft, perhaps already be in one. Yet, wherever he looked, the bombers lay burning or wrecked. His eyes streamed from the smoke that drifted across the airfield.

Through the chaos he watched in fascination as a little tractor, its driver slumped over the wheel, bounced over the grass beyond the farthest hangar, until it ran over a pothole and tipped on its side, two wheels spinning furiously in the air.

His eyes traced its path back through the smoke and it was then that he spotted the mottled bomber, in the lee of the far hangar about two hundred meters away, its camouflage rendering it almost invisible against the mountains beyond.

He lurched toward the Arado. Its nose pointed tantalizingly away from him so that he could not see whether it was manned. His leg gave way. As the pain redoubled, he turned to Herries and pressed a gun up against his temple. "You're my crutch," he shouted. "Get me to that bomber if it's the last thing you do."

The port turbojet of the Arado burst into life with a belch of smoke from its jetpipe. Ignoring the Meteors that prowled above, Hartmann screamed at Herries to make more speed.

☐

Kruze's hands danced over the controls as he fought to remember the start-up procedure of the German turbojet from his flights in the Me 262 back at Farnborough.

As his feet slid onto the rudder-bar pedals, his gaze rested firmly on the port RPM gauge on the right-hand side of the main control panel, which lay directly in front of him. He snatched a quick look over his left shoulder and was relieved to see that the counter was not lying. A steady stream of hot gases poured from the exhaust pipe of the port-side Junkers Jumo 004B axial turbojet as the revs crept up to 800 RPM.

He cursed the rigmarole of the jet ignition process, but reminded himself that to shortcut it would be to invite the disaster he feared most, a catastrophic turbine failure, either there and then, or worse, when—if—he got airborne.

Thanking God that the engine ignition sequence appeared identical to that on the Messerschmitt jet fighter, he watched as the rev needle inched up to the 800 RPM mark, then the moment it passed the magic figure, his left hand darted to the throttle lever, found the button he had prayed was there beneath the knob, and pressed down on it with his thumb. Within the bowels of the Jumo, fuel squirted into the main engine until full ignition was maintained. Keeping his thumb clamped on the fuel-inject button, he pressed the low-reading rev counter again with his right index finger and groaned with dismay when he realized that the revs were only up to the twelve hundred mark, with possibly another thirty seconds to go before the Jumo reached a preflight idle rating of 2500 RPM.

With Oberammergau's destruction being played out beyond the Plexiglas dome, his right hand raced across the panel and pushed the starboard engine starter-motor lever foward for three seconds, priming it into life before pulling it backward. The bang of the Riedel two-stroke ignition was instantaneous. He whispered another oath about the fragility of the turbine blades and then danced his finger back to the low-reading starboard engine rev counter, watching as it, too, nudged toward 800.

With his left thumb aching like hell, stuck to the port fuel-inject button, he checked the corresponding gauge and gave a smile as the needle hit 2,500.

Shit! He suddenly remembered the throttles. Exerting forward pressure with his left hand, he advanced the throttle for the port engine until the lever slipped into its idling gate. He wanted to mop the sweat that trickled from his hairline into his eyes, but knew that to let his hands deviate now would be to throw him out of synch, destroy the concentration that he had to maintain.

Satisfied that the tempo of the port engine was right, despite his delay with the throttle, his right hand clicked off the starter-motor lever, then came across to the throttle gate and switched on the fuel cock. Seeing the "on" signal flash on the indicator panel, he left the switch and pressed the rev counter button once again to check on the status of the port engine. With a yell of satisfaction, he watched it hit 3000 RPM, the speed at which it could idle safely.

Once he had both of them at 3000, he could start taxiing, and get the hell out of there.

Putting half his efforts into getting the starboard engine to the same state of readiness as his left-side power plant, he pulled his seat straps over his shoulder and managed to click the connectors home while he wasn't attending to the functions of the Jumo. He checked the low-reading rev counter once more and saw it pass 1500 just as the aircraft was buffeted from an explosion that ripped through the Ju 52 he had seen earlier, parked on the other side of the apron.

He braced himself for the patter of hot metal fragments that would rain down on the aircraft, wincing as he thought of the irreparable damage that would occur if just one of the pieces from the Ju 52 were sucked into the inlet of a Jumo.

He heard the tinkle of aluminum hail on the Arado's skin.

A crack like a whiplash almost stopped his heart. He saw the silver trace etched across the Plexiglas. His mind was already telling him that it could not have come from the explosion that had torn the Junkers apart when a second bullet ricocheted off the canopy.

He twisted in his seat and looked back over his right shoulder to see the civilian in the long overcoat, propped up by Herries, firing wildly with his automatic.

They were fifty feet behind and to the side of the aircraft. Herries, a manic but triumphant expression on his face, was holding the coat that Kruze had thrown to the ground before clambering into the Arado.

The other man pushed Herries aside, tried to take a step forward, and fell, the pistol clattering across the concrete. The last thing Kruze saw before he turned frantically back to his instruments was the angry bloodstain on the civilian's trouser leg.

Shouting his fury at the traitor, Kruze flicked the rev counter. The needle was still too low, not yet at 2000 revs. He fought the urge to watch the scene off his starboard wingtip; there was still too much to do in the cockpit. 2000 RPM. He pushed the right throttle to the idle detent, all his effort keeping his left thumb on the fuel-inject button just beneath the top of the lever.

He shut down the Riedel starter and looked outside.

The civilian had Herries by the lapels, was pulling his ear to his mouth, shouting over the turbojets. He pointed to the gun, lying six feet across the apron, then to the aircraft.

Kruze tore his eyes away and reached over to the fuel cock, pushing the right-hand one forward to the "on" position.

The low-reading rev counter gave him 2500 RPM. His sweat-soaked thumb slipped rather than eased off the fuel-inject button.

He looked up to see that Herries had run directly in front of him, and was now standing not six feet from the nose of the bomber. The traitor's mouth was wide open, all sound drowned by the whine of the Jumos' compressors as they wound up. Kruze's eyes remained locked on Herries, even when the traitor leveled the Walther at him and squeezed off two shots, both of which easily glanced off the armored Plexiglas. But if Herries moved around to the side where the glass was weaker, or if he put a shot into the engine inlets . . .

His nervous glance to the starboard engine betrayed his thoughts.

Herries saw the look, and suddenly realized why the Rhodesian just sat there with his engines running but did not move the aircraft. He turned from the engine to Kruze, smiled, and raised the Walther level with the inlet.

Kruze could not possibly have heard the click of the empty chamber. He merely saw the look of frustration on the traitor's face. His eyes darted from Herries to the rev-counter and back again. He saw the solution register on Herries' face, the hand with the pistol raised in the throwing position, the careful aim for the inlet, the triumphant smile on the lips . . .

Three thousand RPM.

Bang. He shoved the throttles forward as far as they would go without causing the engines to flame out.

Before Herries could bring his throwing arm down, he sensed the lurch of the bomber. He tried to move, but he was caught completely off balance and the Arado's nose gave him a glancing blow to the side of the head. He fell full-length and lay frozen for an agonizing, hysterical split second as he watched the Arado's nosewheel loom over his body.

Twenty thousand pounds of pressure crushed the traitor's pelvis and testicles to pulp in the same moment. Herries screamed, the noise rising to a howl, audible even above the engines, as the wheel trundled over his chest, splintering his ribs. Every last gulp of air was squeezed from his lungs, the vocal cords rattling until the wheel flattened his face.

Kruze felt little more than a bump as the Arado moved forward. His mind focused on the task ahead. He eased back on the throttles, making sure that the limiting jet-pipe temperature of 650 degrees centigrade was not exceeded. He looked down to his rev counters, saw both needles pass 6000 RPM, and felt the slight change in engine tempo as the governors cut in. Now the aircraft could be handled with a little less caution.

He looked out, pressing the brakes with toe action on the rudder bars to line up the aircraft on the main runway, thankful that the smoke from the burning aircraft on the other side of the field shielded him from the marauders above.

He turned the aircraft onto the runway, set flaps to twenty-five degrees, scanning the instruments once more before opening up the engines to 8500 RPM. Kruze almost stood on the brakes, felt the power of the aircraft as it strained to go. He pushed the power setting up a little more, taking the revs to 8700, quickly checked fuel and burner pressure, as well as the jet-pipe temperature, and then pulled his toes off the pedals.

The Arado shot down the runway like a wild mustang. Suddenly remembering the RATO bottles, he scanned the panel for the switch, found it, and punched it home. There was a second kick as the rockets cut in, ramming him back into his seat.

Out of the corner of his eye he saw a Meteor sweep along the edge of the airfield, then bank tightly to try to get its guns to bear, but he knew he was already in the clear. Once in the air he could give the fighters the signal that showed it was him at the controls.

Kruze pulled the bomber off the runway at 225 KPH and pulled in the flaps a few seconds later. Then he hit the RATO jettison button and felt the aircraft buck a little as the rocket packs fell away from the wingtips. He leaned forward, spotted the undercarriage selector, and pushed it forward, hearing the clunk of all three wheels as they locked into the belly of the aircraft.

Suddenly he was out of the smoke and pulling up into the clear dawn sky. He checked the periscope mirror, saw a gaggle of Meteors about a mile behind him, and carefully moved the horns of his control column from right to left and back again.

The Arado's wings responded to his touch, waggling easily and obviously.

The sign that would call them off.

He settled back in his seat, felt the sweat for the first time soaking his clothes, and banked the jet bomber to the northeast.

□

Fleming pulled up to 1000 feet and held the Meteor in a tight bank over Oberammergau, searching for signs of life below the smoke that hung like a blanket above the airfield.

His first thought was for his fellow pilots. He had seen one of the six Meteors go down, the aircraft taking a direct hit from a thirty-seven millimeter *fliegerabwehrkanone* mounted on a tower at the edge of the base. The fighter's fiery trail as it

307

plowed from two hundred feet into the forest beyond the runway still left a scar across his vision. He blinked again, trying to rid himself of it, but the memory stuck with him.

His second thought was for Kruze. If the Rhodesian had been down there, there was no chance now of him fulfilling his mission. Before the smoke of their strafing run closed in over the airfield, Fleming had witnessed the lines of broken fighter-bombers at their dispersal points on the edge of the runway, in the lee of the woods. There were no more Arados left at Oberammergau; Staverton could have that in his report when he returned to Stabitz.

"Wolf leader to Wolfpack," he spoke into his mask, "break off and head for home. Breakfast time." An empty feeling inside. Was Kruze down there, looking up at them and wondering what the hell they were playing at? More likely he was rotting in a gestapo jail, waiting for another bout with the interrogator, or lying dead in a Munich back street.

Five replies came back over his headset. Four acknowledgments.

One warning. A young pilot's voice, vibrant, excited.

"Wolf leader, there's one of them lifting off now, pulling up through the smoke, off your rear starboard quarter. Christ, the cheeky bastard's waggling his wings at us. Thinks he's got away with it. Can I take a shot at him?"

"No! I have to be sure!"

"Sure? Of what? It's got bloody great black crosses on it!" Bewilderment and frustration in the young fighter pilot's voice. Because of the change in plan there had been no need to tell them about Kruze. How could they understand what he, Fleming, was feeling now?

Fleming strained over his shoulder for a look. The Arado was clearly visible, soaring above the pall of destruction, wings rocking gently in the early-morning sunlight.

He watched the wings a moment too long, willing the lateral motion to be the result of some terrible coincidence, a turbulent updraft from the airfield, or a gust of wind off the mountains beyond.

The signal. As clear as day. Kruze.

He peeled the Meteor off in the direction of the Arado, pushing the throttles to the stops. Despite the range of the German aircraft, a good two miles away from him by now, he still had a height advantage and, while the Arado was still climbing, a little extra speed.

He hit the transmit button. "Get back to base, Wolfpack. This one's mine."

He could still catch him. Had to catch him. Branodz was only thirty minutes' flight time away and Kruze was heading straight for it, three bombs strapped under his wings. Three thousand pounds of high explosive that would rip through the alpine headquarters of the architect of Archangel, turning it into matchwood, then plow into the compound beyond, where the chemical weapons were stored.

He was gaining on the bomber, perhaps halving the range since the moment he had first spotted it pulling away from the airfield. But Kruze's speed was picking up now. The Arado leveled, then scudded between two mountain peaks. Fleming flew on, keeping his eyes fixed on the point where the bomber had entered the valley. He pulled the Meteor around the edge of a gray, jagged peak, his left wingtip dangerously close to the trees that grew intermittently on its rough scree slope. He held his breath for the moment the Arado would spring into view, flipped off the safety catch of the gun button on his joystick in preparation for the warning burst of 20 mm that would make the Rhodesian turn, maybe even turn and fight in the skies above the mountains. But he would see the Meteor, recognize the markings of the aircraft from Stabitz, and know instinctively that something was wrong, that Guardian Angel was finished.

A bank of cloud, like a wall stretching from one side of the valley to the other and as high as the peaks themselves, rushed to meet him. Too late to do anything about it; he saw the two hundred feet of clearance between the base of the thick, rolling mist and the ground, then everything went white.

Fleming fought the panic. The mountains rose around him, invisible, but there. He could almost feel them reaching out to his wingtips. There was no time to look to his horizon indicator, he just prayed his wings were level with the surface of the earth and pulled back on the stick, waiting for the split second of jarring noise—as hurtling metal thumped into bare, gargantuan rock—that would precede infinite blackness.

Sunlight leapt at him like a waterfall, before the blue sky surrounded him. The altimeter read 18,000 feet. The peaks, jutting through the gently undulating swell of the mountain cumulus, fell away behind. He leveled off and began to scour the horizon for a sign of the Arado.

He was alone.

As the panic returned, the vision of the tiny gap between the cloud base and the valley floor leapt into his mind. That was where the Rhodesian had gone, hugging the ground to avoid enemy—Allied—fighters, following his instructions from the countless briefings that had preceded the mission. Kruze had never even seen his Meteor.

He had lost him.

He reached down to the radio and swiveled the dial through all the frequencies.

"Guardian Angel is over. Kruze, if you can hear me, return to base, turn back to Stabitz. It's over, finished."

There was only the hiss of static and the echo of his own voice ringing in his ears.

And Kruze was below him, somewhere, between the carpet of thick mountain vapor and the earth, hurtling toward the target. When he pulled out of the mountains there would only be another 120 miles on the second leg, until the final run-in . . .

The second leg.

A two-stage flight plan to Branodz. One massive course deviation to keep him away from Allied fighter patrols. Kruze flying two sides of the triangle from Oberammergau to Branodz. Fleming's own carefully negotiated flight plan for the Rhodesian seemed to dance before his eyes on the windshield in front of him. Despite the Arado's overall speed advantage, there was a chance, just a chance, that he could intercept him over the target if he flew direct, with no course change, just a straight path: across German lines, across Allied lines, and into Russian airspace.

It was the only option left.

He swung the aircraft around to the north, away from the mountains and the clouds, on a vector that would take him directly to Branodz. He would pick up the landmarks after crossing the river Isar, wide and conspicuous, as it meandered leisurely across the alluvial plain, northeast of Munich.

8

"Careful, careful," Shlemov growled, as he watched the NCOs and enlisted men of the VKhV Military Chemical Forces grapple clumsily with the crates that Shaposhnikov had stored in the corral beside the HQ in Branodz. "You idiots should know better than anyone what's in there," he shouted in the general direction of the nearest work party.

Of course there was no actual danger of the shell cases splitting if the men were to drop one of the boxes. The bastards were doing it deliberately, though, to try to scare him, Shlemov thought. Ever since they found out that he had put Major Ryakhov, their leader, on a truck that would take him to Ostrava and thence to Moscow . . .

It probably wasn't his fault, Shlemov admitted to himself. It was obvious that Shaposhnikov had duped him into transporting the hydrogen cyanide to the front, but he could not be allowed to run around the Motherland knowing what had happened in that place. He was satisfied that the rest of the VKhV troops did not know of Ryakhov's arrangement with Shaposhnikov. They could carry on believing the excuse he himself had given them. There had been an emergency, the fascists had deployed chemicals, but had backed down when they discovered Soviet weapons of equal ferocity had been rushed to the front.

The distant rumble of artillery, their guns, reminded him

311

how close Shaposhnikov had come to pulling it off. Once Marshal Konev learned of Archangel, possibly reacting against the news that he would have been the first killed by the conspirators, he decided to put the offensive into effect right away, with Stalin's blessing.

The unrelenting tom-tom beat of the massive artillery barrage had been going on now for over two hours, more or less since they had begun loading up the trucks. Final victory against the fascists, Konev had assured him, was now at hand. Looking at the frantic activity around him—dispatch riders entering and leaving the HQ every few seconds; troops swarming around the place like soldier ants; hearing the clank of armor rolling from the valley below toward the front lines—personally, he didn't doubt the marshal's words.

Shlemov wanted to get home to Moscow but Beria's unquestionable instructions had come through during the night. Oversee the shipment of the hydrogen cyanide, first on the trucks, then into the rail wagons at Ostrava, and finally get them safely back to Berezniki, a total journey of almost two thousand kilometers. It had not put him in a good mood.

Especially working with these idiots. They were damned lucky not to be joining Ryakhov.

He looked back at the corral and groaned. It was still almost full. Only four trucks had been loaded, another sixteen to go. It would take all day at this rate.

He turned, swearing under his breath, and barged his way past two dispatch riders into the warmth of the HQ to try to find some acorn coffee to drive the sleep from his aching limbs.

□

Kruze held the aircraft as steady as he could between the cloud base and the valley floor, weaving his way around bluffs and points that rushed to meet him with frightening speed and regularity.

He smiled, scarcely able to believe it. He had stolen the Ar 234 Blitz, the "lightning" bomber, from its lair. Despite those idiots in the Meteors, the double treachery of Herries, and the vicissitudes of the aircraft itself. He had done it for Penny and for Fleming. The rest he would do in the name of something less tangible.

The aircraft was aptly named. It felt like riding shotgun on the front of a high-speed locomotive. A few feet of fragile instruments and Plexiglas separated him from 400 MPH of slipstream. That was all. The water vapor that hung heavily in the valley streaked in long rivulets from the glazed nose of the bomber across the Plexiglas over his head. He took his eyes momentarily off his limited horizon and looked through the canopy above him. Fifty feet away wisps of gray, angry cloud flashed past, each reaching down to the aircraft, malevolently, as if they were storm-lashed branches desperately trying to unseat him from his wild, galloping stallion.

Shaposhnikov was less than half an hour away. Just under thirty minutes more of unbending concentration. That was all it would take.

He fumbled for the coat that hid the charts that would get him to the tiny valley that cupped the town of Branodz between its rocky walls.

And then his mind replayed the last minutes of his time at Oberammergau and the terrible moment when he had looked over his shoulder and seen Herries holding up his coat with triumph in his eyes. The traitor, in death, had taken something from him that might cost him the mission. The charts. How could he have been so stupid to have discarded the coat? Yet, in the heat of the moment, it had been a hindrance, something to dispose of; that the charts were sewn into the lining had never crossed his mind.

Could he do without them? He had to.

He looked at the compass. The valley was taking him in the general direction he wanted, but soon he would be out of the mountains and then he would need landmarks, man-made and geological features noted carefully in the briefing room at Stabitz, but now suddenly elusive. The first leg, a vector of oh-seven-oh degrees for eighty miles, then the way point. What was it? The castle, a big Bavarian affair by a lake, Fleming had said. Schloss Ubersee. But it would be like looking for a needle in a haystack unless he found the river Inn first.

Then his eyes fell on the map case, tucked away to his left on the cockpit wall. He pulled at the charts, careful not to take his gaze off the rapidly rolling scenery in front of him for more than a few seconds at a time. On a large-scale map, he quickly found Munich, then Oberammergau.

Ahead, the valley began to widen and, to his relief, the clouds lifted a little.

He pulled the aircraft up to five hundred feet and looked down at the maze of brown, green, and gray topography staring back at him from the paper on his knees. He found the castle, then looked for the river. The Inn stitched its way through the varying contours of the land. He reckoned he was already half-way to it, such was the speed he was traveling.

He plotted the course that had been devised for him by Fleming. Fleming, the mission planner. The route that would expose him as little as possible to Allied and Russian fighters, or their armies' ground fire.

Snatching glances out of the cockpit, he saw the valley gradient level off and the river bed broaden, until the snow was left behind. Wooden chalets flashed past the lower slopes, while higher up, almost level with his wingtips, there were smaller huts, sheds, some of them surrounded by the light and dark dots of the livestock they had housed during the night.

He flashed over a small herd of goats grazing on a bluff touched by the early-morning sun. The pack scattered as his turbojets whistled overhead. As his eyes followed them, a shepherd sprang into view, shielding his eyes from the sun as he searched for the Valkyrie that shattered the peace of the valley. Kruze saw a shake of the fist, then a wave, as the Bavarian peasant recognized the stark black and white *balkenkreuz* stenciled under the wings.

This is how Branodz will look, he told himself. But no one would cheer for him there. The thought jolted him back inside the cockpit.

While he was still in German-held territory he decided to check over the aircraft. It would be the last chance he had. If he managed to find the way point, his hands would be full navigating, looking for fighters, and, more than likely, taking evasive action.

The turbojets were running smoothly at their cruise speed of 7000 RPM, jet-pipe temperature and fuel pressure were normal, and his fuel load was good. He looked around in vain for a headset. Provided he had survived the onslaught of the Meteor strike, the pilot of Ar 234, factory number W.Nr.140219, serial number F1/BB, was probably clutching his flying helmet back at Oberammergau and wondering who had taken his aircraft. Again, it did not matter. To eavesdrop on the airwaves would have served little purpose.

Suddenly he was out of the Bayerische Mountains, the rolling countryside of the Ober Bayern before him. Despite the inherent danger of flying through the peaks, he suddenly realized that they had offered protection, a mask between him and the Mustangs, Thunderbolts, and Spitfires. He felt dangerously exposed, naked to the British and American fighter patrols that he knew to be roaming the area, seeking out their targets of opportunity.

He had no forward-firing armament. He could only fight them with evasive action and a weapon he had never tried before, built into the rear of the aircraft, pointing aft.

The Rhodesian scoured the horizon for a sign of the frontline, a column of smoke here and there which would have signaled the dividing line between Wehrmacht and American troops. There was none. Fleming's flight plan was good, taking him away to the east, deeper into German-held territory, where his Blitz was safe, at least from ground fire.

Until he hit the Russian lines.

A town pulled into view straight in front of him, the spires of its churches clearly visible against the horizon. He looked down to his map. He hadn't crossed the Inn yet, so it had to be Bad Aibling, the only medium-sized population center in the area on the rough course setting he had chosen. As he ripped over the middle of the town, he paid scant attention to the Panther tanks parked haphazardly in the main square. Then he saw what he was looking for, the distinctive confluence where the three rivers joined, the way they did on his map.

He was about twenty miles off course.

He put the aircraft onto a new heading to starboard that would take him directly to Schloss Ubersee, knowing that at any moment the river Inn would flash beneath him, signaling the moment he would have to start searching for the castle. At the speed and altitude he was flying, his glimpse of it would last one second.

An orange and silver trace ahead, the Inn caught in the sun's early morning rays, stretching from left to right, then the river, brown and turgid, shot by beneath his feet. The ground rose rapidly, almost taking Kruze by surprise. He eased back on the stick and noted the brief expanse of arable land giving way to mountains again, although not as steep and craggy as the ones through which he had just flown. As the ground rose up, the Arado hugging its contours at a few hundred feet, so the cloud base moved down to meet it. Kruze swore at the prospect of having his way point obscured by the mountain mist and being forced to set his course to Branodz by dead reckoning instead. With only one pass allowed to him over the target area, he had to get it right.

He pulled up into the clouds and weaved between the steep

sides of the cumuli, avoiding contact with them, as if they were the solid, mountain walls that he had flown between earlier. He stuck to the clear air not out of paranoia but through a desperate urge to maintain contact with the ground. He had to find the castle. He scrutinized every patch of clear sky between himself and the ground for a sign of Schloss Ubersee, or an expanse of lake. They were the only details he possessed, the best he had to go on.

A flash below, like a searchlight in his eyes.

He nosed the aircraft down, below the clouds, keeping a careful watch for high ground, searching, willing what he had glimpsed to be the lake of Schloss Ubersee.

He broke out of the cloud stack about two hundred and fifty feet above the ground. In front of him was the castle, looming above him, almost a mile away, its towers brushing the rolling mountain mist. Below it, nestled in the bowl of a craggy, glacial rock formation was the lake itself, a thin crust of ice on its surface sending shimmering reflections at him whenever the sun's rays forced their way through a gap in the clouds.

Schloss Ubersee, like a lighthouse guiding him in for the final course deviation.

He held the aircraft steady as it whistled over the battlements of the ancient castle, then twisted the horns on the stick to swing him around on the new bearing. He racked his brains for the next landmark. A town. Alten . . .

Altenmarkt. Lying in the fork of the two rivers. He was then to pick up the twisting form of the river Alz, following it for about thirty miles until it met the much larger river Salzach. Thereafter there were only about forty miles to the Czechoslovakian border and another thirty miles to the target. As his confidence grew, the details of the flight plan became clearer. He had forgotten nothing. He was on course.

Kruze pulled the aircraft up to one thousand feet, nosed it toward a patch of clear sky, and set the autopilot. He slid forward into the smooth, glazed nose, and switched on the Lotfe 7H tachometric bombsight and the BZA1 bombing computer.

In other, more conventional Luftwaffe aircraft, the Lotfe was operated by the bomb aimer while the pilot flew the aircraft. In the single-crew Arado, the pilot performed both duties. At altitude, he could keep the autopilot engaged, go forward into the nose, look into the sighting mechanism and drop the bombs under guidance from the sight and computer. At low altitude, however, that was impossible. Kruze would need to employ all his skills as a pilot just to negotiate the terrain around Branodz, even without the problem of the Soviet air defenses.

So how did the Lotfe work under single-crew conditions at low altitude? He looked around the cockpit, his eyes eventually falling on the strange device protruding from the roof above his seat. The periscope; it had to be aligned with the periscope.

He pulled himself back into his seat, decoupled the autopilot and strapped himself in. Then he placed one eye against the periscope sighting system for the rearward firing canon and found himself looking not aft, but forward. He reached down and flicked off the Lotfe and an image of mountains and clouds slipping away from him filled the viewfinder. He thought of Staverton's reaction to his find. A combined periscopic gun/bombsight and rearview mirror.

He looked at the clock mounted in the center of the steering horns on the control column. He had been airborne about twenty minutes. The Russian lines would be coming up soon, very soon.

His right hand reached down to the large dial below the main electrical switch panel. He twisted the dial through two positions and armed the three bombs.

Beyond the nose of the bomber, a river, then another, caught Kruze's eye, their paths converging until he spotted the small village nestling in the bowl where their waters met. Altenmarkt. The confluence of the two streams produced a wide, choppy river, but already he could see calmer water ahead where the Alz began its journey across the lowlands of the Nieder Bayern. He pushed the column forward and increased power, hardly noticing the thumps that rocked the aircraft as it slid out of the last patches of light cloud and turbulence that marked the invisible demarcation line between plain and upland.

Something made him shift his gaze beyond the river and into the haze above the horizon. An almost imperceptible movement, it would have been lost to anyone whose senses were not on full alert for the slightest sign of danger. With the sun rising off the right-hand side of his aircraft, Kruze easily saw the glint of silver off the last of the five Mustangs as they swept in finger formation across the countryside about three miles in front of him.

He slid the Arado down lower, ever lower, conscious of the mountain backdrop, which would shield him from the scrutiny of the American fighters as they swept from right to left across his nose. Sanctuary, he realized, lay between the banks of the river Alz itself. The chances were that this was not the only Allied fighter patrol in the district.

The Mustangs plowed on toward the west, as Kruze watched them carefully out of the corner of his eye, as if even a slight movement of the head would be enough to give his position away.

Kruze brought the Arado down to treetop height. He looked left and right and noted with some satisfaction that he was actually below the tops of the tall, leafless trees that lined the river. Beyond his rudder pedals, through the clear nose, he could see the dark, muddy waters flashing by fifty feet below. He was careful not to look at the boiling water directly. It would be easy to become disoriented, hypnotized, and plow in, he and his aircraft vaporized with the water as his three thousand pounds of bombs exploded on contact with the river's surface.

He flew the Arado down the Alz's invisible center line at 560 KPH, exhilarated by the speed and the agility of the fighter-bomber. As he twisted and weaved through the gradual mean-derings of the Alz, he was overcome by a strange feeling of tranquility.

He saw a group of people rushing crazily toward him on the left-side bank. It was ironic that he found serenity there of all places, in a shuddering, hurtling piece of machinery, flashing through inhospitable countryside at almost 350 MPH. He caught a momentary impression in the midst of the party of the young peasant girl's face, little more than 40 feet below his wingtip, her features frozen as the menacing shape of the Arado headed for her. He thought back to Penny, tried to picture her face, her hair, recall how she felt to his touch. But he could see or smell nothing, save the leather of his seat, the oil lubricating the moving controls, and the paint primer in the cockpit. She seemed a lifetime away from him now. Try as he could to visualize her, he saw only the terrified face of the peasant girl on the banks of the Alz.

Penny's place was with Fleming now.

Rapids ahead of him. Angry water whipped white by the rocks below the surface. Plumes of water rising into the air, lashing the Arado as he flew through them. A curious, bending motion in the pattern of the white water, reminiscent of . . .

Not rapids, but bullets, machine-gun fire snaking across the surface of the water.

He put his eye to the periscope, swearing at his lapse in

concentration, knowing exactly what he would see through the optic sight.

Mustangs. One on his tail and two on either side of the river, hemming him in, waiting for the Arado to pop up so that they too could get their guns to bear on him.

Fifty-caliber bullets punched into his wings. He fought the inclination to take evasive action, for short of pulling up—away from the river and the danger of the trees, and into the gunsights of the Americans' wingmen—there was nothing he could do. If he increased speed he would fly into the ground or the river.

Another snatched glance in the periscope. The lead Mustang was right on his tail, 200 feet behind. He saw the flickering lights along its wings' leading edges and felt the Arado buck once more as bullets hit the fuselage behind him. The American was getting closer.

He pulled the 234 around a bend and immediately saw the bridge, the height and length of a hangar, its two lanes crammed with German vehicles, its arches spanning the river in front of him. For a moment, he froze, thinking that it was too late, that the Arado would be shredded by the great steel girders of the bridge, to fall and plummet through the two columns of retreating Wehrmacht armor before hitting the river in a sea of spray and fire. But with an animal roar he pulled back on the yoke, his whole body sensing the reluctance of the Arado, weighed down by bombs and drop tanks under the wings, to come up.

The pilot of the Mustang that was locked on Kruze's tail never even saw the bridge. In almost one moment, the fighter's wings were pulled off at the roots by the girders, and its 1380-horsepower engine buried itself into the armor-plated turret of a King Tiger tank, the metals almost fusing as one in the explosion. Kruze saw the orange ball of flame in the eyepiece of the periscope and was up to five hundred feet before he even realized he had missed the bridge.

A bullet pierced a Plexiglas panel above his head, narrowly missing the Lotfe sight as it exited somewhere between his feet. Kruze pushed the aircraft back down, knowing that the Mustangs would be lining up for a chance to pull into the narrow river valley and avenge their comrade who had died hugging his tail. A check in the periscope confirmed his worst fears: a second Mustang sticking like glue. He recalled Staverton's words, the ones about the 234 being able to outrun anything.

What the bastard should have said was the 234 could only go into its greased-lightning routine at altitudes approaching its service ceiling, halfway to the stratosphere. At treetop height and with three thousand pounds of bombs below, a Mustang could still pace him.

The left-hand side of his instrument panel, housing the artificial horizon and rate-of-climb indicator, exploded with a crash; the tumbling .50-caliber bullet tore a hole the size of his fist through the Plexiglas. A sharp pain in his arm pulled his left hand off the control horn.

He stared in rage at the periscope sighting system for the rearward firing 20-millimeter cannon. Useless, bloody useless at this altitude, with trees and water rushing around his aircraft. To take his eye off the galloping scenery in front of him would spell the end in a fraction of a second.

Kruze held his breath, waiting for the stream of fire that would end it all. In front of him, the river narrowed, then dwindled into little more than a brook as the hard bedrock split the water of the Alz into small tributaries. He was running out of protection. He started to pull back on the control column as a line of trees rushed to meet him. The nose of the bomber came up, exposing it to the combined guns of the fighters behind; and he realized bitterly that he had never even made the Russian lines.

At 250 feet he could see the smoke and flames stretch the length of the horizon and it made him gasp. If he hadn't been facing the last moment of his existence, it could have been awe-inspiring, magical almost.

In one cogent moment, he knew what it was, knew the reason for his stay of execution.

The Soviet offensive had been launched.

He looked into the periscopic sight and saw the Mustangs peeling away to the west. Had they crossed into Soviet airspace, some thirty miles closer than it had been the day before, they would have been fired on by the Russians, as surely as Kruze would be at any moment.

As the pain caused by the shard of metal from the instrument panel began working its way into his body, a sudden thought, a moment of raging doubt, held it in check.

The smoke and flames of battle that rolled toward him like a tidal wave. The first cries of Shaposhnikov's baby? The birth of Archangel?

It was not too late, he had to tell himself. If the marshal had launched his offensive against the west, there was even more reason now for ensuring that each of his bombs found their mark.

He pushed the throttles forward and caught the first whiff of battle smoke on the slipstream that rushed through the broken Plexiglas on the left-hand side of the bomber's nose.

□

The Yak 9s of Colonel Anatoly Putyatin, military pilot first class, and his wingman, Lieutenant Mikhail Samsonov, swept the sky at three thousand meters, a few kilometers behind the Red Army's advance. It had been an uneventful patrol, but that had been the pattern of things over the last few months, with the Luftwaffe all but destroyed on the eastern front.

Putyatin glanced beyond his starboard wingtip at Samsonov, who was only six weeks out of the air academy at Tanyarsk. He caught his wingman looking admiringly at his own piston-engined Yakovlev 9 *ulutshshennyi*, a masterpiece of Soviet engineering.

Putyatin jabbed his finger downward, the signal that they were to return to Grafen, forward air base of the Thirteenth Guards Regiment, Soviet Fifth Air Force, Frontal Aviation.

The colonel watched as Samsonov pointed his older Yak 9D toward their base. He soon spotted the airfield, clean and untouched by the war, beneath the first line of ridges that gave way gradually to the mountainous region beyond.

He followed Samsonov's aircraft, White 15, as it slipped into the landing circuit, lowering its wheels about a kilometer downwind of the runway threshold.

He was just thinking how easy his first patrol of the new offensive had been, when he saw the German bomber pop up over the trees, its mottled camouflage momentarily stark and conspicuous against the blue, dawn sky. He shouted a warning to Samsonov, whose aircraft had slowed to a few KPH above touchdown speed as it slid over the edge of the airfield, and banked his Yak 9U sharply on a course to intercept the intruder.

□

Kruze was wrestling to keep the Arado 234 on a low-level flight profile parallel with the ground, fighting the waves of pain from

321

the injury to his arm, when he spotted the Yak beyond the next line of trees, its wheels lowered to land. It was too late to change course, or for remorse at his stupidity. Fleming's words about the Soviet fighter base at Grafen were still echoing through his head as the Arado crossed the boundary fence of the airfield.

A row of pristine, single-engined fighters, their fuselages adorned with the red star and white identification numbers of Frontal Aviation, filled his vision. His first reaction was to bank the bomber so that it was lined up on the row of Yaks, his second was to realize the futility of the maneuver because of the Arado's lack of forward-firing armament.

With only a few seconds to think through the consequences of his impending action, but knowing that to do nothing would be to invite the Yak fighter unit to intercept his bomber on the return leg west, he punched the uppermost button on the left-hand horn of his control column. The Arado lifted a little as the thousand-pound bomb on the center line dropped away from the aircraft.

Kruze was so low that the fusing mechanism could not compensate for his height, turning the bomb into a delayed-action device. It skipped once on the concrete in front of the line of fighters, plowed through the first and second aircraft, missed the third, bounced thirty feet above the ground, and then exploded in an airburst over the last five fighters.

The Rhodesian turned the Arado violently away from the destruction in front of him and found himself staring directly into the red propeller spinner of Samsonov's Yak 9D as it wobbled in to land. Both aircraft veered sharply in opposite directions, Kruze narrowly missing a hangar, Samsonov unable to stop his wingtip from catching the ground and sending the Yak into a violent cartwheel across the runway.

Putyatin watched helplessly from eight hundred meters as the German jet bomber, within the space of a few seconds, achieved the almost total destruction of his unit. Then his attention shifted to the wild acrobatics of his wingman's fighter as it rolled, one wingtip after another across the ground, finally disintegrating in a fireball on the edge of the airfield.

The colonel steepened his dive toward the Arado and watched his airspeed hit 640 KPH. He uttered brief thanks that he had been allocated the new *ulutshshennyi*—improved—variant of the Yak 9D, with its boosted 1875-horsepower engine, for otherwise he would have had no chance of catching the fascist bomber.

Kruze had no time to marvel at his lucky escape. Somehow he had veered off course and stumbled upon Grafen. Knowing his exact position now, he eased back on the stick, looking for the Vydra.

For a few long seconds, his airspeed dropped.

Immediately, a line of tracer rose to meet him from some unseen flak emplacement and he nosed the aircraft back down to earth, but not before he had glimpsed the last way point.

Ahead, in the distance, the twin peaks of Leck and Zalednik thrust their way skyward, towering above the other mountains in the range. Trickling between them, athough unseen to Kruze, was the Vydra River, winding its way up the valley all the way to Branodz.

Although flak burst around him intermittently, neither the antiaircraft fire nor the fighter activity was as bad as he thought it would be. With mixed feelings, he realized he had been granted a reprieve from the full wrath of the Russians' air defenses because of the offensive. Frontal Aviation would be busy supporting ground operations with Yaks turned into fighter-bombers. Few Russian fighters would be given over to straight interception duties. Those that had, he had wiped off the map with his bomb run over their airfield.

Kruze winced and looked down at his arm, the blood caked thick around the ripped cloth of the shirt where the metal shard had entered.

"Not bad for a cripple," he said to himself. ". . . except you're one bomb shorter than you were before."

There was nothing else for it, but to make each shot count. The thought of missing the target now, when he had come so far, chilled him far more than the thin blast of icy slipstream that whistled through the cockpit.

With his eye on the peaks ahead and maintaining a steady altitude about one hundred feet above the trees, he leaned forward and found the switch for the Lotfe.

Then he saw a shadow off the right side of the Arado pass across the face of the sun.

Putyatin hurled his Yak around in a tight turn and came in with the light behind him, having taken full advantage of the drop in the Arado's speed to press home his attack from Kruze's front starboard quarter. Kruze never even saw the tracer from the Russian's 20-millimeter ShVAK cannon that tore through his fuselage, cutting a four-foot gash in the Arado just forward of the tail. The controls seemed to slacken in his hands, indicating immediately that his hydraulic pressure was down. A glance to the gauge told him that it had dropped significantly, and the needle was still moving. He peered around, expecting to see a fiery trail pouring from his fuselage, but there was none. Suddenly, the rear-tank low-fuel warning light on the right side of the cockpit began flashing in red, angry pulses. One of the shells must have punctured the cell, miraculously failing to explode on its way through the fuselage, but now giving him a serious shortfall in fuel.

He looked over his shoulder and saw the Russian fighter coming in from the rear, half a mile behind, for another pass. With the bombs weighing him down and his controls at reduced effectiveness, there was little he could do to evade the Yak. He climbed, pulling as hard as he could on the stick with his good arm, suddenly banking the bomber away from the stream of fire that spewed out of the Yak's propeller hub, the bright tracer racing past his cockpit and exploding in the trees five hundred yards in front of him.

Realizing that he could still outpace the piston-engined fighter, Kruze shoved the throttles forward and watched his speed creep up to 650 KPH. He disconnected the Lotfe and peered into his periscope, watching with relief as the Yak began to slip away. In front of him, the mountains loomed, large and impenetrable, except for the gap between the two peaks, where he would point the Arado and fly it up the valley until he hit Branodz and punched the buttons that would release his bombs.

When he looked back to his instruments, the cockpit seemed to be on fire, so bright and so many were the warning lights illuminated on the right side of the control panel. His starboard engine oil-pressure was dangerously low and his exhaust-gas temperature gauge told him his right-hand turbojet was about to explode. A glance in the periscope. The Russian was still receding, leaving him with a choice: try to outrun it to the mountains and risk having the right engine ripped off, or shut it down and wait for the 20-millimeter to knock him out of the sky.

The starboard jet unit fire-warning temperature gauge lit up, making the decision for him. He was a moment away from a catastrophic turbine failure. He willed his injured arm to make haste as it crept perilously slowly toward the throttle. At last he reached it, pulled it back, and shut down the ailing engine.

He looked in the periscope and saw the Yak bound forward.

The Rhodesian reached out to his left, groaning with the stabs of pain to his arm; he hit the first of the three-position flap selector buttons and then pushed the undercarriage selector lever forward.

There was no reaction from the Arado.

Kruze's eyes raced over his instruments. He lunged for the flap and undercarriage emergency hydraulic selector switch and then grabbed the large standby handpump by his right knee, pulling and pushing it furiously until he saw the needle on the hydraulic gauge creep back toward its true position in the center of the dial.

The crippled jet bomber bucked as the flaps and wheels lowered into the airstream.

Putyatin was some way behind the 234 when he saw its wheels lower and the wings waggle. The Russian smiled. With holes that size in his fuselage, the German was finished, his tail looking as if it would fall off if the aircraft made any kind of violent maneuver. The Arado would make a glorious prize, a final testimony to his three years of fighting the fascists. It would also give Soviet scientists a long-awaited insight into the workings of the advanced German aircraft.

Through the periscopic gunsight, Kruze saw the Yak slide in behind his tail. He waited before hitting the button, until the cross centered on its nose and he could see the form of the pilot in the cockpit. Behind him, the rearward-pointing Mauser MG 151 twenty-millimeter cannons fired a controlled burst, striking Putyatin's aircraft first in the engine, then in the fuel tanks as the Yak veered sharply upward, exposing its soft, blue underbelly. There was a flash in the bowels of the Yak and then it plummeted earthward, its rear fuselage lost in the surrounding fireball.

Kruze pulled the undercarriage up again and increased power gently on his good engine, keeping the aircraft lined up on the entrance to the valley. He prayed he could slip the crippled Arado unseen through the Russian defenses as far as Branodz, now less than five minutes' flight time away.

9

Malenkoy swung his knapsack into the back of the jeep, jumped into the driver's seat, and set off at top speed down the forest track, away from Chrudim, the *maskirovka*, and Archangel. He couldn't wait to get on the train at Ostrava. Only then, away from the horror of the last few days, not to mention Shlemov's NKVD, did he feel he could sleep.

Shlemov had been quite specific. When the NKVD major had found him in his tent at Chrudim following his discharge from the hospital, his message was quite clear. He, Malenkoy, was a hero, but an embarrassing one. He was therefore being transferred, with immediate effect, from the front back to Moscow and the academy. And if he wanted to talk too openly about his wartime experiences once he was safely ensconced in the heart of the Motherland, there was always the safety of his family to consider . . .

The early morning sun poured through the trees, the rays glinting on the Order of Lenin that bounced on his chest every time the jeep hit another pothole. Malenkoy sucked in the cool mountain air and the fragrance of the pines. This was how he wanted to remember Czechoslovakia.

□

Fleming patrolled the skies high above the vast forest that lay directly beneath the path that Kruze would have to take on his run-in to Branodz, his eyes scanning the horizon for a sign of the 234 and any inquisitive Yaks. Kruze was already overdue. Although he wanted to see the Rhodesian safe from the Russian's guns, he realized that if the Arado was still airworthy, his Meteor was the last line of defense.

Flying high above the new Russian offensive, Fleming recognized that he owed his safe passage to the fact that Frontal Aviation was running too many missions in support of the Red Army to worry about a lone Meteor crossing into Soviet-designated airspace.

But the assault . . . was it Konev's or Shaposhnikov's?

He double-checked his position. Satisfied that he was maintaining a combat air patrol over the valley that led to Shaposhnikov's HQ, he went back to searching the ground for a sign of Kruze.

He felt desperately alone. He questioned what he was doing there. He could not shoot Kruze down in cold blood. There had to be another way.

It was nothing more than a slight movement, caught out of the corner of his eye, that made him narrow his search to the quadrant on his forward starboard beam. At first he thought it was a Russian aircraft, limping home from a bombing sortie against German positions at the front. But then he noticed the stark black crosses on the upper surface of the wings as it drew closer, sticking close to the contours of the land, and he knew it was the Arado heading straight for Branodz. Although it was still some way off, he could see it was heavily battle-scarred, the great gash in the tail so big that daylight was visible through the hole.

The Arado was flying with one wing down, the starboard wingtip almost brushing the tops of the trees. It was slow, much too slow, he thought; and then he realized why. A thin trail of smoke snaked from the right-hand engine. Kruze had gone for an in-flight shutdown of a Jumo. Either that or it had been knocked out by gunfire.

He increased speed and dived the Meteor toward his quarry.

In the cockpit of the Arado, Kruze was too busy checking the instruments governing his good engine and keeping the damaged plane on a straight and level course to notice the descent of the Meteor. He had the Lotfe sight switched on, and the height and speed of the aircraft fed into the BZA1 bombing computer. Unless he released the two 1000-pounders soon, his aircraft would bury itself into the inhospitable hillside.

He had swept over Russian patrols and vehicles, knew that they would be trying to radio his progress to Branodz. But he also knew that there was more than an even chance that their transmissions would be blocked by the contours of the terrain through which he now maneuvered his crippled aircraft. He gritted his teeth against the pain in his arm. Nothing would stop him from putting his two bombs through Shaposhnikov's HQ now.

The Meteor tore across the front of the 234, missing it by a few feet. Kruze had only the most fleeting impression of a camouflaged blur shooting past his eyes before the shock waves from Fleming's high-speed pass hit him and he wrestled with the stick to keep the Arado under control.

He increased power to his good engine in a bid to put as much distance between himself and the Soviet fighter with which he thought he had just had the near-miss. Kruze could not afford to put his damaged plane into aerial combat. By the time the fighter found him again, if its pilot could at all, he would be those few vital kilometers nearer the HQ.

Just over a minute to target.

Fleming looked back and saw the Arado staying resolutely on course. Kruze was like an automaton, totally locked into the world of his cockpit. His warning had gone unheeded and there had only been time for one. The Rhodesian was almost at Branodz. Fleming pulled the Meteor around for one final pass.

□

Malenkoy almost swerved the jeep off the road when he caught sight of the aircraft coming in low across the valley toward him. He slowed to a stop, fumbled for his field glasses, and brought them up to his face, his hands shaking. He couldn't see any markings, but it had to be a German. The Russians had no aircraft like the propellerless one he had just seen and he doubted whether they had pressed any captured ones into service.

Although it was some way off, he could see from the way the aircraft yawed from side to side that the pilot was in some difficulty; he also saw the massive bombs slung under the pylons on the engine pods and knew immediately that he was heading for Branodz, little more than 5 kilometers from his position.

Branodz, home to Konev's HQ, adjacent to the corral that held the missing Berezniki consignment.

Malenkoy pulled the flare pistol out from under the dashboard and pointed it over the tops of the trees. His finger was poised over the trigger, when he saw the other aircraft hurtle over the top of the valley just behind the German. He looked through the binoculars and saw the markings. It was British! He never asked himself what the RAF was doing in that sector. It offered salvation and that was enough. He threw the flare pistol to the floor, thankful that he wasn't reduced to such a desperate warning. He saw the British pilot drawing up behind the fascist, the whine of their engines growing in his ears. Pinpoints of light flickered in the nose of the British fighter, then the rumble of the cannons rolled across the valley floor. But the tracer missed, the four thin lines of phosphor-tipped shells whistling past the cockpit of the German. The Arado pushed down lower, followed by the Meteor until both aircraft seemed to brush the flat ground. The fighter fired again and Malenkoy watched, horrified as the burst rippled past the other side of the aircraft. It was as if the British pilot did not want to strike the bomber, as if he were trying to issue a warning . . .

As the two aircraft shot past his position, Malenkoy saw the bomber dodge to avoid the tracer. Then the German's rudder seemed to flutter momentarily like a rag in the wind before it broke away completely from the tail. The Arado dropped away behind a cluster of trees and the Meteor pulled up and away from the ground.

The Russian threw the jeep into gear and set off at top speed for the crash site, one eye on the place where he had seen the Arado go in.

□

Kruze fought the Arado with every fiber of his being to prevent it from hitting the trees. With the last of his strength, he pulled back on the stick and felt the tops of the pines scrape the aircraft, then his eyes scouted for some flat, open ground for the belly landing.

He hit the release buttons for the two remaining bombs and they tumbled away to bury themselves deep in the ground, exploding three seconds later in an incandescent orange fireball. The shock waves radiated outward, catching the Arado as he brought it down to earth, the red-hot shrapnel cutting through the cockpit, puncturing his thigh, his side.

He cried out with the pain as the Plexiglas shattered in front of him and the hard, frozen earth tore through the cockpit, hitting his body and cutting his face. He threw his hands up for the final conflagration that would blow him to pieces as the fuel tanks went up, and then all was still.

□

Fleming circled the smoking wreckage at two hundred feet. He had watched in horror, first as Kruze's rudder had broken away from the tail, then in awe as the Rhodesian wrestled with the controls to bring the jet to a belly landing. The huge explosions seemed to end it all, but it wasn't the Arado that had gone up, merely the bombs that had dropped from their racks just before the plane went in.

Well-aimed bursts had narrowly missed the Arado, but Kruze had taken no notice of his warning shots. The Rhodesian had tried to outmaneuver his attempts to shepherd him away from his bomb run into Branodz, but it was the Arado's frail airframe that was finally overcome.

As the dust settled over the scrubland of the Arado's last resting place, his eyes followed the trail of broken metal and engine components until they fastened on the fuselage, which by some miracle was still in one piece. And there had been no fire, only thick, acrid smoke swirling up into the still air.

He pulled the Meteor down for a low pass over the cockpit, afraid of what he would see inside.

The hatch fell off the top of the cabin and the smoke billowed out. In its midst, he saw Kruze pull himself onto the top of the fuselage. He seemed to be clutching his side. Fleming couldn't stop himself from crying out when he saw the Rhodesian inch himself to the ground and stagger away from the wreckage.

Through the dust and the smoke, Kruze heard the sound of the aircraft overhead. He looked up and saw the Meteor, its red, white, and blue roundels clearly visible, despite the swirling clouds that belched from the Arado's cockpit. He thought he was dreaming, but the roar of the jets as the plane swept low across the ground confirmed that he wasn't.

The knowledge that it was the RAF that had finally prevented him from reaching his target cut through the pain. The Meteor was coming around again. The engines were throttled right back, the hood was open and he could see the pilot, waving, no, pointing to the trees.

The pilot was Fleming.

Kruze saw him clearly. There was no mistake. At first he tried to fight it, then he saw it all. Fleming hadn't been trying to shoot him down. He had been warning him off, trying to steer him away from Branodz. And then he no longer cared why it was Robert who had brought him down, or that he had failed to get to Archangel. Fleming was up there and it all seemed to fit. Their lives had come together and the bond had continued, unbroken, in spite of his attempts to cast himself loose from him, from Penny. He had played with fire, basked in its glow for those few short days, and then tried to put it out. Now the fire raged in him, burning him right down to his soul.

He fell to the ground, the pain too much to let him stand. Fleming was circling overhead, his arm hanging from the open cockpit, buffeted by the slipstream, still indicating the way to the nearest belt of trees. Kruze knew that he was showing him the path to escape, away from the Russian patrols that would be there within a few minutes. But he couldn't move any more. He didn't want to. Come on, Robert, finish me off.

Fleming shouted out as Kruze seemed to fall back on the ground. There were tears of frustration in his eyes.

Through the haze he saw the movement off to his left. The Russian, his olive-brown uniform barely distinguishable against the ground, had broken through the trees.

□

Flames had started to lick the twisted fuselage of the Arado by the time Malenkoy reached the crash site. He spotted the pilot, slumped on the ground a few meters from the shattered cockpit, and ran over to him. His gray Luftwaffe shirt was badly torn, there were cuts on his face, and he was moaning softly. The flames were beginning to take a hold on the forward fuselage, creeping toward the large fuel tank just behind the pilot's seat. He had to get him away from there before it all went up.

He grabbed Kruze under the arms and pulled him to safety, away from the heat and the choking smoke. Kruze cried out with the pain as his side bumped over the rough, frozen earth and Malenkoy saw the blood that soaked not just his shirt, but his trousers too. Deep red drops spilled from the wounds, staining the ground.

Away to his right he saw the British aircraft executing a tight turn at the far end of the valley.

Malenkoy did not allow himself to be distracted by the fighter. He pulled off his coat and tunic, ripped the sleeves off his shirt, and packed them tightly against the largest of the pilot's wounds. The German was staring at him wide-eyed, his lips mouthing something that he could not hear because of the noise of the approaching British jet.

Kruze summoned the last of his strength and pulled Malenkoy down to him so that the Russian's ear was almost touching his mouth.

"Archangel . . ."

Malenkoy felt the ghosts of the forest return to haunt him.

The Rhodesian slipped in and out of consciousness. He felt drugged, weary, desperate only to know one thing. The offensive. Archangel. He thought that the man who held him was Fleming, but he could not work out why the hell he was wearing a Russian uniform.

He laughed and looked into the eyes of the Russian, no longer aware of where he was or what he was doing in that strange place.

Malenkoy held the man a little closer. "Archangel . . . *kaput*," he said, drawing his forefinger across his throat.

The pilot stopped his laughing and nodded, once. Comprehension.

Malenkoy's eyes turned to the sky at the precise moment that Fleming's thumb punched the gun button.

The earth seemed to open up as cannon shells exploded all around Kruze and Malenkoy, and when the dust settled, they were both dead.

Fleming bowed his head and pointed the Meteor in the direction of Stabitz. He felt he should be crying, but he couldn't; there were no more tears left in him.

Five minutes later, the Russian patrol arrived on the scene of the crash. They found the body of the Soviet major lying on top of the German pilot.

The sun rose a little higher over the mountains at the far end of the valley, its rays catching the metallic object that lay on the ground close to the Russian's outstretched hand. The patrol leader picked up the Order of Lenin and let it glitter in the bright mountain light. He looked back down at Malenkoy and issued the command for the burial party to begin its work.

The Order of Lenin. Whoever he was, the major must have been quite a hero.

10

"You'll have my resignation, of course," Staverton said, putting down the decoded transcription Deering had brought with him from the prime minister's War Cabinet.

"I think it would be best, Algy," Deering said. "I'm afraid the admiral's on the warpath this time. He's in with Churchill at the moment."

"And?"

"We were damned lucky with Guardian Angel, damned lucky. I don't need to tell you that." He paused. "But that doesn't alter the fact that a good man died for nothing, and that he died because you hid the 163C crash and activated a totally unauthorized operation. You lied, Algy. You lied."

Staverton said nothing. He thought back to Fleming's call twelve hours ago, telling him of Kruze's death. And now this.

He stared at the message from the military attaché in Moscow again.

7659843ZHN374/TOP SECRET/PM CABINET ADVISERS EYES ONLY/
BERIA REPORTED STAVKA YESTERDAY RED ARMY COUP AVERTED
EASTERN FRONT/CGS SHAPOSHNIKOV RINGLEADERS EXECUTED/
OTHER RESISTANCE SQUASHED/JOE SAFE/DETAILS UNKNOWN/WILL
FILE LATER/VEREKER

☐

When Beria entered the office, Stalin did not get up from behind his desk and he did not invite the chief of internal security to sit.

"Comrade Marshal Shaposhnikov's body will be brought back to Moscow immediately," Stalin announced. "He will be buried with full military honors."

Beria fought to remain impassive. Until he had stepped through the door, he had been sure that he had been summoned to receive Stalin's congratulations. The NKVD, his NKVD, had uncovered and thwarted a major coup and laid the corpse of Archangel at Stalin's feet.

"Why did you not tell me from the start about your investigations into Archangel?" Stalin continued.

Beria was aware of General Semyon Sabak at Stalin's shoulder, and the pleasure Sabak felt at his discomfort.

"Comrade Stalin, we were operating on little more than guesswork at first. As soon as we discovered Shaposhnikov's intentions it was necessary to act quickly. I believe we were only just in time."

"Perhaps I could have helped," Stalin said.

"With respect, Comrade Stalin, my investigation began on the slightest of suspicions. I sent Shlemov to Czechoslovakia because I had to be absolutely sure before you were informed. However, within mere hours the enormity of the plot was clear—"

"Archangel, you mean?"

"Yes, Comrade Stalin, and more. I believe that your own life was in serious danger."

"I thought the objective of Archangel was the military defeat of the British and the Americans."

"That is true," Beria said. "But without your endorsement of their plan they would have had to . . . move against you. The NKVD ensured that you were never in any danger . . ."

Stalin held Beria's gaze.

"The NKVD had nothing to do with it. Shaposhnikov was working for me."

Beria blinked. He tried to control his voice. "For you?" The question came too quickly, the tone too high.

Sabak allowed himself the ghost of a smile.

Beria felt his gut twist. "But he was going to launch Archangel against our allies. He was twisted by hate . . . right to the end. He was acting beyond the control of the state. Even he did not protest his innocence—"

Stalin cut him off. "Enough," he said, pushing his chair back and moving to the window. Then he turned. "You are looking at the true architect of Archangel. Here, now."

Beria was too stunned to speak.

Stalin pressed on. He had Beria just where he wanted him. "As soon as we began our counter-attack I knew we would beat Hitler. But Russia could not win on her own. We needed Churchill and Roosevelt; we had to have the second front." He paused. "But that created a new problem for us.

"If the Red Army failed to take Berlin, if we let the Allies get there first, Russia would be no better off than she was before the war. The race for Hitler's bunker was one we could not afford to lose."

"But what about the Yalta agreement? The Allies as good as gave you Eastern Europe."

Stalin shook his head. "What was Yalta, but a piece of paper? Roosevelt and Churchill gave us nothing but the territory they knew would be ours. Poland? Was there any way Poland would not already be behind our lines at war's end? But as for the rest of Europe, Eisenhower's forces were moving too fast. I had to find a way of stopping them."

"So you created Archangel, a sham to keep the Allies at bay, to slow their progress to Berlin . . ." Beria's voice was a whisper.

"My master plan," Stalin said emphatically. "Executed with the help of my chief of general staff, the late Marshal Shaposhnikov. It was arranged that Major Paliev would drop Archangel into the hands of the Allies when we wanted them to know," Stalin said. "It was the ultimate maskirovka."

Beria nodded slowly. It was brilliant.

Stalin turned to Sabak. "Tell him what Archangel achieved, Comrade General."

Sabak gestured to a small-scale map on Stalin's desk. He traced a line from the Baltic to Czechoslovakia. "All along the western front the Allies have dug in. Even though the British and Americans now believe that the Archangel emergency is over, they are slow to abandon their trenches. Berlin is ours."

"Why did you not tell me about Archangel, Comrade Stalin? You could have trusted me."

"I thought it was the NKVD's business to know everything," the generalissimo said. "Besides, the fewer who knew the better. It had to appear to be Shaposhnikov's own plan. If Churchill and Roosevelt were ever to suspect my own involvement, what credibility would we have had at the negotiating table? Apart from Sabak, here, there is only one other person in the world still alive who now knows the secret of Archangel." He paused. "See that it stays that way."

Beria felt the power draining from his body. "But what about the chemicals—the hydrogen cyanide? He was going to launch, Comrade Stalin, I am sure of it."

Stalin moved back to the desk and sat. After busying himself for a moment with a sheaf of papers he looked up once more. "As I said, the marshal will be buried with full military honors, Comrade. That will be all."

Sabak let the sound of Beria's footsteps fade in the corridor outside. "Among other things, Comrade Stalin, it appears you have brought the wolf to heel."

"A necessary bonus," Stalin said. "Beria's appetite for power has to be curbed."

"There is still something that intrigues me," Sabak said. "Was Shaposhnikov planning to take your orders a step farther? Was he really going to launch?"

Stalin eased himself back in his chair. "Shaposhnikov was a dangerous man. That was why he was ideal for the job, why Paliev had to watch him, and why we were always going to have to hand him over to Beria at some point. The Nerchenko girl played her part admirably."

"And the murder of his family . . .?"

"All too real," Stalin said "It appears you dropped the details into Beria's lap just in time."

Sabak's look hardened. "Then you . . .?"

"Yes, I think Shaposhnikov was going to do it. Why else did he ship the hydrogen cyanide to the front? I ordered no chemicals. He was consumed with loathing for the British. I underestimated that hatred."

"But why did he not tell the NKVD that he was acting on your orders, that Archangel was just a *maskirovka* before he was shot?"

"Because to him Archangel had become reality," Stalin said solemnly. "That's why Paliev headed east instead of west. He was trying to warn us."

"Poor Yuri Petrovich," Sabak said. "He ended up doing the most effective job of all."

EPILOGUE

It was a strange place for a reunion.

Fleming found them standing at the edge of the cemetery. The ranks of marble tombstones stretched in one direction toward a small chapel, and in the other to the road out of London. He had barely noticed it before, even though he had driven past many times on the way to the cottage.

He picked his way through the stones, the vicar's last words drifting over to him as the box was lowered into the ground. Penny had her back to him, but he had no trouble picking her out.

On the other side of the grave, a young woman cried softly, the blue uniform visible beneath her overcoat telling him that she must have been one of the little boy's nurses. A young man, standing close by, moved his arm gently around her shoulders.

Apart from two old gravediggers, their faces chapped from years of wind and rain, there was no one else there.

He reached Penny's side just as the first spadeful of earth was cast on top of the rough wooden box.

She raised her head, the hair falling away from her face. It was as if he was looking at her for the first time. Although there were tears in her eyes, she smiled and took his hand.

He stood, gazing at her. In the two days he had been back, during the endless hours of debriefing from Deering and Welland, he had thought of little else but this moment. When finally he had been able to talk to her on the telephone, he promised he would come as quickly as possible.

Penny put her arms around him. They stood there, holding each other, he did not know for how long. Fleming felt her body give, heard the sound of her crying into his shoulder.

"Are you really home, Robert?"

He held her at arm's length and wiped the tears from her cheeks.

"I'm home," he said.

She squeezed his hand again, then released it, turning back toward the grave. A small corner of the coffin was still visible.

Penny pulled something from her pocket and threw it tenderly into the hole. The handkerchief landed on the last exposed patch of wood, the loosely tied knot parting the moment it did so.

"God bless you," she said.

Fleming caught a fleeting glimpse of the medal ribbons before they were covered by another spadeful of earth and buried forever.

Penny lifted her eyes to his, searching his face.

Fleming nodded, then turned her gently toward the far-off gates, beyond which the car was waiting.